Her Highness *the* Traitor

Her Highness the Traitor

Susan Higginbotham

sourcebooks
landmark

Published by Sourcebooks Landmark, an imprint of Sourcebooks, Inc.
P.O. Box 4410, Naperville, Illinois 60567-4410
(630) 961-3900
Fax: (630) 961-2168
www.sourcebooks.com

Library of Congress Cataloging-in-Publication Data

Higginbotham, Susan.
  Her highness, the traitor / Susan Higginbotham.
     p. cm.
  (pbk. : alk. paper) 1. Grey, Jane, Lady, 1537-1554—Fiction. 2. Women—
England—History—Renaissance, 1450-1600—Fiction. 3. Great Britain—
History—Tudors, 1485-1603—Fiction. 4. Great Britain—Kings and
rulers—Fiction. I. Title.
  PS3608.I364H47 2012
  813'.6—dc23

                      2012003465

       Printed and bound in the United States of America.
          VP 10 9 8 7 6 5 4 3 2 1

Characters

The Royal Family

Edward VI, King of England.

Mary, his half sister, later Queen of England.

Elizabeth, his half sister, later Queen of England.

Catherine Parr, Queen of England; sixth wife of Henry VIII, later married to Thomas Seymour.

The Greys

Henry Grey, Marquis of Dorset, later Duke of Suffolk.

Frances Grey (née Brandon), wife of Henry Grey, Marchioness of Dorset, later Duchess of Suffolk; niece to Henry VIII.

Jane Grey, daughter of Henry and Frances Grey, later married to Guildford Dudley.

Katherine ("Kate") Grey, daughter of Henry and Frances Grey.

Mary Grey, daughter of Henry and Frances Grey.

The Dudleys

John Dudley, Viscount Lisle, later Earl of Warwick, later Duke of Northumberland.

Jane Dudley (née Guildford), wife of John Dudley, Viscountess Lisle, later Countess of Warwick, later Duchess of Northumberland.

John ("Jack") Dudley, son of John and Jane Dudley, later Earl of Warwick, later married to Anne Seymour.

Ambrose Dudley, son of John and Jane Dudley, later married first to Anne "Nan" Whorwood, then to Elizabeth Tailboys.

Robert Dudley, son of John and Jane Dudley, later married to Amy Robsart.

Guildford Dudley, son of John and Jane Dudley, later married to Jane Grey.

Henry ("Hal") Dudley, son of John and Jane Dudley, later married to Margaret Audley.

Mary Dudley, daughter of John and Jane Dudley, later married to Henry Sidney.

Katheryn Dudley, daughter of John and Jane Dudley, later married to Henry, Lord Hastings.

Andrew Dudley, younger brother of John Dudley.

Jerome Dudley, younger brother of John Dudley.

The Seymours

Edward Seymour, Earl of Hertford, later Duke of Somerset ("the Protector"). Brother to Jane Seymour, third wife of Henry VIII.

Anne Seymour, wife to Edward Seymour, Countess of Hertford, later Duchess of Somerset.

Anne Seymour, daughter of Edward and Anne Seymour, later married to Jack Dudley, known as Countess of Warwick after October 1551.

Jane Seymour, daughter of Edward and Anne Seymour.

Edward Seymour, son of Edward and Anne Seymour, later Earl of Hertford.

Thomas Seymour, later Lord Sudeley ("the Admiral"), younger brother to Edward Seymour, later married to Catherine Parr.

Others

John Aylmer, tutor to Lady Jane Grey.

Katherine Brandon (née Willoughby), Duchess of Suffolk; widow of Charles Brandon, Duke of Suffolk; stepmother of Frances Grey; later married to Richard Bertie.

Bess Cavendish, friend of Frances Grey, later known as Elizabeth Talbot, Countess of Shrewsbury.

Susan Clarencius, lady-in-waiting to Mary.

Ursula Ellen, gentlewoman to Jane Grey.

George Ferrers, courtier and Lord of Misrule.

Henry Fitzalan, Earl of Arundel, nobleman.

Maudlyn Flower, gentlewoman to Jane Dudley.

Edward Guildford, father of Jane Dudley.

Joan Guildford, wife of Edward Guildford, stepmother to Jane Dudley.

Francis Hastings, Earl of Huntingdon, father-in-law of Katheryn Dudley.

Henry, Lord Hastings, son of Francis Hastings, husband to Katheryn Dudley.

George Medley, half brother to Henry Grey.

Elizabeth Page, mother of Anne, Duchess of Somerset.

William Paget, royal councilor.

Anne Paget, wife of William Paget.

Elizabeth Parr, Marchioness of Northampton.

William Paulet, Lord St. John, later Marquis of Winchester.

Adrian Stokes, master of the horse to Frances Grey, later her second husband.

Elizabeth Tilney, gentlewoman to Jane Grey.

Anne Throckmorton, friend of the Greys.

Anne Wharton, lady-in-waiting to Mary.

The Tudor Succession

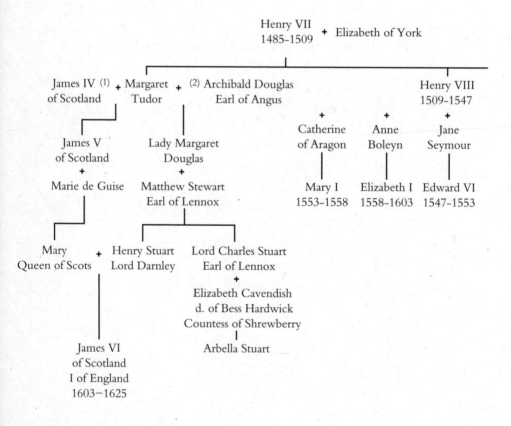

Henry VII
1485-1509 + Elizabeth of York

James IV (1) + Margaret + (2) Archibald Douglas
of Scotland   Tudor   Earl of Angus

Henry VIII
1509-1547

+
Catherine
of Aragon

+
Anne
Boleyn

+
Jane
Seymour

James V
of Scotland
+
Marie de Guise

Lady Margaret
Douglas
+
Matthew Stewart
Earl of Lennox

Mary I
1553-1558

Elizabeth I
1558-1603

Edward VI
1547-1553

Mary
Queen of Scots

+

Henry Stuart
Lord Darnley

Lord Charles Stuart
Earl of Lennox
+
Elizabeth Cavendish
d. of Bess Hardwick
Countess of Shrewberry

Arbella Stuart

James VI
of Scotland
I of England
1603-1625

The Tudor Succession

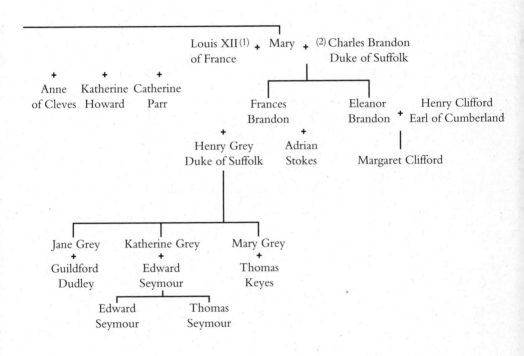

Louis XII (1) + Mary + (2) Charles Brandon
of France   Duke of Suffolk

Anne   Katherine Catherine
of Cleves Howard   Parr

Frances   Eleanor   Henry Clifford
Brandon   Brandon + Earl of Cumberland

Henry Grey   Adrian
Duke of Suffolk   Stokes   Margaret Clifford

Jane Grey   Katherine Grey   Mary Grey
+   +   +
Guildford   Edward   Thomas
Dudley   Seymour   Keyes

Edward   Thomas
Seymour   Seymour

Part I

1

Jane Dudley
January 1555

IF THERE IS AN ADVANTAGE TO DYING, IT IS THIS: PEOPLE HUMOR ONE'S WISHES. I could ask for all manner of ridiculous things, and I daresay someone would try to oblige me, but instead I simply call for pen and paper.

"Here follows my last will and testament, written with my own hands," I begin, and then I stop, frowning. I am not learned in the law, and the thought occurs to me that perhaps I should give up my task and call in someone who is. But he would charge for it, and that fee would make my children, who have lost so much already, that much the poorer. So I press on. I can say what I need to say as well as any lawyer can, though I might not be as verbose about it. If these last few months have taught me anything, it is how to fend for myself, which is more than I can say for some women I know.

But there is a phrase I am searching for. What is it?

Being in perfect memory, of course. I smile to myself, for although I have forgotten that phrase, there is not much else I have forgotten.

January 1512 to January 1547

I was not born to high estate. My father, Edward Guildford, was only a knight—and he was not even that when I was born, but a mere squire, albeit one high in the young king's favor. It was owing to this royal esteem that one chilly day in January 1512, my father strode into our hall at Halden in Kent with a black-haired boy in tow. "This is John Dudley, Mouse," Father said, using the pet name I had been given to distinguish me from my stepmother, Joan, whose name was sufficiently close to mine as to cause confusion sometimes. "He is to be my ward—that is, in my care—now that his father is dead and his mother's remarried. He'll be staying here a long time."

John, who was seven years of age to my three (almost four, as I liked to point out), executed a respectful bow, but did not match my stepmother's welcoming smile. "You look cold, John," my stepmother said then, her voice lacking its natural warmth. "Why don't you sit by the fire?"

It was an order rather than a suggestion, and the boy said, "Yes, mistress," and obeyed. His voice was not a Kentish one, even I at my young age could tell.

"He seems very ill mannered," my stepmother said when the boy was out of earshot.

"He's coming among strangers, and he's tired. He's a London boy, don't forget, not used to riding." My father chuckled. "Stared at my horse as if he were at the menagerie at the Tower. I had him take the reins for a time while coming here, though, and he did quite well. He's sharp."

"Aye, like his father. And look where that got *him*, speaking of the Tower."

"Where's that, Mama?" I could not resist asking. "What tower?"

"Never you mind," said my stepmother briskly as my father gave her what I had begun to recognize as a meaningful look. I was a quiet child, which meant adults often said interesting things in my presence they might have avoided saying in front of a more talkative girl, but sometimes to my disappointment they remembered themselves. Pitching her voice in a manner that informed me that future comments would not be welcome, she said to my father, "How much does he know of all that, by the way?"

"Most all, I fear. Some of the neighbors talked before they stopped speaking to the family altogether, and he figured out the rest for himself. He's sharp, as I said."

"Oh." My stepmother's voice softened. "Poor lad." She glanced at me. "Jane, why don't you join Master Dudley by the fire?"

I obeyed. John was sitting on a bench and staring into the flames. Shy as I was, I was being brought up to converse properly, as became a well-bred young lady. "Hello," I said brightly.

John looked at me with apparent reluctance, though in my opinion, I was at least more interesting than the fire, crackle as it might. "They called you 'Mouse' just now," he said with the air of one feeling bound to say something. "That's a strange name."

"That's just what they call me here. My real name is Jane." I paused. "Jane and John. They sound almost alike."

John grunted.

"I have my own pony," I went on, undaunted. How I had forgotten to mention this to John immediately I had no idea, for there was no creature I loved more than my new pony, which I was just learning to ride. I'd tried my best to let everyone in Kent know of my new acquisition. "Father said you don't know how to ride yet."

"No. Why should I? I'm from London."

I did know something about London. Father was often at the king's court there. But I didn't know all that much. I contemplated this apparently horseless place for a time before asking, "How do you go places there? Walk?"

The boy gave me a pitying look for my ignorance. "Just for short distances. People do ride, especially if they're coming in or out of the country, but if you're traveling from one part of London to another, it's best to take a boat down the Thames."

"Really?"

"My father used to take me all of the time before he died."

"My mother's dead," I offered companionably. "She died the same day I was born." (I thought at the time only that this was rather an interesting coincidence.) "They say she got sick. What did your father die of?"

"They cut off his head."

I stared at him in bewilderment. I vaguely knew that men who did wrong things could get hanged, though I had never seen such a dreadful sight. But cutting a man's head off? "Like a *chicken*?"

"Yes."

I placed my hands on my neck and determined that losing one's head would not be an easy accomplishment. "But why?"

"Mouse," said my father, putting his hand on my shoulder and looking at John apologetically. "That's enough questions for now. Your mother needs you to help her with—well, she needs you to help her with something."

"Yes, Father," I said, but I could not resist looking back at the boy as I scurried away. I had good reason to look back, after all; without knowing it, I had met my husband.

No, I was not born to high estate, and neither was my husband, the eldest son of a man who had been executed as a traitor. The titles we held were gained, and will die, all in a single generation. Yet if we were upstarts, we were no different from many others of our day. Dukes, earls, even queens— the court of Henry VIII was plentiful with those who had owed everything to one man, and in January 1547, five-and-thirty years after little John Dudley entered my life, that man, King Henry, lay dying at Whitehall. Henry VIII was an upstart in his own way, as well: his dynasty had sat on the throne for only two generations.

Upstart he might be, but I could not remember another king; I'd been but a babe in arms when Henry VIII came to the throne. I had known all six of his queens, if only well enough to bend a knee in some cases.

I mused upon this as I made my way from the queen's side of Whitehall, where I had been attending the sixth and last of the king's wives, Catherine Parr. There was no sign here that anything was amiss: meals were still being brought into the sick man's chamber, accompanied by the sounds of trumpets. They would stay in the chamber for a decent interval, I supposed, before being brought out and distributed to the poor, who surely by now must have been wondering about all of this extra bounty they were receiving.

As I had hoped, my husband was inside the chamber we had been allotted at court. He rose from the desk at which he had been working and kissed me. "What brings you here?"

"I came to check on the king's health."

"Did the queen send you?"

"No, but I expect she will be glad to hear a report."

"Then you must keep this secret, my dear, at least for a little while longer. King Henry is dead. He's been dead for two days."

I stared. "Why has no one been told?"

"The Earl of Hertford wished there to be no difficulties until King Edward was brought to Westminster. He, of course, has been told, along with the lady Elizabeth. The earl brought the news himself. Tomorrow it will be announced in Parliament."

King Edward. It seemed a strange title for the nine-year-old I'd known since he was christened, whose mother's funeral procession I'd ridden in. "Why was the queen not told? Why not the lady Mary?"

"They will be, very shortly." My husband gave an uneasy cough. "I suppose Queen Catherine is expecting to be made regent."

"Yes."

"Then she will be disappointed, I fear. The king did not wish a woman—even a woman as able as the queen—to have the rule during the king's minority. Don't glare at me so, my dear. I am only the messenger. In truth, the council won't have the rule of England either, not completely anyway. The council has agreed. There will be a protector."

For a moment, I paused to admire the industriousness of the men who had settled all of this in just two days, while keeping up this façade of a living king. But I knew my chronicles. I frowned. "A protector?"

For the first time, my husband smiled. "Shades of Richard III! And yes, it is to be an uncle. But Hertford has no kingly ambitions, and it's wise to have a single man in charge, even though he will be answerable to us on the council. And in any case, it's a different world now than it was in 1483."

"Well, it is that," I conceded. I sighed, thinking how disappointed the queen would be not to be named regent for the young king. She'd been closer to him than any of the other queens, for Jane Seymour, Edward's mother, had died soon after giving birth, the good-natured Anne of Cleves had lasted only a few months as queen, and poor Katherine Howard had been badly in need of a wise mother herself. Catherine Parr had been on good terms with all three of King Henry's children—no easy task, as each was as different as their respective mothers. Surely she had deserved the honor of a regency after putting up with her increasingly lame and ill-tempered royal husband. Worse, Anne Seymour, Countess of Hertford, was completely insufferable. Being the protector's wife could make her only more so. "What of Thomas Seymour?" He was the younger brother of Edward Seymour, Earl of Hertford; the two were Jane Seymour's brothers. "Is he to have a role in all of this?"

"Something, I'm sure." My husband yawned. "That's to be discussed. These things take time."

I stared out the window, my mind still trying to adjust itself to an England without Henry, who'd reigned nearly eight-and-thirty years, nearly as long as I had been alive. Softly, for I knew I was treading on delicate ground, I asked, "John, did you ever hate him for what he did to your father?"

"I never really thought about it." My husband tipped my chin up gently and brushed his lips against mine. "I've got some time to spare before I return to the council. Do you have to hurry back to the queen?"

I smiled. It was not uncommon of my husband to avoid talking about a topic by making love to me. It was a tactic that might have been employed more often than I realized, and generally with success, for I had borne him thirteen children.

⁊

To a man's eyes, I must have looked seemly enough as I returned to the queen's lodgings at Whitehall. To a woman, it was obvious that unskilled hands had put me back into my clothes; all my fastenings were slightly awry. I hoped I had sent John back to his council meeting in somewhat better repair, though he had servants nearby who would probably step in to make him presentable.

Anne Seymour, Countess of Hertford, gave me a knowing look as I entered the outer room of the queen's private chambers. The queen was in an inner chamber attending to business, it being the time of the day when she did this, but most of the other great ladies of England were here: the lady Mary, the new king's eldest sister; the lady Frances, King Henry's niece; a dozen or so others. I had known them all for years: together we'd buried Jane Seymour; greeted Anne of Cleves; watched helplessly as poor Katherine Howard giggled and flirted her way to the scaffold; speculated on who would be the king's sixth, and it would prove, final, bride.

"Did you hear anything, Lady Lisle?" asked the lady Mary. Just shy of her thirty-first birthday, she was still reasonably attractive, despite her voice, which was oddly gruff for a woman's.

I quaked at lying to a princess, but I did it anyway. "I have heard nothing new, Your Grace," I said smoothly, sensing Anne Seymour's eyes upon me. If I knew, she must certainly know, as well; her husband would no more leave her out of his confidence than mine would me. "I saw my husband, but he could tell me nothing more than that the king was doing poorly." That, I consoled myself, could be viewed more as a gross understatement than as an outright lie.

"I can't believe they have told us nothing. I know my father wished to make his peace with the Lord in private, but he is dying, for mercy's sake! I simply cannot fathom that he would not want his queen or his children by his side." Mary's thin face hardened. "I am not putting up with this lack of communication any longer. When the queen finishes her business, we are going to go to the king's lodgings togeth—"

A knock sounded upon the door, and a grave-looking man entered the room. "My lady," he said, kneeling to Mary. "I am grieved to tell you that His Highness King Henry has departed from this life."

Mary closed her eyes, then opened them again. What went through her head? After King Henry had repudiated her mother, Catherine of Aragon, and married Anne Boleyn, he had treated Mary horribly, declaring her a bastard. Only in the past several years had she been treated as a princess ought to be. Even after that, her father had been lacking: he'd not made a suitable marriage for her, so she was a maid at an age when many women were mothers ten times over; he'd not given her a household of her own, but seen fit to subsume hers within the queen's. Her voice gave nothing away. "Has the queen been told?"

"Yes, my lady. She is being brought the news as we speak."

"When did my father die?"

The man bowed his head even farther, perhaps as much out of caution as respect. "The king died two days before, my lady. Parliament will be informed tomorrow morning. The Earl of Hertford is aware that your ladyship might find the delay unsettling, and he has given me a letter explaining why he acted as he did."

Mary took the letter and read it slowly, a flush on her pale complexion the only betrayal of the anger she must have felt. "Take me to see my father's body."

Followed by her most trusted attendants, Jane Dormer and Susan Clarencius, Mary left the room. As the sound of conversation filled the chamber, the Countess of Hertford whispered to me, "You knew."

"Yes. Surely you did, too?"

"Yes, but I am the new king's aunt, after all. It is different. How long have you known?"

"Since John told me this afternoon."

The countess shook her head. "And he swore you to secrecy."

"No." I resumed the work I'd left behind, a handkerchief for the young prince—no, the young king. "He didn't have to *swear* me to anything. He is my husband."

⁂

The old king's death had been officially proclaimed, and the young king was on his way to the Tower to take up his duties. As the executors of the king's will and their wives collected to greet their new sovereign, Thomas Seymour, the younger of the king's maternal uncles, hurried up to John and me. "Fool bargemen," he panted. "Why, the king and my brother are not here yet? It's not like my brother to be unpunctual."

"The clock has not struck three yet," I said as John nodded distantly. Like many men, he was somewhat cool toward Thomas Seymour, although Seymour never flirted with me as he did with some women. I could not help but feel slightly insulted by his neglect in this regard.

"No, my lady, but it is my brother's habit to always be slightly ahead of his time. So when a lesser man might be punctual for arriving on time, my brother is late for arriving on time. A deeply irritating habit, don't you agree?" Without waiting for my reply, he asked, "The queen is not coming to greet King Edward, my lady?"

"No. She and the lady Mary have gone into seclusion until King Henry's funeral, as they thought was proper."

"Pity," said Thomas Seymour thoughtfully. "I was hoping to offer my condolences in person."

John quirked an eyebrow.

Just as the clock struck three, a distant rumbling announced the arrival of the king. As we ordered ourselves into tidy lines and sank to our knees, King Edward VI, accompanied by his uncle the Earl of Hertford and a host of other dignitaries, rode through the gate.

Ginger-haired like his father and sisters, the new king was a handsome child, well grown for his age and looking around him with obvious interest. He listened patiently as the Constable of the Tower, Anthony Kingston, welcomed him. When we had all paid our respects, the king asked, "Where shall we stay?"

"Why, in the palace," the Earl of Hertford said. Plainly puzzled by the king's unwonted ignorance, he stroked his brown beard, which grew less luxuriantly than his younger brother Thomas's, and added, "That is where kings usually await their coronation, of course. The rooms are ready and are quite spacious. Were you never told?"

Thomas Seymour pushed forward. "I believe Your Highness was pointing at the Garden Tower as you rode in."

"Yes!" Edward looked up at the younger of his uncles eagerly. "Where the princes were murdered by Richard III. Can't we stay there? Or at least see it?"

"That is hardly appropri—"

"Oh, for heaven's sake, Brother, what's the harm? I was always keen to look at it when I visited the Tower as a youngster; isn't any boy? I am sure that it is too small for Your Highness to lodge in"—the constable nodded—"but I daresay Sir Anthony will allow you to go inside."

"It is ill omened," said Hertford dismally. "And probably full of lumber."

"We have read much about it," said the king in a good approximation of his father's tone. He squared his legs in the manner that had made King Henry's courtiers quake. "We have never been inside it, as it happens, and we wish to see it."

"And so Your Highness shall immediately," Thomas Seymour promised. "I shall take you myself. Do you trust yourself there with your wicked uncle Thomas?" Seymour contorted his stance to give the appearance of a hunchback.

The king unsquared his legs. "Oh, yes!"

"I shall come, too, then," said Hertford resignedly.

"Ah, see? Now Your Highness has *two* wicked uncles. What king could want more? Lead on then, Sir Anthony."

I supposed it was an honor that the queen, usually the most self-contained and dignified of women, thought highly enough of me to include me in the small circle of ladies who were privileged to hear her rant like a fishwife. "The nerve of my husband! Letting me think for months—nay, years—that I would be regent for King Edward in case of a royal minority, and what does he do? Changes his will without a word to me."

"The king mentioned Your Grace in his will with great affection," I said.

"Dry bones!"

"It was not ingratitude, Your Grace, I am sure of it, or lack of natural affection. The king merely wanted a man—men—to have the guiding of the kingdom."

The queen scoffed. "Say 'man,' Jane. The Earl of Hertford seems to have grabbed all for himself." The queen flicked her elegant hand, adorned with a mourning ring in the shape of a death's head. "Oh, they had the right to elect Hertford as protector, I suppose. But that's not what the king planned. If he had wanted a lord protector, with a council to guide him, that's what he would have created in the first place. And I am not the only one who has been treated shabbily in this business. Sir Thomas Seymour is every bit as much the king's uncle as Hertford, and just as capable, I daresay, and he is not even a councilor! Only an advisor to the council. He might as well be a stick of wood."

A knock at the door sounded, and the stick of wood himself was announced.

Thomas Seymour, dressed more somberly than was his wont, entered the room, measuring his usually buoyant steps to the solemnity of the widow's bereavement. "Your Grace, I wanted to give you my condolences on the king's death," he said, brushing his lips against the queen's hand. "I know my brother will do his utmost to be of service to you, as well."

"On the contrary, the Earl of Hertford—or the Lord Protector, as we must call him now—has been of no service to me whatsoever," the queen said. Resentment lit up her face, making her appear rather younger than her five-and-thirty years. "He sent his man to inform me of King Henry's death only the night before the news was proclaimed to the public. Two solid days after he died. He should have told me and the lady Mary immediately, as a courtesy." She nodded at the lady Mary, who had joined her in her seclusion, which would continue until the old king was buried. "After all, the lady Elizabeth was told at the same time as King Edward."

"My brother moves in mysterious ways," Thomas said. "Much like the Lord, and trust me, the comparison is not one that would displease him."

The queen let out a sound much like a snort of laughter and clapped her hand to her mouth.

Mary was not so easily amused. She said, "It does not auger well, if those who have the keeping of the kingdom cannot be bothered with the common courtesies."

"I could not agree more," Thomas said, inclining his head.

"Why, you have been treated shabbily yourself," said the queen. "We were just saying."

"Well, I am to be a baron." He glanced at me with more interest than was his wont. "By the way, my lady, I understand congratulations are in order."

"My lord?"

"You mean your husband hasn't told you?"

"I have been attending the queen over the past few days, and have not seen or heard from him."

"Oh, yes. Well, it's known by all and sundry now—except here, I suppose. There was a clause in King Henry's will stating that gifts which had been promised but not perfected were to be fulfilled. Well, lo and behold! Lord Paget came before the council, and what do you think he announced? He announced that the king would have doled out new titles and lands if he had lived a little longer to amend his will. I myself am to be Baron Seymour of Sudeley—so I can hardly complain, I suppose. Your Grace's brother is to be Marquis of Northampton."

The queen blinked. "Why, he has told me nothing!"

"It has only just come out. And as for you, Lady Lisle, your husband is to be an earl."

"An earl?"

"Old title, dating back to Anglo-Saxon times," Seymour said cheerfully.

"I believe Lady Lisle knows the origin of the title," said the lady Mary, who had a certain literal cast of mind.

I said nothing but gripped the sides of my chair.

The queen asked, "That is well deserved on Viscount Lisle's part, I daresay. But what, pray tell, is the Earl of Hertford gaining out of this?"

"Merely a dukedom. Of Somerset, to be precise."

"Your brother to be a duke, and you to be a mere lord," mused the queen. "Something is wrong there." She turned to me. "But I will not keep you here. You have matters to discuss with your husband. You may go home—Countess."

༄

It was a bitterly cold day, but I barely noticed the wind biting into my cheeks as I made my way to the house we'd rented in London. It was a large place, but it seemed much smaller, for John liked having the children residing with us in town instead of staying on our estates in the country. All seven of them were waiting for me as I entered. "Father is to be an earl!"

"An earl, Mother! You are to be a countess!"

"That means Jack is to be Lord Lisle. Doesn't it?"

"Do we get new clothes?"

"Will there be a ceremony?"

"What is an earl?"

My husband pushed past the mob surrounding me and embraced me.

"When were you going to tell me?" I asked after we had hugged for a long time.

"Tonight, as a matter of fact. I was going to send for you and break the news to you over a private supper." He glanced at our brood, whose ages ranged from four to twenty. "Quietly."

⁓

"You have well and truly deserved this earldom."

John smiled. "Do you know where I went today after the news was announced? Candlewick Street, my father's house. I remember the day he was arrested, just after the seventh King Henry died. I was five years of age, full of excitement about the new king being crowned, and my father had said he would find a good place for me to see the coronation procession—he was sure the king would oblige, as he'd been in such good favor with Henry VII. Instead, I woke one morning to hear my mother crying, our servants shouting—absolute chaos. The king and his council had ordered their men to surround the house just before the break of day. They seized my father like a common criminal. My nurse tried to keep me from seeing them rough handle him out of the house and into the street, but I was too quick for her. Then a few days later, the rest of us had to leave. I loved that house. They had to drag me out kicking and screaming."

"John, in all the years we've known each other, you've never talked of this."

He shrugged. "You know I've never cared to speak of those days. Father was guilty of nothing more than collecting money too well for Henry VII, but he'd made enough men angry doing that, and the new king couldn't resist such a sop to the people. So my father had to lose his head, after he had spent more than a year sitting in the Tower, hoping the king would change his mind. I never saw him again after they took him out of Candlewick Street that day, and I never saw his house again until this morning. It's strange. They say the places you've been in childhood look smaller when you see them as an adult, but this place didn't. It was just as I remembered it. I found myself missing it again, just like I had when I first had to leave."

"Maybe you could buy it or lease it. We surely could afford it."

"No," John said dryly. "Too small for us now. Besides, some other young boy might be attached to it. I wouldn't want to be the one who took him away from it, even in exchange for a handsome sum."

He fell silent. I indeed had never heard him speak of his father before, save in passing. Instead, John, after his first evening at Halden, had thrown himself into country life: learning to ride and to hawk and hunt, going for long outings with my older brother and returning muddy and cheerful. After my brother died, John had become practically a son to my father. At age thirteen, he had gone with my father to court, where he had made a good impression and fit in easily with the other youths his age; it was I, when I came to court, who had felt awkward and shy.

John continued. "You once asked me if I hated King Henry for executing my father. Yes, until I saw him for the first time. Then I couldn't. He was kind to me, interested, pleasant. I didn't feel like a lowly page in his company. Sometimes I wondered if he remembered who I was, the eldest son of the first man he had executed. But he never forgot things like that. I've wondered if all of the honors he gave me over the years, all the trust he placed in me, weren't his way of apologizing for putting my father to death. But it's not the sort of question one can ask a king." He squeezed my hand. "Do you know what else is amusing? I never did see King Henry's coronation, of course, following my father's arrest as closely as it did. So when King Henry died, the first thing that popped into my head was that this time, I would get to see the new king's coronation. It shall be my first."

2

Frances Grey
December 1555

IT IS DANGEROUS TO SPEAK OF MY DAUGHTER JANE TODAY, AT LEAST HERE IN
England. Men can die, and have died, for holding the beliefs she held. Nonetheless, people sometimes turn up at my house to tell me of their admiration for
my daughter. Some ask me for a memento of Jane. I hand them the few things I
can—a hair fastening, an old pen—while hoarding a few such mementoes myself.
As I do, I sometimes ask myself, are these things really much different from the
relics of the saints these people scorn? Are they not pilgrims of another sort?

Whatever I give them, however, my visitors leave disappointed. The mother
of an extraordinary daughter, they think, must surely be extraordinary herself.
How wrong they are! For wherever my daughter got her great gifts, I know it
was certainly not from me. As a young woman, I could embroider beautifully,
carry a tune respectably, play a pretty melody upon my virginals—but I could
barely speak French, much less the ancient languages. Indeed, my French was
atrocious, which was a matter of some embarrassment for me, because my
mother, Mary, had been that country's queen.

How my sister, Eleanor, and I loved hearing my mother tell about her days
in the French court! Her brother, King Henry VIII, had married her at age
eighteen to Louis XII, a man in his fifties. Not a robust man, and nearly three
times her age, Louis had nonetheless done his best to make the wedding cel-
ebrations as lively and festive as possible for his vivacious new queen. There
had been tournaments, dancing, and feasting, and while it all delighted my
young mother, it had proven the undoing of poor Louis, who, after just a few
months of all of this, dropped dead from sheer exhaustion, leaving his son-in-
law Francis as the king and my mother fair game to be married off to some
French nobleman or the other. But having married one aging man for policy,
Mother was not inclined to do so again.

Charles Brandon, Duke of Suffolk, an Englishman, was a fine jouster and a handsome man and the king's closest friend; he was also, it was noted, an upstart duke who had not a jolt of noble blood in him. But he had caught my mother's eye long before she married the King of France, and when King Henry sent Suffolk to England to check on his newly widowed sister, my mother wasted no time in renewing her acquaintance with the duke. My mother had the rare ability to look pretty while she cried, and when she turned her tears upon Charles Brandon, they were so effective that in just days, the pair were secretly married, to the scandal of the French court and the fury of King Henry. But in those days, the king did not bear a grudge for long, and soon all was right once again between the king and my parents.

My nurse loved to tell my younger sister and me about this runaway match, so naturally, I would dream of making a romantic marriage like that of my mother and father. But what my parents had practiced in their own case was very much different from what they practiced in mine. At age thirteen, I was dangled before the Duke of Norfolk, who to their great chagrin (and mine, for I could not help hearing about it) thought my dowry too meager for his son. Then my father turned to the young Marquis of Dorset. There was an impediment in that the marquis was already contracted to the Earl of Arundel's daughter, but this obstacle was quickly surmounted for the benefit of the king's close friend, my father. So a couple of months before my sixteenth birthday, I was married to Henry Grey, Marquis of Dorset, who was just a few months my senior.

I had heard that my new husband was careless with his money and fond of gaming, which I had expected, and that he had a strong interest in the New Learning, which I had not. The first I could cope with readily, as my father was such a man; the second I found more daunting. My husband had been educated in the household of the late king's natural son, the Duke of Richmond, and there had learned Latin and Greek. Though in many ways we were compatible, he scoffed at the handful of English books, prettily illustrated and teeming with romance and chivalry, which I brought to our marriage. To them, he would not even grant space in his study.

But my Jane—my poor, dear Jane—surpassed him. By the time she was four, she was well beyond the instruction I could give, and my husband was obliged to get a master just for her. Her special gifts, I think, were what reconciled him to God calling our little son to Him. For our younger daughters, though they were loved by my husband, are pretty, ordinary creatures.

Much, as those pilgrims who came to Sheen years later would discover, like me.

February 1547

By the time Jane was almost ten, our household had divided into two unacknowledged but distinct sets: my husband and Jane, and me and my two younger daughters, Katherine and little Mary. That was how it was in the days after God called my uncle, Henry VIII, out of the world.

There was but one aspect of Jane's studies upon which I was qualified to instruct her—sewing. Every day at the appointed time, Jane would take out her hated workbasket and join me and her younger sister Kate in my chambers, where she alternated between pricking her finger and casting baleful looks at Kate, who, despite being more than three years younger than Jane, already exceeded her as a needlewoman. Even my Mary, who at a year and a half was too young to do more than empty my workbasket of the bright cloth it contained and then fill it again, showed more promise, I thought.

As Jane sat beside me, frowning as she sewed a shirt that would surely have to go to the poor, as it was by no means worked well enough to grace my husband, the door to the chamber opened slowly. In walked my husband, Harry, clad in black and pulling a long face. At a funereal pace, he plodded from one end of our solar to the other, then turned to Jane and Kate, sitting side by side on the window seat. "Well, chickens, do you think I'll pass muster as chief mourner?"

"Oh, yes!" Jane clapped her hands together, letting her work fall to the ground. Kate dutifully applauded in turn. "You'll be splendid, Father."

"I am relieved to hear that." He nodded toward me. "Now, take yourselves off, chickens. I have something I must discuss with your mother."

"Really, Harry," I said as the girls dropped a curtsey and left, "I wish you would treat my uncle's death with more solemnity."

"I am merely practicing for my role. As it's the only role of substance I've been given in living memory, I must perform it well, don't you agree?"

"More will come, Harry, with this new reign."

"Well, we shall see. In any case, that brings me to what we need to speak about."

Inwardly, I groaned, expecting yet another diatribe about ceasing to hear Mass. In the past few months, Harry had become almost as bad as my friend and stepmother, Katherine Brandon, who could not so much as look at an innocuous loaf of bread without holding forth on the sheer stupidity of the doctrine of transubstantiation. The Mass was still heard in our household, but I knew its days were numbered. "What is it, Harry?"

"King Henry's will. Quite interesting. He lays out the order of succession, as

Parliament allowed him to do by testament a couple of years back. There aren't any surprises in the first part. If King Edward dies without heirs, the crown should go to the lady Mary, and then to the lady Elizabeth."

"And then to Queen Margaret's line?" Margaret, King Henry's older sister, had married King James IV of Scotland. Her little granddaughter, Mary, was now that country's queen.

"No. That's where it concerns us. He knocked that line out altogether. Didn't want a little Scottish lass on the throne, I suppose."

I did a quick calculation. "So that means *I* am next in the succession?"

"No, it means Jane is. King Henry passed you over, but he willed that if the lady Elizabeth died without heirs, the crown will pass to your heirs." Harry forestalled my next question. "I don't know why he chose to skip over you, but my guess is that he preferred not to have a woman on the throne, and was hoping you'd have a son by the time that contingency came to pass. But for now, that leaves our Jane as third in line to the throne."

"Such a thing might never come to pass. It is bound never to come to pass. King Edward will certainly marry and have children, as will the lady Elizabeth. The lady Mary—well…"

"She's missed her chance," Harry said bluntly. "She might yet get a husband, but a child at her age?"

"It hardly matters, with a healthy young brother and a healthy young sister." I resumed my sewing. "Jane's chances are as remote as mine ever were. And I am glad of it. A woman should not rule."

"Spoken like a good niece of King Henry," Harry said. "But I am surprised to hear you hold your own sex in such low regard. And Jane is a brilliant girl. Perhaps most women could not rule, but she could be an exception."

"I pray it never comes to that."

"But with Mary a Catholic, and both she and the lady Elizabeth still officially bastards…"

"Harry! Men have died for saying such foolish thoughts aloud." I looked around to make sure we were alone.

Harry stared out the window. "Well, it's very remote, as you say," he said briskly, with the appearance of pulling himself back to earth. "But I do know this: a girl with as good a claim to the throne as our Jane should be able to make a very good marriage. A very good one."

"That idea, I like," I confessed.

"I thought you would. Now, let me tell you what else I have heard. The

Earl of Hertford—or the Duke of Somerset as we must begin to learn to call him—is giving consideration to ceasing to hear the Mass. Don't you think it's time we thought more seriously about doing the same ourselves, my dear?"

∽

The old king had been buried; the new king had been crowned. A few days after the latter event, Harry came to me again. "Tom Seymour's man has been to see me."

"Since when did Tom Seymour become too important to come himself?"

"Since he asked for our Jane to come live with him. He wants to broker a good match for her."

"What match could he broker that you could not broker yourself?"

"One to the new king."

I stared at my husband. "He is offering to make Jane Edward's queen?"

"That's the sum of it, my dear. Think of it. They're the same age, they're well educated, and they're Protestant. And then there's the matter of the succession. What better bride for King Edward than the girl who's third in line to the throne?"

"What does the Duke of Somerset have to say about it?"

"Oh, nothing, because Tom hasn't mentioned it to him. No doubt he'd disapprove if Tom did, just by dint of the fact of Tom being the one to mention it."

"Tom Seymour is unmarried. Is he suitable to care for a young girl?"

"Why not? We'd be sending her suitably attended. But why not express your concerns to him yourself? He has asked us to meet him at his place."

∽

Seymour Place, as Tom Seymour had renamed Hampton Place when it was granted to him several years before, was just a short ride down the Thames from our own house, Dorset House. The smile Tom bestowed upon me far exceeded the one he gave to my husband. "Doubly blessed! My friend Harry and his lovely lady. I suppose your lord has told you why we are here, my lady?"

I nodded. "Yes. You wish to marry my daughter to the king."

"Can you think of a worthier bride, my lady, than your fair daughter?"

"No, but there will surely be others pushing a foreign bride upon the king."

"The king will remember that his own mother was an English bride, as were his grandmother Elizabeth of York and his great-grandmother Elizabeth Woodville." Tom Seymour turned another smile upon me. "And believe me, I shall be active in reminding him. Mind you, I don't plan to push your daughter upon him, as he's so young; I want to ease them into marriage slowly. Give the young people a chance to get better acquainted, for the king to see your daughter's fine points, so he naturally thinks of her as his first choice. That shouldn't be hard. After all, she's a brilliant girl, and a pretty one, too. She takes after her mother in that respect."

I took the wine cup that was offered to me, embarrassed to find myself actually blushing at this compliment. Though I had never matched my own mother in beauty, and was approaching my thirtieth year, I knew myself to still be comely, with reddish-gold hair and a slender figure, and it was pleasant to be reminded of it occasionally by a man not my husband. But Tom Seymour, I reminded myself, was no doubt profligate in paying his compliments, as he was rumored to be in other matters, as well.

"And, of course, she is third in line to the throne," said Harry. "And indisputably legitimate, not to mention having received a godly upbringing. That can only increase her appeal to the king. He has decided views as to religion, I understand."

"Indeed he has," said Tom Seymour rather gloomily.

"What of the Protector?" I asked.

"What of him?" Seymour's good-natured face darkened, and I realized I had made a conversational misstep. "He can't rule the king, as much as he'd like to. Or England." His face cleared, and he said more lightly, "He might be the king's protector, but I'm the king's favorite uncle. Always have been. That counts for a great deal, whatever Ned might say."

"Ned?" I asked. "You are still speaking of the Protector?"

"Yes. It's what they called him at home when he was a boy." He anticipated my next question. "No one calls him that now but me."

"I am surprised he tolerates it."

"Oh, he hates it," Seymour said breezily. "So what of it, my lady? Will I have the privilege of welcoming your daughter into my house?"

⁓

"I think it's a fine idea," Harry reiterated as we rode back to Dorset House.

I pulled my cloak closer around me. "I know. You all but agreed to it."

"So what's the harm? Our Jane's of the right age to go to another household, after all. The worst that can happen is that the king marries someone else. Even if Seymour can't bring it off, it's bound to lead to a good match."

"Harry, have you considered that Tom Seymour might mean to marry her himself?"

"You would think that, with your father's history," Harry said, grinning at me. Just three months after the death of my mother, my father, nearly fifty, had shocked his family by marrying fourteen-year-old Katherine Willoughby, whose wardship he had acquired. Katherine, to whom I'd become close after she had joined our household, had been intended for my brother. Father, on due consideration, had decided that matching himself with the young heiress was too advantageous to be passed up, especially as my brother had long been ailing (and indeed died not long afterward). If he had thought to have the upper hand in the marriage, he was sorely mistaken. Katherine, as Duchess of Suffolk, had used her status to fill the house with clergymen who shared her reformist religious views. Poor Father had eventually found himself surrounded by them. "But in this case, you'd be wrong." Harry lowered his voice. "I have it on good authority that Tom plans to marry, but it's not to our daughter."

"So who is the bride-to-be?"

"The queen."

I gasped. I was well familiar with the gossip that, years before, Seymour had set his cap at Catherine Parr, only to have his suit curtailed by the king's own interest in her—but back then she'd only been a baron's widow, quite suitable for Seymour. "On whose authority?"

"Tom Seymour's own authority. And she's not at all unwilling." Harry gave me another grin. "Think of the advantages to Jane from being in the queen's household." Harry winked. "After all, your mother stooped to marry your father."

He was a duke, at least, I thought to myself, albeit one who owed his dukedom solely to the late king's affection for him. But I knew when I was beaten. "Very well. We shall send Jane to his household."

∽

"What are you translating?" I said, looking at the open book on my daughter's desk.

"Latin."

"Well, I guessed that much. What author?"

Ten-year-old Jane gave me a pitying look, knowing as she did that one was the same as the other to me. "Cicero."

Harry, standing next to me, nodded approvingly, and I knew if he had been alone, my daughter would have elaborated. Sparing me the embarrassment of asking who Cicero was, he said, "We have news for you, Jane. You are to go live in Sir Thomas Seymour's household."

"It will be a great opportunity for you, and you will be able to visit us regularly," I put in. "I think you'll like it there."

"When am I to leave?"

Even Harry seemed nonplussed by my daughter's matter-of-factness. "Why, as soon as it can all be arranged, I suppose. Sir Thomas stands ready to receive you at any time."

"Might I bring my books?"

"Yes." My second daughter, Kate, would have asked whether she could bring her pets.

"Then I shall write him and thank him for his gracious invitation," Jane said, as usual anticipating me.

☙

My daughter had seemed perfectly content as we parted from her at Seymour Place. In the days after our parting, it was I who paced the halls at Dorset House, wondering how the absence of one quiet girl could make them seem so empty.

3

Jane Dudley
May 1547

WITH THE OLD KING BURIED AND THE NEW KING CROWNED, QUEEN Catherine moved from court to her dower house at Chelsea, to which I was invited toward the end of May. As my servants escorted me off my barge, newly painted with the bear and ragged staff of Warwick, and through the gate, I looked around appreciatively. The queen's gardeners had applied all of their arts, and nature had done the rest; this place smelled like Eden before the Fall.

Catherine Parr stopped me short from kneeling to her when I was shown into her chamber. "There's no need of that here at Chelsea," she said, allowing me to salute her on the cheek instead. "Why, look at you! Being a countess agrees with you, I think."

I smiled. "And I believe the air at Chelsea agrees with you, Your Grace," I said, thinking it might be the queen's widowed state that agreed with her instead. In the last year or so of King Henry's reign, when poor Anne Askew had been roasted alive and the religious conservatives had tried their best to alienate the king from the queen, she had looked tense and wary, even when the attempt failed and Henry had showered her with gifts.

"It is pleasant here indeed." Catherine hesitated then put her hand on my shoulder. "My lady, I have a secret I wish to confide in you. I trust you, and I know you can keep one very well." The queen smiled a little archly at me. "As you did when the king lay dead."

"Your Grace, I beg your forgiveness. My husband—"

"There is no need to do so. You are right to be loyal to him. And that is why I am telling you a secret that you can share with him. Tom Seymour and I have married."

"Married?" I squeaked in a manner suitable to my nickname of old.

"We married at my sister's chapel at Baynard's Castle just a few days before. Well, my lady? Are not congratulations in order?"

"Indeed they are," I managed. The queen, married after just four months of widowhood! And in a secret ceremony! "I suppose the king doesn't know?"

"No, and neither does the Protector nor that shrew he has for a wife." The queen's eyes narrowed. "Do you know what that—that *hell* is doing? She has encouraged her husband to keep my jewels, the jewels the late king willed to me, on the ground that they are the Crown's! I've no doubt she wants them for her own skinny neck." Catherine glowered, then recalled herself. "No, I have not told them, and I shall not. Only my sister and her husband and the priest who married us and a couple of my ladies know. We want to secure the king's approval for the match."

"A little late for that," I ventured.

Catherine shrugged. "We can always have a public ceremony."

"How long have you been courting?" I could not resist asking.

"Since just days after the king's funeral. Have I shocked you?"

"Yes," I admitted. "But I understand the temptation."

"No, you probably don't, having known your husband since you were three, and having been married to him since you were sixteen." Queen Catherine was beginning to melt away before my eyes, and I was seeing Lady Latimer as I had known her years before, when she was newly arrived in London from the North and was eager for a taste of court life. "I wanted to marry him years before. Everyone knows it; why should I lie about it?" The queen settled back on her stool and smiled reminiscently. "Tom came to me not long after the funeral on the Protector's business, as he put it. I knew there was no such thing, and I did not care. Soon we had picked up where we had left off before King Henry married me."

I was rather more grateful than otherwise that the queen's confidence did not extend to telling me exactly what they had been doing with each other when they left off.

Catherine was continuing, in a more regal manner than previously. "I am telling you these things because I know your husband is friendly with the Protector. Tom and the Protector have been at odds since they were boys, and you know what I think of his wife. How I detested having that woman in my household! So we are neither suited to the task of gauging his feelings. But if your husband could not tell the Protector, but sound him, getting a sense of how he would receive my marriage, I would be most grateful."

"I will speak to my husband."

"Thank you, my dear. I know he is clever enough to manage the business. In the meantime, my husband plans to write to the lady Mary, asking her to urge me to the match."

"She is no longer in the household here?"

"No, she left in April. I don't believe she suspected anything; her chambers are far off." The queen's eyes positively twinkled. "And Tom came at night and left in the morning."

I was only a few years older than the queen, yet I felt hopelessly old-fashioned. The intrigues and amours of King Henry's court had passed me by; I'd lain with but one man in my life, even in my imagination, and I could not imagine lying with another, not to mention having someone sneaking to my house in the middle of the night. My distaste for the whole business must have shown, for the queen said, "We always did intend marriage, you know. And we *are* married now."

"Of course," I said brightly.

"In any case, he is coming for supper today, all quite in the open. Will you stay? He is bringing his new charge with him, the Marquis of Dorset's eldest daughter, and she is quite an interesting little thing. Have you met her?"

"Only in passing."

"Well, you and she ought to get on well together."

"I would be happy to stay."

"The lady Elizabeth will join us, too, of course. She never likes to miss a sighting of Tom." Catherine shook her head. "Indeed, keeping her in the dark has been far harder than it was the lady Mary. The lady Elizabeth misses nothing."

∽

The Admiral, as Thomas Seymour was known because of the position he'd been given when the new king came to the throne, kissed the queen's hand decorously as two pairs of young eyes observed him: those of the lady Elizabeth, the king's thirteen-year-old sister, and of Lady Jane Grey, Dorset's ten-year-old daughter. Elizabeth's alert eyes were indeed focused upon the Admiral, while Jane, dressed expensively but very plainly for a girl of her high station, crinkled her brow in disapproval at the queen's bright summer gown.

I turned my own attention upon Lady Jane. In the last century, it had been Jane's great-great-grandmother, Elizabeth Woodville, whose beauty had led Edward IV to make her, a knight's widow and a mere commoner, his queen. This girl was descended from Elizabeth Woodville's first marriage, to one

John Grey, as well as from her royal marriage, and the family's good looks had not been much diluted over the generations. Jane was a pretty child, with reddish-brown hair, much darker than that of her kinswoman the lady Elizabeth, and she was slender and pale skinned, like her mother, Frances, and her grandmother, the French queen. If she'd been my daughter, though— and I had two living—I would have put her in a gown of a more flattering color. If I'd not learned to play at the game of courtly love during my time at court, I had at least learned to dress well. But the Marquis of Dorset was a strong evangelical, more so than his wife, and evidently it was he who had influenced the manner of his daughter's dress. "Are you enjoying staying with the Admiral, Lady Jane?" I asked when we were seated side by side at table. "He is a charming man."

Lady Jane looked toward her guardian, who was chatting animatedly with the queen and with the lady Elizabeth. "He is," she allowed in a low tone of voice. It was clear she had never thought of such a thing.

"They tell me you are quite a scholar," I ventured.

"My tutors say I get on well," Lady Jane acknowledged.

"You will like the queen, then. I suppose you have heard that she has written and published her own book of prayers? And the lady Elizabeth translated it just last year for the king, into French, Italian, and Latin."

Jane's little nose wrinkled in unmistakable jealousy. "I know French and Latin, and I am to learn Italian."

"Of course you will," I said reassuringly.

My companion's well-bred silence told me I had presumed.

After my disconcerting trip to Chelsea, it was a relief to return to our new home in Holborn: Ely Place, which John had acquired after years of leasing lodgings in the city. It was the grandest house in which we'd lived, and we had been staying there for so short a time that I still could get lost in its tangle of staircases and corridors. I managed, however, to make my way to John's chamber without incident and to tell him the news.

"The queen has married?"

"Yes, and I confess it made me uncomfortable."

"It should have," said John. He shook his head. "Why couldn't she have waited a year? I daresay the king wasn't a model husband, but she owed him that much respect."

"So you won't speak to the Protector?"

"No. What can I say? If they hadn't married already, I would have been willing enough to say a word; it's none of my concern if the queen wants to marry a rascal. But now that they have married, I can hardly speak to Somerset as if they hadn't done the deed already. All I can promise her is to keep silent. That is as much deceit as I care to practice. He is, after all, my friend." John snorted. "And it won't be a secret for long, with the Admiral going back and forth to the queen's place night after night. Especially with the lady Elizabeth in her household, and Dorset's daughter in his. The lady Elizabeth is too sharp to miss such antics, though I know little enough about the lady Jane."

I smiled. "The lady Jane would not approve of such romantic folly, but I doubt she pays much attention to anything that is not within the covers of a book. She's very bright, but a rather frosty little creature."

"I wonder whom Dorset is considering as a husband for her?"

"Someone with a good-sized library." I snickered. "And with a great deal of patience, I daresay."

4

Frances Grey
September 1547

I HARDLY RECOGNIZED MY JANE WHEN I NEXT CAME UP FROM OUR HOME OF Bradgate in Leicestershire to London. Not only had she had a slight growing spurt, but she also was dressed in the height of fashion, in a green that became her very well. "The queen gave me the material," she said as she spun around, almost coquettishly, for me to better admire her. "Don't you think it's pretty?"

"It's lovely. But I have tried to get you to wear such colors before. You never would."

"The queen ordered it," Jane said sensibly. "I could not refuse. And the Lord Admiral pressed it upon me, too. He hates dark colors."

Just as Harry had predicted, Tom Seymour had married the queen, having been allowed to do so by the king himself—unaware the couple had married long before the royal permission was obtained. That piece of news when it leaked out had been the scandal of the summer, and I had been all for removing my girl lest she be touched by it. I'd expected a proper marriage with the blessing of the king and the Protector, not this clandestine affair. Harry, however, had mandated that Jane stay put. "They're properly married, after all, and any damage has already been done. And besides, Jane shall now be living in the same household as the lady Elizabeth, the king's favorite sister. What better way to the heart of the king than that?"

As usual, I had not been able to muster an argument. Instead, I had had to hope Jane would be so uncomfortable with the newlyweds, she would beg to be sent home when I visited. Perhaps the couple themselves might like some privacy, instead of having two young girls underfoot.

But the visit did not match my hopes. Having shown off her new dress to me, Jane turned to Harry. "I like being here so much," she bubbled. "The Lord Admiral is so pleasant, and the queen is so kind!"

"How are your studies coming?"

"Wonderfully," said Jane, raising herself up on her toes to better emphasize her point. "The lady Elizabeth has an excellent tutor in Master William Grindal, and he teaches me as well on occasion. I know that your lordship sent me very good tutors," she hastened to add. "But Master Grindal excels even them in Greek."

"We must not distract him from his duties to the lady Elizabeth," I put in.

"Oh, but the queen quite encourages it! And did you know that she will soon be publishing another book? *Lamentations of a Sinner*. She has even let me read the manuscript! I hope that the queen might even allow me to collaborate with her sometime," Jane confided, her pretty brown eyes taking on a dreamy look. "When I am older and more accomplished, of course."

✺

If I must say so myself, I sew a shirt beautifully. On many a New Year's Day, I had presented my creations to my uncle King Henry, who confided to me once that they excelled his first queen's handiwork, and she was a capital shirt maker. I also made smocks, which graced the forms of both the ladies Mary and Elizabeth. I did not neglect to keep my own family well supplied with these garments, and I was hard at work on a shirt for Harry when he joined me in my chamber later that evening. "I am doing something new with the embroidery this time. See?"

"Lovely," Harry agreed. "So what did you think? Were you pleased to see our Jane getting on so well in the queen's household?"

"It appears that Jane has become very fond of the queen." I sighed slightly.

"So what is wrong with that?"

What was wrong with it, I longed to say, was that I wanted her to love me. "Nothing, of course. I just wish she paid the same respect to me as she did the queen."

"When has she been insolent toward you?"

"Never in so many words. Well, not at all, really. She is a good girl. But—"

"Collaborating with the queen when she gets older! Did you hear that? I say, this has opened up a world of opportunity for our Jane."

"I just hope it doesn't give her an inflated idea of herself," I ventured. "Modesty is an accomplishment in itself."

"Well, of course." My husband yawned.

I continued to work on my husband's shirt, my thoughts not on my stitches but on my first child, my little Henry, born when I was still just sixteen. What a sweet baby he had been! But he had lived only six months, and at seventeen, I had watched as he was laid in his tiny grave. I had been too drained from days of watching him fade away to cry. Harry had stood beside me, weeping openly, and his hateful mother had stood there, too. She had let it be known I was a burden on her son, with the large retinue my father insisted I have as a duke's daughter and his attempting to renege on his promise that he would support us until Harry came of age. This mother of several healthy grown sons had stared at the little coffin dispassionately, plainly thinking I was proving even worse of a bargain than she thought. I could not even bear her Harry a healthy male child.

My husband and I had been too young to know how to offer each other the comfort we each needed. After our little boy was buried, he had turned to his books and to his gambling and to his life at court, and I had turned to my relations and friends, whom I had visited for weeks on end. Somehow, though, we had come together often enough for me to conceive a second child, who had lived only hours. But whatever God's plan had been in depriving me of my first two babes, he seemed to have changed it with the birth of my third, for Jane and her sisters after her had been thriving infants, gulping their nurse's milk and protesting vigorously against the indignity of being swaddled.

Yet I could not stop thinking about my lost children—especially about my son. It was foolish, I knew, for he had died so young that I had no way of knowing what sort of boy he would have become, but I pictured him as an affectionate, kind young man who would have never scorned my ignorance and who would have written to me regularly from his place at court. I pictured him much like my younger half brothers, who were nearly as learned as my Jane but with a taste for archery and tennis, as well. Or perhaps Henry might have been like the lads of Jane Dudley, Countess of Warwick. The countess had lost several of her boys, two as young children and one during the siege of Boulogne three years before, but five had survived: handsome sons who outshone their plain little mother in every respect but who never treated her as an embarrassment.

My little Henry would have proudly worn my shirts, I thought as I sighed and turned my attention to my work.

5

Jane Dudley
September 1547

IN THE SUMMER OF 1547, THE DUKE OF SOMERSET HAD MOUNTED A SCOTTISH campaign, on which he was joined by my husband as second in command. I was left behind at Ely Place, undefended from the Duchess of Somerset as she spoke of her brother-in-law.

"Thomas Seymour should be in Scotland, fighting alongside his brother, instead of lounging around London with the queen," she informed me when she visited me early that September.

"I can't imagine why he chose to stay here. He's no coward."

"Can't imagine? Let me supply your deficiency, my dear. He wishes to stay here so that he can work his malign influence over the king, and undermine my husband's role as the Lord Protector."

"Surely not."

"Why, does Thomas Seymour have you under his spell, too?"

"Certainly not," I said. "But he is the king's uncle as much as the Protector."

"You needn't tell me that," said Anne Seymour, glaring at a book that lay on a table near us. "Do you know what he keeps beating upon? The minority of King Henry VI, where one person had the governing of the kingdom and the other of the king's person. Or so Thomas Seymour claims. And look how that king turned out." She snorted. "Why, Thomas Seymour can't even govern a young girl properly. Do you know what I saw the other night? The lady Elizabeth, floating down the Thames on a barge by herself, as though she were a wherryman. It's a disgrace. The queen is too besotted with Seymour to chaperone the girl properly."

I decided not to mention that I myself had seen the lady Elizabeth in her barge; with her fine head of hair she was unmistakable, especially when she made a point of waving and calling out greetings to the occupants of the vessels that came near hers. "I'm sure it was merely a lark. The lady Elizabeth is a sensible girl, and it seems that her tutors are quite demanding. And the weather here has been so fine."

"I don't see your girls being allowed to drift up and down the Thames on a barge all by themselves."

"Well, no. Mary prefers her books and her verses to the Thames, and Katheryn is but four years of age. How are your daughters doing, by the way?"

Anne was undeterred from her course. "In any case, I gave that Kat Astley"—the lady Elizabeth's governess—"a good scolding. What kind of governess calls herself 'Kat,' anyway? If the young lady is to make a respectable marriage, she can't afford to have any blemish on her reputation."

"She told my boy Robert once that she didn't want to get married." I smiled reminiscently. "They have known each other since they were young, you know. Robert says she was quite determined."

"Bah! A girl of that age is too young to know her own mind about anything. But it may turn into a self-fulfilling prophecy, if she's not more carefully guarded. The lady Elizabeth already has the stigma of being that Anne Boleyn's daughter."

Try as hard as she might, Anne, as sister-in-law to the queen who had supplanted that Anne Boleyn, could not help but sound rather smug.

◦ℐ◦

I saw Anne Seymour off, feeling guilty as I watched her barge, only a shade less grand than the king's, pull away. Our husbands had been friends since 1523, when as young men they had served together in France under Charles Brandon, so it had been natural when Edward Seymour married Anne as his second wife that the two of us would spend time together. He was very fond of her, for good reason: his first wife, pretty but ill suited temperamentally to her solemn husband, had been an adulteress. He had had her put away in a house of religion, after which she had had the decency to die and leave him free to take another wife.

The attractive Anne, bearing his children almost yearly and loyally supporting his career, had been the balm he needed after the hurt and shame of having been cuckolded. But even in the early days of their marriage, Anne, with the smidgen of royal blood she had through her mother, had been prone to give herself airs, and when her sister-in-law Jane became Henry VIII's third queen, it had well and truly turned her head. Yet she had good points: I just had to make an effort to remind myself of them.

Robert, who at fifteen was the third of my five living sons, entered my chamber and looked around. Then he called back, "It's safe! The duchess is gone. Come on in!"

"Really," I protested as my children ambled in, trailed by their uncle Jerome, "you should not speak of the Duchess of Somerset in that manner. She is a faithful wife, a loving mother, a pious woman, a—"

"Battle-axe," said Robert. "They should have left the Duke of Somerset here and sent her to Scotland. The Scots would turn tail."

"Robert!"

"Did she tell you about the Great Barge Incident?"

"Yes," I admitted.

"The lady Elizabeth told me what she said to poor Kat Astley." Robert turned to his brothers, ten-year-old Guildford and nine-year-old Hal, and to his thirteen-year-old sister, Mary. Only my youngest child, Katheryn, napping in her nursery, was not here for the fun. He pitched his voice high. "'An outrage, Mistress Astley, an outrage! Do you want a princess of the blood to marry a mere knight? For this is surely what will happen if you let her run around so!' Poor Kat Astley was prostrated for a day after the duchess's visit."

"She means well."

"What were you doing visiting the lady Elizabeth?" asked Hal.

"What's the harm? She just likes seeing someone now and then besides her ladies and the queen and the Marquis of Dorset's daughter. Now that is a frightening little miss, by the by. Deadly earnest. Knows at least three languages, they say, and can't laugh at a joke in any of them. I pity the man who marries her. He'll probably have to translate a passage from the Greek before he's allowed in the lady's bedchamber. At least the lady Mary wasn't there."

"Do the lady Mary," my own daughter begged.

Robert crossed himself, dropped to his knees, and lowered his voice to a growl. "*Ave Maria, gratia plena, Dominus tecum*—Oh, Jesu, my knees are sore!"

"Robert!" I protested, though not without first admiring the accuracy of the imitation. "I cannot have you treating the king's sister with such disrespect, even in the privacy of our home."

I could not be too angry at Robert, however, for I knew he spoke in part to distract me from my worry. Three years before, my husband and my son Henry had set off for war in France; there, my handsome, high-spirited boy, knighted just weeks before, had fallen ill and died during the siege of Boulogne. I had lost five other children to illnesses in early childhood, and I grieved for them still, but with them I'd had time to prepare for their deaths, to clasp them in my arms and offer them what comfort I could, to say good-bye. With Henry, I'd had to hear the news from a messenger, bringing what I had hoped at first was an ordinary letter from my husband. When my husband returned from France by himself a few weeks later, strained and grieving, I'd had to relive my misery again. Three years later, I now had to fear for the safety of my sons Jack and Ambrose in Scotland, not to mention that of my husband, for he was not a man to spare himself in battle. If there was fighting, they would be in the thick of it.

My husband's brother Andrew was fighting for England, too; of the three Dudley brothers, only Jerome was at home. I smiled at Jerome, who as usual was sitting on his favorite stool, enjoying the hubbub around him without taking part in it. He had been very young when his father, Edmund Dudley, was executed, so young that Edmund had had hopes he could train for the priesthood. But it had become apparent in another year or so he would not have a career in the Church or any place else, for his mind would never be more than that of a young child. He had been a docile lad who had grown into a sweet-tempered man, and as he liked company better than anything and was no trouble, John had brought him from his lodgings in the country to live with us at Ely Place.

"Please let Robert do the lady Mary again, at least," begged Guildford.

"Please," echoed Jerome in his voice that always startled me, so much like John's as it was.

I sighed. "Oh, very well. But only if he does the Duchess of Somerset again, too."

⁓

"You are here to see the king, my lady?"

I nodded at Thomas Seymour, coming out of the king's outer chambers at Hampton Court just as I was coming into them. "Yes. He summoned me. I hope nothing is wrong in Scotland."

"Not that I know of," Seymour said lazily. "Ned's alive and well, as far as I know."

"And my husband and sons? Have you any news of them?"

"No, but I imagine Ned would have told even me if there were any cause for concern. I daresay the king will tell you what you need to know." Seymour bowed and hurried away.

"He could have been more forthcoming, don't you think?" I asked my companion— Maudlyn Flower, one of the gentlewomen who served me. "But I suppose nothing can be so very wrong."

King Edward awaited me in the chair where he received visitors, his feet dangling well above the floor. I dropped a curtsey. "Perhaps you have seen our uncle, my lady?"

Though I am a short woman, it was still necessary for me to take care when I arose that I did not look down at the king. "Yes, Your Majesty."

"He brought us some money," said Edward cheerfully. "He's always bringing us money. But did he tell you the news?"

I bit my lip. "No, Your Majesty. I hope things are well with us in Scotland?"

"We had a victory!" the king announced. He slid off his chair and waved me over to a map lying on a table. "Here, at a place called Musselburgh. We killed ten thousand Scots. My lord of Warwick was ambushed before the battle," he added.

I froze.

"But he escaped," the king assured me quickly. "Oh, I would have told you immediately if he had not! He charged at one of them—Dandy Carr—and chased him for twelve score at spear point. He would have run Carr's horse straight through if his horse had been just a little slower. They must have very fast horses there."

"My lord was not hurt, then."

"No, no. The battle was joined the next day. See, my lady?"

I gazed at the map as the king recounted the battle with boyish gusto, my mind focusing only on the news that my John was safe.

Only when I was on my knees in my chapel, giving thanks for my husband's safety, did it occur to me to wonder why Thomas Seymour was giving the king money.

6

Frances Grey
December 1547

"I KNOW YOU'RE TAKING ME INTO THE CHAPEL, HARRY," I PROTESTED, ADJUST-ing my blindfold. "There are those two steps. Where else could I be?"

"Patience, my dear, patience." Harry led me forward a step or two, and I brushed against something that could only be a chapel pew. "There!"

Harry untied my blindfold, and I stared around me.

While I had been visiting friends, Bradgate's chapel had been completely whitewashed. The images of saints that decorated the walls had been obliterated; the altar had been stripped of its finery. "Well? How do you like it?"

"It's bare," was all I could manage.

"Well, of course it's bare," Harry said reasonably. "All of that frippery gets in between us and the Lord."

I turned my eyes again to the blank wall on my left. It had borne an image of the Virgin, commissioned by Harry's grandfather, the first Marquis of Dorset, when he built Bradgate Hall in the last century. He must have found the best workman in Leicestershire for the task; perhaps he'd even chosen someone from London. Probably he'd come in regularly to check the progress of the work. His children and grandchildren had gazed at it countless times over the years as they squirmed in chapel; some had seen it when they were married or when their own children were christened here. And now with a brush stroke it had vanished, to be replaced by blankness. Bradgate was Harry's ancestral home, not mine, but I felt as if I had been robbed of something. "It shall take some getting used to."

"Better sooner than later, when abolishing idolatry and superstition is concerned. And this is only the beginning." Harry looked around our stark chapel with satisfaction. "It's a new world, my dear. Our Jane will be so pleased when she sees it."

"No doubt she will."

"Oh, and I hate to have you go away so soon, but you've an invitation, and I suppose it must be accepted. It's from the lady Mary. No doubt you'll get your share of images at her place."

✐

The lady Mary and I were first cousins, and close in age; aged one-and-thirty that autumn of 1547, she was only a year or so my senior. She was, in fact, my godmother, though of course being a mere babe herself at the time, she had christened me by proxy. When she was small, I had been brought to the princess's household to play with her from time to time. Even when the failure of her mother, Catherine of Aragon, to give the king a living son had combined with the dark eyes of Anne Boleyn to turn the king against his queen, I'd still been able to visit my cousin occasionally. Then the king had married Anne, just a few months before my own wedding to Harry, and my poor cousin Mary had become more and more estranged from her father the king.

Harry might scoff about Mary's fondness for the old religion, but it was her faith that had pulled her through those horrid years. Without it, she never would have had the courage to face up to her father the king when he tried to get her to recognize the validity of his marriage to Anne. Goodness knows, he had frightened me enough—and he had never been anything but a kindly uncle to me. He had even pinched my cheek at my wedding and told me what a beautiful bride I was. That was more, I reflected, than what my husband had done.

At Hunsdon, I was just in time for Mass. Mary held at least two a day, sometimes four. Mary gave me a disapproving look afterward; I'd stumbled on some of the responses and had coughed when the incense grew particularly strong. "I hear that your household has ceased to hear the Mass."

"Yes." I considered mentioning Harry's other changes but thought better of it.

"The Protector has ceased to hear it also, as well as the Earl of Warwick. And the queen herself has joined the apostasy. I suppose I could have expected no less of her, however, after that marriage of hers. I just hope she does not corrupt my sister. But I must say that I am disappointed to hear that you have joined that crew. Your father would not have approved."

I wondered if he truly would have cared; one theology had been much the same as another to Father, as long as it didn't interfere with a good day's hunting. "I have no choice, my lady. It was my husband's decision."

Mary looked wistful. I wondered now, with her father dead, whether she would at last find a husband. It was odd, not to mention a little sad, to see a king's daughter past thirty and still unwed. She looked around at her little band of ladies, who had followed us from the chapel. "Well, shall we play cards?"

We walked into a chamber where a series of card tables, all neatly laid with cards and counters, awaited us. Susan Clarencius and Eleanor Kempe, who had served Mary for years, joined us. "How is the lady Jane?" Susan asked after we had played a round or two, Mary handily winning.

I found it much easier to speak of my daughter than to her. "She is faring very well in Queen Catherine's household. She has not written recently, but when she did, she seemed quite happy. The queen is a stimulating companion, and the lady Elizabeth is quite learned herself, of course."

Mary's face clouded. She and her younger half sister were not very close; indeed, Mary had been known to wonder aloud whether Elizabeth might have been the by-blow of one of Anne Boleyn's supposed lovers. I bit my lip and added hastily, "Of course, my Jane spends far more time with the queen than with the lady Elizabeth. They share only a few lessons, being several years apart. There is some gossip, though." I looked at the queen for her approval, received it, and went on. "The Protector and the queen are still quarreling over the queen's jewels, and now the Protector's wife is in the middle of it all."

"I'll have nothing said against the Duchess of Somerset," Mary said coldly. "She is a woman of virtue and a friend of mine."

"Indeed," I said, suddenly wishing myself back at Bradgate with its bare altars.

7

Jane Dudley
April 1548 to September 1548

Thomas Seymour patted the Queen of England as if she were a particularly fine heifer. "Well, Lady Warwick? Do you think the mouse will crawl nicely out of its hole?"

"I do indeed," I said as the queen gave a strained smile and my son Robert, who had decided I needed a manly escort to Chelsea, looked slightly ill. The couple's wards, the lady Elizabeth and the lady Jane, tittered.

To everyone's shock, the queen had announced her pregnancy a few weeks earlier. Now in her mid-thirties, she'd never quickened with child before, although Seymour was her fourth husband. Catherine had been miserable for the past few weeks, her early pregnancy sickness exacerbated by her having conceived for the first time at such a comparatively advanced age, but she had come out of her worst time and now had a healthy glow to her.

The queen took me by the arm. "Would you walk in the garden with me, my lady?" She smiled at her husband and at my Robert. "You can entertain the ladies Elizabeth and Jane. There are maternal matters I wish to discuss with Lady Warwick."

I let the queen lead me away toward some rose bushes, the flowers just a few weeks from bloom. The men, I saw, had paired off also: Thomas Seymour with the lady Elizabeth, Robert with Lady Jane. I suspected my Robert was not entirely happy about this situation. "I hope Your Grace is not overly concerned about this pregnancy?" I eyed the queen as appraisingly as Seymour had earlier. "There are risks, as you hardly need me to tell you, but you are not delicate look—"

"No, it is not that. For that I will trust in the Lord." The queen looked over her shoulder, but we were well out of sight of the others. "It is my husband and the lady Elizabeth who concern me. Tom is flirting outrageously with the girl, and I know not what to do."

"Flirting? A man married to a queen, flirting with a princess of the blood?"

Catherine nodded grimly. "At first it was mere pleasantry, I thought. Tom is not the sort of man who can let a pretty girl go unnoticed—I knew that when I married him. But lately, his behavior has been most unseemly. He comes bare legged into her chamber, surprises her in bed—even pats her on her buttocks. It is all quite open, mind you. Her whole household is aware of it."

"Does he do the same with the lady Jane?"

"No, not at all. He is very kind to her, very friendly—but no more. But then, he hopes to match her with the king. It would not do to demean her. And she is very young, too."

"Has he done more with the lady Elizabeth than flirt, do you think?"

"I don't believe he is lying with the girl, and I don't believe he will try. That would be too much even for Tom."

"Does she resist his advances?"

"Not in the least. I believe she was taken aback at first, but now I believe she looks forward to them, from the way she giggles. The lady Elizabeth has the strangest giggle, by the way. Almost like a neigh. I never heard it until Tom started his antics with her." She sighed. "I quite expected this from King Henry. Sooner or later, I thought, some pretty young girl would make her way into my household, and he would be after her. He did no such thing, though; he must have had his fill of young girls with Katherine Howard. But I never expected this treatment from Tom Seymour, who professed to love me so!" The queen broke off a sprig that was beginning to bloom and twisted it in her hands.

"There is no need to think that he no longer loves you, Catherine. Men sometimes act foolish when their wives are expecting a child," I offered gently. "Even loving husbands."

Catherine snorted. "What would you know about such matters? Your husband is notoriously faithful to you. My brother once tried to entice him into visiting one of the finest brothels in Southwark. There was no harm in a little paid pleasure, he said, and it would only improve the enjoyment of the marital bed. Your husband was horrified at the very idea."

I had never heard this story, and I paused a moment to savor it. "Well, I am lucky. Most other men have their lapses. Have you considered sending the lady Elizabeth away?"

"Yes, but it would surely cause talk. And I am half afraid Tom would follow her."

"Follow her? You saw him today. He is looking forward to his coming child. Why would he sacrifice that for a fourteen-year-old chit?" I patted the queen on her arm. "He is anxious about the babe, that is all, and this is his foolish way of putting his mind off it, I'll wager. Let him have his horseplay for a few months. It will all be over soon, and you will be a proud mother, and he, a doting father."

"Perhaps you are right."

"Of course I am right! Now let us speak of happier matters. Where are you going to spend your confinement?"

Despite Thomas Seymour's folly, I could not help but feel rather smug as I rode in my barge toward home, for it was true John had never been unfaithful to me. It could be no great credit to my own charms, for I knew well I was not beautiful—not even pretty. Though my figure was tidy for a woman who had borne thirteen children, the most that could be said about my face was it was pleasant. On my best days, I could just manage something approaching prettiness, and that was only with the assistance of two ladies, the best tailor and hoodmaker in London, and a little bit of art.

I smiled, ignoring the sights and sounds of the busy Thames as my barge lumbered along. My looks, or lack thereof, had never kept John from my bed; indeed, we had anticipated our wedding day, though naturally this was not a fact I had advertised to my sons and daughters, particularly my daughters. It was the Castle of Loyalty tournament that had been our downfall, so to speak. Over Christmas of 1524, when King Henry's court was a more cheerful place than it became later, sixteen young men, including John, had proposed to defend their castle against all comers. The king had responded with enthusiasm, and soon after New Year's of 1525, a team of workmen had dutifully built a mock castle, with a mount on which stood a unicorn. Standing on each of the castle's turrets was a lady, who was expected to clasp her handkerchief to her heart at appropriate moments and in general look romantic and worried at the same time. It was a drawn-out tournament that took place over a series of days, so instead of the same four ladies sighing upon the turrets day after day, different ladies were used on each occasion.

Having just recently been appointed as one of the first of Queen Catherine's maidens, I was a newcomer to court, and not one of its ornaments. My father, however, was master of the armory, who helped arrange the king's tournaments. He had said a word to the right people, and so I had been chosen as one of the ladies of the castle.

I had never been dressed so thinly in my life. We were supposed to look like damsels from King Arthur's court, which must have been a chilly place. I wore simply a flowing tunic with an under tunic, with a hooded mantle to keep the cold off. The garments clung, which was not a bad thing, as I had a pretty figure, but the idea of the entire court seeing just how pretty was so daunting to me that at the feast afterward, I was slipping away when a slender hand pulled me back. "Where are you going?"

Anne Boleyn was about nine years my senior, and whatever people said about her afterward, she was never anything but kind to me. Perhaps because I was so much younger than she, and such a novice at court, she had taken a liking to me. It was Anne who had helped me arrange my costume after putting on her own robes in a careless, jaded manner that reminded all of us she had spent time in the splendid courts of Burgundy and France, where grand spectacles were the order of the day.

"To change," I said.

"Change? What on earth for?"

"I feel naked."

"You look fine. It's a costume; everyone expects it. And what are you going to put on? That terrible gable headdress that you had on earlier, I wager."

"I had it made for me in Kent. It's almost new."

"It should have stayed in Kent. It's not a style that suits anyone under thirty, don't you see? You should wear a French hood. Your hair is your greatest beauty; it should be displayed as it is now."

In my distress at my clinging costume, I had forgotten about my dark brown, hip-length hair, which was bared for all of the court to see. "But—"

"It's too late, anyway. Who is that young man staring at you?"

"Sir John Dudley." He'd been knighted by Charles Brandon, Duke of Suffolk, while serving in France just over a year before. "He is my father's ward. I am to marry him."

"Have you known him long?"

"Since I was three. We were raised together. We are almost like brother and sister."

Anne snorted. "My brother assuredly does not look at me the way that Sir John is looking at you." She raised her chin. "Get Sir John over here. Do *this*." She tilted her head slightly and sent a signal with her eyes.

I obeyed. My version of *this* was a poor one, but it actually did bring John over. I had not seen him in a number of months, as I was a recent arrival at court, and he had been there for some time now. At the tournament, he had just been another knight in armor; now that he was in his ordinary clothes, I saw he had grown lean and muscular. I felt the stirring of a feeling I did not fully understand, except to know it was not sisterly.

Men's eyes usually lingered upon Anne; John's did not. Instead, he nodded to her politely and turned to me, barely acknowledging her departure as someone claimed her for the dance that was just beginning. "Jane?" he said as ladies and gentleman milled around and jostled us. "You're beautiful."

"It's just the dress."

"No. It's you. Let's dance."

This was odd, indeed. John was a passable dancer, but he had never been an enthusiastic one. I obeyed him without comment, however, and we joined the pavane.

I could perform all of the intricate steps without thinking about them, which was fortunate, because John and I never took our eyes off each other. The odd feeling I had when I'd looked at John earlier was spreading throughout my entire body. I could not imagine how it was not visible to the entire company. When the dance was over and we had made our obeisances to each other and to the king and queen, John took my hand and we hastened, without a word, outside the great hall and into a dark corner, where we came instantly into each other's arms and kissed until we were breathless.

"Do you want to go back to the feast?" John whispered at last.

"No."

John said nothing more, but took me by my hand and led me off. I knew instinctively where he was taking me, and I did not care. His chamber was not in the palace itself, but in some outbuildings built to handle the excess of courtiers. The twists and turns and flights of stairs we had to take to reach our destination did nothing to dilute our passion; indeed, once in a while we would stop our progress at a particularly inviting dark spot and kiss again. At last, John stopped in front of a door, turned a key, and guided me inside. It was the tiniest of chambers, just large enough to hold a stand and a narrow bed. There was nowhere to sit but on the bed, and after we had sat there and kissed a while, there was nothing for us to do but lie upon it and kiss some more. Nothing, once we lay down and the only thing that stood between John and me were two flimsy layers of cloth, for him to do but to strip me bare of them and then, at my soft urgings, to take my maidenhead.

I blame the dress completely.

The next day, John had a word with my father, and a month later, we were married. No one could have suspected, as we exchanged our vows and as the guests watched us shyly settle into our marriage bed after the priest blessed it, that we'd already consummated our relationship. No one, that is, except for Anne Boleyn, who had winked at me as I crept back in the direction of the maidens' chamber late that night.

I had winked back.

ॐ

"Mother, are you listening to me?"

I blinked my way back from the twenty-three-year excursion into the past my thoughts had been taking. "No," I admitted.

"Well, it's about the lady Elizabeth. She hardly said a word to me, and we've been friends for years."

"Yes, she seemed rather taken up by the Admiral." I decided not to tell my son about the conversation I'd had with Catherine Parr. It was bad enough having the queen upset while she was great with child, and Thomas Seymour running around Chelsea bare-legged, without Robert deciding he had to uphold the lady Elizabeth's honor. I envisioned him traveling down to Chelsea, sword in hand, while Thomas Seymour ran around in his nightshirt, and despite myself, I snickered at the sight my thoughts were presenting to me.

"It's not amusing. She's hanging on every word the Admiral says, as if he weren't thirty years her senior. It's disgusting."

"I am sure she is merely being polite, as one should be to one's elders."

Robert ignored the pointed tone in which I'd spoken the last part of my remark. "Even that little lady Jane goggles at the man. So does Kat Astley, for that matter, and she's married, for God's sake. You'd think the three of them had been shut up in a nunnery for twenty years, the way they act."

"He is an inveterate charmer, that is all. Don't worry so."

Three weeks later, Queen Catherine caught Thomas Seymour with the lady Elizabeth in his arms. Her reaction could be felt all the way up the Thames to Greenwich. Elizabeth was sent in haste—or as much in haste as a princess and her entourage could be sent off—to Cheshunt, where Kat Astley's married sister lived.

I visited the queen at her manor at Hanworth, near Richmond, a couple of weeks later. The queen and Lady Jane were hard at work sewing baby things, while Thomas Seymour bustled around preparing for the queen's move to Sudeley Castle, where she would spend her confinement. The queen and

Seymour seemed their old selves; even when they railed about the still-ongoing battle with the Protector and his duchess about the queen's jewels, they did so with a happy sense of mutuality. The Admiral beamed at the lady Jane paternally from time to time and effusively praised her stitches (which hardly deserved it, Jane not being much of a needlewoman), but otherwise kept his charm well within the bounds of propriety. The lady Elizabeth, the queen told me in private, had written a contrite letter expressing her gratitude for their friendship, as well as a friendly but entirely decorous letter to Seymour himself. I left Hanworth content in the thought that all had worked out and that I and the rest of Catherine's friends would soon be hearing of the queen's safe delivery.

In September, we got the good news: Catherine had given birth to a girl, Mary, at the end of August. Then, just a few days later, another message arrived. The queen was dead.

8

Frances Grey
September 1548 to October 1548

JUST A DAY AFTER THE TERRIBLE NEWS ARRIVED THAT QUEEN CATHERINE had died of childbed fever, a messenger rode up with a letter from Tom Seymour, written in his own hand. It was tear stained and barely coherent. His aged mother would be taking charge of his baby girl, and the Protector had invited him to stay with him at Sion House so he would not have to face his sorrow alone. Our Jane had been chief mourner at the queen's funeral and had done her duty with much gravity and honor. Which brought him to his main point: with the queen gone, he could no longer maintain our daughter in his household. The very sight of the girl for whom his dear wife had had so much affection was too much for him to bear. In fact, Seymour said in a postscript, our daughter was on her way to Bradgate now.

I had barely had time to make my daughter's chambers ready for her, when I heard Jane was just a mile or so off. Not long afterward, my girl stood before me. She was dressed in mourning for the queen, which made her look older than her eleven years, and I could see she was beginning to develop a hint of a bosom.

Jane allowed me to embrace her. "I was very sorry to hear of the queen's death," I said. "I know she was very fond of you."

"She was very kind to me. I shall miss her."

"When you are ready, we can talk more of—"

"Jane! Come here, my girl!"

Jane rushed to Harry's arms. He ruffled her hair. "Tell me about the queen, lass. I know it must have been dreadful. Wasn't it?"

"It was. At first everything went so well. I didn't see the poor little baby being born; the queen said I was too young. But it didn't take that long, and I saw the queen soon afterward. She looked so happy, and the Admiral was so proud. He said he had the finest baby girl in all of England."

Harry said, "Well, he was wrong about that, because I had the finest baby girl in all of England, but we can make some allowances. Go on, child."

"Everyone thought the queen was going to be well, and then suddenly she fell ill. The Admiral said later the very same thing happened to his sister Queen Jane. She became feverish and started to rant—accusing him of treating her badly, of not allowing her to be alone with her own physician, so many foolish things she never would have said if she had been in her right mind, for he was never unkind to her. Anyway, he lay in bed beside her and tried to ease her, and toward the end, she did become calm. She dictated her will and left him everything. She said she wished her possessions were a thousand times more in value than they were. And then she started to fade away, almost, and in a few hours, she died."

Jane put her handkerchief to her eyes, and Harry patted her back. "She is in heaven, Jane."

"Oh, I know," said Jane. "But I miss her, and I feel so sorry for the poor Admiral. He was crying—even when he shut himself away, we could hear him. I think he loved the queen dearly. I never saw them have an argument—well, only once. It was right before the lady Elizabeth left. They were shouting at each other—I don't know about what. But later, the Admiral came to me and told me that he was sorry I'd overheard that, but that I shouldn't worry, all married people fought once in a while, and that they usually made it up. And I think they did make it up after the lady Elizabeth left. The Admiral had the cooks make the queen's favorite foods, and he sent for anything that she wanted that he couldn't supply. He ordered magnificent things for the baby's chamber. When he had to leave, he sent letters to her every day." Jane brightened. "The queen did have a very nice funeral, though. Doctor Coverdale preached the sermon in English and said that the offering was not for the dead, but for the poor."

Harry nodded approvingly.

∽

In a few days, it was as if Jane had never left us. She approved thoroughly of our stripped-down chapel—I still found myself walking in there and thinking a thief had been to Bradgate—and she took it upon herself to improve her younger sister Kate, who was not entirely grateful for the attention.

Jane had been back at Bradgate for several weeks when a messenger delivered a letter from the Admiral. Unlike the tear-laden missive he had last sent us, this was written in a clerk's trim hand and came straight to the point. So grieved by the queen's death that he had had little regard for his own doings, and believing his household would have to be broken up, he had sent our daughter home, but now he had reviewed the situation and felt he could retain the queen's household. Therefore, he was able to take Jane back into his care, and what was more, his mother would treat her as her own daughter. As soon as he could manage it, he would come to talk to Harry and me in person.

I frowned at the letter. Tom Seymour was planning to retain all of the women who had waited on the queen, plus a hundred and twenty gentleman and yeomen. How on earth could he keep up such a household, with no queen to justify it? Even I could see the impossibility of it all.

Katherine Brandon, Duchess of Suffolk, my childhood companion who had become my stepmother, was paying us a visit at Bradgate that day. "So, what does Tom Seymour want?"

"He wants us to send Jane back to stay with him."

"So soon? I saw him at his brother's house a couple of weeks ago, and he could hardly hear the queen's name without weeping. Or maybe it was just the company of Somerset and his duchess. I declare, I shall be heartbroken if my two boys end up rubbing along as miserably as those two brothers do. I told Somerset that he really ought to give his brother a little more power, to keep him sweet."

"You told the Lord Protector that?"

"Oh, I tell everyone everything, you know that, Frances. Not that everyone listens. Somerset didn't, anyway. But at least I got the cold stare instead of the blank look, so I knew he heard me at least. Maybe one day he'll actually remember what I said and act on it, thinking of course it was his own brilliant idea." Katherine snorted. "Mind you, I like Somerset; he's a kind man in that remote way of his. I trust him, which is more than I can say for his brother Tom."

"Harry trusts Tom Seymour."

"Do you?"

"I don't know what to think. Harry—"

"Why did the Lord give you a brain if not to think? Really, Frances! You've more common sense in your little finger than what's in the whole of Harry Grey. It's high time you realized that. So what do *you* think?"

"I was going to tell you, if you'd allowed me to speak. I believe Harry is still keen on marrying Jane to the king, although he hasn't said as much to me lately."

"Of course not. When does he consult you, and bring common sense into the picture?"

"He consults me. It is not quite as bad as you say."

"Certainly he consults you. On what to serve your guests and where to lodge them, no doubt, and no more. And you allow it, even though I'll wager this household would fall apart in days were its managing left up to your Harry."

"It's easy for you to say how married people should get on together," I snapped. "You are, after all, a widow, and I don't recall you having things entirely your way when Father was alive."

"No, but I was making inroads. But do go on."

"It's not that I trust or mistrust the Admiral anyway—it is Jane. She took a very high opinion of herself in the queen's household. She has great gifts, I know, but she has become almost arrogant. She treats my poor Kate as if she were the household fool instead of her younger sister, and me—well, she has never had much to say to me, you know, but now she is almost insolent. Even Harry noticed."

"If Harry Grey noticed something amiss about his darling, she must need a good boxing on the ears, Frances. Give it to her. I would, if my lads were acting so."

"I fear that if I send her back to Tom Seymour—particularly without the queen—she will take an even higher opinion of herself."

"Quite possibly." Katherine snorted. "You ought to send her to the Duchess of Somerset."

⟨ornament⟩

To my surprise, Harry was also reluctant to return Jane to Seymour's care. He wrote a long letter to the Admiral, explaining that Jane needed to be under my guidance. "As I do think she ought to be, my dear, because she has been a bit pert as of late, one can't deny it. But there are other reasons, too, of course."

"Which are?"

"Quite frankly, I don't think the Admiral's the right man to entrust Jane's education to. Why, they say even the queen became more frivolous in his company in those last few months. She might lose interest in her studies."

"Nothing could turn Jane from her books." My tone held a conviction so firm that even my stepmother would have been impressed.

"Well, perhaps you're right, my dear. Perhaps you are. But I'll not chance it. Seymour has asked to visit and will no doubt try to persuade us, but we must stand firm."

That was easier said than done.

After a further exchange of letters, in which even Jane herself joined, Tom Seymour arrived at Bradgate in October. He was accompanied by Sir William

Sharington, who ran the mint in Bristol. My husband entertained Seymour, while I entertained Sharington.

They must have rehearsed for their conversations with us. To every objection I raised, Sharington had a rejoinder that made me feel utterly unreasonable for having entertained it, and Harry fared no better with Seymour. Forgotten was the fact that the king had not shown the slightest inclination to marry our girl; Seymour was still laboring to bring it about. All he needed was time and more access to the king. Harry had debts? They would all be taken care of by Seymour, who offered to loan him two thousand pounds. Jane was still but young to be pledged in marriage? The Protector's girls were even younger, and had I not heard they were fine scholars? If we let our daughter languish at Bradgate, there was every chance the Protector would marry one of them to the king. Would I want to attend that royal wedding, knowing my gifted young daughter should have been standing in the bride's place? What of my daughter's feelings? There was no young lady more suitable to be Edward's queen. Why, if I let such a chance slide by her, I might as well marry her to a mere knight's younger son this very afternoon and be done with it.

If I was the well of common sense Katherine claimed, the well had run dry by the time I came out of our interview. "My lord, your lady has expressed her willingness to return the lady Jane to you," Sharington announced triumphantly as we emerged from our conference.

"Then I cannot but agree," Harry said. I surmised from his dazed look, he had survived Seymour's bombardment no better than I had survived Sharington's.

Yet the misgivings we could not entirely suppress might have won out had not Seymour begged to pay his respects to Jane herself. "My lord Admiral!" she said, arising from the table where she had been working. There was no mistaking her genuine delight. "I hope you are doing well, as is your baby girl?"

"Little Mary is thriving, and I am as well as can be expected, but my household has been empty without its ward, Jane. It is not the same. I have been attempting to persuade your parents to have you come back to me. My work is done; I can only hope they say yes. Won't you put in a good word on my behalf?"

"I very much enjoyed staying with you, my lord." She looked up at him, and at us, in a fetching way that she could have inherited only from my own mother. "I should be most pleased to return—if my lord father and lady mother consent, of course."

Harry and I looked at each other and at Jane, and we knew we could do nothing else. A week later, we watched as Jane once again left Bradgate.

9

Jane Dudley
December 1548

AT THE CHRISTMAS MASQUE AT WHITEHALL, THE KING VISIBLY STIFLED A yawn, his third such effort in an hour. For the sake of the masquers, I hoped it was the lateness of the hour and not the quality of the entertainment that was afflicting the king so.

Yet I suspected that even had this been the grandest of masques at the most splendid of courts, it would not have been enough, for there was something very odd about the court this Christmas. All of the men, including my husband, seemed distracted, and tones were hushed. It reminded me, now that I thought of it, of the days a dozen years before, just before Anne Boleyn and her supposed lovers had been clapped into the Tower. The same wary glances, the same conferences in corners, the same desperate jollity as everyone tried to pretend nothing was amiss.

I turned my eyes from the masquers and toward the dais where the king sat, flanked by the Duke and Duchess of Somerset. Despite his grand clothing, only a trifle less splendid than the king's, the duke had a weary, strained look about him. The duchess—resplendent in jewels I recognized as the late queen's—was patting his hand in a tender way that reminded me why I sometimes liked her.

As I gazed toward the duke and duchess, I felt a pair of eyes on me. But no, they were not fixed upon me; rather, they were staring in precisely the same direction. They were those of Thomas Seymour.

The masque over, it was time for dancing—starting with a galliard, which my own generation wisely left for the younger among us to enjoy. The king promptly arose and led out the Protector's eldest daughter, Anne, while one of his companions, nineteen-year-old Henry Sidney, partnered my daughter Mary. While I watched the latter pair attentively, noting they seemed more interested in each other than in the dance, Thomas Seymour pushed forward, Lady Jane Grey in tow. For a moment, I thought they might join the dance as a couple themselves—a shocking breach of etiquette for the Admiral, who had been widowed but a few months—but instead, my eldest son claimed Jane Grey, and the dance began as Thomas Seymour stood with the rest of the spectators.

The Duke and Duchess of Somerset had joined the throng and stood there hand in hand, watching their own daughter dance with the king. Then the duke walked over to his brother and took his hand with a smile that seemed genuine, if wary. "I am glad to see you here this Christmas, my brother. Is this a portent of a better year between us to come?"

"You say 'I,' Brother, not 'we.' Are you slipping?"

I could not help but smile at this, for John, too, had commented on the alacrity with which the Protector had taken to using the royal "we" in his letters. Somerset said in an injured tone, "I use 'we' in correspondence, as befits my position. I do not use it elsewhere."

Thomas Seymour snorted. "Well, I have come here to see my nephew the king. I cannot see him in private. I must make do at public occasions like this one."

"I have never prevented you from seeing the king," Somerset said. "I have asked only that you see him when he is at leisure to receive visitors and that you refrain from giving him the presents of money that you have brought him in the past. He has plenty in hand."

"Yes, and you have plenty of my late wife's jewels in yours. Or on your wife's person, I should say."

Somerset's hand went to his left hip, where he would have worn his sword had this not been a feast. With obvious difficulty in controlling his temper, he said, "We have been through this. The jewels became the Crown's upon the king's death, and even if there was the slightest bit of doubt, which there is not, they certainly became the Crown's upon the death of the queen. Until the king marries, the Duchess of Somerset has every right to wear them. It is fitting, as my wife, that she do so. She graces them by placing them on her person."

"Indeed," said Seymour. "I see that your daughter is wearing some of them, too. Have your youngest children some tucked inside their cradles, as well?"

"I will not have you speak of my daught—"

The music stopped, and Somerset flushed as heads turned to see why he had raised his voice. The king released his partner with a bow that made her beam and run to her mother to recount her triumph. Young Anne Seymour had barely left the king when Thomas Seymour, the queen's jewels forgotten, swiftly disengaged the lady Jane from my son and propelled her firmly in the king's direction. "Your Majesty, might my young ward be allowed to demonstrate the tutelage of her dancing master?"

The king smiled down at Lady Jane. She was a small girl; the Protector's gangly daughter, by contrast, was slightly taller than her royal partner. "Why, we shall be honored."

With Seymour and Jane's father, the Marquis of Dorset, beaming nearby, I watched as the king and the lady Jane danced together. I had expected such a studious young lady would have no interest in such frivolity, but I was quite wrong. Jane danced beautifully, though she seemed to be enjoying the music more than the dance itself. As for the king, his father had been a fine dancer in his youth, and Edward evidently took after him in this respect. I turned to the Somersets, who were talking together unintelligibly but obviously angrily. "They make a pretty pair, don't they?"

"Lovely," said the Protector. He put his hand on my husband's shoulder. "Let us talk," he said quietly.

By midnight, the king himself had begun nodding off in his chair, and the Protector gave the signal he be escorted to his bed. The rest of us, some more sober than others, straggled to our chambers.

John would have kissed me and rolled over to sleep, but I would not let him. "What on earth did the Protector have to discuss with you, on Christmas day? Why does the man look so miserable? Why is everyone acting so strangely?"

My husband gave half a smile. "Can I choose which question to answer, or must I answer all at once?"

"You can answer any one of them, because I suspect that they all have the same answer."

"You would suspect right." John lay on his back, staring up at the canopy. "The Admiral is becoming truly dangerous. It is not just that he wants to marry the king to that lady Jane Grey, which would be harmless enough, as the king can't be forced to marry any girl he doesn't wish to marry. The Admiral aspires to marry the lady Elizabeth."

My first foolish thought was my son Robert would be furious at that. Then I realized the deeper implications. "Marry the girl who's second in line to the throne?"

"Yes. He seems to find no incongruity in the idea at all."

I winced. "I knew he had flirted with her outrageously while the queen was alive; Catherine told me so. But I thought there was no harm in it, so I said nothing."

"How could you have thought there was harm in it? After all, the queen was living and was getting ready to bear Seymour a child. He couldn't exactly put her aside. In any case, that's not the worst of it. The worst is that I, and several others, believe, on good information, that he intends to take both the king and Elizabeth into his custody and imprison and perhaps kill the Protector."

"John?"

"I don't believe Seymour is entirely sane where the Protector is concerned. I'll freely admit that Somerset has his faults, but he's never held any ill will toward the Admiral. He was kindness itself to Seymour when the queen died. But Seymour has convinced himself that the Protector has some grand scheme to alienate him from the king and to ruin him. The more he speaks against the Protector, the less the Protector is inclined to let him near the king, and then the more the Admiral speaks against the Protector. And so it grows worse and worse."

"Has someone tried to speak to the Admiral?"

"Many have tried to reason with him. I have myself. I couldn't make any headway; I'm too close to his brother, so he thinks I have sinister designs against him, as well. But no one else has succeeded either."

It was fortunate, I thought, that poor Jane Seymour had not lived to see her brothers fighting for control over her son. "What is the Protector going to do? I suppose that is what you were talking about tonight?"

"He would rather not do anything. Paget wrote him a letter this very day, complaining that he was trying too hard to please all men and has not been firm in upholding the laws. And those are against ordinary men, not his own brother. But he can't tolerate this much longer. Something will have to be done." John put his arm around me. "I cannot tell you how I long for the day when the king is old enough to rule on his own."

"What does the poor boy think of all this?"

"Somerset has tried to shield him from it. Unfortunately, that also means trying to shield him from Seymour, and you know how charming Seymour can be when he cares to exert himself. Somerset can't compete with that; he's never had the gift of speaking to young boys. So the king's unhappy with the Protector because he wants to visit with his favorite uncle." John shook his head. "It's a thankless job, being Protector. I wouldn't have it. Sometimes I wonder whether Somerset regrets having taken it on."

"You are friends. Why don't you ask him?"

John sighed. "I could have a year ago. Now I can't. This discussion we had tonight—it was like a king speaking to a councilor, not two old friends who fought together. I was the one he told when he discovered his first wife had been unfaithful to him. I was the one he told when he became engaged to his present wife; he was excited as a boy. All that's changed now. He has subjects, not friends. One doesn't confide in mere subjects."

"Maybe when the king comes out of his minority and Somerset is back to being another advisor, he will be more like his former self."

"Maybe." John wrapped his arm around me tighter, and I pressed my lips to his. He smiled in the darkness. "Shall we make it a merry Christmas for two people, at least?"

10

Frances Grey
January 1549

MY FIRST THOUGHT WHEN MY HUSBAND'S MESSENGER GALLOPED INTO Bradgate was that something had befallen Jane or my husband in London. "What on earth is it?" I called as I hastened to meet him. "Is someone ill?"

"No, my lady, but the marquis wants you and the girls to come to London immediately." Before I could get out a question, the messenger added, "It is the Admiral, my lady. He is under arrest."

∞

As I neared London, I began to hear the rumors about the Admiral's downfall. The closer I got to the city, the wilder the rumors became. At one milestone, the tale was that he had been plotting to kill the Protector; at the next, the story was going about that he had been planning to kill the king himself, followed by the lady Mary, and then to marry the lady Elizabeth and jointly rule England with her. One account even had it that he had been caught breaking into the king's bedchamber and had killed the king's faithful dog when it barked at him. One thing was certain: he was a prisoner in the Tower, but my Jane was safe at Dorset House. So was Harry.

"I am a lucky man," he said when I arrived. "I was with Seymour the night before he was arrested—staying at his house, as a matter of fact. I would ride to and from Parliament with him, dine with him. They arrested him when we were preparing to leave for Westminster together. His house is being searched on orders of the council, and I've no doubt our bargain about Jane will be brought out. I'll have to give evidence, I suppose."

"Harry, tell me you knew nothing about any plans to do violence to the king."

"I'll tell you, and I'll mean it. Seymour went on a great deal about building an affinity; you'd think we were in the last century. The worst I ever thought he would do would be to get the king declared to be out of his majority and the Protector removed from power. And I never heard any plans about precisely how he was going to do it."

"But you encouraged such talk."

"If Tom Seymour wants to talk about something, he's going to whether one encourages him or not. I listened. He's been telling all and sundry these things, it appears."

"How did the council find out?"

"The Earl of Rutland. Something Seymour said made him nervous, and he went to the Earl of Warwick—he admires Warwick—and told him. Warwick brought him to Somerset immediately. But you haven't even asked about Jane yet."

"I haven't had the chance, Harry." It was late, and Jane was already asleep in her chamber. "You started speaking as soon as I entered the room."

"True, my dear," Harry conceded. He made a motion with his hand that served as a sort of apology. "I'm concerned about the effect all of this will have on her. I just hope she doesn't have to give evidence against him. They say the lady Elizabeth might be questioned. It seems he had hopes of marrying her." He snorted. "Poor Seymour. He did aim high. But I suppose after you've bedded a queen, the girl who's second in line to the throne is the next logical choice. I'm surprised he didn't try for the lady Mary, but then again, perhaps not."

"Harry, promise me, if he gets freed from prison, you will not let our daughter go back to him."

"Don't fear. I've no intention. From henceforth, Jane stays with us—until she goes to her husband."

Encouraged, I went on. "And that you will have nothing to do with him. Harry, you could have ended up in prison yourself."

"You don't need to tell me that," Harry said huffily. He sighed. "But yes, I have learned my lesson."

❧

Over the past few weeks, it seemed as if every man in London was called upon by the Protector to depose as to what he knew about Tom Seymour and his doings. There seemed to be no one whom he had not confided in at one time or another. Harry had had to go before the Protector several times—each time he was summoned, I paced my chamber, fearing he would not come back—and the letters he and I had written to Seymour were duly dragged out. Even Jane's letter to Seymour did not escape Somerset's sharp eye, but she herself was not called upon to give evidence, the Protector having satisfied himself she knew nothing of any interest to him.

As it became clear neither Harry nor Jane would suffer for Seymour's folly, I relaxed, then marveled at all that had gone on in the past couple of months while my girl sat quietly at Seymour Place, practicing her music and improving her Latin and Greek. Seymour had come to the king's chambers at any odd time he pleased, examining the locks and windows to gauge how easily a boy could be smuggled out. With the help of his friend Sharington, the man who'd so handily persuaded me to send my daughter back, he had been plotting to coin money with an eye toward paying an army to help him overthrow his brother. He had bragged of how well he would govern England once the Protector was locked up and he himself was in power. Less sinister, but more disturbing to me as a mother, were the stories that emerged about a flirtation with the lady Elizabeth. Seymour had popped into the princess's room in the morning, bare-legged, and had made as if to pounce on the girl. With the queen assisting, apparently with the notion that this was simply Seymour having his fun, he had held Elizabeth down and cut a black gown of hers he disliked into shreds. Then the queen herself had caught her husband embracing Elizabeth, and the fun had ended. Might he have been engaging in such conduct with my Jane? She was young—but not so young that such behavior by a man was beyond belief.

"There is something I must talk to you about," I said, half stammering, as I came into Jane's chamber at Dorset House. "The Admiral. He seems to have been very familiar with the lady Elizabeth while you were both there."

"Yes, my lady. He was."

"In what way?"

Jane's face puckered in puzzlement. "The same way he was with me, I suppose. He would pay her compliments on her music. He liked to dance with her—with me, too. And with the queen, too, of course, before she became great with child and preferred to sit and watch. He never spoke much about what we were reading; I don't think he cared for it himself. He would go riding with us and the queen quite often. The lady Elizabeth is a good horsewoman, better than me; he always would praise her. Sometimes they would make a game of seeing who could ride the fastest, but it made the queen worry too much, so they stopped."

"And after you came to live with him again after the queen's death? Was he familiar with you?"

"No, my lady. Not like the old days. I spent most of my time with his mother, doing needlework and practicing my music when I wasn't having my lessons. He seemed very busy, much more than he had been when the queen was alive. He was always coming and going. Even when Father stayed there, I hardly saw him. The most I saw of him was when he took me to court for Christmas. I enjoyed that."

"Jane, I must ask you a delicate question. Did he ever lay his hands upon you?"

"My lady?"

"Like—like a lover might."

"No, Mother! Nothing like that." Jane's expression, half indignant at this insult to the Admiral, half puzzled at my asking such a strange question, was worth a thousand denials.

I let out my breath with relief. "Then I am glad to hear it."

"Mother, is the Admiral in trouble? Am I the cause of it?"

"You are not the cause of it, but he is in very serious trouble. It has to do with the Protector and things that he has been saying against him."

"Oh, the Protector," Jane said offhandedly. "The Admiral hates him."

11

Jane Dudley
March 1549 to October 1549

WITH THE LAST OF THE DEPOSITIONS COMPLETED, THE KING'S COUNCIL HAD made the painful choice to bring formal charges of high treason against Thomas Seymour, which he refused to answer, and a bill of attainder had passed both the Lords and the Commons. An ashen-faced Somerset had signed his younger brother's death warrant, his hand shaking, and on March 20, 1549, the Admiral, debonair as always, walked to the scaffold at Tower Hill.

His brother was not there to see his last moments on earth. He and the duchess had gone with the king to Greenwich, where the duchess had invited my husband and me to stay lest Somerset give way at the last moment and halt the execution. But as we sat down to breakfast on bacon, eggs, and cheese, it was clear the Protector's mind was not on the delicious-smelling food, not even on the quince marmalade made by his own duchess, who liked to potter around in the kitchen from time to time.

"The fourth Edward had to put his brother to death," said the Protector. "I wonder if he felt as I do today."

"The Duke of Clarence was a menace to the king," said John. He laid an arm upon Somerset's sleeve. For the occasion, the Protector had dressed in black. "And your brother was a menace to our king—and to you. You heard what he was plotting."

"The man gave you no choice," the duchess said briskly.

"He would never have stopped plotting against you," I added for good measure.

The duke sighed and stared toward the window, then at the clock on the mantle. "It must be about to take place." He slowly spread some marmalade over his bread and took the smallest bites. "Delicious," he said tonelessly.

For the next hour or so, the men talked about the other problems in the realm, of which there were many at the time. John, normally a taciturn man, hardly stopped talking long enough for the Protector to form a thought, much less a response, while we women discussed our gardens and our children in false, bright voices. Then one of the duke's servants knocked on the door and entered. "The Constable of the Tower wishes to inform you that the sentence has been carried out, Your Grace. The body has been taken to the chapel for burial."

I felt the Admiral's shade glide into the room and make himself comfortable.

"Go back and make certain that the body is treated with all due respect, as befits an uncle of the king," Somerset said.

"Yes, Your Grace." The man bowed and backed out of the room.

Somerset pushed his untouched food away, propped his elbows on the table, and wept into his hands. Anne left her seat and knelt next to him, her arm around him. "If he had asked to see me, this never would have happened," Somerset said, his words barely intelligible through his tears. "I would have never allowed him to be put to death. Why did he not ask? Why did no one offer to bring him to me?"

"Edward, let us go to our estates for a few days. You need some rest and quiet; these past weeks have strained you unbearably. Come. Let us get ready now. The Earl and Countess of Warwick will understand." We nodded our assent.

"No. I must tell the king that the sentence has been carried out. He cannot be allowed to hear it from someone not in the family. He will hate me for it, but he deserves to hear it from me." Somerset chuckled bitterly. "He already hates me anyway. Do you know what the king said in his deposition? My brother told him that he would be able to rule without a protector within a couple of years, as I was growing old and would not live long. The king replied, 'It were better for him to die before.'"

"The king did not mean what you think," I put in even before the duchess could. "He is a boy, for all that he is a king, and boys speak callously in that manner. He merely meant that if you were truly ill, you should not suffer."

Somerset ignored my gloss on the king's comment. "And I must tell our mother. She will never forgive me. Thomas was her favorite son." Somerset rose and ran a hand over his face. "She never liked me nearly as much as she did him. Just like the king."

The duchess took her husband's hand again. "But the people love you, Edward. They call you their good duke."

The Protector's face cleared, and something of a faint smile broke through. "It's true," he said. "They do."

The summer of 1549 was one of the most frightening ones ever seen in England. Not since the Pilgrimage of Grace twelve years before had the country seemed so much in danger. There was anger in Cornwall and Devon about the new prayer book put out by the government and about the other religious changes, anger in Norfolk about oppressive and corrupt local government. Discontent in one county seeped into the next county, and there were a number of small risings, but the best organized had been in the area around Norwich. William Parr, Marquis of Northampton, had been sent to deal with it, and had failed miserably, losing many of his men in the process.

It had been left to my husband—newly risen from a sickbed, for his health had been poor that year—to save Norwich from its fate. It was not from John but my sons Ambrose and Robert, who had served under him, that I had learned of my husband's deeds: how he had told the city officials he would either save it or die in its service; how he had urged the rebels to accept a pardon and save their own lives; how, having been refused, he had proceeded to slaughter the rebels; how, wishing to spare the survivors, he had ridden into their midst in person to demonstrate the sincerity of his renewed offer of pardon; how he had executed the leaders of the rebellion but refused the demands of the town officials that he punish even more widely. From my sons, not my husband, I had learned the city of Norwich had declared that each year on the anniversary of the battle, its citizens would close their shops and give thanks for Norwich's deliverance.

The Protector had not shown similar gratitude. When John asked that our son Ambrose, who had been one of the first to ride against the rebels, receive as a reward for his good services the reversion of certain offices, he'd been refused in favor of one of Somerset's own friends. Every request John made of the Protector, no matter how easy it would have been for him to fulfill, was refused.

After these slights, John said little to me, and I did not question him. I knew it was just a matter of time before he came to me, and in mid-September, he did. "I don't know what to do, Mouse."

Even though I had been anticipating that John would confide in me sooner or later, I blinked, both at the admission and the use of my childhood name, which I'd begged John to stop using when I became a grown-up young lady of twelve. "John?"

"The Protector. This can't continue as it is, Jane. He's unfit for his office. I have kept telling myself he'll grow into the position; it's not what he was raised to do, after all. He was raised to be an ordinary knight—as was I." John's mouth twitched upward faintly. "He's been far too willing to make concessions to the rebels, at the expense of the gentry. He's carried on about their grievances so much, one would think he's one of them. Jane, I care about the people! I truly do. Do you think I don't feel for the common man? But Somerset takes it too far; the rabble can't have the rule of the land. Is he trying to make his own nephew less secure on the throne? And it's not just his behavior toward the rebels; it's his behavior toward those who are governing the realm with him. Once—twice—I have seen him reduce grown men to tears. Not weaklings, but men who have fought bravely on the battlefield. He doesn't seek advice from the council very often, and when he does seek our advice, he ignores it. He's become worse since he executed his brother, too. More prone to anger, more sharp tongued, more uncompromising. Maybe he'll be more like himself when the guilt over Thomas Seymour's death eases, but when? We've some years to get through until the king comes of age or is old enough to be declared to be of age. Can we afford to wait all these years on the hope the Protector improves? If we keep letting him drag us into the mire, can we pull ourselves free?"

"Are you saying he should be removed as Protector?"

"Yes, I am, and I am not the only one. Trust me, much of the council is of the same mind. But it is tearing at my soul, for we have been friends, and I know him for a good man. I know also he means well toward the king, too; he loves the boy, for all he can't show it that well. But he is sowing the seeds of disaster, and if this keeps up, it will be left for the king a few years from now to reap them, if he hasn't already."

"Do you think he will agree to step down?"

"Aye, that is the crux of the matter. Probably not; he's too proud." John snorted. "Paget has taken it upon himself to send him long letters of advice, he tells me. I saw a copy of one. I can't say I'd be pleased to get such letters myself, but Somerset hardly seems to notice them. I suspect he doesn't even read them."

"So he will have to be forced out."

"Yes. I don't want to do it. More than anything, I don't want to shed blood—his or mine or anyone else's. But this can't go on. I'm torn, Mouse."

"You must choose between your friendship with Somerset and your duty to the kingdom—and to the king. That's what it comes down to, isn't it?"

John looked at me and sighed. "When you put it that way, there's no choice at all, is there?"

"None indeed," I said sadly.

No one wanted bloodshed, but for a few frightening days in October, it seemed as if that would be exactly what we would get. Forces gathered around John and his allies in London, while others gathered around the Protector at Hampton Court. Every spare chamber at Ely Place was crammed with the council members and their entourages, to the puzzlement of both my youngest daughter, Katheryn, who could no longer play hiding games in its once vacant spaces, and of Jerome, who asked plaintively one day when all of the grim-faced strangers could be expected to leave. "Soon," I said hopefully, while I hurried off to ensure yet more provisions were brought in for our many house guests. Civil strife, I was finding, lessened no one's appetites.

The war over the few days, however, would be fought not with swords, but with pen and paper. From Ely Place, the council sent letters to Somerset; from Windsor Castle, where he had hastened with the reluctant king, Somerset sent letters to the council. Everybody, it seemed, was writing to everybody. The printers of London had never been happier; both sides were furiously produc-ing handbills, which still could be found gracing the walls of sundry buildings weeks after all had ended. As the days wore on, John received a letter from the Protector himself, begging him to remember their old friendship, and I received a letter from the Duchess of Somerset, begging me to use what influ-ence I had with my husband. But there was nothing John could do other than to assure Somerset he did not seek his blood, and nothing I could do other than to send a similar message to the duchess. Meanwhile, the men at Windsor were rapidly deserting Somerset's cause, and on October 11, he was arrested without putting up any resistance.

Three days later, Somerset was escorted to London as a prisoner. John did not watch him enter the city, half because he felt it unseemly, half because he could not bear to see his old friend brought low. I was of a baser nature, though, and of a more curious one, so I went. I have been repaid threefold for my idle gawking that day.

The council had taken care not to humiliate the duke—no longer Protector, for that position had been abolished the day before. Somerset wore fine clothes and was mounted on a good horse, and the only thing that marked him as a prisoner was the armed guard of three hundred men that ringed him. He gazed at the men surrounding him reprovingly yet sadly, as if they were well-loved children caught in a bad act. Only when a group of poor people cheered did his austere features soften into a smile.

Not far from me, a plainly dressed woman stifled a sob as the duke passed by.

I stared at her, and stared at her even harder when, the duke having ridden past us, she began weeping openly. The Duchess of Somerset might have stripped off her jewels and hidden her carefully tended face and figure underneath someone else's drab clothes, but she could not conceal the love she plainly bore for the prisoner heading off toward an uncertain future.

I moved to her and touched her on the shoulder. She gasped then turned a ravaged face to me. "You are enjoying this, Lady Warwick?"

"No. I am very sorry for all this."

The duchess stared after her husband. "He thinks I am at my brother's house in Beddington. I promised him I would not come to see him brought to London as a prisoner if it came to that. I little thought that it would. But it may be the last I ever see of him alive."

"I told you, Anne, my husband does not seek his life."

"He cannot bear to be in the Tower long. He will be miserable and cold there. His health will suffer."

"I have it on good authority that the council is arranging for him to be comfortably housed there. He will be treated as his rank deserves. You have nothing to fear."

"I miss him."

I had no response to that. Instead, I said, "I will do everything in my power to see him freed."

"And restored to his protectorship?"

I had to smile at the duchess's presumption even in the face of disaster. "That I cannot promise. But I will try my best to have him restored to you and your children."

"I thank you," Anne said. For the first time I could recall in our long acquaintanceship, her expression was a humble one. She looked back toward her husband, but his figure had long disappeared from view. "And can his favorite cook be with him in the Tower? My husband is very particular in his eating habits."

✑

"I have made a promise today, John."

"Oh?"

"To the Duchess of Somerset."

John groaned eloquently.

"I promised her that I would use my influence to see her husband released from the Tower."

"Released from the Tower? He's not even there yet; his quarters won't be ready until tomorrow. I'll say one thing for you women—you don't waste time."

"I couldn't bear it, John. She had gone to watch Somerset being brought into the city, and she was weeping. I felt pity for her." I put my arms around John in the bed we were sharing. I could feel the bones in his back more easily than I could a couple of months ago; he'd been hardly eating, and some days could scarcely keep anything on his stomach. Somerset, at least from my vantage point on the street, had looked less worn for his ordeal than did my husband. "I told her that you would receive her if she came and spoke on his behalf. Did I presume?"

"Yes, to put it mildly. Tell me, my dear, have you made any other promises on my behalf to the duchess, or to anyone else, I should know about? Issued pardons?"

"It is only seeing her, John."

"And seeing her again and again, no doubt, until this business is resolved. It won't be quick, I suspect, no matter what you and the duchess must think."

"She loves Somerset very dearly and is utterly devoted to him. It is her best quality." I ran my hand along John's back. "Surely she can't be blamed for trying to help him. I would do the same for you if you were in trouble, John."

John sighed. "Very well. I'll see the woman."

A few days later, Robert and Guildford wandered into my chamber. Robert cocked his head in the general direction of the chamber where John received visitors. "Is she still here?"

"Still," I said grimly. The Duchess of Somerset had presented herself at Ely Place that morning, dressed in a less matronly fashion than usual and wearing, I suspected, a bit of paint on her face. Though she always was impeccably dressed and groomed, this was a step too far. I had said she could come to see my husband, not that she could look beautiful doing it.

"How long has she been here?" asked Guildford.

"Too long," I muttered. "I fear she will be taxing your father's strength," I added hastily. "He has not been able to shake off that stomach disorder of his."

Robert, from whom I could hide nothing, shot me an amused look. "What if we send Guildford in there?" he suggested. "I'd go myself, but it would look too obvious. Guildford can go in there to retrieve something he's left. He's always leaving things around the house, anyway."

"Not lately," Guildford protested.

"But you have that reputation. Go in there for—for your Greek grammar.

That's it! Stay there and search for it a little, so you'll be able to tell us what feminine wiles and snares the duchess is using."

"Feminine wiles and snares?" Guildford's brow crinkled.

"Never mind about that," I interjected. "Just tell us what she's doing in there."

"And there's a bonus," Robert added. "Father will think you're actually working on your Greek."

"I do work on my Greek."

Robert and I rolled our eyes in unison.

"All right," Guildford said. "I'll go." He headed out of the chamber, then turned. "What if Father asks me about my Greek tonight?"

"I'll cover for you," Robert promised.

Presently, Guildford loped back into the room. "It was *tragic*, Mother. She was kneeling before Father. I think she had been crying."

As long as she wasn't sitting in his lap, I thought.

"She had a bunch of letters in her hands, from the duke, I guess, and was reading from one of them. Father was listening and nodding."

"Agreeing with her?" Robert asked. "Or trying to stay awake?"

"I don't know," said Guildford. "The duchess started telling me about her brilliant daughters, and I decided it was time to leave. I couldn't find a good excuse to linger, anyway, once I found my book." He held up a volume that showed little signs of wear. "It was there, actually."

"Maybe you should study it, then," said Robert. "In case Father asks about it."

"You promised—"

"Well, yes. But now, there's something I need to speak to Mother about. Privately." Robert practically pushed Guildford out of the room. "Go play a game of tennis with Hal."

A baffled-looking Guildford left the room. Robert let the sound of his departing footsteps fade away. Then he said in a low voice, "I'm in love."

My heart sank. "The lady Elizabeth. Robert, she is not for you. The second-highest lady in the land—"

"Calf-love," Robert said firmly. "No. Amy Robsart."

"Who?"

Robert reached in the pouch at his side and pulled out a locket. "I sent a man to paint this of her," he said reverently, carefully opening it and laying it on my outstretched palm.

I gazed at a limning of a pretty blonde girl of about Robert's own age of seventeen. Though the artist was obviously skilled, the girl herself looked to me much like every other pretty blonde girl in England, but I kept quiet on this point. "She's lovely. But who is she? I don't know of any Robsarts."

"She's John Robsart's daughter." He anticipated my next question. "He's a man of substance in Norfolk. He's been sheriff there. We stayed at his place at Stanford Hall while we were marching to Norwich this summer. Amy and I got to talking. When Father had finished that business with Kett's men, we stayed at Stanford Hall again, and we got better acquainted."

"Robert. Have you got this girl with child?"

"No! She is a virgin. I don't want to seduce her. I've never even tried. I want to make her my wife."

I stared. Substantial John Robsart might be, but his daughter was no suitable match for an earl's son, even an earl's younger son, and Robert knew it as well as I did. "Robert—"

"I know, I know! I could find a bride with better breeding or a better dowry. But I don't want such a bride. I want Amy. I'll be miserable without her. And she wants me. Not marrying me will break her heart." Robert gave me his most earnest look, one he had perfected over the years and that never failed to work its intended effect. "She might pine away without me and die. It does happen, you know."

"The streets of London weren't piled high with unhappy lovers the last time I looked." But Robert had me, and he knew it. "It will be your father's decision, in any case. But for what it's worth, I won't oppose the match."

"I knew you wouldn't."

"I suppose you want me to speak to your father."

"Yes. Oh, I could speak to him—but you're a woman. He'll see reason more quickly if it comes from you."

"I should think that you wouldn't want him to see reason, because if he does, he'll never approve of this unsuitable match. But I will speak to him. I seem to be much in demand for that type of thing lately."

"That's because you're good at it, Mother."

"Flatterer. Save your blandishments for Amy."

∽

"Oh, her," John said.

I found myself mildly disappointed I had not provoked more of a reaction. "You know?"

"I guessed. They spent a lot of time in each other's company that evening, I noticed, and when he found out that she helped brew the family ale, he took an inordinate interest in the brewing process. So he fancies himself in love with this girl?"

"Yes. I am to intercede with you for their marriage."

"A love match. I can't say that I put much faith in them. Look at King Henry, besotted with Anne Boleyn and later that silly Howard girl. And Queen Catherine, losing her good sense over that rascal Thomas Seymour. I could think of others if I put my mind to it, I daresay."

"But there were so many other things wrong with those matches besides them being made for love. Robert and Amy are alike in years, with no prior attachments or entanglements like the king had, and they are doing the right thing by seeking our blessing, instead of marrying in secret like the queen did. And how is their love match different from any other? They will have to mature together, just as we matured together when we were first married."

"I don't remember us being that immature when we married."

"Well, I do. Do you remember how I could not do the household accounts to your satisfaction until two years into the marriage? How hateful I was to you when I first got with child?"

"True. You were a terror. And I was a tyrant." John smiled fondly. "I'd shut it out of my memory. But we are getting away from our son. It's hardly the sort of marriage I wanted for him. He could do better."

"We have other sons who can make good marriages."

"Unless they all decide they need love matches, too, with the first pretty girl they see."

"Does that mean you give your consent?"

John grimaced. "Probably, unless I have an attack of common sense. The lad did good service at Norwich; I suppose he deserves something as a reward. Besides, he's headstrong. If I forbade the marriage, he'd probably marry the girl secretly. Some Norfolk connections wouldn't hurt our family, I suppose, and Robsart's a sensible man. One could have worse relations. So I suppose we might as well make a fine wedding of it."

I hugged John.

"But this is as low as it goes," warned John. "If Guildford or Hal decides to marry a tavern maid, he'll get no sympathy from me."

12

Frances Grey
November 1549

WE'RE GOING TO SEE UNCLE GEORGE!" KATE CHANTED AS OUR ENTOU-
rage set out from Bradgate. "We're going to see Uncle George!"

Mary took up the cry. "We're going to see Uncle George!"

"So we heard," muttered Jane. She rolled her eyes at Elizabeth Tilney, a
relation of ours who was being brought up as one of Jane's companions.

"I like Uncle George," protested Mary, and I smiled at her. At four, she was
a pretty child, but very small for her age, with a slightly misshapen back. She
was seated on a pillion behind a groom, and bystanders in the towns through
which we passed would stare, wondering how such a tiny creature could ride
a horse so calmly. "He's jolly."

George Medley, Harry's older half brother, was indeed jolly, and I was
looking forward as much as my daughters to spending a few days at his Essex
estate of Tiltey. We needed some merriment this year. During the summer,
there had been dreadful unrest, and three thousand rebels had been killed by
the Earl of Warwick's men at Dussindale alone. Harry had managed to keep
the peace in Leicestershire, and a sullen calm had settled over the rest of the
country, but I still found myself looking around uneasily for angry mobs as I
passed through countryside that was normally as safe and familiar to me as my
own bedchamber.

Riding near me and my ladies was Adrian Stokes, a man of around thirty
who had recently become my master of horse. He had been serving with
Harry's brother John in France as marshal of Newhaven, which had fallen
to the French a couple of months before. When Master Stokes returned to
England, Harry promptly hired him at the recommendation of his brother,
without consulting me, of course. Although it had irritated me to have Harry
interfere with the management of my own household in this manner, I could

find no fault with the conduct of Master Stokes himself. Indeed, I could not remember when we had left for a journey in such good order and good time.

I also could not help but notice that Master Stokes was an exceptionally good-looking man. He was of average height and of a strong build, with dark brown, curly hair, a short, neat beard, and dark blue eyes. The young ladies who served in my household liked nothing more than to watch him get upon his horse, where he struck an especially good figure. Had he been inclined to lechery, he certainly could have found partners with whom to exercise his tastes.

Thanks to Master Stokes's excellent planning for our travel, we arrived at Tiltey in good time. The younger children ran off to play, while we adults caught up on the news of the family. Then George Medley shook his head. "So, Frances, what do you think is going to happen to the Protector? Odds has it that he loses his head. Evens has it that he's in for a long spell in the Tower."

"What do you mean?"

"You don't know?"

"No. I have heard nothing since Harry went to London, except about our travel arrangements. No news of any sort."

"Well, there's news, all right." George shifted on his feet. "I don't know why he didn't tell you; it's no secret. The Protector is in the Tower, you see. After the disaster this summer, the Earl of Warwick and others started talking about ending the protectorate. You really can't blame them, I suppose. Anyway, Somerset got wind of this and dragged the poor king to the gates of Hampton Court. Ranted about how the council was trying to destroy him and the king—even started carrying on about Richard III, for heaven's sake. Why an uncle would want to mention that particular king is beyond me. Summoned the commoners to his side."

George Medley paused, presumably so I could ask a question, but as all this was news to me, I could only say, "Go on."

"So now we have the Protector and the king surrounded by a mob of devoted peasants, as if we hadn't had enough of that this summer! Not that they were kind to his duchess; Somerset decided he had to send her to safety, and she left in tears. The peasants jeered at her. Some blame the whole of the duke's troubles on her and her sharp tongue and meddling ways. I think it's nonsense myself; the duke is capable of mucking things up without a woman's help, from what I hear. Finally, the Protector hauled the king from his warm chamber at Hampton Court and took him to Windsor Castle in the dead of the night. A mistake, as it's not been used as a royal residence for years and wasn't provisioned to receive him. The king was miserable there. Caught a cold, as a matter of fact. Letters started to go back and forth between the Protector and the council, each accusing the other of all manner of evil doing. Finally, the Protector gave in. He didn't have enough men to win a civil war, if that's what he was thinking, and to his credit, maybe he didn't want one either. So he gave up the king and let himself be taken a prisoner to the Tower, where he's sitting today."

"I never heard any of this. It is important, surely, and yet Harry told me nothing!"

"Well," George said. "Perhaps—"

I turned to look at my oldest daughter. There was not a trace of surprise on her face. "Jane, had you heard of this?"

"Yes, Mother."

"You mean that your father told you?"

"Yes, my lady, everything." Even Jane could not look me quite in the eye. "I am sorry, my lady. I thought Father would have told you, and when you did not mention it, I assumed you were not interested. It did not occur to me that—"

"No. How could it?" I gave George Medley, standing there awkwardly, a radiant smile. "I suppose Harry simply omitted to tell me."

✺

Although it was only late November, there was already a feeling of Christmas in George Medley's old-fashioned great hall. Only at court in the days of my uncle Henry had I seen more food—every animal that could fly, swim, or run appeared to be represented on George's table, along with the fruit of every tree imaginable. The fruit of the vine was also there in abundance.

I am normally temperate, to the point of sometimes being the only sober person at a banquet, but with my anger at Harry festering, I took the opportunity to overindulge that night, especially after the children were sent to their beds and the company became conspicuously merrier. I sampled every variety of wine and joined in every toast, and when it came time to dance, I stumbled my way through three numbers, each time using the excuse of being overheated afterward to reward myself with a gulp of wine.

By the time the fourth dance started, even I recognized I was in no condition to join it. Instead, I was stumbling toward my seat when I saw my master of horse approaching. "Master Stokes!" I called. "Will you get my horse ready for me? I wish to ride."

"Ride, my lady?"

"A horse," I said, a little irritated at his denseness. "You are my master of horse, and I wish to ride a horse. Ergo—" I giggled. "Ergo. It sounds like something my daughter Jane would say."

"It is a little late to ride, my lady, but I think some fresh air might do you good."

"My horse is not ready? Is that what you are saying?"

"Yes, my lady."

"Well, that is quite a disappointment to me. You are my master of horse, after all."

"Yes, my lady."

"You could at least make yourself useful and bring me some wine, then."

"No, my lady."

"You refuse me?"

"I think you might have had just a bit too much already, my lady. Come. Let us walk a little."

Unable to muster further argument, I let him haul me out into the chilly autumn night. Suddenly I had an irresistible urge to sit, and did. "Master Stokes," I said dreamily as he joined me on the ground, "I do believe you are correct. I have had a trifle too much wine."

"Yes."

"Don't tell Harry. He would be angry."

"I won't."

"Good. He would be shocked, actually, for I am not a habitual drunkard, Master Stokes."

"I did not think so."

"My mother had a poor head for wine, and she drank little of it as a consequence. Usually I try to follow her example. But..." I lost track of what I was going to say and giggled instead.

"I remember seeing your mother once or twice. She was a beautiful woman."

"Yes." Half to confide, half because I badly needed the support, I leaned against Master Stokes. His belief in the sobering effects of fresh air had been woefully misplaced; I felt giddier than ever and more reckless than I ever had in my life. "Did I ever tell you that my mother seduced my father?"

"No."

"Well, she did. It was easy, I suppose. She was the Queen of France, after all, and she was very beautiful. Mind you, she was a widow, and they married immediately. But it was still a seduction." I snorted. "She used to tell me the story of their marriage. She made it sound so very respectable, but I could read between the lines. I am not entirely stupid, no matter what Harry and Jane say."

"They say that?"

"Not in so many words. But they think it. Why, he did not even bother to tell me about the Protector. And yet he told Jane!"

"Perhaps he did not think you would be interested. Your ladyship is not a friend of the Protector, are you?"

"No. But it is the principle of the thing! Husbands should tell their wives these things. Not only their daughters. I am nothing to him, Master Stokes, but something to get with child now and then, and as of late, I have failed even at that." I shrugged in a way I had learned from my mother, who in turn had learned it from her brief stay at the French court. "But of course, to get a woman with child, you must lie with her, and he hardly ever does that. He says it is because I almost died giving birth to Mary, but in truth, Master Stokes, I think it is that he simply does not care."

"My lady—"

"Oh, I know, I should not be telling you this. But who else can I tell? It is not the sort of thing one wants to tell another woman. We have our pride. And, too, I am the Mar...Mar... Mar... the something of Dorset. Many a woman would like to be me. Why should I disillusion anyone?" My head was beginning to hammer. I made an effort to rise. "I am going to go and get some more wine."

"No. That would be unwise."

"But I am unwise. In fact, some think me downright stupid." I leaned back against Master Stokes's shoulder and closed my eyes. "I may be stupid, but at least I am not ugly. You don't think me so, do you?"

"No." Master Stokes gently dislodged me from my resting place. "I am going to find your ladies to help me escort you to your chamber. You need to sleep."

"My ladies think you are quite handsome. Do ladies ever tell you that, Master Stokes?"

"No."

"Well, they should. You are handsome. And very, very kind." Master Stokes attempted to raise me to a standing position, but I shook him off. "And you won't tell Harry about this?"

"No."

"You swear?"

"Yes, if you promise to let me help you up so I can find your ladies."

"Very well," I said, attempting to rise also and instead sinking back to the ground. I giggled again. "But it will not be as easy as you think."

Somehow, Master Stokes got me to my feet at last and back to the hall, where I sagged on a bench as he went in search of my ladies. Fortunately, my sodden condition went unnoticed: all eyes were on the hobbyhorse prancing about and emitting guttural neighs that sounded suspiciously like George Medley.

Master Stokes quickly arrived with my ladies, who had been looking for me. I blew him a parting kiss good-bye as they steered me toward my chamber. "Good night, kind and handsome Master Stokes," I said. "Don't let some lady seduce you. You are innocent about such matters, I fear."

"I won't, my lady," Master Stokes promised.

Mercifully, my ladies managed to haul me away before I could give any more parting advice to Master Stokes.

I longed to spend the rest of the next day in bed, nursing my hangover and my shame, but I was the Marchioness of Dorset, after all, the highest-ranking lady present, and I had to act up to my station. So I struggled into my riding dress—even the feather that adorned my cap drooped as if hung over—and rode out to the hunt with the rest of the household, Master Stokes by my side. How many times had I told him the previous night he was handsome? At least, I consoled myself, I had not tried to seduce him. As we rode at the tail end of the hunting party, every step my horse took feeling like a hoof on my head, I said, "I believe I asked you several times last night not to tell my husband of my foolishness, Master Stokes, but I will ask you again nonetheless."

"There is no need, my lady." Master Stokes smiled. "Indeed, my lady, I must confess that after our encounter last night, I myself overindulged. I have very little recollection of what happened before and afterward."

I looked into Master Stokes's deep blue eyes, which bore no sign of recent dissipation at all, and shook my head. "You are a poor liar, Master Stokes, but I thank you."

◈

Our next stop on our journey to London was worlds away from George Medley's house: Beaulieu in Essex, a home of the lady Mary also known as Newhall. "Will we have to go to Mass?" asked Jane as we rode side by side.

No inkling of my regrettable behavior at Tiltey seemed to have reached Jane, or anyone else besides Adrian Stokes and my ladies: the Lord was certainly entitled to some heavenly thanks for that, Mass or no Mass. "Yes, if she wishes us to attend with her. She is our hostess and is entitled to that courtesy."

"Perhaps she won't let us be present," Jane said hopefully. "We are heretics in her eyes, after all."

Mary was indeed at Mass when we arrived at Beaulieu, which gave my daughters and me time to freshen up after our journey and to admire a special feature of my own luxurious chamber: the bathing room. Even Jane looked awed as we stepped inside and played with the faucets: one for hot water, one for cold. "May we take a bath tomorrow, Mama?" Kate asked.

"Of course," I promised. I turned to my youngest daughter, who appeared wary. "It's quite safe," I assured her. "Just like the tubs we use, only this one has its very special room."

We could have enjoyed admiring the bathing room and the other luxuries of Beaulieu for a while longer, but shortly thereafter, Lady Anne Wharton, one of Mary's waiting women, came to lead the four of us to her mistress in the great hall. We walked past the indoor tennis court, once enjoyed by Anne Boleyn's brother George, and by the side chapel. Sitting on the altar in a splendid receptacle was something that had long been banished from our own altar and from nearly every other altar in England: the Host.

Lady Wharton genuflected in front of the Host and made the sign of the cross. I was about to follow suit, out of respect for the lady Mary, when Jane spoke up. "Why do you do that?" Exaggeratedly, she looked around. "Is the lady Mary out here?"

"I make my curtsey to Him who made us all," Lady Wharton said coolly.

Jane widened her eyes in mock puzzlement. "Why, how can he be there that made us all, when the baker made him?"

"Jane!"

Kate tittered under her breath while Lady Wharton flushed with anger. "The lady Mary awaits you," she said. "Come."

I glared at my daughter, but there was no time to reprove her, for Mary, clad splendidly in a red gown that appeared almost gaudy, stood before us. She embraced my girls and me in turn. "So you are on your way to London," she said. "The Tower menagerie has taken over the government there, you know."

"I have heard but little of this business, actually. Harry has been much concerned with his own affairs."

"Oh? Well, time will tell, but in my opinion, there is but one motive behind this action against the Protector. Envy and ambition, namely, that of the Earl of Warwick, the most unstable man in England. I have never liked him." She put up her hand, and the ladies around us all stopped what they were doing to hear her speak. "Don't ask me why. He has never been less than civil to me, and his countess is very pleasant. But there is something about the man I don't trust. Perhaps it is simply that he is the son of a traitor. Such things will out." She lowered her voice. "They tried to involve me in their scheme, you know. They told me that if I gave them their support, I would be allowed to act as the king's regent. I refused. I want no part of their plots, and how long would I last as regent anyway? They harass me about performing my religion now, far away from court. What would it be like if I tried to practice my religion at court?"

I was silent, not knowing what to say. Although the matter had been over-shadowed for a time by the drama surrounding the downfall and execution of Thomas Seymour, the council had made sweeping religious changes that year—abolishing the elevation of the Host and the doctrine of the sacrifice of the Mass, dear to Catholic hearts and anathema to Protestant ones. Every house of worship was to follow the new Prayer Book, a copy of which was tucked into my own coffers, and the Mass was to be said entirely in English. Harry and Jane had been delighted at the changes—wishing only that they had been more extensive—as had the king. But Mary had been appalled. She had continued to hear the Mass exactly as it had been heard in her father's lifetime, and when the king's council ordered that she conform to the new laws, she had increased her two daily Masses to three. The king himself, writing a couple of months before he had been dragged by the Protector to Windsor, had scolded her for her intransigence. Yet the matter had gone no further than a scolding, and the government, wishing to maintain good relations with Mary's uncle, Charles V, had left the matter there. Harry had sniffed, "Mary might like to think of herself as a potential martyr, but the council isn't obliging the poor dear." Even I could not help but think she was being treated rather leniently under the circumstances.

Mary turned to look at my daughters. Kate and my own Mary had looked politely bored during our exchange, but Jane had clearly been fighting to keep herself from speaking. "But that is enough of that. What fine girls you have, Frances! And I have a gift for each of them." She nodded to Susan Clarencius, who handed a velvet box each to Kate and Mary. They lifted the lids and squealed their thanks at the sight of the golden cramp rings inside. "You, Lady Jane, have a gift more suited for your years." Mary indicated a large coffer at her side.

With Susan's help, Jane dutifully opened it. Inside was an ensemble of tinsel, cloth of gold, and velvet, materials so rich that the garments could have belonged only to Mary herself. "Why, it will hardly need altering," I said as Jane held the gown against her slim figure. "And that color suits you wonderfully."

"Yes, I thought it would," Mary said with satisfaction.

"I thank Your Grace," Jane said. She handed the garment to a servant, who carefully placed it back in its coffer.

She might as well have been thanking King Henry's sister for a piece of fruit.

After dinner, Mary went to conduct some business. As we were on our own for the time being, I went to Jane's chamber to survey Mary's gift once again.

"It's beautiful," said Elizabeth Tilney. She fingered the velvet wistfully.

Jane looked at the clothing coolly. "What on earth can I do with it?"

"Why, wear it," Elizabeth said.

"You are so similar in stature, you could wear it at dinner tomorrow," I put in. "Rose could have it ready for you by then with no difficulty at all."

"I'm not going to wear it," Jane said. She shut the coffer resolutely.

"Why on earth not?"

"It is not fitting to wear such outlandish material. The lady Elizabeth, who follows God's word, eschews such frippery, and so shall I."

"You most certainly will wear it, and you will wear it here in the lady Mary's household," I said. "It is an honor to be given such a gift from the king's sister, frippery or no frippery. Why, it is finer than any of my own gowns!"

"Father will not expect me to wear it."

"I don't care what your father expects. I am your mother, and the lady Mary is my cousin! I will not have it said that I have not raised you to treat her with the respect she deserves. She is next in line to the throne. Have you forgotten that?"

"I hope she never sits upon it. She is a Papist. She has no busin—"

I reached for Jane and shook her hard, then dealt her a smart slap across the cheek. "You have behaved abominably since we have come here," I said when I had released her. "Do you think I didn't notice how insolent you were to Lady Wharton? Are you so stupid—yes, that is right, stupid—so as to think that she will not tell the lady Mary what you said to her? And this dress! It is worth a fortune, and beautiful besides that, and you acted as if you were conferring a great favor upon the lady Mary by accepting it! Well, this has come to an end. You will allow Rose to make the necessary alterations, and you will wear it at dinner tomorrow, and you will smile and be pleasant to Mary. Do you understand?"

Jane's face bore a white mark where I had slapped her, and she was fighting back tears. Looking at her, I longed to take her into my arms, but I forced myself to stare at her coldly. "Yes, my lady," she whispered.

"Good. I will send Rose to you shortly. If you are anything less than cooperative, I assure you I will hear about it. Do you understand?"

"Yes, my lady."

"Good. Tonight after supper, there will no doubt be card playing. You will probably be asked to join the lady Mary and me at her table. If so, you will give no sign that you are not enjoying yourself, or the slap I dealt you just now will look like a pinch as compared to what you will receive. Do you understand?"

"Yes, my lady."

"Good. Stay here until you are sent for. I wish to see no more of you for now." I touched Kate and little Mary, who were staring at me with unmitigated terror. They'd never seen me scold Jane, or anyone, with such fury before. "Come along, girls."

❧

That evening, we did indeed play cards, and Jane indeed sat with the lady Mary, Susan Clarencius, and myself. She was a model of good deportment, speaking only when spoken to by her elders, smiling graciously at all the appropriate moments—and trouncing the princess mercilessly. Furious at my daughter as I still was, I could not help but smile as I watched Mary's servant duly hand Jane her winnings. I hadn't, after all, instructed her that she had to lose.

The next day at supper, Jane appeared in Mary's dress. So well did it suit her, it was difficult to believe it had been made for another woman. "Why, you look beautiful," I whispered as Jane took her place beside me, her back rigid and her smile fixed. "Like a young lady of fifteen. If your father could see you now! He would be so proud."

"Thank you, my lady."

Mary entered and took her place of honor in between us, smiling her approval at Jane's garb. She took a dainty sip of wine, and I followed suit. Jane picked up her own wine cup and lifted it to her lips. As I watched, the heavy gold cup tipped in her hand, spilling its contents all over Jane's elaborate gown. "Oh, no! How clumsy of me." Jane turned toward Mary, her eyes pleading. "I have ruined it, and you were so kind—"

"It is no matter," Mary said, her smile as fixed as Jane's had been a few moments before. "A mere accident."

❧

"I didn't mean to, my lady! Truly!" Jane looked up at me pleadingly as I, in the privacy of her chamber, jerked her to me. Suddenly I realized she looked a great deal like my mother in times of distress. "It was an accident, just as I told the lady Mary. I was flustered with all of those people looking at me in my dress, and it was a heavier cup than usual. Please, my lady, believe me."

I relaxed my grip upon Jane. Was she telling the truth? After all these years of motherhood, I could not read her well enough to guess. Perhaps Harry could have. The thought wearied me so much I released her and let my hand drop to my side. "Very well. I shall take your word for it and not punish you. It is only the front panel that was ruined, after all. But if I ever find out that you acted deliberately…"

Jane cautiously stepped back and dropped a miniature curtsey. "My lady, I promise, I did not. In truth," she confessed in a low voice, "I am sad I spilled the wine on it. I thought I looked pretty in it."

"You did look pretty in it." I put my hand on Jane's shoulder and was gratified to see she did not flinch. "There is no shame in being a pretty girl, Jane. Nor is there any shame in being pleased about it or in wearing colors that suit you, as long as you don't let your head get turned. After all, you wore bright colors when you lived with Queen Catherine and Thomas Seymour."

"But he was a traitor. Wasn't he?"

I'd never spoken to Jane about Tom Seymour's death, I realized suddenly. "Yes, but he had some good qualities. Were you sorry when he died?"

Jane looked at me with troubled eyes. "A little."

"That is natural. He was kind to you, after all."

A knock sounded at the door, and one of my men entered, rather to my dismay, for I could have gone on speaking to Jane in this confidential manner all afternoon. "My lady, the lady Mary has asked that you and the lady Jane accompany her to Mass."

Jane looked so horrified, I had to smile. "Tell her I will gladly do so, but that my daughter will not be able to. She is er—being punished." I glared at Jane, who dropped her eyes hastily. Was she suppressing a conspiratorial smile?

I would be glad to get to Dorset House, I decided as I readied myself for Mass. The Grey women had not had much luck with wine on this journey.

∽

At Dorset House, our servants dutifully came out to greet us, but there was no sign of my husband, although I had sent word we would be arriving. "Where is the marquis?"

Harry's steward said, "He is at a meeting of the king's council, my lady."

"The council? He is not a member of it."

"He is as of today, my lady."

I looked over at Jane. There was no need to ask whether she had heard this news; for once, she looked as bewildered as I did.

"It has something to do with this business of the Protector being removed from office, my lady. Out with the old, in with the new."

I nodded, grateful that thanks to George Medley, I knew what he was talking about.

Harry came home a few hours later. "The king's esteemed and trusted councilor, at your service," he said, sweeping a bow after he had embraced all of us. "A sudden change, eh? Well, I must tell you how it came about. The Protector—"

"Your brother told me about that," I said crisply. "It is a good thing someone deigned to, or I would be in utter confusion at the moment."

Harry smiled sheepishly. "My dear, I meant—"

"Never mind that now. What happened?"

"It's simple, really. The Earl of Warwick and a couple of his friends approached me. Told me that it was a disgrace that a man of my rank and religious sympathies wasn't on the council—and there you go, on the council! I don't flatter myself that the earl suddenly was overcome with respect for my wisdom, mind you. Truth is, with Somerset in the Tower and some of his allies booted off the council, it's too lopsided in favor of those who want to go back to the old religion. The king doesn't have much use for the Protector, especially after being hauled to Windsor like a hostage, but he does have strong feelings against the old religion, and Warwick prefers the new himself. So here I am, and about time, I must say."

"Harry, I am glad you are a councilor; do not mistake me. I think it is about time, too. But do you think the Protector will be executed?"

"Hard to say. Warwick at least doesn't want him executed, and he seems to be the man in charge at the moment. He's been ill, so the council's been meeting at his home over at Ely Place."

"You trust Warwick? After all, wasn't he Somerset's friend?"

My husband shrugged. "He was. Still is, perhaps. But Warwick's first allegiance is to the king." Harry looked at me more closely. "Mary hasn't been poisoning you against him, has she?"

The most unstable man in England, I heard Mary's voice telling me. "She doesn't like him," I acknowledged.

"No wonder, with her insisting that she be privileged above everyone else in England to hear the Mass! You didn't stoop to that, did you?"

"Oh, no," I lied, and I was glad to see that Jane shook her head with equal vehemence.

⁂

When I had told Adrian Stokes that Harry seldom came to my bed, I had been exaggerating, but not by much. It was true having Mary had nearly killed me and left her slightly misshapen, but I had recovered quickly, and no one had told me I couldn't have another baby. And it wasn't as if Harry were consistent, anyway. When he felt like sleeping with me, he seemed to be able to put aside his worries about my health easily enough. He just didn't feel like sleeping with me all that often. I could console myself that he didn't seem to feel like sleeping with anyone else, either, as I'd never seen signs that he had a mistress or consorted with whores, but on nights when I longed to feel a man's arms around me, it wasn't much consolation.

Tonight, however, Harry paid me a visit. Usually I welcomed him, but tonight I resisted his attempts to remove my night shift. "You didn't tell me about the Protector, Harry. Why?"

"Really, my dear, it was just a foolish omission."

"Yet you told Jane."

"Well, yes. She is interested in that type of thing."

"And what makes you think I am not? I am not a dolt, Harry. But in any case, I am your wife and have been for sixteen years. I should hear these things from you, whether or not you think I am interested in them."

"Well, yes," Harry conceded. "There's logic in that." He grinned at me. "I've rarely seen you angry at me, Frances. It makes you rather interesting."

I snorted, and Harry drew me to him, then removed my clothing and began to caress me in a manner that made me gasp and clutch him to me. He was not always so attentive to my own desires, and if this was the result of the council's promotion of him—well, the council deserved the heartiest thanks. Perhaps it was also his way of apologizing; if so, I would accept it.

But as I climaxed, my mind was not on Harry. It was, I realized to my shame, on Adrian Stokes.

13

Jane Dudley
December 1549

"THE COUNCIL HAS AGREED THAT YOU CAN SEE YOUR HUSBAND ON CHRISTMAS Day," I told the Duchess of Somerset.

"Only for that one day? I had hoped for more."

"It is the best I can do," I snapped. "Really, as there are members of the council who would like to put him to death, I consider it a victory of sorts."

Anne lowered her eyes. "Yes," she said quietly. "I am sorry. I truly am grateful beyond words for what you have been able to do for us. It is just that I miss him so much, and I fret so about him. You cannot know what it is like, not knowing whether he will be alive a month from now." She brushed a hand across her eyes, which did show the signs of many sleepless nights.

I patted her other hand. "The men who want his death are in the decided minority, I am told."

The duchess bristled. "Why should anyone want my dear Edward's death? He has done nothing, except to be too kind and forbearing to the peasants." She rose from the chair in my chamber in which she had been sitting. "But I must go and make ready for my visit. There is so much to do. Do you think the guards will let me bring in my jam for him? And some new shirts and handkerchiefs?"

"I am sure of it. In fact," I added archly, "you might want to get some new things for yourself, as well. You will want to look your best. The council has agreed that you may be alone with him when you visit."

Anne let out a girlish squeal of pleasure. Then she kissed me lightly on the cheek and hurried away.

༄

A few days later, John developed a fever, which confined him to his bed. After a miserable day, he was at last on the verge of resting for the night when a knock sounded on his chamber door and William Paulet, Lord St. John, was announced. "Tell him to come back at another time," I said to our servant. "My lord is ill."

"My lady, Lord St. John says it's urgent."

I sighed. All the commotion at our house that had taken place since Somerset's removal had given me a certain appreciation for the man's burden of office. I might have protested further, but John said sleepily, "Well, send him in, then," and sat up. Quickly, I helped him adjust his nightcap to more statesmanlike effect.

"My lord—my lady—I apologize for coming at this bad time. But I did not think this could wait." John nodded for him to keep talking, and Paulet continued, "Today I accompanied the Earl of Southampton and the Earl of Arundel to the Tower, to interrogate the Duke of Somerset, as you instructed. To several questions, he stated that he had acted by your advice and counsel."

"No doubt he did, in some instances," John said wearily. He coughed.

"After we left the duke, my lord, the Earl of Southampton said that you and he should both be found traitors, and that you were both worthy to die."

I rose. "My lord!"

"Go on," John said.

"The Earl of Arundel agreed. They talked a little more and decided that on the day the Duke of Somerset was executed, you would be arrested and put in his chambers at the Tower. Then you would soon be tried yourself, and, undoubtedly, executed."

"Undoubtedly," agreed John. "Is there more?"

"They talked of having the lady Mary made regent, my lord, but I didn't get the sense that they had approached her. The long and short of it, they want Somerset dead, and you with them."

"That information was worth disturbing my sickbed for," said John calmly. He squeezed my trembling hand and smiled at Paulet. "I shall keep it in mind. But for now, my lord, I must get some sleep, or the Earl of Southampton won't have to take the trouble of plotting against me."

✑

John slept that night; I didn't. It was the Earl of Southampton—Thomas Wriothesley—who had interrogated Anne Askew, even turning the rack himself, it was said, when she was not forthcoming with the information Wriothesley sought. What he had sought was information that would link Catherine Parr herself, and some of her ladies as well, to what had then been regarded as heretical practices. I had been one of those women who stood in danger, for I had possessed books, passed around among us ladies-in-waiting and read aloud in the queen's chambers, that were illegal then. Anne Askew's brave silence in the face of torture had surely saved some of the rest of us from the flames.

Unable to get Anne Askew to implicate anyone, those who wished to see a return to the old religion had tried another tack—turning King Henry against the queen herself, even to the point of procuring an order for her arrest. It had failed miserably when the queen, advised of her enemies' schemes, had groveled so humbly, and so cleverly, before the king, he had turned on the ones who had sought to destroy her. It would have been almost comical to see the king throwing the arrest warrant in Wriothesley's own face, had we not been aware of how close Catherine might have come to sharing the fate of her predecessor: poor Katherine Howard.

And now Wriothesley had my husband in his sights. "Why would they want to execute you and the duke?" I demanded the next morning as soon as John awoke.

John shrugged and obediently swallowed the physic he had been given. "Terrible stuff. Simple, my dear. Wriothesley has held a grudge against Somerset since being deprived of his office as Lord Chancellor after the old king died. I stood with Somerset at that time, so he bears a grudge against me, as well. As for Arundel, he's probably hoping for a restoration of the old religion—hence the lady Mary."

"John, what shall you do?"

"Enjoy the Christmas festivities as much as I can in my state of health."

"I don't—"

"Wriothesley's a fool. If he could only count, he'd know that there aren't enough men of his stamp on the council to send Somerset to the block, or me either. I shall beat him at his own game, never you fear." John looked at me straight on, and for the first time I saw real anger in his eyes. "And speaking of fear, I have never forgotten the fright he gave Queen Catherine, or you and the rest of her ladies. When I take him down, I promise you, you shall be there to see it."

∽

The Duke and Duchess of Somerset had their Christmas visit, and afterward went to hear a sermon at the Chapel of St. Peter ad Vincula—sitting on the same pew, the guards later told us, without so much as an inch between them, and gazing into each other's eyes more than into their respective prayer books. The next day, Somerset's children by Anne—he had eight living at the time, all of them under the age of twelve—paid their father a noisy visit. Uxorious as the duke was, he was rather less at ease among the brood of offspring that had resulted from his marriage, and I suspected he might have found his Tower lodgings peaceful after the last of them straggled out of the fortress's walls.

Then, as December was about to fade into January, the council met once more in a conference chamber at our house, where John, wrapped from head to toe in furs against the sharp cold, croaked his way through the proceedings as I, at his bidding, brought physic in from time to time and plumped the pillows at his back. The meeting had been droning on for some time, the pillows were no longer plump but downright fat, and I was beginning to run out of excuses to stay in the room, when Wriothesley said, "My lords, now that the New Year is almost upon us, we must decide what to do about the traitor."

"Traitor?" asked Henry Grey, Marquis of Dorset. A newcomer to the council, he had contributed little to it thus far, but did occasionally make remarks like this to remind the rest of the council he was still breathing.

"I refer, of course, to the Duke of Somerset."

"He's an incompetent," said William Parr. A flush passed over his handsome features as he remembered his own ignominious performance at Norwich before John had been appointed to clean up the situation. "But not a traitor," he continued lamely. "And I say this as a man whose own marriage he tried to invalidate."

"He is a traitor," said the Earl of Arundel. "What else would you call a man who all but handed the government over to the rabble?"

"Look at these," said Southampton. He waved a sheath of papers: the charges to which the duke had agreed to plead guilty. Everyone in the council room looked up obediently, as did I from placing a warm brick against John's feet. "Are these not the admissions of a traitor?"

"There is no treason in any of the charges against Somerset," said John. "Only folly and mismanagement."

"The man has acted traitorously; he must suffer the fate of traitors. It is time we started proceedings to attaint him, and to sentence him to death."

"You seek his blood, my lord?"

"Haven't I made it clear enough? I do."

"Do you seek mine also?"

"I—"

John rose and placed the hand on the sword that was propped up against his chair. "Know this, my lord: I am well aware that he who seeks his blood seeks mine, as well. You shall have neither, I tell you."

He had never raised his voice. No one else in the room spoke. Then Southampton rose from his seat, his chair scraping the floor as he moved it backward the only sound in the room. Without a word, he left the room. Another chair scraped backward, and the Earl of Arundel followed.

No one else stirred from his seat. After a moment or two, John sat back down. "Shall we turn to the next order of business, gentlemen?"

✑

That night, I saw John off to bed as I always did when he was ill, not trusting his comfort to our servants, devoted and competent as they were. Having seen that everything in his chambers was to my satisfaction, I kissed him good night and walked to my own chambers, where my ladies helped me to undress. (It amused me sometimes to remember there was a time not so long ago when I'd done that and almost everything else for myself.) It was an ordinary night, and yet as my ladies brushed out my long, heavy dark hair and braided it for bed, I sensed what had happened in that council meeting had changed our lives forever.

My husband, John Dudley, son of a man who had died upon the scaffold, held the rule of England in his hands.

14

Frances Grey
June 1550 to August 1550

D O I HAVE TO COME?" ASKED JANE, LAYING DOWN THE WEDDING INVITA-
tion we had received. "I am extremely busy with my translation."

"Of course you have to come," I said. "It will be the grandest wedding seen
in years. The king himself will be there."

Jane looked at Harry, who nodded. "I'm afraid your mother is right this
time, my girl. Duty calls. Besides, you haven't seen the king in a while."

"There will be dancing and masques and a tournament," I said coaxingly.

Jane looked unimpressed, but Kate, coming up in the middle of our conversation, said, "A grand wedding? Whose, Mother?"

"Anne, the eldest daughter of the Protector—"

"Frances," Harry prodded.

"The Duke of Somerset," I corrected myself. I had found it hard to break the
habit of calling him by his former title. "She is marrying the Earl of Warwick's
eldest son, Lord Lisle." Somerset had been freed from the Tower in February
and, after a brief period of house arrest, had been restored to the king's council,
albeit in a position subordinate to Warwick, who as head of the king's council
was now known as the Lord President. "This marriage is proof of their good
will to each other."

"I can come, can't I?"

"Of course you can, and Mary, too. The entire family has been invited."

"Good," said Kate. "The Earl of Hertford will be there, don't you think?
He's good-looking."

"Is that all you think of, Kate?" Jane asked. "At your young age?"

"He is a good-looking boy," I said of Somerset's oldest son. "It is no harm
to say so."

"Perhaps as proof of good will between the Duke of Somerset and our family, a match could be made between one of us and the Earl of Hertford," Kate said. "Preferably me, as Jane is above such things."

"It is not your place to suggest matches for yourself," said Jane.

"Jane—" I began.

"Well, why not? That way, Jane is saved for the king, and I can marry an agreeable boy."

"There is no intention of marrying Jane to the king, or any of you girls to anyone just yet," Harry said. "Negotiations are afoot to marry the king to a French princess. As for the rest of you, Jane is correct. All of this speculation is unbecoming for maidens."

Behind her father's back, Kate stuck her tongue out at Jane, who magnificently ignored her. I should have reproved Kate, I suppose, but I did not.

∽

"They can marry off all of Warwick's boys to all of Somerset's girls if they like, but does Warwick really think that Somerset's going to be content with being a humble member of the council?" Katherine Brandon, Duchess of Suffolk, asked as we waited for the king to appear at Sheen, which he had offered for the wedding. "Like it or not, he's still a duke, and the king's only living uncle. He can't forget it. Neither should Warwick. And where is Warwick, by the way?"

"Perhaps he is ill. Poor man, having to miss his son's wedding."

The Duchess of Suffolk was about to snort a reply when a quiet voice said, "My husband is ill, my ladies. He regrets his absence keenly, but his health has been so uncertain these past few months, I begged him to keep to his bed."

I stared at the Countess of Warwick before I caught myself. Though not unpleasing in her appearance, she could not be called anything but ordinary looking, but today, dressed elegantly in wrought velvet, she looked almost pretty and a couple of inches taller. She almost showed up the Duchess of Somerset herself. Was her transformation a temporary one due to her son's wedding, or was this a consequence of her husband's elevation? "I am sorry that your husband was not able to come," I managed.

"Well, we have Robert's wedding tomorrow. I hope he will be able to attend that." The countess smiled as we glanced in the direction of a handsome, tall young man who was strolling arm in arm with a very pretty blonde of whom no one in London appeared to know anything but her name. Harry and the rest of our household (including me, I am ashamed to admit) had amused ourselves on the barge, trying to figure out her possible origins. "A love match," the countess said simply. "It happens."

"I daresay your husband will make the best of it," said the Duchess of Suffolk. Even I recognized the acid in her voice.

Jane Dudley heard it, too, but chose not to let it spoil her good humor. "Yes, as a matter of fact he has. He will establish Robert in Norfolk, though of course I imagine he and Amy will be spending much of their time in London." She glanced around. "Ah, the Duchess of Somerset. I *must* speak to her about the musicians."

"My, that little woman creeps up on one," muttered the Duchess of Suffolk after the Countess of Warwick had hurried away. "I wonder if the Earl of Warwick is absent because he doesn't share his wife's enthusiasm for this match with Somerset's girl? They say it was chiefly the work of the countess and the Duchess of Somerset. Who, I see, has not lost a single pearl as the result of her husband's ill fortune."

"Katherine! I thought you and the Duchess of Somerset were friends."

"Oh, we are, but there's no denying that Anne Seymour likes her jewels. And look at her! Six months gone, I'd say. It looks as if that visit she paid to her husband on Christmas Day bore fruit."

I stole a look at my daughters to see if they had caught any of the Duchess of Suffolk's cheerfully malicious commentary, but Kate was talking to Katherine's two sons, who were my younger half brothers. Mary was admiring the brightly dressed courtiers and the foreign dignitaries who had been invited to witness this bonding between the two old friends turned enemies turned friends again. Jane, too, was eying everyone's clothing, but not in the way I might have hoped. "Peacocks," she said dourly.

"Peacocks?" I looked around for the exotic birds.

"These ladies, Mother. Look at them! Why, some of them are even painted. The Countess of Warwick certainly was."

"She could use the help," said the Duchess of Suffolk with a smirk. "But I would hardly say she looked like the Whore of Babylon, my dear girl. A spot of color to the cheeks or to the lips is a harmless thing, especially for a celebration. You must amend your opinions, child, to accommodate us mere mortals, or you will never get on in the world."

"That is what I tell her," I said.

Jane thrust out her lower, unpainted lip in a gesture I alternatingly found endearing and irritating. "John Aylmer says that it is vulgar and ungodly."

"I really wonder sometimes why we keep that man," I said. "He finds everything vulgar and ungodly. I marvel how he puts up with us."

"No doubt through the stipend your husband pays him," said the Duchess of Suffolk. She winked at me.

"Master Aylmer was not speaking of Your Grace or my lady mother," Jane said. "Nor was I."

"Well, good," said the duchess. "I should hate to displease you, my dear."

It was a rare thing to have an adult ally in my skirmishes with Jane, especially one as clever as Katherine. I would have been content to go on some more in this vein, but the sound of trumpets announced the approach of the king's barge.

Edward stepped out, smiling at the assembled company. He was ruddier than he had been the last time I had seen him, for the Earl of Warwick, believing his knightly upbringing had been neglected, had arranged his schedule to give him more time for outdoor pursuits. This put me in mind of King Henry, my late uncle, especially when the young king looked around and frowned. "Where is my lord Warwick?"

The Countess of Warwick stepped forward. "Your Majesty, I am to blame. He removed to Hatfield for the sweet air, and I begged him to remain there, as his health has been so uncertain."

"We fear the Earl of Warwick has been exerting himself too much on our behalf. It is a pity that he must miss his son's wedding."

"I am pledged to tell him all about it." The countess smiled. "Though it is true, Your Majesty, that he wants none of the details that we women savor, so it will be a quick telling."

"Do give him our best wishes, my lady."

"I will, Your Majesty."

"We miss him," said the king softly. He turned to the Duke of Somerset, who had been standing near his duchess, just far enough apart from the rest of the council to look a little awkward. Somerset and the king had dined together recently, Harry had told me, but it had been a rather stiff, formal affair. "Your Grace."

Somerset's face brightened. "My dear nephew, I am grateful you can honor my daughter's wedding with your presence."

The king nodded a little distantly, then turned back abruptly to the Countess of Warwick. "Perhaps we can send the earl our physician?"

Behind the king, the Duchess of Somerset opened her mouth, then shut it again as her husband sent her a glance.

"It's been like that since January, my friends in high places tell me," the Duchess of Suffolk said later in her chamber at Sheen, where the two of us had gone to freshen up after the ceremony. The Duchess of Somerset and the Countess of Warwick had joined each other in weeping sentimental tears over the marriage of their offspring, though not, as Jane had snidely observed, so many tears that they affected their carefully painted faces. The Duke of Somerset had given a rather long speech alluding to his own happy marriage and, rather irrelevantly, it was thought, to the spiritual growth he had experienced in prison. The young Earl of Hertford had said something to Kate that had sent them both into silent giggles during the finest part of the speech, and Will Somers, the elderly fool who had previously served King Henry, had protested that Somerset had spent more time making the speech than he had in the Tower. "The king would trail after Warwick like a dog after a master, if he were allowed to. To the earl's credit, he doesn't exploit it—much, though I dare say he enjoys it. I can't say I ever thought of Warwick as being a brilliant man, but he appears to be the only person in England who has had the sense to figure out that the king wants to be treated as a king, not like a little boy."

"I do feel sorry for the Pro—Somerset, I mean. The king hardly spoke to him just now, and I think the Countess of Warwick or the earl's brother Andrew must have prompted him to do that much."

"It'll sort itself out. Mind you, I'm not saying how it will sort itself out, or whether anyone will be the better off for it. But tell me, Frances. You are friendly with the lady Mary. Was she not invited? Or did she choose not to come?"

"She was invited," I said uneasily. "I suppose she chose not to come."

The lady Mary had refused the king's invitation to visit his court the previous Christmas, although the lady Elizabeth had arrived and had had great fun playing hoodman blind with Robert Dudley over New Year's. I could still hear Harry fuming about her absence, which he and much of the rest of the king's council had regarded as a personal affront. "She's got this absurd idea in her head, such that it is, that if she comes to see the king, he will lock her into the Tower for hearing Mass. Doesn't it occur to her that if that was what he wanted to do, he could simply send men to arrest her?"

The Duchess of Suffolk followed the line of thought Harry had been arguing in my head. "Why she has to be so stubborn is beyond me. The council allows her to hear Mass, which is more than it really should be doing, in my opinion. All they ask is that she not allow half of the countryside to hear Mass with her. It seems quite reasonable."

"Her religion means a great deal to her. It was what helped her through those days when King Henry was ridding himself of her mother."

Katherine gave me an odd look. "Sometimes, Frances, I wonder if you don't have Papist sympathies yourself. Though I suppose Harry Grey would have thrown you out of your house long before if you did."

"It is not that. It is simply that my mother and the lady Mary's mother were friends, and we have been, too, of sorts. And she has been kind to my daughters." I looked out the window to where the servants were putting the finishing touches to the hall, made entirely of boughs, where we ladies were to dine with the king. "I shall go see her after these weddings, I believe. After all, she is my cousin."

&

"The goose was the idea of Amy's family," said the Countess of Warwick ruefully the next day. Suspended between two posts, the poor creature was squawking in terror as a group of young men took turns at trying to decapitate it. The king and most of the men were watching this display with a certain enjoyment, but the countess had her fingers half over her eyes, and the Duchess of Somerset, putting her hands on her belly significantly, had declared herself ill and demanded that the duke take her to their chamber. The countess turned to her fourth son, standing nearby. "Guildford, you are good with your sword. For God's sake, go there and put that poor thing out of its misery this very instant."

"It's not my turn."

"Make it your turn. Tell them I ordered you to, as the mother of the groom!"

Guildford, a tall young man who was about thirteen, nodded and went to do his mother's bidding. In one swift stroke, the goose's head was severed from its body.

"Thank the Lord," said the Countess of Warwick. "Such folly men engage in." She turned to my eldest daughter as Guildford ambled back. "They tell me you are remarkably skilled in languages, my lady."

"I speak several, my lady," Jane said without a great deal of modesty.

"I speak only French, and little enough of that," the countess said. "It was not fashionable when I was young for ladies to learn more than that, unless they were very great indeed. But all of our children are learning French and Italian, and our sons know the ancient languages, as well. Or at least some of them do." The countess looked at Guildford indulgently. "You would put Guildford to shame in Greek, my lady, but he speaks Italian quite well. Don't you?"

Guildford dutifully said something in that language to Jane, who responded in kind. Though I could not understand a word either was saying, or judge how well they were saying it, I sensed the conversation was a forced one. When another lady claimed the countess's attention and steered her away, Jane abruptly switched to English. "Is your mother tipsy?"

"Of course not," Guildford said huffily. He smiled, a gesture that revealed him to be easily the most handsome of the five Dudley sons. "She is naturally retiring, you know, and at affairs like this she becomes ill at ease and starts to babble, especially with my father not here. And the goose did upset her."

"Such pastimes are foolish and idle," Jane said. "Like hunting for pleasure."

"I like hunting for pleasure," admitted Guildford, who had suddenly acquired the look of a trapped deer himself. "It is good exercise, and it helps with the art of war. Of course, it might not help all that much, as the deer isn't shooting a crossbow," he acknowledged. "But I am sorry, my ladies, I must go. My brother is waving to me."

"He seems a pleasant young man," I commented after Guildford had left us.

"A ninny," said Jane. "Deer not shooting a crossbow!"

"He was trying to be amusing, Jane."

"And his Italian conversation is commonplace. Do you know what he said to me?"

I shook my head.

"He said that my dress was very pretty and that the color suited me. And then he asked me if I would dance with him later today!"

"Really, Jane, the poor young man was only trying to make gallant conversation. It can't be as easy for men as women think it should be, in English or Italian."

"He could have saved himself the trouble and not made such conversation at all."

"I hope you did not refuse to dance with him. That would have been quite rude."

"No, I agreed. Though I am not looking forward to it." Jane gazed over to where Guildford was talking with his brothers. "Perhaps I could get sick, like the Earl of Warwick."

⁂

When I wrote to Mary, asking to visit her on my way to Bradgate, I received a strangely noncommittal response, to my distress. Had I angered my cousin in some way? I wrote back to that effect and was told I had not offended in any way and to come as soon as I wanted.

"Perhaps she is ill," I told Harry.

"Perhaps," said Harry without a great deal of concern. "Don't let her trap you into attending her Mass this time." He winked at my guilty look. "Oh, you can't fool me, my dear. I know she inveigled you into going the last time you visited her. Jane told me."

&

Mary, it turned out, had moved for the summer to Woodham Walter in Essex, which was not on our way to Bradgate, so I sent the girls on to Leicestershire with a suitable entourage and went to Woodham Walter by myself. Jane, for one, put up no argument about being deprived of a visit to the lady Mary.

Woodham Walter, about two miles from the sea, was an attractive manor, but it was small for a person of Mary's station—the sort of place one might use for a few days while en route to somewhere else. It seemed odd to be there for over a month, as Mary apparently had been, but as I drew closer to the manor, I found that the air that blew in from the sea felt good across my cheeks. Perhaps that was the appeal for Mary.

I was shown to Mary's private chamber just moments after I came through the manor gates. To my surprise, she dismissed her ladies and servants as soon as I knelt to her. When they had all cleared the room, she said, "Rise. Why are you here?"

I started. Never had Mary greeted me so rudely. "To visit you, my lady."

"You have not been sent here by my brother's council?"

"The council? Why on earth would they send me to your ladyship?"

"Your husband is a member, and a favored one from what I hear."

"My husband trusts me with the management of the household and the management of my younger daughters. Nothing more. He certainly would not send me on the council's business. Nor would anyone else on the council."

"You are truly not here at the council's bidding?"

"Mary, what is this? Our mothers loved each other. We played together as children. As adults we have been friends—or so I thought until now. I came here only because I heard that you had refused to come to the weddings, and I thought you might be ill or troubled."

Mary stared into my eyes. But I was as much a Tudor as she, and I met her gaze without flinching. Finally, she lowered her gaze. "Perhaps I am wrong. So you will swear that you have not been sent by the Earl of Warwick and his crew?"

"The Earl of Warwick?"

"You were at his sons' weddings."

"So was almost anyone else of any consequence. Mary, I should not have to swear to anything. When have I ever given you reason not to trust me? I came here solely out of friendship. No one sent me. No one so much as gave me a message for you. Except for Harry and our household, I doubt if anyone knows that I am here, or would care if he or she did." I fiddled with the gloves I held in my hand. "I have overstayed my visit. With your permission, I shall be gone within the hour."

Mary shook her head. "No, stay. I have wronged you." She stared past me toward the window. "But I cannot help it. Everything has been poisoned for me. I trust almost no one in England now."

"Why?"

"How can I? They have tried to deprive me of the one thing that matters most to me, my religion."

I hesitated, then got up my courage. "Harry says that they have only asked you not to hear the Mass. Forgive me, but couldn't you conform like so many others do, and make your life so much easier?"

"Conform?" Mary put her hands behind her back and began to pace around the room. "You and I are cousins, Frances, yet so different. You speak of conforming as easily as you might talk of replacing a French hood with an English one. As if these differences between my faith and the new one were mere trivialities."

I dared not utter the thought I sometimes had, which was that they were. "Still, couldn't you ease your conscience by saying you acted under duress, as you did when you agreed with King Henry that your mother's marriage was unlawful?"

A look of pain crossed Mary's face. "That is the most shameful thing I have done in all of my life. I still regret it."

"You were young and dependent on your father. What else could you have done? It did bring you happiness, did it not?"

"No. It brought me security and wealth. They are poor substitutes when you know yourself to have once known something better." Mary gripped the rosary she carried at her side as a man might grip a sword. "I dishonored my mother's memory that day, and for very little purpose. I will die by my own hand before I do such a thing again."

"Mary!"

"No, I lie. I would not do such a shameful act. I would do something else."

"What do you mean?"

Instead of answering me, Mary turned, bidding me with a motion to follow her. Stopping outside of the manor's small chapel, she went inside, leaving me to stand self-consciously by its door. When she returned after some moments, her face was entirely at peace. "We may return to my chamber."

I obeyed. When the door had closed upon us once again, Mary spoke. "I do trust you, Cousin, and I will tell you of my plan now that I have prayed for guidance. But you must promise—I will not make you swear an oath, but merely promise me, as my cousin and my friend—that you will tell no one of this."

My heart thumped. What in the world had I gotten myself into? "I cannot promise if it involves anything that would bring harm to my husband or to anything that concerns him. Harry and I are not as close as some couples," I admitted, "but he is kind in his own way, and he has the highest claim upon my loyalty."

"It will not harm your husband. Indeed, he might welcome it. So do you promise?"

"I promise."

"I believe it is no longer possible to marry out of England, so I plan to flee. The emperor has agreed to help me."

My mouth fell open. "What on earth are you thinking? England is your home. Your brother and sister are here."

"Elizabeth? Sometimes I doubt we even have the same father. In any case, she is the darling of the council, now that Thomas Seymour is safely gone, and can be no friend to me. As for the king, he is Warwick's and the council's creature now. They are turning him against me. It will only be worse for me as time goes on, I fear. I see no hope but to leave, and in secret."

"I can't believe the king or his council means you any harm."

"You are naïve," was the short answer.

"What did the king say when you saw him in February?"

"He was very loving, very friendly. Of course, Warwick was sick and not at his side."

"He is quite often sick. He missed his own sons' weddings. Perhaps he does not have the absolute hold over the king that you fear, since he is not constantly around him."

"It does not matter. If he is not there, his creatures are, like his brother Andrew Dudley." Mary looked at me stonily. "I believe I made a mistake in telling you this. You will go to the council."

"No," I snapped. "I promised, and I will not. But I cannot help but think you exaggerate the danger to yourself. If you confine the Mass to yourself and your women, how can that antagonize the council? It has conceded that much, hasn't it?"

"For now." Mary lifted her chin. "You think me mad, don't you? But I tell you, the council means me ill."

I was silent, for in a way, I did think Mary mad—or partly so. I could not believe the king, or the council for that matter, wished her harm. They might rail against Mary's sharing Mass with any traveling stroller who happened to be in the neighborhood, as Harry put it, but most of these men had been servants of King Henry. Surely they would not want to see any harm come to his old-est daughter.

Mary read my thoughts. "You think the king will be bound by his love for me as his sister, but remember what happened with Thomas Seymour, and what almost happened to Somerset. Both of them the king's uncles."

"Thomas Seymour was courting disaster. It could not have ended otherwise for him. As for the Duke of Somerset, no permanent harm came to him."

"For now. That could change."

"And the emperor approves of this plan of yours to escape?"

"Yes. Not wholeheartedly, I think, but his sister has given her support, as well." The Holy Roman Emperor, Mary's first cousin, Charles V, had once been engaged to Mary when she was very young. The match had fallen through, as had all prospective matches for Mary, but Charles had continued to take an interest in Mary's affairs, both for political and personal reasons. His sister, Mary of Hungary, the regent of the Low Countries, was said to be more vigorous than he these days. However misguided I might think Mary's plan was, it certainly had supporters in the highest places.

But that was not enough to make me feel better about the plan. "You will never be able to come back to England if you accomplish this. You will be an exile, and what kind of life will that be? If you ask me, this is a foolish idea. I would abide here to see what happens."

"I did not ask you, and I do not want to abide here to suffer more."

I knew nothing else to say. Catherine of Aragon had been a legend for stub-bornness in her time, and it was evident her daughter was no different. I did not even ask for details, half because I feared Mary would take this as evidence I was spying, half because I truly did not want to know.

"I don't know why I told you this," Mary mused. "You could hardly be of help even if you supported the idea. Your husband is too prominent for you to escape notice. Perhaps I want to be talked out of it. I don't know. I was born in England. I love the English people, for they loved my own mother. And if I leave, those who stay behind will be left with no livelihood, no way of upholding the true religion. I will be deserting them. But I have told myself all of these things, and all of the things you told me, and in the end it makes no difference. I want to leave."

"You have made definite plans, then, I gather?"

"Yes."

I supposed the convenience to the sea was the reason Mary had chosen this manor as her residence, but I asked no more questions. "I hope that you will think upon this more and not act impulsively. You said just now you have doubts. I think you are wise to have them."

"There is time yet to think, but I know I shall not change my mind. But we have done with this. Let us have a game of cards with my ladies."

Back at Bradgate, I spent the days in a high state of restlessness—and guilt— waiting to hear news of Mary's flight. I had not thought of it at the time, naturally, but what if the emperor had a sinister reason for wanting Mary out of England? Was he planning to send her back at the head of an invading army, to depose her young brother and establish herself as a Papist queen? I could not imagine Mary agreeing to such a scheme, but if her trusted cousin proposed it, and framed it as a matter of religious duty...

But I had made Mary a promise, and I kept it.

Then, toward the end of July, Harry came from London to Bradgate, all smiles. "It seems as if you missed some excitement when you visited the lady Mary."

I managed to keep my voice level. "What do you mean?"

"The fool woman had plans to escape from England! Don't ask me why— she's got it into her fool head that she's being persecuted. Actually, my dear, it's rather embarrassing. She almost succeeded."

I put a hand to my throat. "She is a prisoner?"

"No. She's not in custody at all. From what the council can make out, she laid these plans to leave the country—and then, when men and ships from the emperor arrived to help her, she dithered. Kept coming up with excuses why she couldn't leave immediately, why she had to pack every trinket she owned, why she couldn't leave certain ladies behind. The locals were getting suspicious, with these foreign ships lurking about, and the emperor's men couldn't stay indefinitely, waiting for her to make up her mind. She kept wailing, 'What shall I do? What is to become of me?'" Harry chuckled. "The emperor's men had to keep inventing all sorts of stories to explain their presence—that one was a corn chandler, that another was looking for pirates—but the men of Essex were too intelligent to be duped. They told the council, and we sent Sir John Gates into the area to put a stop to any more of that nonsense. So now, the emperor's men are heading back to Flanders where they belong, and the lady Mary is no doubt wishing that she'd acted sooner."

"What will happen to her?"

"Nothing, although she's a fool if she thinks this has helped her in the matter of her ridiculous Masses. As much as she would like to see herself as a martyr, the council isn't willing to oblige by imprisoning her. The king would like to have a word with her, that's all. He's not happy about his kingdom being painted as a place from which one must flee, as you can imagine, or about the emperor and his sister sticking their noses and their Hapsburg jaws into our affairs, but he prefers to speak to Mary quietly rather than to create a stir over this."

I could not help but sigh in relief.

Harry looked at me sharply. "You were visiting Mary during the planning, or part of it. Did she confide in you?"

I lied with more ease than I quite liked. "She did tell me of some of her fears for the future and talked rather wildly about getting out of England, but I did not take her seriously."

"No, how could you?" Harry snorted. "I hope this little episode teaches the lady Mary that she has no head for intrigue. Or a head for governance, lest, God forbid, anything should ever happen to the king." He raised the glass of ale from which he had been sipping. "Long life to King Edward."

∽

"I must talk to you."

Since my indiscretion of the autumn, Adrian Stokes and I had been on cordial, if formal, terms. I did not know why I was confiding in him now, except something told me I could trust him, just as Mary had felt she could trust me.

"Perhaps you have heard of the lady Mary's plan to escape, and its failure."

"Something of it, my lady."

"I knew of it and said nothing. I made a promise to her that I would not, and I kept it."

"That must have been a painful position for you to be in, my lady."

I relaxed a little under Adrian Stokes's sympathetic gaze. "Yes, it was. We are friends as well as cousins. I did not ask for her confidence, but when she gave it to me, I felt bound to uphold it, even though I thought her plan was unwise and advised her against it."

"Does my lord know that she told you?"

"No. I concealed it from him, and when he asked me this very day whether I had had knowledge of it, I lied to him. I am not proud of that, but..." I looked down at my feet, then up again. "But that is my own problem. What I am concerned about is that word did get out about Mary's escape plan. It distresses me to think that Mary might believe that I betrayed her."

"And you wish me to tell her?"

"Yes, but I do not wish you to risk going yourself. Harry is not an ill-tempered man, but I don't know if—"

"I have brothers and friends. I will find a way to get a message to her—a verbal one. It would be foolish to trust something to writing." Adrian Stokes paused, then added, "I should tell you, my lady, that I have no sympathy with the lady Mary's religious ideas or, indeed, with her contumaciousness toward the king and his council. I share the views of my lord Dorset. But it distresses me that her folly has troubled your mind."

I thanked him. A couple of weeks later, Master Stokes came to me. After we had discussed business for a short time, he said, "My brother William made contact with the lady we spoke of. She assured him that she knew you had nothing to do with a certain matter becoming known. I hope that eases your mind, my lady."

"It does, very much, and I am grateful to you."

Master Stokes bowed his head, apparently expecting to be given leave to depart. Instead, I asked, "I gather you and your brothers are close, Master Stokes?"

"Yes, my lady. We have each other's confidence."

"Harry is fond of his brothers too. I wish my daughter Jane and my daughter Kate were on friendlier terms with each other," I confessed. "There is nothing like having a sister or brother one can confide in."

"I believe your ladyship's sister, the lady Eleanor, died several years ago."

I nodded. "I still miss her. Have you ever been married, Master Stokes?"

"No, my lady. I had intentions once, but the young lady died."

"I am very sorry to hear that. Have you ever thought of marrying?"

"No, my lady, until recently I have lived the life of a soldier, and it would not have been meet to take a wife. And in truth, I had no desire to marry. I took my betrothed's death very hard. I loved her, you see. But forgive me, my lady, that is probably more than you wished to hear."

"Why? I asked a question, and you answered it. I hope you are happy with us, Master Stokes."

"I am very happy in this household."

"Well, good." I could hardly go on asking Master Stokes personal questions, I realized, though something in me longed to keep on doing exactly that. Reluctantly, I said, "You may go now, Master Stokes."

                        *

Despite my worry about being found out, our life at Bradgate went on as normal. Harry's brothers often visited, and one day in August when the weather had been especially fine, we decided to go hunting.

It seemed too fair a day for any young person to spend indoors, so once I had donned my riding habit, I went to Jane's chamber. "We are going hunting, Jane. Would you like to join us?"

"No, Mother. You know I think that folly."

"I didn't see you turning down the venison the other day," I said mildly. "It came from our own park, and the deer certainly didn't walk into the kitchen and offer itself up as a sacrifice. Besides, you needn't actually hunt. Just riding in the fresh air would benefit you. You have been cooped up with your books too much lately."

"I am working on Father's New Year's present. It is a translation from Latin into Greek of Heinrich Bullinger's treatise on marriage. I must get on with it."

"Very well," I said. I looked at Jane's handiwork: a page covered with what I could only assume was flawless Greek. "What does Bullinger have to say on marriage?"

"I can hardly summarize it in a sentence, but in short, he believes it a state to be most desired. There is an English version," Jane suggested. "Perhaps you might want to read it."

"No, thank you," I said. "Having been married for many years, I do not think I need instruction on the subject."

                        *

I did not last long at the hunt. As the dogs spotted their prey and yapped ecstatically, I felt a familiar pain in my gut: the cramps that presaged my monthly course. Some months I scarcely had pain at all; others, the cramps were so bad that I could not speak through them. I decided to ride back to the house and rest. As I made my way back to my chamber with Bess Cavendish, who had been one of my waiting women before her marriage and often visited me as a friend, one of the servants approached. "My lady, Master Ascham arrived in your absence and is paying a call on the lady Jane."

I sighed, wondering whether I should postpone my rest and greet Master Ascham. Such men were common guests at Bradgate, for over the past couple of years, Harry had gained a reputation as a friend and patron of scholars, who naturally flocked to our house. My Kate regarded them as a bore, while little Mary generally took their visits as a time to scuttle off onto the grounds of Bradgate if she could manage it. Jane, naturally, delighted in their company, especially as they shamelessly flattered her and Harry. I, of course, was a different matter. Though the scholars appreciated a well-kept chamber and a well-cooked meal as much as did lesser mortals, it never occurred to them I might bear some responsibility for the quality of this hospitality. They confined their exchanges with me to pleasantries, if that much.

Today's arrival, Roger Ascham, had tutored the lady Elizabeth but had left her household after the uproar about Thomas Seymour. He was not a recipient of Harry's generosity, but he had been impressed with Jane's scholarship and had suggested some books for her to read, and he was friendly with her own tutor, John Aylmer. As a result, Jane and Ascham had corresponded now and then. He was on such terms with Jane that I could greet him and then take to my bed without causing offense, leaving Jane to be his hostess, I decided. I made my way to her outer chamber, the door of which had been left slightly ajar.

"So your ladyship decided not to join your family on their hunting trip?" Ascham was saying.

"Yes. Such idle pastimes are not to my liking. Mother urged me, but I was absorbed in my translation for Father, and in this Plato."

"Your parents must be very proud of your dedication to learning, my lady."

"Father is, but Mother has no appreciation for such things. She is a woman of limited intellect, you see."

Bess gasped. I opened my mouth, then shut it as Jane's voice continued relentlessly.

"She is entirely absorbed in such pastimes as gambling and hunting. She can barely speak French, which is astounding, considering that my grandmother was its queen. All she can do is sew shirts and make comfits and the like, and then she presumes to criticize me when I fall short at these things." Jane's voice dripped with scorn. "As if there are not servants to do those tasks, and do them better than she ever could."

"With respect to your ladyship, I think you judge your mother too harshly," Ascham said. "She was not educated in the fashion that you have been, and even if she had been, few have been blessed with your gifts, my lady."

"True, but she is so insufferable! I am glad you have come here today. I have longed to speak to someone about this, and there is no one here who would understand. They are all so commonplace. If Father were here more often, it would not be so bad, but with him gone on business so much now, there is simply no one I can talk to, except about inanities."

"My dear lady—"

"She has even laid hands upon me in anger," Jane continued. "Do you see here, Master Ascham? This was where she pinched me the other day, when I did not sew one of her precious shirts to her satisfaction. There seems to be no pleasing her, for no matter whether I am speaking, keeping silent, sitting, standing, sewing, playing, dancing, or anything else, I must do it perfectly, just as God made the world. I cannot count the pinches she has given me, as well as the nips and bobs, over the years. It is sheer hell! And then my mother wonders why I have no interest in being in her company! I would much rather be in the company of John Aylmer. He makes learning so agreeable, it is all I can do to keep from crying when I must leave him and spend time with my mother."

"Your ladyship hardly needs any inducement to learn, however."

I had heard enough. I turned away from the door, tears fogging my vision. Bess took my arm and helped me toward my chamber.

How could my daughter think so ill of me? I had pinched her arm the other day, it was true, but not because she had sewn her shirt poorly; it was because I knew she could have done a much better job if she had bothered to take the time. The poor people who were the intended recipients of the shirts would hardly appreciate having them fall apart after a couple of days' wear. Nips and bobs I had given her, too, usually when her arrogance was too insufferable, or when she had spoken slightingly to her younger sisters or to a servant. I had received plenty such in my own day when I misbehaved, most usually from my nurse, but also from my beautiful mother herself on the occasions when my conduct was so bad as to merit it. It had never occurred to me to complain of such treatment, or even to resent it. I had simply determined to be a better girl so it would not happen again.

When we had reached my chamber, Bess said, "My lady, that is blatantly unfair! You spoil the girl, if anything, if you do not mind my saying so, and you know that I am fond of her. You should confront her."

"No," I said. "I would have to tell her that I was listening, and that would only add eavesdropping to my list of sins." I sank into a chair.

Bess patted my shoulder. "In any case, my lady, you should not take this too much to heart. Girls are like that, my lady, about their mothers. They believe them stupid and hopelessly old-fashioned, until they have children of their own and suddenly realize they weren't so stupid after all. Lady Jane is just a more extreme example."

But I had never thought my own mother was stupid. Neither had my sister Eleanor. For us, she had been a fairy queen come to life, a woman who had married both the King of France and the man she loved. How many women could say that? Our favorite activity as girls had been to go into our mother's wardrobe, not to try on her clothing, for that struck us as a sacrilege, but to finger each garment carefully and to wonder to what glamorous occasion she might have worn it—despite that my mother had lived a relatively retired life since her marriage to my father. When she died, soon after my wedding to Harry, Eleanor and I had been desolate, even though her health had been poor for some time. I even tormented myself with the notion that traveling to attend my wedding had caused the final crisis, although nothing could have kept her away.

"Maybe I could speak to the lady Jane, as we're not that far apart in age," suggested Bess, who was in her early twenties. "She likes me well enough. If she knew how she had hurt you…"

"No. I shall let it pass." I wearily rose and allowed Bess, stepping back into her role as my waiting woman, to help me out of my riding clothes. "At least now I know exactly what she thinks of me."

15

Jane Dudley
November 1550 to April 1551

HAVE YOU HEARD THE LATEST GOSSIP ABOUT FATHER?" ROBERT SAID.

I sighed. In the past year, I had discovered that John's newfound power brought with it a heavy price: the rumors that dogged him. Each was more absurd than the last, which stopped no one from believing them. "Evidently not. So tell me. He is planning to murder Somerset? Somerset is planning to murder him? He is going to lock the lady Mary in the Tower?"

"No. He's planning to cast you off, marry the lady Elizabeth, and make himself king through her."

I turned to stare at Robert. I could laugh off the other rumors, but this one… "Who told you this nonsense?"

"The lady Elizabeth, actually. The imperial ambassador heard the rumor and passed it along, and it made its way to her, so naturally she wrote to ask if I was indeed going to become her stepson. She thought it an excellent jest."

"It is not the least bit amusing, Robert."

"It's just the same old rubbish, Mother. Don't look so concerned. The imperial ambassador would pass along a rumor about his own mother if he heard it in the streets of England. You know that."

"But he believed it. Did he not?"

"Who knows? He's terrified that there might be a pearl hiding in a pile of horse dung, so he passes along the dung and leaves it to others to find the pearl." Robert kissed me on the cheek. "Amy and I are off to dine with friends tonight. Don't worry about this fool rumor, Mother. I'm sorry I spoke to you of it."

⁓

"What's wrong, my dear? You've been very quiet tonight."

"It is just a cruel and stupid rumor."

"Cruel, maybe, but it can't be all that stupid if it has you brooding about it. Tell me, Mouse."

"Very well. The—the imperial ambassador—says you mean to divorce me and marry the lady Elizabeth."

"The imperial ambassador is an ass. Where does he come across these things? Surely you don't believe this rumor."

"No." I stared at the large salt cellar in between us; we were dining privily. "But it could happen. I mean—" I faltered, then pressed on. "I am no longer young, and I never was all that pretty, and I do not believe I can bear you children anymore—I have some of the symptoms of the change of life. I hardly knew what to say to people at Jack's and Robert's weddings. I was so nervous, I just babbled. The lady Elizabeth is so striking and young and clever—"

"Jane! The lady Elizabeth is nothing to me, and you are everything. You know that."

"I should, but we have hardly seen anything of each other lately. You are so often ill, and when you are well, you are meeting continually with people. This is the first time we have dined together in weeks, just the two of us. And"—I swallowed—"we have not had marital relations in weeks. Months, maybe. I know you have had so many new responsibilities, and that you cannot shirk your duty to the king and to your country, but I have been so lonely, and when one is lonely, it is easy to believe stupid rumors. Or at least not to dismiss them out of hand."

John rose from his chair.

"I have offended you," I said.

"No. I will be back presently."

A while later John returned, followed by a man bearing a large, covered cage. John nodded, and with a slight flourish, the servant swept off the cover. Inside the cage sat a handsome green parrot. "He was to be an early New Year's gift to you, my dear, but now he is to be a very early New Year's gift to you. It's just as well. I couldn't have kept him hidden here indefinitely."

"Can he talk?"

"He most certainly can. We've been working on some things." John bent and looked at the parrot. "Pretty Jane."

"Pretty Jane!"

"I love you."

"Love you," croaked the parrot.

"John!"

"John?" queried the puzzled bird.

I wrapped my arms around my husband. "John, he's wonderful!"

"I can't take that much credit for him, in truth. A petitioner brought him to me, as an inducement to show him favor. I would have helped him without the parrot, but I thought it was the type of thing you might like. But there's more." John opened the cage and stretched out his hand. With complete self-assurance, the parrot hopped onto his wrist. "He'll do the same for you after he's come to know you, my dear." He turned and faced me, the parrot perching on his arm. "Now, answer me, Jane. Do I look like the sort of man who would cast off my wife, the mother of my seven living children, for a seventeen-year-old girl?"

I shook my head. "Assuredly not."

"And as soon as I get this bird off my hand, we shall go to bed. Just make sure the parrot's in the other room; God knows what words he might pick up."

∽

In April, we had a visitor at Ely Place: Henry Sidney, a young man of one and twenty who had been part of Edward's household since the king's infancy. He was a great favorite with the king, and had recently joined his privy chamber. He had asked to see both of us. "I hope nothing is wrong with the king," I said as he was shown in.

"No, my lady. His Majesty is well. My business concerns myself—and another." Henry Sidney swallowed. "In short, I have taken a wife."

"Who?"

"Lady Mary." In a small voice, Sidney added, "Your lord and ladyship's daughter, that is."

My first instinct was to marvel that Mary had at last found something other than a book to command her attention. The second was to gape at Henry Sidney. "Our Mary?" I said stupidly.

John rose. He was a tall, powerfully built man, and it must have taken a great deal of courage for Henry to stand his ground when he asked, "Did you dishonor my daughter, boy?"

"No, my lord! She came to the marriage bed a virgin, I swear it! I would not treat her—or your lordship—with such disrespect."

"But there was a marriage bed," I said.

Henry's voice grew small again. "Yes, my lady. We did... er... consummate the marriage."

"Several times," said a voice behind me. I turned as Mary strode into the room, her face devoid of its usual dreamy expression. "We married at Esher," she said. "On the twenty-ninth of March."

Esher was a manor in Surrey that John had been recently granted by the king. Mary had been ailing after New Year's and had been sent there to recover her health. "Do you mean to tell me you were feigning illness?"

"No, Mother. I was ill. Henry came there to see about me, and we decided to get married. I was feeling better by then," my daughter added.

"No doubt," I muttered. I looked toward John, but for some reason he was leaving me to handle this matter on my own. "Why didn't you simply ask your father and me before making this match? Your brother Robert showed us that much respect."

"I knew you had been considering other matches for me," Mary said. "I feared you would say no."

"As we might well have done," I said. "What do the two of you plan to live on?" Henry Sidney was the eldest son, but his father was still alive.

"My father might allow me something," Henry said. "Or even the king."

"You were married by a priest?" I asked.

"Yes," Mary said. "And we had witnesses, too. *Say* something, Father."

John shrugged. "What can I say? Congratulations? You've behaved deceitfully and disrespectfully. If you're expecting any largesse from me, I would put that idea out of your heads. I hope you weren't expecting my blessing for this carnal marriage of yours, for you'll get no such thing."

He stalked out of the room, letting the door shut behind him with a thud. Mary started weeping, while Henry stared after John in bewilderment. "My lady, I am truly sorry. We meant no harm, I assure you. My motives in marrying her were not mercenary—"

"Comfort your wife," I said, almost shoving poor Mary in Henry's direction. "I must speak to John."

∾

"John, what on earth is the matter with you? I know Mary did wrong in marrying as she did, but did she deserve such unkindness? Henry Sidney is from a perfectly good family, and the king is fond of him. He will inherit a more than adequate estate. You had not promised her in marriage to someone else, had you?"

"No."

"Then why speak to her so harshly? It is unlike you."

John stared straight ahead.

"Please, John. Don't be like this. Mary was weeping as hard as a girl could weep after you left. Think of all of the romances she reads. It must have seemed like such to her. I know she did not think she was dishonoring you. After all, they revealed the marriage to you themselves. They were honest, if only after the fact." I touched John's hand. "Something else must be on your mind, to make you act so. Don't hide it from me."

"They chose an ill time for this escapade of theirs. I had not wanted to frighten you, but I suppose it's best that you know. The Duke of Somerset is plotting against me."

"John?"

"It is true. He has been discontent for some time, I knew, about being just another member of the king's council, and we have quarreled over matters of policy, as well, but I did not believe there was anything to be concerned about. But today, I found just how far it has gone. There was a plan to stir the people of London to rise up, and tonight one of my men was in an affray at Holborn Bridge. There are bills being put around the city urging rebellion. If Somerset is not behind these plots, they are at least being organized in his name." John sighed. "There is no shortage of men to come to his side. You know our difficulties. King Henry left little in the treasury, and Somerset depleted it even further with his vainglorious Scottish wars. The coinage is debased; the harvests have been poor. You hardly need me to tell you these things, though. Our government is trying to improve matters, but it is a slow process. Too slow for the people, who either cannot or will not understand the difficulties involved, and Somerset has been exploiting this."

"But do you have proof that he is plotting against you?"

"Not enough, and that is the problem. If I return him to the Tower, it must be with good reason and clear proof. If he were tried and found innocent, it would be my own death, either at the hands of the people or on the order of the king. And in truth, I do not want to act against him without good proof. The king has lost one uncle to the axe; I would not have him lose another without the best of reasons." John stared out the window. "And Somerset has children. I know all too well what it is to have a father executed as a traitor. I am not eager to make his own children suffer so."

"You could imprison him and keep him there, like the Duke of Norfolk." The old duke, imprisoned when King Henry was alive, had been spared execution by the king's own death, but the council had rejected all calls for his release.

"I have thought of that, but Somerset has been imprisoned and released once, with the consequences you see now. No. If he goes into the Tower, I cannot risk ever having him come out alive again." John stared bleakly into space. After a while, he said, "They shall be married here at Ely Place, in public. Soon."

"John?"

"Mary and Henry Sidney. I don't like this secrecy. It could be used against them or their children someday. It won't be as grand as Jack's wedding, or even Robert's, but it will be better than this clandestine affair at Esher. He's a fine young man. I suppose she could have chosen worse, after all." He rang for a servant. "Send my daughter Mary to me, along with Henry Sidney if he's around. Don't hurry. Let them worry a little while longer about the consequences of their headstrong behavior."

I wrapped my arms around John and kissed him as the puzzled servant departed. "No goose, please. I hated that."

"No goose," John agreed. He sighed. "I wonder if I should invite Somerset to the wedding."

16

Frances Grey
July 1551

IN EARLY JULY, AS I SAT SEWING WITH MY DAUGHTERS, I RECEIVED A MESSAGE from Harry, who was with the king: the sweating sickness was about. By no means were the girls and I to leave Bradgate, unless the sickness reached Leicestershire, in which case we were to move to one of our more isolated manors.

I stared at Harry's scribbled message and fancied I was sweating already. "What is the matter, Mother?" Kate asked.

"The sweating sickness."

"The what?"

"Like the plague," Jane said knowingly.

"Not quite," I said. "It does not produce the tokens the plague does, and it is not as deadly as the plague, but it is close. A person can be dead from it within hours. It causes lethargy and a great deal of sweating. That is why it has that name." I looked at Jane, almost expecting her to contradict me or roll her eyes at the obviousness of my remark, but she merely nodded.

"Have you had it, Mother?"

"No. There has not been a major outbreak since 1528, when I was about Kate's age. I was lucky. Some people in my father's household did contract it. They died." I stared at my sewing. "It is a strange illness. It is more likely to strike rich households than poor ones. Indeed, the lady Elizabeth is lucky to be here. Her mother, Anne Boleyn, was stricken when she was, er...being courted by the king." I put down my sewing. "It is odd the way things work out. Had the sweat taken Anne, as some certainly hoped it would, King Henry might have never remarried, and Mary might be queen today."

"And we would all be clutching rosaries and praying before saints," said Jane acidly. "Thank goodness the sweat spared Mistress Boleyn."

⚭

We were lucky at Bradgate. No one fell sick, although some of our neighbors in Leicestershire were not so fortunate.

Then a messenger wearing the livery of Katherine Brandon appeared at the house. I knew as soon as I saw his downcast face that some misfortune had befallen my stepmother. "It is the Duke of Suffolk and his brother, my lady."

My fifteen- and thirteen-year-old half brothers, my father's sons by his marriage to Katherine, had been studying at Cambridge. "They are ill?"

"They are with the Lord, my lady. They perished of the sweat."

"Lord have mercy," I whispered. They were Katherine's only children.

"When the sweat came to Cambridge, they left immediately for Buckden, but it was too late. They fell ill hours after their arrival. Their death was very quick. My lady was sent for, but they had expired before she arrived. The eldest died first, and the younger followed just a half hour later."

The twins, we had nicknamed my brothers, for even though they were a couple of years apart in age, they had been inseparable. "They died together, at least. It would have been cruel for the Lord to have left only one alive."

"Aye, my lady, and they both died as dukes, as the younger inherited the elder's title in his remaining half hour of life. They will be buried as such."

I nodded sadly. My father's dukedom, awarded him by King Henry before my parents married, had died with my brothers. There would be no other Duke of Suffolk—unless, as Harry pointed out when he came to Bradgate a few days later, the king chose to give Harry himself that title.

"How can you think of such a thing at a time like this?"

"I'm sorry, my dear, but the possibility does spring to mind." Harry patted me on the hand. "Be honest, Frances. You probably thought of the matter yourself."

"Yes," I conceded. "But it's poor taste to speak of it at this time."

"All right, my dear."

We were to leave the next day to visit Katherine at Grimsthorpe. Harry, hearing of my brothers' deaths, had hastened to Bradgate, heedless of the sweat still ravaging the countryside. That had to count in his favor, I reminded myself.

"Sometimes, I wonder which is worse," said Harry. "For a child to be taken as an infant, like our Henry, or for one to be taken as a young man, like your brothers. At least the Duchess of Suffolk got some time with her boys, got to see how they turned out. Not that I'm trying to make light of her grief, or yours. I know they'll be sorely missed. I was fond of them myself."

"You still mourn for our Henry?" I asked.

"Most certainly I do. Every day. You never realized that?"

I could not say the word "no"; it sounded as harsh as the July sun boring through our windows. "I suppose I never did."

"Well, I do. Give me credit for some feeling, Frances."

I said nothing, and we went about our separate business for the rest of the day until late in the afternoon, when I appeared in Harry's study—usually forbidden to anyone but my husband. He was not reading one of his books, but weeping into his hands. "I'm sorry, Harry," I said.

Harry nodded and took me into his arms. Holding each other, we cried for different things—him for our loss of many years before, me for my brothers—but we cried, at last, together.

17

Jane Dudley
October 1551

SINCE THREE OF OUR SONS—JACK, AMBROSE, AND ROBERT—AND OUR daughter Mary were now married, and some of our sons were attending the king, we had begun setting aside one day a week to dine together, just John, our children, and their spouses. It was a time for each of us to tell the others our news, if we had any. With so many children married, I deeply hoped one or more of the couples would soon have news of a coming child. Having reached the end of my own child-bearing years, it appeared, I looked forward to spoiling a line of Dudley grandchildren.

But the news that night belonged to John. "The king is to make several knights next week," he informed us. He nodded at Henry Sidney, who after his initial misstep in secretly marrying our daughter had become a favorite of John's. "Henry is to be one of them."

Mary squealed. "This calls for a kiss," she announced and turned her attention, and her mouth, to Henry. Since Henry Sidney had joined our family, I had discovered there was very little in life Mary did not deem worthy of a kiss from her husband.

Robert, Jack, and Ambrose obligingly followed suit with their own wives, while Katheryn sighed romantically. Hal, my youngest son, rolled his eyes. "Why did you seat them together, Mother?"

"When do I get to be knighted?" Guildford asked.

"All in good time," said John. "You are but young yet. But there are more honors to be given out that day, some of which you may find of interest. If I may have your attention—"

"Yes," muttered Hal. "Save this for the bedchamber."

My married children obediently turned flushed faces to their father. "William Paulet is to be made the Marquis of Winchester." This was the William Paulet who had informed John of Thomas Wriothesley's scheme. John had previously made him the Earl of Wiltshire. "William Herbert is to be made the Earl of Pembroke. The Marquis of Dorset is to be made the Duke of Suffolk." John coughed. "And I am to get a new title myself—the Duke of Northumberland."

I dropped my napkin. Even Mary was too stunned to kiss Henry Sidney.

"Well, it was likely to happen sooner or later, given my position," John said.

"Will you have a coronet, Father?"

"Yes, Katheryn."

"With jewels?"

"No doubt. And your mother shall have one, too."

Katheryn sighed rapturously.

"Did the king give this to you of his own, my lord, or did you demand it of him?"

We turned as one to Anne, Jack's wife, who as Somerset's daughter had come to fill the role of a skeleton at our family meals. I tried to be kind to her—it could not be easy, I knew, being Somerset's daughter at a Dudley table now that relations had turned so cool between John and her father—but there was a whole string of topics that could not be discussed around her, and even seemingly innocuous remarks could be taken the wrong way. It did not help to ease the tension around the table that Anne was not only her mother's namesake, but also her virtual double, minus some years and her mother's mature figure.

John said calmly, "I demanded nothing of the king, Anne. He is a young man with a mind entirely his own. He chose to honor me for my service to England, as well as others who have served him, and I am grateful."

"With John a duke, Jack shall be the Earl of Warwick," I added. "You shall be a countess, Anne."

"I can only hope to fill the role as well as you have, my lady," Anne said. She turned back to John. "Will my father be at the ceremony?"

"Certainly."

"No doubt that will delight him."

"Anne—"

"What? Today there is one duke in England—well, two if you count the Duke of Norfolk in the Tower—and soon there will be two more. Why wouldn't my father be delighted of the extra company?"

Amy, who had a certain talent for rescuing conversations, said, "Will we ladies be allowed to attend?"

"Yes," John said gratefully. "The king is allowing the ladies to witness the ceremony, though it will be crowded, I daresay. And there will be a banquet afterward."

"Delightful," said Anne. "I must plan what to wear."

∽

"The Duke of Northumberland," John commented when he came to my bed that night. "What would my poor father have thought?"

"He would be proud beyond measure, as I am." I looked through the opening in the bed curtains, where I could see the parrot in his covered cage. "I shall have to teach him how to say, 'Duke.'"

"'Northumberland' might be a bit much for the poor creature," John agreed. He kissed my cheek. "'Duchess' he will be able to manage, I'm sure."

"The sooner the better, for there will be a new countess in the household." I bristled. "I was furious, I must say, that Anne was so rude to you at supper. I know that it is hard, with her father—"

"Don't speak of him," John said. He took me into his arms and began fondling me in a way he had not done in some time. "Let me remind you of how an earl makes love. Then you will have a fresh basis for comparison when I become a duke."

∽

On October 11, my children and I joined the press of courtiers in the king's presence chamber at Hampton Court. John's younger brother Andrew was not present, as he was serving as captain of Guines, but Jerome was there, dressed in his finest clothes and agog at the sight of the king sitting under his canopy of state, surrounded by noblemen. Next to our family stood Frances Grey, Marchioness of Dorset, and her three daughters, the youngest so tiny at age six that a servant had been deputed to hold her upon his shoulders.

With a flourish of trumpets and a burst of color, the king's officers of arms processed into the great chamber, followed by the Garter herald, who bore the patent creating Harry Grey the Duke of Suffolk. Lord Cobham, bearing a golden verge, the Earl of Rutland, bearing a cap of estate and coronet, and the Earl of Bedford, bearing a sword, followed. Behind them walked Harry Grey himself, wearing the crimson velvet, ermine-trimmed robes of estate of a duke. He was flanked by the Duke of Somerset and the Marquis of Northampton.

Harry Grey knelt before the king. Impulsively, I squeezed Frances Grey's hand as the king vested the new Duke of Suffolk with his sword, coronet, and rod. She turned to smile at me.

Crimson robes trailing behind him, Suffolk moved to stand on the right side of the king as Frances wiped a tear from her eye and her daughters gazed at their father. Even Jane Grey, who had struck me as a girl who could not easily be moved, appeared to be impressed by the ceremony.

Then the officers of state and the attendant lords left the chamber. With another flourish of trumpets, they returned, this time with John walking between an expressionless Somerset and a smiling Northampton. John's face was solemn, as befitted the occasion, but his eyes glowed with pleasure.

Robert put his hand on my shoulder as John knelt before the king, his head bowed low. Already, tears of joy were streaming down my face, and the king hadn't even placed John's coronet on his head yet. "Happy, Mother?"

I turned my tear-stained face to Robert and smiled. "Beyond words."

⁓

Five days later, the Duke of Somerset was arrested and imprisoned once again in the Tower.

"Four dukes in England," said Jerome, who had become somewhat obsessed with the topic since his brother had been raised to his new status. "Two in the Tower. Two out."

18

Frances Grey
November 1551

W HAT ON EARTH ARE YOU DOING TO YOUR HAIR?" DEMANDED HARRY. My serving woman withdrew an iron from my hair and wound out a perfect red-gold curl. When all was done, my French hood would be covering a mass of ringlets. "For Mary of Guise, we ladies are dressing in the French style," I said mildly. "One wouldn't want her to think that Englishwomen are dowdy. Especially English duchesses."

"Haddon—"

James Haddon, Harry's chaplain, had made it his mission to improve us all, reminding us in his sermons about the vanity of dress and the evils of card playing for money. While I accepted that this was his duty, I could not help but find it annoying, especially since I had always been rather lucky at cards. Haddon had found even Jane wanting, much to her amazement. "He will just have to live with us tonight," I said, nodding at my woman as she prepared to put a touch of color on my cheeks. "Trust me, the Duchess of Northumberland will be just as splendid. Why, even Jane has consented to wear that lovely gown that the lady Mary gave her." She was also sporting a head of wanton curls, I started to add, but decided against it. Harry would find that out for himself shortly.

Mary of Guise, dowager queen of Scotland, was the mother of Mary, Queen of Scots. Having paid an extended visit to her native France, where her daughter was living, Mary of Guise had decided to visit the English court on her way back to Scotland. Jane and I were among the ladies who had been appointed to greet her, and as Mary was a member of the powerful Guise family and had been used to the luxurious courts of France, it would be unthinkable for us to meet her in anything less than the highest of style. Since the news had come that the dowager queen had arrived on England's shores, we ladies had been frantically refurbishing our wardrobes. The Duchess of Northumberland and I had sent several messages back and forth to ensure we were not wearing gowns that were too similar, and even Jane had been inclined to spend less time with her Hebrew and more time with her dancing master.

There were conspicuous absences from our ranks, however. The lady Elizabeth, who was having a bout of ill health, was not present. The lady Mary, who had been specially urged to come by the king, had also pleaded ill health. "Feigning illness," Harry had commented, and I knew he was probably right. Mary and the council had been quarreling about the Mass all year.

My poor stepmother was not there, but that was no surprise; still mourning the loss of her sons, she was living quietly at Grimsthorpe, though the last letter she had sent to me showed she was coming to terms with their deaths. By far the most glaring absence, however, was that of the Duchess of Somerset. How she would have liked to have put on her finest clothes and jewels and meet the dowager queen! But two days after the Duke of Somerset had been seized on his way to a council meeting and taken to the Tower, the duchess had been arrested, along with her half brother and a number of the duke's men. The duke and duchess were now in separate quarters at the Tower, their children—the youngest a mere babe—lodged with various relations. It was said the duke and his allies had conspired to arrest the Duke of Northumberland and shut him in the Tower, or even to murder him while he sat dining at a great banquet.

I found the rumors hard to believe, though I kept my thoughts to myself—especially around the Duchess of Northumberland. Instead, I concentrated on Mary of Guise's visit and my jewels and my clothing and my hair, and hoped that somehow everything would sort itself out without bloodshed, as it had the first time the duke was arrested.

Somehow, though, I doubted it.

"Which gloves would you like to carry, my lady?"

"My newest ones," I said. "I wouldn't want the queen to think we are savages."

∽

At dinner, the king and Mary of Guise dined under the same cloth of estate, Mary's words lost to me in her strong French accent tinged with a Scottish burr picked up during her stay in her adopted country. I sat at a table slightly below them with my old friend and first cousin Margaret Douglas, Countess of Lennox, whose mother, Margaret, was my mother's elder sister. As one of Anne Boleyn's ladies, Margaret Douglas had scandalized the court by becoming secretly engaged to Anne's handsome uncle, Lord Thomas Howard, and both she and her fiancé had been sent to the Tower by an outraged King Henry. Thomas Howard, poor man, had sickened and died there, but Margaret had been released, only to fall in love with yet another Howard. King Henry had finally found her a suitable husband, Matthew Stewart, Earl of Lennox, and she had obligingly fallen in love with him, too. Safely married, she now spent most of her time at Temple Newsam in Yorkshire. It was rumored her household was crawling with Catholics and Margaret herself could be found praying the rosary in the privacy of her own chamber, but Margaret, unlike our cousin the lady Mary, kept the matter of religion to herself. Instead, she chattered about her son, Henry, Lord Darnley, whose limning she kept in a locket around her neck, in readiness to show off at any opportunity.

"Do you miss being at court?" I asked after having duly admired the very pretty five-year-old Lord Darnley from every possible angle.

"Sometimes," Margaret admitted, lovingly closing the case containing Lord Darnley's portrait. "Yorkshire is beautiful, as is Temple Newsam, but sometimes it is too isolated for me, especially when my husband is gone." She lowered her voice. "But every time I come to London, it seems someone new is in the Tower. Will they try Somerset soon?"

"I think so."

"There are so many missteps one can make around here," Margaret said. "The Lord knows, I made enough of them in my day. And the poor duchess is imprisoned, too, isn't she?"

I nodded.

"Do you think they will execute her?"

"Surely not."

"The duke?"

"I cannot say." I dropped my voice even lower. "But I fear the worst."

"So do I, and I have always been one to expect the best," Margaret said. She sipped her wine. "No. This time when I go back to Yorkshire, I think I shall be quite pleased to be away from court."

19

Jane Dudley
November 1551 to January 1552

WHATEVER THE PEOPLE SAID LATER—AND THEY SAID PLENTY OF THINGS— the Duke of Somerset was no Anne Boleyn, brought down by mere slander. There was evidence against Somerset, and it was damning. Sir Thomas Palmer claimed Somerset had been planning to invite my husband, the Marquis of Northampton, and others to a banquet to cut off their heads. Somerset was planning to raise the apprentices of London—a potentially unruly lot—in his favor. William Crane testified that my husband and other lords were to have their heads stricken off while dining at Lord Paget's house. The Earl of Arundel, no friend to my husband, said he and Somerset and the duchess, meeting in the garden of Somerset House, had conspired to arrest John and the Marquis of Northampton, then throw them into the Tower. John Seymour, Somerset's bastard brother, had seen Arundel, clad in an inconspicuous black cloak, visiting Somerset House. Michael Stanhope, the duchess's half brother, had taken messages between Somerset and Arundel.

In the days before the trial, John conducted many of the interrogations of the witnesses himself, including that of Somerset. Each day he returned to Ely Place looking more disheartened, and a little older.

"I had no idea the man had come to hate me so much," he said one evening. Then he went to his chamber and shut himself up there until the next morning.

∽

At five in the morning on the first day of December, a barge, shrouded in fog, carried Somerset from the Tower to Westminster for his trial. Eager to catch a glimpse of their hero in his barge, two men leaned so far over the Thames that they plunged into the water and drowned.

I stayed at my brother-in-law's home at Tothill Street, hard by Westminster, waiting for news. It came in fits and spurts from John's men.

Somerset defended himself at the trial, batting back the charges against him with an ease that suggested, had life given him a different start, he could have found a career in the law. He had raised men, certainly, but only for his own protection for these uncertain times. He had never planned to raise the North, where his influence was but small. He scoffed at Palmer's story of the banquet, saying his tale was more suited for Boccaccio than to the pleasant land of England. He demanded that Crane, whose confession was read at the trial, be produced to testify in person. But when questioned about whether he had planned to kill John and the rest, he said quietly, "I did speak of it, and think of it, but changed my mind."

Hearing the account of his testimony from the messenger, I shivered in the warm chamber in which I sat.

The afternoon dragged on as the lords deliberated Somerset's fate. Now and then, the cry would go up, "God save the Duke of Somerset!" Then I heard the pealing of bells, followed by shouts louder than any heard yet.

I flung open a window. "What news is there?" I shouted like a fishwife to the crowds passing below.

A man turned up an exultant face to me. "The good Duke of Somerset has been acquitted. He will go free!"

"Northumberland will hang within a week, I reckon," added his companion. "We'll see who's the traitor now!"

I slammed the window shut and collapsed to the window seat, shaking.

Feet ran up the stairs. "It's true?" I said to the messenger. "Somerset was acquitted?"

"Yes, Your Grace—but only of the treason charge. He was convicted of felony. What those dolts don't realize is that he can still hang for that. If I were you, Your Grace, I'd get home before they figure that out."

"The people love Somerset that much?"

"I'm afraid they do, Your Grace."

⸰⸱⸰

Toward Christmas, John flung into my chamber and placed a coin in my hand. "What does this look like to you?"

I studied the coin. It bore the three royal lions, but they looked misshapen. "They look odd. What happened?"

"The die broke. Tell me. Do these lions look like the bear and ragged staff of Warwick?"

"No."

"Tell that to the people. That is the latest lie they are telling, that I have produced coins at Dudley Castle bearing my own insignia. It is a sign of how I am aspiring to the crown."

"John, no."

"I am gathering together vast amounts of money—like my father did—and I am listening to prophecies saying the king will not live long. Nay, I am commissioning them! There is no end to my evil and perfidy now that Somerset has been convicted of felony. I just wonder how I find enough time during the day to accomplish all of it."

He tossed the coin on the floor, where it fell with a clang. "They are saying now that I have planned to try him for treason since he was first put into the Tower back in '49, that I have been poisoning the mind of the king against him. Are they fool enough to think that I would have married his daughter to my eldest son, if I meant ill to him? As for poisoning the king against him, it was not I who dragged the king to Windsor Castle without warning and terrified him with tales of the wicked King Richard. It was not I who never bothered to ask the king for his opinion on a matter. It was not I—"

"John! Calm yourself, my dear. No person of intelligence could possibly believe you meant harm to Somerset. We all know you tried your best to work with him."

John sighed. For a few moments, the only sound in the room was the clock, its case etched with representations of the planets, which ticked on the mantle. I loved clocks, and John had faithfully bought them for me ever since we had first become wealthy enough to afford them. "One thing you can say about my wife," he had joked, "she always knows what o'clock it is."

He retrieved the coin and turned it in his palm several times. Then he said, "I've been talking with Somerset in the Tower."

"What about?"

"At first, I just wanted to know if there was any unfinished business—any men lying in wait to murder me. He said there weren't, other than the man Berteville we already had."

I shuddered. Berteville, a French mercenary, had confessed to being approached by Somerset and his men, but had never reached the point of carrying out his scheme. For giving evidence against Somerset before his trial, he had been freed.

"Since then, we've just been talking. Mostly about our old days fighting together, and about the situation now with Scotland and France. He did apologize for plotting against me. He swore he would have never given the order to kill me if it came down to that. Sometimes we just play a game of cards together. He worries about his wife a great deal. I've promised that she shall come to no harm, although there's probably evidence enough to convict her of felony, too." John stared at the clock. "He's never asked me to intercede with the king for a pardon or asked that his life be spared. He expects death."

"Would you intercede with the king if he asked?"

"Yes."

Then why, I almost asked, did my husband not tell that to Somerset? But the question died on my lips. John had pardoned Somerset once, and he had abused his kindness. Why should John risk pardoning him yet again? Instead, I said, "Then I hope he does not ask. Do not think me hard. It breaks my heart to think of Anne and the other children he will leave behind. Even to think of the widow he will leave behind. But I would not have you risk your life again to assuage your conscience. In fact, I pray you do not urge the king to pardon him. You cannot trust him, and even if you could, what if his friends decided to carry out what they thought were his wishes? Don't tempt fate once again. I love you too much for that, John."

John turned his face to mine and kissed me gently. "Even if all of England hates me?"

"Especially if all of England hates you."

Somerset's fate was not the only thing that preoccupied the court that season. The king, remembering the pleasure his father had taken in masques and disguisings, had decided to revive the old custom of having a Lord of Misrule preside over the Christmas revelries. John, eager to please the king in all things, especially with Somerset in the Tower, had duly appointed George Ferrers, a courtier of literary tastes, to that position. For the past couple of weeks, the elaborate preparations had engulfed the entire council, and the king had taken the greatest interest in their progress, even reviewing the various scripts and altering them to his satisfaction.

On Christmas Day, the court gathered at Greenwich, where we heard the king's chapel. The music, composed by Thomas Tallis, put us all in a reflective mood, but not a downcast one, and even John seemed in good spirits. As we proceeded into the hall to enjoy the evening's entertainments, he squeezed my hand in a way I knew meant we would have a happy night together in my bedchamber.

"Today is the day Misrule will make his appearance," the king said with an eagerness that made him appear suddenly younger than his fourteen years. "Yesterday, he sent an embassy to us to announce his coming. It should be splendid!"

"I have every hope that it will be, Your Majesty," said John. "Sir George has been laboring mightily."

"We don't know how Misrule will appear," the king confessed. "We asked purposely not to be told of any of his plans for his entrance."

Will Somers, the king's fool—still spry despite his advanced years—juggled and jested, then let out a fart of such resonance that the king jumped in his seat before breaking into enthusiastic applause. This was followed by a procession of men and boys dressed up as the Pope, bishops, and priests—I recognized my younger sons, Guildford and Hal, among them—who paraded through the hall, bearing a tabernacle in a shape that made the men in the hall roar with laughter and the ladies blush. The French ambassador passed a hand over his eyes, and the Venetian ambassador shook his head grimly and muttered something in a tone that made me grateful I did not understand Italian.

The Pope bowed to the king and the court. "The body of the Lord," he announced and opened the tabernacle with a flourish to reveal a monstrance, shaped similarly to the tabernacle, containing a bright red Host. The Duke of Suffolk roared with laughter, and even his bookish daughter, the lady Jane, let out a squeal of delight. Only the Duchess of Suffolk appeared not to be amused. She was, I remembered, on the friendliest of terms with the lady Mary, who fortunately had stayed away from court.

Another bishop stepped up and gave an exaggerated sniff. "Your Holiness," he announced. "The Lord's body stinks."

The priests and bishops gasped and held their noses. The king clapped.

"What can we do, Your Grace?" wailed Guildford in his acting debut. (I could not help but give motherly applause here.)

The Pope pondered while the other players strutted around him, similarly in deep thought. Then two courtiers, dripping with jewels and wearing doublets with sleeves that hung so low they almost tripped them up, minced into the room. "When my lady love tells me I stink—"

The younger of the two courtiers asked, "Your lady love tells you that you stink?"

The players murmured behind their hands, then went up to sniff the older courtier. "He stinks," they announced.

"My lady love never tells me that I stink," said the younger courtier. He held up a perfume decanter. "Generous applications of this elixir keep me smelling sweet, so much so that the ladies cannot stay away from me. In fact—"

Three boys, dressed as young ladies, rushed into the room and to the side of the younger courtier. One dropped at the courtier's feet and gazed up at him worshipfully, while the other two each draped herself over the courtier's shoulders and glared at her rival.

The Pope stared thoughtfully at the perfume bottle, then at the monstrance. After an interval of staring back and forth, he raised his finger in triumph. "I have found a solution!" he proclaimed. "May I, good sir?"

The young courtier, occupied with his three women, nodded in boredom and allowed the Pope to take the perfume. Accompanied by chanting in Latin, the Pope bore the perfume to the monstrance, then took the wafer from the monstrance and solemnly dipped it in the perfume. To the sound of trumpets, he held the wafer aloft and sniffed it. "Perfection!" he pronounced.

The bishops and priests turned from the audience, dropped on their knees, and began worshipping the wafer drenched with perfume. Then the young ladies abandoned the courtier, giving him a parting kick of contempt. Pushing their way into the ring of bishops and priests, they arranged themselves into a trio by the monstrance in the same adoring pose in which they had surrounded the courtier. "The body of the Lord! And what a body!"

The king clapped wildly, and the rest of us followed suit.

Bowing, the company left the room, to be replaced by Diana, the moon goddess—this time, represented not by a boy, but by a shapely, beautiful woman in a sheer gown. She bowed to the king, who ogled at her and her two female attendants.

Diana took her attendants by the hand, and the three executed a graceful dance. Then a curtain was pulled up, revealing a huge crescent moon on wheels.

The goddess swept her hand toward the moon. As a fanfare played, a door concealed in the moon opened, and a platform swung out. On the platform stood George Ferrers, wearing a crown and robes of purple and carrying a scepter. "Your Majesty—my lords—my ladies. The season of misrule has begun!"

⟡

The Lord of Misrule kept the court busy beyond belief over the twelve days of Christmas. There were interludes, masques, jousts, banquets with so many dishes I lost count. Each night I fell into my bed at Greenwich, exhausted from all of the merriment. But the prisoner in the Tower could not be forgotten, especially when a scaffold was erected by the Eleanor Cross at Cheapside. There, a group of young knights were tried and convicted for not having obeyed Misrule the day before, but the sentence of execution was carried out on a hogshead of wine and a bag of coins instead, and the contents of each distributed among the crowd. I could not help but feel pity for Somerset, kept closely in his prison this time (no Christmas visits from the duchess), as the headsman swung his axe against the barrel.

Even when Twelfth Night passed, the festivities did not end, for on January 17, twelve gentlemen, including my three eldest sons and Henry Sidney, tilted at Greenwich. Snug in furs, I watched as Jack, Ambrose, and Robert rode out, feeling altogether too much maternal pride as the January sunlight glistened upon their armor.

Near me were Robert's wife, Amy, and Ambrose's wife, Nan. Seated next to me, or rather on my right with the width of a good-sized human being between us, was Jack's wife, Anne, Countess of Warwick. Feeling for the poor girl, whose parents, the Duke and Duchess of Somerset, were both in the Tower, Jack had made much of her over the past couple of months, giving her fine clothes and many pretty presents, and I had tried to fill the role of a mother to her. But our efforts were to no avail, and indeed, how could they be, under the circumstances? I wished the girl was not so slender; before her wedding, her father had asked that the consummation of her marriage be delayed until she was sixteen because of her physique, and we had honored his wish. If she had borne Jack a child, or was expecting one, she might have been, if not happy with us, at least less unhappy.

The countess stared blankly at the knights, neither appreciating nor troubling to admire Jack's skill as he ran against his opponent. (Jack took after his father, who had been a fine jouster in his younger years.) I touched her shoulder and attempted to draw her closer to me. "I see Jack is wearing your favor."

"He took it from me. I did not give it to him."

"Oh."

"My head aches. I would like to return to my chamber."

"Of course, my dear."

"I am not your dear."

"It is only a manner of speaking, Anne. I meant no harm. Shall I send our physician to you?"

Anne rose and shook out her skirts. "No, I need no physic for my headaches. I often get them, and the only thing that helps them is to lie down in

darkness and quiet, as Mama could tell you if she were not in the Tower."
She looked over her shoulder as her page began to help her away. "Besides, I
would not trust any physic which came from a Dudley."

I sat there open mouthed. No one else had heard the insult, spoken in a
low tone; Amy and Nan were discussing Amy's new gloves, while Guildford
and Hal, both slightly too young and inexperienced to joust publicly, were
consoling themselves by criticizing Jack's every move. Mary's mind was back
somewhere in the court of King Arthur, where it would reside until her own
husband took his turn in the lists, and Katheryn, her father's darling, was
leaning on his shoulder contentedly as he explained to her the various strate-
gies Jack was taking. For a moment, I thought of following the girl and giving her a well-needed shaking: how dare she speak of me and my family so
disrespectfully—and slanderously—even in her present difficulties? It was not
something that should be borne.

Yet I did bear it, knowing what distress hearing of the remark would cause
John, who with Katheryn at his side looked at peace, as he had not been for
weeks. Instead of confronting my daughter-in-law, I sat still on my bench and
prayed to myself that whatever Fate had in store for Somerset, it would be
determined soon, so Somerset's shadow would no longer hang over our every
family gathering.

Four days later, I got my wish: King Edward signed Somerset's death warrant.

For anyone who had been a member of King Henry's court, it had been almost
impossible to avoid attending executions. Indeed, some courtiers had become
virtual connoisseurs of death, critically eying each performance upon the scaffold as if the condemned were a new player come to court. Had the doomed
person dressed perfectly, as had Anne Boleyn? Had he managed a witty quip,
as had Sir Thomas More? How large a crowd had he attracted? Did he falter in
his last speech, or deliver it clearly and well? Had the executioner been given
a generous sum of money by the deceased?

I was not one of those who delighted in such ordeals. True, I had attended
the executions of Katherine Howard and her accomplice in adultery, Jane
Boleyn, but that was out of pity for a queen I had once served and had found
it impossible to dislike, exasperating as her royal whims and as foolish as her
actions had been. My one concern had been to keep from fainting or vomit-
ing. I had managed to avoid both, though only because I averted my eyes at
the proper time. Never again, I had vowed, would I attend another execution.

Yet on the morning of January 22, the day set for Somerset's execution, I rode to Tower Hill to watch the duke die.

I was not supposed to be there. John, who had moved to Westminster with the king the day before, had not forbidden it, but he had not anticipated I would make such a trip, either. Why I felt impelled to witness this I did not know; I had never been close to Somerset, even at the height of my husband's friendship with him, and I certainly had no warm feelings toward him after he had plotted to destroy my husband. But his wife and I had once been friends of a sort, and his fourteen-year-old daughter was my son's bride.

Somerset's execution had been scheduled for eight in the morning, slightly earlier than was the custom, and the council had ordered the London constable to tell the populace to stay in their homes until ten in the morning. Despite this, as I rode from Ely Place to Tower Hill, the streets were full of people, all of them headed in the same direction as I.

Knowing it would be unwise to make my identity known, I was accompanied by only one manservant, and I had worn a plain gown. Were it not that some of the officials recognized me and gave way to allow me to ride near to the scaffold, I might have been unable to see anything but a figure in the distance. Instead, I was close enough to see the duke's face as he was led out to Tower Hill. It was slightly before eight; Somerset was punctual to the last.

His hair and beard had been trimmed carefully, and he was elegantly and richly clothed; I'd not seen him dressed so finely since his daughter Anne married my son. Having climbed the scaffold, he knelt and prayed, raising his hands upward as naturally as if he were in his own chapel. As he made his devotions, the people stood still and silent, their faces solemn or streaked with tears. No one was jostling for a better view; instead, men stood with their arms around their wives, mothers with their hands on their children's shoulders, supporting each other through this ordeal. Even the cutpurse I spotted nearby abandoned his prey to concentrate on the duke.

Somerset rose and walked to the east side of the scaffold. For a moment, he and the crowd gazed at each other adoringly. Then Somerset sighed sharply and began his speech, the same sort of speech that had been heard on Tower Hill too many times. "Dearly beloved friends, I am brought hither to suffer death, albeit that I never offended against the king, neither by word nor deed, and have been always as faithful and true unto this realm, as any man hath been."

"Hear, hear!"

"But I am condemned by a law whereunto I am subject, as are we all, and therefore to show obedience I am content to die, wherewith I am well content, being a thing most heartily welcome unto me, for which I do thank God, taking it for a singular benefit, and as great a benefit as ever might come to me any otherwise. For as I am a man, I have deserved at God's hand many deaths, and it has pleased his goodness, whereas he might have taken me suddenly that I should neither have known him nor myself, thus now to visit me and call me with this present death, when I have had time to remember and acknowledge him, and to know also myself, for which thing I do thank him most heartily."

Somerset had begun to urge the people to stay steadfast to the king's religious reforms and was warming to his theme, when there was a sudden noise, like a clap of thunder or an explosion of gunpowder. People who had been listening to the duke in utter silence screamed in terror. Some fled to nearby houses; others flung themselves into ditches. It was all my man could do to keep my own horse from bolting. Then Anthony Browne—the man who had helped me to my favored place near the scaffold—galloped up to keep order among the crowd.

"A pardon!" a bystander shouted. "The king has issued a pardon!"

"God save the king! He has issued a pardon!" The crowd, on the verge of riot a moment before, screamed with joy as men threw their caps in the air.

"There is no such thing," said a quiet voice from the scaffold. Somerset raised his hand, and the crowd froze. "There is no pardon," he repeated. "I pray you all to be quiet and to be contented with my death, which I am most willing to suffer. Let us now join in prayer unto the Lord, for the preservation of the King's Majesty, unto whom hitherto I have always shown myself a most faithful and true subject. I have always been diligent about His Majesty in his affairs both at home and abroad, and no less diligent in seeking the common commodity of the whole realm."

"It is true," muttered the crowd.

"I wish His Majesty continual health, with all felicity and all prosperous success."

"Amen," murmured the people.

"I do wish unto all his counselors the grace and favor of God, whereby they may rule in all things uprightly with justice. Unto whom I exhort you all in the Lord, to show yourselves obedient, as is your duty under the pain of condemnation, and also most profitable for the preservation and safeguard of the King's Majesty," Somerset continued. He gave a faint smile. "Forasmuch as I have had oftentimes affrayed with divers men, and have found it hard to please every man, therefore if there have been any offended or injured by me, I

most humbly require and ask him forgiveness. Especially almighty God, whom
through all my life I have most grievously offended. And whoever has offended
me, I do with my whole heart forgive them."

"He speaks of Northumberland," a man called. "The wicked Duke of
Northumberland, who has put him wrongfully to death!"

Somerset raised his hand again. "I once again require you, dearly beloved
in the Lord, that you will keep yourselves quiet and still, lest through your
tumult, you might trouble me. For albeit the spirit be willing and ready, the
flesh is frail and wavering, and through your quietness I shall be much quieter."

The crowd obeyed instantly, and Somerset said, "I desire you to help me
with my prayers," then knelt and prayed. Rising afterward to shake hands
with everyone on the scaffold, including the sheriff and the Lieutenant of the
Tower, he presented the executioner with a bag of coins and stripped to his
doublet and shirt.

With the rest, I watched in awe as Somerset slowly untied his shirt strings
and allowed the executioner to turn down his collar, then covered his face
with his handkerchief. He laid himself flat on the ground, only to have to rise
again and remove his doublet, which was obstructing his neck, at the command of the executioner. "Lord Jesus save me," he said, lying down once
again. "Lord Jesus save me. Lord Je—"

Even before the executioner raised Somerset's head, the crowd surged
toward the scaffold, terrifying my horse. As I struggled to bring her under
control, and to fight down the nausea that was engulfing me, I realized what
they were doing: dipping their handkerchiefs in the duke's lifeblood, which
was seeping through the boards of the scaffold. The bloodstained handkerchiefs
would become relics, like the bones and fingernails of the saints the faithful
used to treasure.

"My lady? Shall I take you home now?"

I shook my head. My cheeks, I realized, were damp with tears. "No. Take
me to the Tower. I wish to see the duke's widow."

In those days, John's power was such that I could go almost anywhere in
England I chose, except perhaps to the king's private apartments. No one
challenged me, therefore, as I passed through the Tower gates, having finally
managed to make my way through the crowd that was still trying to catch
the very last droplets of Somerset's blood as Somerset's body and head were
bundled into a cart and taken to the Tower chapel for burial. But the guards

outside of the Duchess of Somerset's lodgings did shake their heads warningly as they ushered me inside. "My lady, she may be trouble."

"I will take my chances."

Surrounded by her ladies, Anne Seymour was slumped on a chair, her luxurious brown hair wild around her face. She was not even dressed properly, but was in her nightclothes. "Get out," she hissed.

"I came to see if you needed anything," I said, realizing as I spoke how stupid a remark that was. What could I do for her? Resurrect her husband? "I mean, to see if you needed any physic, or some spiritual comfort."

Anne shook her head vaguely and gathered her robe around her more closely. She seemed to have forgotten she'd ordered me out. "I saw them bring him back just now," she announced.

I looked to her ladies for confirmation. "Aye, Your Grace, she did. She wouldn't let us keep her from the window."

"There was so much blood," Anne said, staring at the wall. "He must have left most of it on the scaffold, but there was plenty in the cart." She gave a macabre laugh. "Who knew that a man could hold that much blood? Not me. Now I do. They didn't even bother to wrap his body in a sheet. Just the head."

"How in the world could you let her see that?" I whispered.

"We would have had to hold her by force to stop her. She was wild."

"They let me visit him last night," Anne continued. "We read to each other for a while and we held each other tight and kissed, just like it was when he first started courting me. He married me for love, you know. Other men didn't want me. They said I was too outspoken and that my father couldn't give me a large enough portion to make up for that, and then when I turned twenty, they said I was too old." Tears were spilling down her cheeks. "But he never thought any of those things. He thought I was perfect. In all the years we were married, he never raised his hand against me, or even raised his voice to me. He loved me."

"I know he did," I said gently. Anne's shoulders were shaking, and I put an arm around her.

"I loved him, too. I knew he would advance, but that's not why I married him! I could have been happy to stay plain Lady Seymour. I would be happy to be that now, if that would bring him back to me." She touched the pillow beside her. On it laid a little book. "He must have given me something to make me sleepy, because I fell asleep in his arms when I was in his chamber, and when I awoke, I had been carried back here. He told his guards that he couldn't bear to say good-bye to me and asked them to tell me not to be angry with him for not waking me." Anne shook her head. "As if I was ever angry at him in his life. With plenty of other people! But never with my dear Edward. And he did leave something for the children and me to remember him by. The constable sent it to me this morning."

She picked up the little book—a nondescript almanac. Written in Somerset's careful handwriting was:

> *Fear of the Lord is the beginning of wisdom*
> *Put thy trust in the Lord with all thy heart*
> *Be not wise in thine own conceit, but fear the Lord and flee from evil*
> *From the Tower, the day before my death*
>
> E. Somerset

On the verge of tears again, I cleared my throat. "Anne, I will do my best to see that you are freed soon. Or at least sent to live with one of your sisters-in-law, or your mother, where you will have people who can ease your grief and offer you comfort. I shall talk to my hus—"

"Your husband!" Anne pushed my arm away and stood. "How dare you mention that devil to me? He was the one who brought my dear husband to this, with all of his plots."

"He did not! Your husband was plotting against mine, and you know it."

"Only after your husband poisoned the king's mind against my husband. My Edward loved the king. He was the apple of his eye. He used that very phrase! But first Thomas Seymour sought to tear them apart, and then your beast of a husband did. They ruined everything." Anne balled her hands into fists. "He sent you here, didn't he, you vixen? To taunt me, or was it to spy upon me? Did the two of you hope I would betray some secret? Well, I'll give you your money's worth. I want your husband dead for what he did to mine, and I'll have you dead, too, if they let me out of here. Is that enough for you?"

I backed into a corner. "You don't mean what you're saying, Anne. You have undergone a great shock. I know in a day or so you will think better of it."

"Don't mean it? By God, I'll strangle you here, you bitch!"

She grabbed me by the throat, evading her ladies' efforts to stop her, and shook me while I screamed for the guards and tried to shake her off me. Finally they prized her away. She stared at me in pure hatred as they dragged her back. "I curse you," she said. "I curse the entire house of the Dudleys. May you suffer what I have suffered today!"

"You had best go, my lady. She's wild."

I needed no persuasion. I picked up my skirts and stumbled down the staircase, Anne's curses and screams ringing in my ears.

∽

"She threatened you?" John stared at me.

I'd not wanted to tell John about my encounter with the duchess, but my manner when I returned to Ely Place had been too agitated to escape the notice of my household, someone in which had sent for John. I had been too shaken to formulate a lie when John arrived in my chamber, where I had been put to bed with a warm brick next to my feet. "She is half-mad with grief over her husband, John."

"And what's this?" John's hands found the marks of Anne's fingers on my neck. "Christ! Did she attack you?"

"She did not know what she was doing."

"By God, the bitch should hang for this!"

"No!" I sprang out of bed and sank to my knees. "Please don't harm her," I begged, looking up at John. "There has been so much death. Please! Promise me." My voice reached a higher pitch. "Promise." I turned my head and started sobbing.

John lifted me up and helped me back into bed. "I will not harm her. I promise."

"Oh, thank you, John."

"But I'll be damned if I ever let her see the outside of the Tower. She can rot there."

I made no argument.

John sat in bed next to me, stroking my hair as I calmed down. "Jane, you should not have gone to the execution. It could have been dangerous for you."

"I know. I am sorry."

"He died bravely, I suppose?"

"Yes. Very bravely."

"One day I will ask you for the details. Not today."

I nodded as John went on talking. "There were good reasons not to go. One was that I might appear to be gloating. The other one was that the crowd might riot if they saw me. But the real reason is that I am a coward. I could not bear to see him die. He was the first true friend I had as a young man."

I took John's hand. "England will be more at peace for this, John. We will move past this. We have to." I hesitated. "Did you see the king today?"

"Yes. I asked for his forgiveness. He frowned and said, 'What else could you do, my lord?'" John rose and kissed me on the cheek. "I must go back to Westminster. There's business to do before Parliament opens tomorrow. You sleep, and stay out of trouble." He headed toward the chamber door, then turned with a slight smile. "Did you know where they buried Somerset?"

"In the Chapel of St. Peter ad Vincula, of course."

"Yes, but do you know who he lies between?" I shook my head. "Anne Boleyn and Katherine Howard. If those aren't an odd threesome, I don't know what is."

20

Frances Grey
January 1552 to February 1552

WITH THE COURT FESTIVITIES OF CHRISTMAS OVER, THE GIRLS AND I returned to Bradgate. I was glad to be there, for despite all of the determined gaiety, London was a gloomy place that January, the impending fate of the Duke of Somerset casting a pall over everything.

Even in the comfort of my home at Bradgate—my husband's inheritance, but a house I had come to love as my own—I was despondent after the duke's death, not so much for the duke but for the sake of his eldest son, Edward, Earl of Hertford. I had met him at court a time or two and had found him to be a charming yet serious-minded young man, who might be particularly suitable for Jane as a husband. Indeed, after the Thomas Seymour debacle, Harry, anxious to make amends with Somerset, had suggested Jane might marry Hertford, but the negotiations had been desultory at best and had died out altogether when Harry aligned himself with Northumberland. Now the Earl of Hertford, son of a traitor, was worth little as a husband, unless the council chose to restore him to his father's forfeited estates. But I was sorry not only for the loss of the young man as a potential match for Jane, but also for his own bereavement.

Jane did not give any indication of what she thought about the loss of her potential suitor, and I did not ask her. Since I had overheard the conversation she had had with Ascham the previous summer, my manner to her had been more distant and cool. I no longer lost my temper with her, but I no longer asked the sort of questions about her studies that had always made her roll her eyes at me. My manner at times toward her had been so astringent, I had seen her blink in puzzlement, which I am ashamed to admit gave me a certain petty satisfaction. When Aylmer, distressed at the pleasure Jane had taken in decking herself out in fine robes and curling her hair for the visit of Mary of Guise, asked that his mentor in Zurich, Heinrich Bullinger, address a few words to Jane about the manner of dress suitable for a young lady professing godliness, I did not even protest that Jane hardly needed such instruction. Even when the lady Elizabeth was named—much to Jane's annoyance—as an example to be followed, I kept my counsel. "Master Aylmer knows best about these things, and you must follow his advice," I said sweetly.

"But he is telling me I spend too much time with my music, and you have always encouraged me to spend more time on it!"

I had, not only because I loved music, but also because it was something I could understand. "He knows best," I repeated. "Not me."

∞

In early February, John Aylmer hurried into my chamber. It was about the time of the week that he usually reported on my daughters' studies, and in which I tried to formulate intelligent questions, so I at first thought nothing of it when he was announced. Then I saw his face. "My lady, the lady Jane is acting very strange. I have never seen her thus."

I asked no questions, but followed him to the chamber where Jane had her lessons. She was in her usual place, surrounded by books, pen, and parchment, but she was slumped over her desk listlessly. "I don't want to study," she said, lifting her head at my approach. "I'm tired."

Her sulky voice was slurred. For a moment, I thought she might have smuggled some of our wine to her room and drunk it undiluted, as my sister Eleanor and I had once done in our youth on a mutual dare. But no. There was no smell of wine, and John Aylmer had been at university; he would know the effects of drink when he saw them. I looked at Jane more closely. She was perspiring, though the February day was a particularly bitter one. Suddenly fear clawed at my heart. "Don't you feel well?"

"I told you, I'm tired." Jane suddenly pulled off her French hood, revealing her fine auburn hair. She rose, unsteady on her feet. "I'm going to bed."

"No, you are not."

John Aylmer stared at me. "My lady!"

"She cannot go to bed. She has the sweat. If she sleeps within the next few hours, she will die like my brothers did." I grabbed Jane, who had actually started to unfasten her gown, totally indifferent to the presence of a man in the room. "Stop that! You shall not go to bed. You must study. I insist."

"But Mother…"

"Go inform the household that my daughter has the sweat," I told Aylmer.

"See if my other daughters are ill. If they are not, make sure they go nowhere near Jane and me, and make sure that their ladies watch them closely for any signs of the illness. And have a physician sent for," I added. But physicians were next to useless against the sweat, I knew. "Then come back and help me keep my daughter awake." I shook Jane, whose eyes were shutting. "Read to me."

"I want to sleep."

"Read to me. I care not what you read. Just read it." I glared down at my daughter, grateful for my advantage in height. "Read, or I will take a switch to you."

Jane picked up a book—I recognized it as Plato—and stumbled her way through its pages, half reading, half crying with frustration. When Aylmer came back, she looked to him for rescue but got none. When her voice grew hoarse, he hauled her to her feet and walked her in circles around the room, then sat her down after a while of this and ordered her to write out a translation of what she was reading. All this time, she was sweating and having the utmost difficulty catching her breath.

For a couple of hours, we kept up this parody of a normal day's study, until the physician arrived to confirm what I had guessed for myself. He allowed Jane to take to her bed, but bade me to continue to keep her awake and to make her sweat even more. Obediently, I swaddled Jane as tightly as a newborn babe in layers of blankets, ordered that the servants who had bravely ventured into the sickroom stoke the fire, and poked and prodded Jane every time she showed an inclination to shut her eyes.

Late in the evening, Jane begged to use the chamber pot. The physician nodded in satisfaction as she did so. "Copious urination. A good sign."

Settling back in bed, Jane glared at him as he studied her prodigious output. "I wish you would go away."

"Disrespect to one's elders," the physician said. "An even better sign."

Jane turned her glare on me as I tried to wrap her blankets around her again. "Would you stop that, Mother?"

I nervously touched Jane's forehead. It was cool. The physician followed suit and gave another nod of approval. "I believe the crisis is over, my lady. If the lady Jane continues as she is for another hour or so, she may sleep."

⁓

When the physician at last consented for Jane to sleep, I watched her nervously, expecting every breath to be her last. But she grew visibly better as she slumbered through the night, and when the sun rose, she looked almost her usual self, except that after waking she was content to loll back against her pillows and doze some more. Her condition was so promising, I, too, could sleep for the first time in four-and-twenty hours, leaving Jane under the eye of our servants. When I returned to her side, Jane was sitting up against her pillows, sipping ale and staring at what she had written when her tutor and I had kept her awake. "I wrote this? It's barely coherent, complete nonsense."

"I will have to take your word for it, because it all looks like nonsense to me."

"Little Mary could have done better."

"You were very ill."

Jane looked up at me with eyes that were mercifully clear and bright again, if weary. Then she lowered her gaze. "The physician told me that you kept me awake," she said to her paper.

"They say it is dangerous to sleep when one has the sweat."

"He said that you probably saved my life."

"The Lord saved your life. I did only what he enabled me to remember was necessary."

Jane raised her eyes back to me and gave me a rare smile. "Thank you, Mother."

"There is no need to thank me for doing what I desired most as your mother."

Jane said nothing, and I did not want to break this happy moment by speaking further, and possibly saying the wrong thing. My daughter had lived, and lived to smile at me. That was enough.

21

Jane Dudley
April 1552 to May 1552

IN EARLY APRIL, THE KING GAVE ALL OF ENGLAND A TERRIBLE FRIGHT: HE FELL ill of the measles and the smallpox. Some cruel people said it was God's wrath, punishing him for allowing the death of Somerset; others openly won-. dered whether the lady Mary would soon become queen. But the king soon shook off the illness. By St. George's Day, there was almost no sign he had been ill, except for a few stray pocks on his face.

With the king well mended, John and I traveled to Otford Palace in Kent, to spend a few days relaxing in the country before John went to the North on the king's business. With us were our children and their spouses. Even those who served the king, like my older sons and Henry Sidney, had obtained a few days' leave. There was more than enough room for us. Otford had once been the palace of the Archbishops of Canterbury, one of whom, William Wareham, had built a palace there to rival Cardinal Wolsey's Hampton Court. So successful had he been that some years later, King Henry had taken a fancy to Otford, and the current archbishop, Thomas Cranmer, had obligingly, and sensibly, given him the palace. Recently, King Edward had given it to John. I could not walk around the vast expanse of Otford without thinking of my childhood home of Halden, also in Kent but a world away from the grandeur here.

"Is it true that you're to marry the Earl of Cumberland's daughter?" Robert asked Guildford one evening as we had settled in what once had been the archbishop's private quarters.

"Father wants me to," Guildford said gloomily.

"Most men wouldn't complain about marrying an earl's only child," John said dryly. "Particularly men who are fourth sons."

"But the girl's never been out of Yorkshire!" Guildford said. "I hear that her father's practically a recluse there."

"There's a romantic story about that," said Mary. "Do you want to hear it?"

"Oh, please!" said Katheryn.

"His father built a tower and a gallery just to welcome his wife, the lady Eleanor," Mary said. "She was the younger sister of the lady Frances, you know. The earl fell passionately in love with her."

"'Passionately!'" mimicked Hal. He gave a mock bow when Mary glared at him. "Go on, Sister."

"He fell *passionately* in love with her," continued Mary. "But then she fell ill and died. The earl was heartbroken. He would not eat or take drink, and finally he fell so ill that he was given up for dead. He was actually laid out for burial, when his men saw signs of life in him and managed to revive him. But he was so weak after that, he could drink only milk from a woman's breast."

"Ugh," said Hal.

"I hope he paid the lady well," said Robert. He nudged Ambrose. "What sort of annuity do you think that would rate?"

"Depends on how handsome the earl is," Ambrose said.

Mary raised her voice. "After a few weeks of that, he recovered, but he has never ceased to grieve for the lady Eleanor, whom they say was as fair as her mother, the French queen. His daughter is very dear to him, as her only child, and they say he is reluctant to see her married."

"Thank God for that," said Guildford. "Perhaps I won't satisfy his tastes."

"He has an excellent library," Mary offered consolingly.

"If he does consent, I'll most likely have to live at Skipton Castle with them, among the sheep," Guildford said. "And the girl probably speaks with a northern accent."

"And kills and skins her own supper each night," said Robert.

"And has a tail," added Hal.

"Look on the bright side," Jack advised. "If all she's seen are the northern men, you'll probably look to her like King David."

"The negotiations are not far along at all," said John, who had been enjoying this banter thoroughly. "There will be plenty of time to civilize the young lady before your wedding, should her father and I reach an agreement."

"Just don't drink the milk at Skipton Castle," Hal advised. "God only knows where it comes from."

I decided it was time to take this conversation to a higher level. "Perhaps we might have some music," I suggested. I looked at Ambrose's wife, who played the lute beautifully. "Maybe you can play for us?"

Nan, who was always glad to perform, obliged, and soon all of my daughters and daughters-in-law were singing, even the Countess of Warwick. Her scratchy little voice was not exactly melodious, but thanks largely to the kindnesses of the other ladies in my family and Jack, she had become a little more amiable lately, so I listened and forced myself not to wince when she hit a high note. Besides, I had a surprise planned. When the singing was done, I held out a book to Anne. "I obtained this the other day, Anne. I thought you might want to read it to us, as we have not heard it."

Anne stared at the book. It was of her own authorship, a collection of verses she and two of her younger sisters had written to commemorate the death of the learned Marguerite of Navarre. It had been published in Paris two years before. "How did you get a copy of this?"

"Jack gave it to me. Will you read it? The French verses," I added hastily. "I do not know Latin, and I would like to understand what is being read."

Anne hesitated, but the vanity of authorship proved uppermost, as I had hoped, and she stood to read us her and her sisters' production. I wondered at the beginning, when her voice faltered when reading of Marguerite's death, whether I might have been opening a wound, but she quickly regained her composure and read with a feeling that touched me.

> Begin to bear in your hand the honor of the victorious palm branch, both
> because you won and because you were strong.
> By this time you are standing before the stronghold of the throne; now
> you are adoring the Might of God; you shout greetings to the One
> Alone who sits in the stronghold.
> You are holding in your hand true offerings, a casket of real incense and
> simple prayers not without understanding.
> Now a Divine One joined to the celestial choir, you will not fear thirst or
> hunger, cold or heat.

"That was beautiful," said Mary before I could speak. "I wish I could do as well as you and your sisters, Anne, and I am older than you."

Anne blushed and looked pleased. That night, for the first time since her marriage to our son, she let me give her a good-night kiss on her cheek as we made our way to our various bedchambers.

☙

I fell asleep that night in the arms of my husband. Late, late that night, a scream awakened me from a pleasant dream. "What is it?" I said, blinking as John and I untangled ourselves to sit up and stare around. Then the first thought of a loyal courtier came to mind. "The king? Is the king ill?"

My door slammed open without a knock. "My lady—my lord—forgive me. The lord Ambrose's lady is dreadfully ill."

Throwing on just enough clothing to hide our nakedness, we rushed to Nan's chamber, where Ambrose sat clutching his wife in his arms. She was shivering and covered with sweat. As we came in, she glanced at us vaguely, as if not quite understanding who we were. "She was fine earlier tonight. We even…" Ambrose's voice trailed off. "Her illness came on just a short time ago."

John's physician pushed into the chamber and pried Nan out of Ambrose's arms. After examining her, he told us what we had all suspected: our daughter-in-law most likely had the sweat. John promptly gave orders that the rest of the household be kept far away from Nan's rooms, which was a simple matter, given the size of Otford.

For the rest of the night and day, we attended on Nan. To John's fury, in our absence, one of Nan's waiting women allowed her to rise to sit upon the close stool, which brought on a fainting fit, and, we thought, certain death. She quickly revived, however, and by midmorning seemed to be past the most serious part of her illness. But by noon, she was markedly worse. Finally, at six in the evening, she breathed her last in Ambrose's arms.

Every now and then, I felt an ache for the old religion, for the practice of saying prayers for the dead. I felt it now as I saw this lovely young woman, who less than four-and-twenty hours ago had been strumming her lute and laughing at my sons' jokes, lying motionless and cold on her bed. Superstition such prayers might have been, perhaps, but—

I touched Ambrose's shaking shoulder. "*Now a Divine One joined to the celestial choir, you will not fear thirst or hunger, cold or heat,*" I recited softly.

Ambrose nodded dumbly, my words small comfort to him. Then Robert—who like the rest of my children had been barred from the sickroom—walked in and knelt beside his brother. "Come with me," he said after a while, and gently led Ambrose away.

A few days later, we left Otford Palace, never to return. The next spring, John exchanged it for other land. It was too large to keep up properly, he explained to the king.

22

Frances Grey
August 1552

HAD SOMEONE TOLD ME IN THE SUMMER OF 1552 THAT IT WOULD BE THE last one I would spend at Bradgate, I surely would have lived it differently. I would not have passed my days indoors, sewing or listening to music or reading or playing cards, for those were things I could do anywhere. Instead, I would have spent my days in our gardens and in our parks, breathing in the sweet fragrance none of our other properties, no matter how grand, could match. I would have sat on the grounds at dusk and watched the rays of the dying sun cast a mellow glow upon the red brick walls of the manor house. I would have taken off my stockings and waded through the cool streams like a young girl, and tried to see if I could balance myself on the thick log that had fallen across one of them. I would have said a last good-bye to my little Henry, sleeping in the chapel with his father's ancestors. But no one around me could foretell the future, so I spent that summer like any other.

It was indeed a rather ordinary summer. Harry was with the king on his progress through his southern estates. Jane was devoting herself to her latest course of study, learning Hebrew, and had quite pushed Plato aside, which I thought would undoubtedly have annoyed that august gentleman. Twelve-year-old Kate was rapidly developing into a young woman, and a very pretty one at that; it was clear she would be the family beauty. To her mixed irritation and pride, she had started her monthly courses. Mary, at seven, was the size of a girl two years younger, but she was perfectly intelligent and could sew almost as well as I could. For myself, I enjoyed paying and receiving visits from my various friends and relations.

In early August, my stepmother was one of my visitors. The last time I had seen her, soon after the death of my brothers, she had been almost immobile with grief and shock. Now, no longer wearing mourning for her two sons, she had gone further and put on an elegant green gown, which made her look younger and more handsome than she had appeared in several years. "There is something I must tell you, and I won't dawdle about it," she said before she had barely cleared the threshold of my private chamber. "I am remarrying."

I mentally surveyed all of the eligible single men and widowers among the nobility. No name came instantly to mind: all I could summon up were either too old, too young, too poor, too Catholic, too remotely situated, too testy, or (it had to be admitted) too homely.

"Don't trouble yourself," Katherine said, seeing my difficulty. "I am marrying Master Bertie."

I goggled at her. Richard Bertie was Katherine's gentleman usher, who had handled her business affairs since the death of my father. An Oxford graduate, he was unquestionably a clever and trustworthy man of business, but… "Master Bertie?" I said stupidly.

"No doubt you are going to tell me that he is not of my station, that he aspires to my hand only for my wealth, and that I am disgracing my title by marrying him."

"I—"

"Well, I say fie on that! Master Bertie is a gentleman of good abilities and unimpeachable character, who has been kindness itself since my poor boys were called to God. Why shouldn't I marry him? It is true, as you say, that he is meanly born—"

"Katherine! I haven't had a chance to say anything yet," I protested. "You are carrying on this argument quite adequately all by yourself."

"True," Katherine admitted.

"But I must admit I am shocked. With your beauty and wealth—"

"I could marry a man who would perish on the scaffold. I want no nobleman who will involve himself in this miserable business of running England. I want only to be left to enjoy my estates in peace, and perhaps to bear more children. Master Bertie can help me do the first most adequately, I have learned, and as for the second, I shall be quite happy to find out. I have been lonely since your father died, for all my resources, and I shall be glad enough to have a pair of warm feet in bed next to me once again."

"Have you asked permission of the king?"

"Yes. I have not received a reply yet, but he is on that progress of his. I have no doubt that he—or that is, Northumberland—will approve the match, unless perchance Northumberland was minded to marry me to one of that brood of his. And that I think most unlikely, given the young ages of his sons. Now that I think of it, actually, I am surprised that Northumberland hasn't tried to match up your Jane or Kate with one of his boys. Is Harry arranging a match for your Jane?"

"Not that I know of." I found that although Jane was certainly of a marriageable age, I did not want to think of the matter of her wedding, of my girl lying in a stranger's bed. "But we are getting off the topic. How did Master Bertie propose to you?"

"Well, as a matter of fact, I asked him to marry me. Oh, it wasn't quite as bold an undertaking as you might expect. He'd been making sheep's eyes at me for some time, although in the most discreet and proper way."

I snorted with laughter.

"In light of our positions, I suppose he just couldn't come out and ask, as a man of my own station might do. So I finally just called him to me on business, and after we had finished discussing the revenues of Grimsthorpe, I said, 'Master Bertie, have you ever considered marrying me?' And he admitted that he had. And so it was all arranged."

"What if he had said no?"

"Oh, I doubt he would have dared," said Katherine cheerfully. She smiled. "But I would have been very sorry if he had. For the truth is, I love him."

⌀

Soon after Katherine left us, we moved to our house at Sheen, not far from London. No sooner had we arrived than it began to rain constantly, keeping us confined inside. When a clear morning finally dawned, therefore, I was eager to venture out for a ride, especially as I had developed a headache. My daughters were as restless as I was. Even Jane asked that her horse be brought out.

The fresh air, however, did nothing to ease the pain in my head. Instead, the ache spread to the rest of my body, and I found myself having to think about the simplest details of riding my horse, as if I were a novice.

"Mother?"

I blinked. "What, Jane?"

"I asked if Father had told you when he might be coming here." Jane looked at me more closely. "Are you unwell?"

"It will pass." I clutched the pommel of my saddle as a wave of dizziness suddenly overtook me. "If we can just rest for a moment—"

Jane brought her horse to a halt. "My lady mother is ill," she called. "We must turn back."

"It is really not—"

"Now," said Jane.

Master Stokes, who had been riding a little ahead of us with my daughter Mary, wheeled around. In almost a single motion, he dismounted his own horse and swung himself onto mine, taking the reins as I slumped back against his shoulder.

⁂

By the time Master Stokes carried me into my chamber, I was burning with fever and had a sharp pain in my chest. "Don't disturb Harry," I begged as my ladies stripped me of my clothing. "He is so busy on the king's affairs, and he will be annoyed if he is called for nothing."

In hours, however, I was past caring if Harry, or anyone else, was called or not. I saw figures that I vaguely knew were my daughters and servants, and I was conscious of people giving me physic from time to time, but otherwise, I was oblivious to all that went on about me.

At some point, I felt someone stroking my hair, followed by the pressure of a large hand on mine. *The Lord himself*, I thought dreamily, and drifted off into a tranquil sleep. When I woke, the hand was still upon mine, and my mind felt clear. I blinked. "Harry?"

"The one and the same, my dear."

"You came."

"Of course I came. They told me you were ill. Indeed, we thought you would die. The chaplains have been praying for you, day and night. The girls have been miserable, worrying about you."

"Even Jane?"

"Especially Jane. She's worn herself out, tending you."

"I am glad to hear that. I mean—"

"I know what you mean." Harry lifted his hand from mine and patted me on the cheek. "Don't tire yourself with talking. All sorts of people have been inquiring about your health. The lady Mary, the Duchess of Northumberland, your stepmother, the Marchioness of Northampton… The marchioness has an idea in her head about our Jane's marriage, by the way."

"Marriage?"

"She thought that we might consider matching her with one of Northumberland's sons. Guildford, perhaps; they're close in age."

"But he's the fourth son! Jane can do much better than that."

"True. I think she was just talking to divert my attention. Anyway, we can speak more of it later. I won't tire you with it at present." Harry started to rise, then sat back down. "I've been thinking. When you get strong enough again, my dear, maybe we can start trying for another child, more often than we have lately. If, of course, you're willing. Perhaps after what happened to Queen Catherine, you might find it risky—"

"I am willing, Harry. Very." I took his hand in mine. "I love our daughters, as I know you do, too, but I should like to give you a son. We could name him Edward, like every other little boy in England."

Harry smiled.

"And," I said daringly, "even if I were not to have a child, I would like to lie with you more often. We did a great deal of that when we were first married."

"Nearly every evening." Harry took a strand of my hair in his hand. It was a point of pride with me that it had not faded much with age, but was still as bright as it had been in my girlhood. He stroked it, as he had before. "We were quite the pair in those early days."

"We can still be so."

Harry stood. "Then I must let you rest now, my dear." He kissed me lightly on the cheek and headed toward the door. Then he turned. "I was frightened that I would lose you, Frances. I'm thankful to the Lord that I didn't."

So was I. I settled down to sleep, dreaming of new beginnings.

23

Jane Dudley
January 1553

L ADY PAGE IS HERE WITH YOUR LADYSHIP'S NEW YEAR'S GIFT."
I sighed. I myself had prepared a New Year's gift for Lady Elizabeth Page, a pair of gloves, but I knew full well this was not the present she was hoping for. She wanted her daughter, the Duchess of Somerset, released from the Tower.

It had been the surprise of my life to meet Lady Page, for only in coloring was she like her elegant daughter, the duchess. Where Anne Seymour was tall and slender, Lady Page was short and ample, what men called "comfortable," and their differences did not end with their lack of physical similarity. Only in one respect were the women alike: they both made excellent comfits, as I had found over the past year when Lady Page first began to cultivate my favor—though I like to think I would have been kindly disposed toward her even without the jams she brought me.

Her efforts had brought her only partial success. I had prevailed upon John to let her visit her imprisoned daughter, and she now came and went from Anne Seymour's Tower cell as she pleased, often spending days at a time there. Over the summer, she had made it her mission to "cheer up" her daughter's quarters with her own tapestries, of the sort last fashionable in the seventh Henry's time, and she was known to disapprove of the Turkey carpet Anne had been allowed to take with her into captivity. It bred fleas, she had told anyone in the Tower who would listen, and it had been a triumph for her in August when she had found one nestling in its folds.

Try as I did, though, I could not move John to release the duchess. It was not just that she had threatened me, he explained—though I suspected this lay at the heart of his intransigence. The duchess had plotted against him with her husband, and might plot some more if freed. If she were a man, she would have certainly been executed, as had her half brother.

I had no answer for this, for John was entirely correct. Indeed, I was not certain why I kept pleading for the duchess's freedom, save that I pitied her in her widowhood and felt sorry for her children, especially the Countess of Warwick.

Besides, it would take a heart of stone to refuse Lady Page, now being ushered into the room and bearing the usual jar. She curtseyed to me, which always made me feel guilty, and handed me her gift—strawberry jam. "A little token, Your Grace, in appreciation of your kindness to me this past year."

"Thank you. I know I will find it delicious," I said, quite truthfully. Also quite truthfully, I said, "I wish I could have done better for you. I know your daughter wishes she could be with her children."

"She misses them, but I must say it is her husband she grieves for, every day." Lady Page sighed. "And her brother." Her half brother, Michael Stanhope, was Lady Page's son. He, too, had died on the scaffold a few weeks after the Duke of Somerset.

"Perhaps the council will agree to free the duchess this year," I said encouragingly. "I will certainly do all I can to promote it."

"I know you will, Your Grace." The old lady gave another sigh. "But sometimes I despair. My daughter has a good heart, but she can be difficult. I often tell her that if she could have kept a civil tongue in her head, perhaps she would have been freed by now. But of course she doesn't want to hear it. Daughters don't, as you probably know."

"I do indeed. I will keep trying. And in the meantime—" I handed Lady Page the gloves. Dutifully, she tried them on. They fit—barely—but I knew well she would never wear them. They would go instead to her glove-loving daughter in the Tower. "Happy New Year, my lady."

"And a happy New Year to Your Grace, as well. I hope it is a good one for you."

"And for you as well, my lady."

❦

George Ferrers had proved such a successful Lord of Misrule the Christmas before, the king had invited him to reprise his role. He had worried openly he might not be able to repeat his triumph of the previous year, but so far the festivities had exceeded expectations. On New Year's Day, there had been a joust of hobby horses, and tonight, Twelfth Night, there was a triumph of Venus, Mars, and Cupid.

With my daughter Katheryn at my side, I settled back contentedly, watching the small boy who was playing Cupid, complete with golden wings, try desperately to evade the clutches of the marshal and his band. This New Year's was so much happier than the one before. Somerset lay peacefully between his two queens at the Chapel of St. Peter ad Vincula. England was more stable and prosperous than she had been for several years, thanks to John and the council. The king himself, who had turned fifteen in October, was becoming more active in government each day. There were plans to declare him of majority when he turned sixteen, a day I looked forward to desperately. Then John—home sick at the manor of Chelsea the king had given us as a country home near London—could lead a more tranquil life. His continuing ill health and the melancholy it always inspired in him were the only things that troubled my mind that Twelfth Night.

A burst of laughter made me turn my attention back to the stage, where Venus, trailed by her ladies, was attempting to rescue Cupid. Having employed all of her considerable charms upon the marshal without success, Venus retreated and conferred with her ladies. Then, as the court cheered them on, the ladies pelted the marshal and his band with tennis balls. Soon the marshal and his cohorts lay vanquished on the field.

Cupid ran into the waiting arms of Venus, while the sound of trumpets signaled the grand but tardy entrance of Mars, who surveyed the carnage around him shamefacedly. Heaving a noble sigh, he slowly lifted his helmet off his head, as if to crown Venus with it, but Venus would have none of it. Backing away in terror, she was on the verge of being cornered by Mars, when Cupid, having rushed around behind the god of war, shot an arrow at him. Pierced by it, Mars put his helmet back on his head and embraced Venus and Cupid at once.

The audience clapped, none more vigorously than the king. As the applause died down, I heard another distinct sound. The king coughed, and coughed again.

He sounded, I realized as the players took their final bows, perfectly horrid.

Part II

24

Frances Grey
February 1553

"ARE MY BROTHER'S PHYSICIANS QUITE SURE THAT HE IS WELL ENOUGH TO see me?" the lady Mary asked as we rode through Fleet Street toward Westminster, I on her left and the Duchess of Northumberland on the right.

"Very sure," I said, and Jane Dudley murmured her assent. "It is nothing more than a cold."

We had at least two hundred horse in our procession, the palfreys bedecked as brilliantly as the lords and ladies who sat astride them. Colorful as our company was, however, we were almost swallowed up by the gloom of the February day. And yet this was a joyous occasion: the king and his sister Mary had put aside their differences regarding religion for the time being, and the king had decreed that Mary be received in London with the highest of honor.

Unfortunately, the king had taken ill on the same day Mary entered London, so she had had to wait several days before she could see him. With London so damp and gray, I was not at all surprised the king was ailing, nor was I worried about his health. It was only surprising that we were not all in our beds.

The weather, however, had not kept the Londoners from enjoying the fine show of the lady Mary riding to court. "How kind they are to cheer," Mary said now as we left behind one particularly enthusiastic street corner. "It is for my mother's sake, you know. The Londoners always did love her. Unlike that Anne Boleyn creature," she added.

The Duchess of Northumberland, who had been friendly with Queen Anne, looked at her horse's mane.

My husband and the Duke of Northumberland, flanked by scores of knights and gentlemen, awaited the lady Mary outside of the gates of Westminster. No sooner had our party pulled within sight than the dukes and the rest sank to their knees, doing reverence to Mary. Almost, I thought as we made our slow, stately way past the kneeling men, as if she were queen.

∽

"My brother and I had a very nice visit," Mary said as my daughter Jane and I sat with her and her ladies that evening. Mary had issued the invitation outside of the presence of the Duchess of Northumberland, who no doubt would be hurt later when the inevitable court gossip informed her she had been excluded. But Mary and I were, after all, first cousins, while Jane Dudley was a mere knight's daughter from Kent. "We talked only small talk. I did not bring up the subject of the Mass, and that is just as well, I suppose."

"The council is not interfering with your hearing it?"

"No. For now, anyway." Mary sighed. "Perhaps it was just as well my brother was ill. He might have lectured me about my beliefs if he was stronger." She frowned. "He was ill just last year. Do you think Northumberland is making him do too much work?"

"It was the measles. Anyone might have them. And there was a great deal of sickness last year. Northumberland's daughter-in-law, my own Jane, myself…"

"Well, I cannot help but worry. But he did seem to be amending, thanks be to the Lord." The lady Mary crossed herself, then turned to Jane, who had been docilely listening to our conversation. "Have they found a husband for you yet, Cousin?"

"No, my lady."

Mary looked at me inquiringly. "There was talk of the Earl of Hertford, but with the Duke of Somerset's attainder and death, that is no longer a possibility," I said. "But my daughter is still young."

"That is what they said about me at one time," Mary said bluntly. "Don't let her chance slip by."

"My daughter should have no difficulty attracting a husband. She is learned and extremely accomplished."

"But some men may not like a woman who is too learned."

I had to give Jane credit for maturity; two years before, she probably could not have endured this conversation in silence. "Harry's great pleasure has been to bring up Jane as an educated woman. He would not match her to such a man."

"No doubt," conceded Mary. She glanced at Jane critically. "She's a pretty young lady, in any case. But it is a pity you can't do anything about the freckles. Have you tried the sap of a birch tree?"

Out of the corner of my eye, I watched Jane clench a dainty fist.

"So she told Mother she would send for some recipes to get rid of my freckles," Jane told Kate back at Suffolk Place, the grand home, once my father's, which we had inherited when my brothers died. "As if we haven't tried them all! And it's not as if my face is one mass of freckles anyway." Jane held up a mirror and frowned into it. One flaw Mary had not mentioned was that she was slightly shortsighted. "Only a few scattered around my nose. They aren't large."

"I can't believe she's giving anyone lectures on her appearance," Kate said. "She's no beauty herself. If she weren't the king's sister, people would call her downright plain."

"Kate!"

"Well, it's true, Mother." Kate, the reigning beauty of my three girls, shrugged.

Jane continued in Mary's gruff voice, "'Some men may not like a woman who is too learned, little cousin.' As if Father would marry me to some cowherd! Any man I would wish to marry would be pleased to have a learned woman as a wife," said Jane. She traced the finger on which she would have worn a wedding ring. "Mother, are there plans to marry me?"

"It is as I told the lady Mary, there are none at present. But you are almost sixteen. That was the age when I married your father. There will most certainly be men seeking your hand for their sons."

"But what of my studies?"

"There is no need to stop your studies when you are married. Queen Catherine did not, and you yourself have corresponded with William Cecil's wife, haven't you? But they must take second place to your duties as a wife— and eventually as a mother." Jane looked so stricken, I patted her on her shoulder. "You will adapt, as all of us must do."

25

Jane Dudley
April 1553 to May 1553

DESPITE BEING URGED BY THE KING AND BY THE COUNCIL, THE EARL OF Cumberland had not accepted Guildford as a match for his daughter, to my irritation and to Guildford's relief. "I would have caught my death of cold up north, Mother. You should be glad."

"Oh, Guildford, for heaven's sake, it's not that bad up there."

"I believe he was speaking of the girl," Robert said, and my sons guffawed.

I could not quite see the humor. Why wasn't Guildford good enough for Margaret Clifford? He was our fourth son, to be sure, and Margaret was the earl's only child, but she was not necessarily a great heiress, for Cumberland was young enough to still father sons if he chose to remarry. Worse, there had even been rumors, spread by a former servant of the Duchess of Somerset, that my husband had been plotting to gain the throne through the marriage—even though Margaret Clifford was behind Mary, Elizabeth, and the three Grey girls in the line of succession.

Silly and stupid as the rumors were, they had begun to revive this spring, for the king was not well. The cough that had troubled him on Twelfth Night had never disappeared entirely, and for a few days in February, he had been bedridden with a fever. Though he had recovered well enough to visit with his sister Mary, he had spent much of March confined to his chambers. Yet by early April, he seemed well on the mend, and I trusted the nonsensical rumors would soon die the death they deserved.

Meanwhile, my son Ambrose, after months of mourning his pretty Nan, had begun to take a healthy interest in women again, and in that same April, we held a dinner to celebrate his betrothal to Elizabeth Tailboys, an heiress a few years his senior. "I had rather hoped to be celebrating Guildford's betrothal by now," I confided to Elizabeth Parr, Marchioness of Northampton, as we stood watching the young people dance. "But it seems that the Earl of Cumberland is adamant against him."

Elizabeth, whose husband was the brother of Queen Catherine, glanced at Guildford, capering with one of William Cecil's daughters. "The girl's loss, I daresay. He's a fine-looking lad." She looked around at the dancers. "I am surprised you never considered the Grey girl for him. Especially now that both your husband and her father are dukes."

I looked in the direction of the girl in question, Harry Grey's daughter Jane. I had seen a great deal of her in February when the lady Mary came to court, as the lady Jane was nearly sixteen and of an age to be seen at such affairs. She was fully marriageable, and looked pretty and healthy, but I had somehow never thought of her as a potential match for Guildford or for my youngest son, Hal. "Wasn't she intended for the Earl of Hertford?"

"So it was said, back when he had prospects." The marchioness snorted. It was Somerset who had forced William Parr to separate from Elizabeth on the grounds that their marriage was invalid, and it was Somerset's fall that had enabled the couple to finally have its validity affirmed. Plainly, Elizabeth's dislike for the former Protector extended to his family, as well. In a somewhat kinder tone, she said, "In any case, their fathers never got beyond the talking stage. So that's no obstacle. She's a brilliant girl, they say, and you don't need me to tell you about her lineage."

"No. I wonder how she would get on with Guildford, though. I don't remember them having much to say to each other at my eldest son's wedding."

"They would learn to get along like other couples do. You surely don't intend to let another of your children marry for love."

I refrained from pointing out she and William Parr had done just that, but she did have a point. Besides, there was no logical objection to such a marriage. The would-be spouses were well educated, close in age, healthy, and Protestant; their fathers were the only two dukes in England in power; money was no problem. Royal approval would have to be secured, but I could not think of a single reason why it would not be forthcoming.

Yet something about the arrangement made me uneasy. Was it just that I had always found the lady Jane to be a rather chilly young woman? That hardly seemed good enough grounds to reject the match outright, especially as my contact with the girl had been only superficial. She was young, after all, not to mention very bookish, and the court could be intimidating. Perhaps her manner was more pleasing in the privacy of her household. "I will mention it to my husband."

"Do so," said the marchioness. She laughed. "And if he likes the idea, be certain to give me full credit."

✍

"The lady Jane Grey? Funny. Northampton suggested her to me tonight as well. I didn't realize he and his wife were such determined matchmakers. I must say she seems a logical choice. But—"

"But what?"

"Nothing."

"It is a woman's prerogative to say 'Nothing' when asked such a question. Not yours." John did not laugh. "John, what is it?" I grabbed his arm when he remained silent. "Tell me, for heaven's sake!"

"You must not tell this to a living soul. I should not be telling you, actually. I believe only the king and I know about this. You will be the third."

The realization of just how much my husband trusted me made me fall silent. I took his hand. After a while, he said, "A couple of weeks ago, the king was feeling very ill. So ill, he told me afterward, that he had thought he might never recover. He was wrong, thank the Lord, as he was much better in a day or two. But just a few days ago, he called me to him again and showed me something."

John looked around. Sensing what he wanted, I rose and bolted the door.

"Thank you. You remember King Henry's will. The crown to Edward and his heirs, then to Mary and her heirs, then to Elizabeth and her heirs, and then to the lady Frances's heirs."

"Yes."

"He's proposing to alter that." John made his voice even lower. "Should the king die without heirs, God forbid, the crown will go to Lady Frances's male heirs. If there are none, to the lady Jane's male heirs. And so on to the lady Jane's younger sisters, and then if none of them has male descendants, to Margaret Clifford's male heirs."

My head swam. "The lady Mary? The lady Elizabeth?"

"Cut out of the succession entirely. King Henry declared them both bastards, King Edward pointed out, and never had them legitimated."

"But King Henry provided for them to succeed to the crown!"

"That's what I reminded King Edward. He just shook his head and gave me his father's glare—he's getting quite good at it. He said that besides being a bastard, Mary would bring us back to Rome, and that although he did not believe the lady Elizabeth would do our religion harm, she was as much of a bastard as her sister. Perhaps not even King Henry's child, given the accusations against Anne Boleyn."

"John, you know all that was lies."

"Maybe. But that's not what the king believes. To him, King Henry's first proper wife was Jane Seymour. That's the one thing both of the Seymour brothers agreed upon, and they never missed an opportunity to tell the king so."

"But the lady Frances has not borne a child in years, and the last have all been girls."

"Precisely. So under the king's devise, as he calls it, if Lady Jane marries and has a son, that boy could be the king of England."

So if Guildford married the lady Jane and sired a son, our grandson would be King of England. I sank into a chair.

John continued, "Of course, this all supposes the king will die without issue of his body, which is most unlikely. His French match is sure to go through now that we're at peace. And his health will certainly improve now that spring is here. I told the king these things."

"And what did he say?"

"He said that he believed that God would be merciful and let him reign for many years, but that it was best to be prepared. Then he put his devise away in a chest he has, away from prying eyes. He likes to tinker with it from time to time, he said."

We were silent for a short while. Then I said with some relief, "You could not possibly ask him now to approve Guildford's marriage to Lady Jane, even if they wished it. It would make it appear that you had ulterior motives."

"To the contrary, the king has urged it upon me. He said that should his line happen to fail, he believed that England would be safest in the hands of my grandson." John looked out over the Thames. "I set out to win the trust and affection of the king, and I have succeeded, it appears."

"Do you intend to marry our son to the Grey girl?"

"I can think of no good reason to refuse the king. Even without that devise of his, it is, as the Marchioness of Northampton says, an eminently suitable match. I will talk to the Duke of Suffolk."

"What about the king's devise? Can't you persuade the king not to disinherit his sisters? It seems so unnatural, and it is bound to lead to trouble."

"I can try. But the king is not a child who can be distracted from one bauble by handing him another. He has thought about his sisters' legal status, read about it, even asked that the records of Anne Boleyn's trial be brought to him. I fear it will not be an easy task. I can only hope that the necessity does not come to pass."

"And if it does come to pass? John, you must think of this!"

John reached for me. "I really don't want to," he said quietly.

⌘

"Jane Grey? That sour little girl? I tried to carry on a civil conversation with her—in Italian, mind you—and it was sheer misery. Of all of the women in England, why must I marry her?"

"She was younger then, Guildford," I said. "You have seen her at court. She's perfectly polite and civil."

"Like a stick of wood."

"She's pretty."

"Not enough to make up for the rest." Guildford looked at John, who had been standing silently by. "Father, must I marry her?"

"It is the king's own wish."

"Why? What is it to him whom I marry?"

"She is of royal blood, and the king wishes to honor the Dudley family by bestowing her upon us in marriage," John said.

"Then why not bestow her on Hal? He's a better scholar."

"You are the oldest of our unmarried sons. It would be perceived as an insult, perhaps, if we offered him our youngest in your stead. Besides, you and the lady Jane are nearly the same age."

"Fourth son, fifth son, what's the difference? And Hal's but a year younger. Please, Father."

"I am sorry. It must be."

"You let Mary and Robert marry people of their own choosing."

"Have you contracted yourself to someone else?"

"No," Guildford admitted. "But I wish I had. Then you couldn't make me marry this self-important little chit."

"Guildford, many marriages start in dislike, and end in deep love. The two of you will come closer together when you get to know each other better. Especially when you have children."

"I'd rather not even think about that, if you please," Guildford snapped.

"She is a far more prestigious bride than any of your brothers' wives."

"If only Ambrose hadn't remarried so quickly. He could marry her." Guildford suddenly brightened. "Why not annul Jack's marriage? The girl doesn't care for us, and it's never been consummated. Then the lady Jane could have an earl for a husband, not just Lord Guildford."

"We are not going to throw the Countess of Warwick out of our household just to oblige you," John said. "Lady Jane is for you and for no one else. Most fourth sons I know wouldn't complain of getting a duke's eldest daughter for a bride. I have overindulged you, I fear. There shall be no more comment from you about the subject."

He turned and walked out of the room, leaving an open-mouthed Guildford. "Mother? Isn't there anything you can do to make him change his mind?"

"Not this time."

"I don't understand. What is so important about this girl? She's of royal blood, but she's not the only girl in England who can say that. She's not an heiress. She's not beautiful. She's clever, but there's such a thing as being too clever. Why does my marrying her mean so much to Father?" He frowned. "Is there something that you're not telling me?"

"Don't be absurd. It is simply a good match, that you are too blinded by your prejudice against this girl to realize. You have been overindulged."

Just as John had, I turned and left the room, leaving my son doubly puzzled.

Guildford's betrothal to the lady Jane—a match to which the Duke of Suffolk had eagerly assented—seemed to inspire everyone in the court to begin match-making. Suffolk, not content with arranging the marriage of one daughter, promptly began negotiating for the marriages of the other two; in addition, he proposed his niece Margaret Audley as a wife for Hal. The Earl of Huntingdon suddenly decided that no one but our little Katheryn would do as a bride for his son, Henry, Lord Hastings. Even the Earl of Cumberland, having in time-honored fashion decided that Guildford might make a suitable husband for his daughter after he had been promised elsewhere, agreed to a match with the one remaining Dudley—John's younger brother Andrew, whom I had considered destined for perpetual bachelorhood.

There was to be a triple wedding on May 25—Guildford and Jane, my Katheryn and Henry Hastings, Kate Grey and the Earl of Pembroke's son, William Herbert. In preparation, the king showered presents on all of us—cloth of gold, cloth of silver, and jewels, most of which had come from the goods forfeited to the Crown by the Duke of Somerset. There seemed no end to the cloth the duke had acquired: produced for him by the finest workshops in Italy, it came in every imaginable shade of blue, green, tawny, yellow, and crimson, and in a variety of patterns, so no one at the wedding would be in the same garment. As my dressmaker transformed some green cloth into a gown that would flatter even me, I could only wonder at why

Somerset had amassed so much uncut fabric. Had he been saving it for his own children's weddings? For his daughter Jane's longed-for marriage with the king? It did not seem a good omen, but the cloth was too lovely to let superstition stand in the way of wearing it. Instead, I gloried in the way it set off the fine tablet, bearing the face of a clock, which had also come to me from the Somersets' goods.

Guildford and Katheryn were also being fitted for their wedding garments. Guildford would stomp into his fittings, allow himself to be draped with fabric, and stomp out again, but ten-year-old Katheryn had given herself entirely over to the bridal preparations. She kept a limning of her seventeen-year-old husband by her side constantly and tucked it under her pillow at night; I could only hope the live original matched her expectations. Just the day before, when I went to her chamber to check the progress of her lessons, I had found written on an entire page that should have contained an Italian translation, the following, in various sizes and scripts:

> *Katheryn Hastings*
> *Katheryn, Lady Hastings*
> *Katheryn, lady to Henry Hastings*

At the bottom, my daughter, whose father-in-law the earl was still very much alive, had been unable to resist the temptation of trying out:

> *Katheryn, Countess of Huntingdon*

"I wish I could dress like this every day," Katheryn sighed now as she stared at the blue fabric billowing around her. "Is this what King Henry's sisters wore to their weddings?"

"Something very like it, no doubt."

"I will be afraid to eat in it," Katheryn said happily. She hopped down from the dressmaker's stool on which she had been standing and stared out the window. "Oh, I can hardly wait until my wedding day! I wonder if the lady Jane and the lady Katherine are finding the wait as long as I am finding it. It must be *excruciating* for them."

26

Frances Grey
April 1553 to May 1553

GUILDFORD DUDLEY?" I SAID AFTER HARRY BROKE THE NEWS TO ME OF MY daughter's betrothal. "You cannot be serious."

"I certainly am, my dear. What's to be said against him? He's a presentable young man, with no mean share of learning, and his father's the virtual ruler of England. It's a pity, I admit, that his older brothers are married already, but there's the chance he'll be created the Duke of Suffolk in right of his wife one day, just as I was created the Duke of Suffolk in your right. In any case, they won't be poor."

"His grandfather died on the scaffold!"

"Quite a few families can now claim that distinction."

"But Edmund Dudley was not a nobleman who fell on the wrong side of King Henry. He was a money-grubbing lawyer!"

"Whose skill at it left your uncle quite wealthy, one could add. And if it makes you feel any better, Northumberland's mother was of noble stock. But whatever Edmund Dudley did, it hardly matters now, does it? The king regards Northumberland as his father, practically, and he wants this match. So does Northumberland. He's not even demanded an unreasonable dowry, as I thought he would. For a man with three daughters, that is a consideration."

I said nothing. Harry took me in his arms. "I know it's sudden, speaking of having our girl married, but you know I wouldn't match her where she would be miserable. I've talked to the lad. He's not a scholar like she is—how many men of her station are, really?—but he's well educated and presentable. They must come to know each other. We did."

"Just the other day, I told Jane that we didn't have a match planned for her."

"Well, we didn't then. This has come up quite suddenly. Shall we tell Jane now?"

"You tell her," I said.

∽

"I am to marry Guildford Dudley?" Every single one of Jane's freckles stood out upon her face as she stared at her father and me. "You cannot be serious."

"And you, young lady, cannot be serious in speaking to me like that."

"I beg your pardon, Father." Jane lowered her eyes, but only briefly. "But Guildford Dudley! A traitor's grandson."

"Your mother has already reminded me of that. He happens to also be a duke's son."

"A duke's fourth son! A virtual nobody. And he speaks terrible Italian. It was painful to listen to him."

"And how often will you be speaking Italian with him? Jane, if you are going to oppose me, at least do so with reason."

Jane turned an accusing pair of brown eyes on me. "You told me, my lady, there were no plans to marry me yet."

"I spoke the truth. There were none that I knew of."

"What if I refuse? I cannot be forced to marry him. Our marriage would be invalid then."

"Do you set yourself up as a canon lawyer now, child?"

Jane stared at the ground. "I don't wish to marry him, Father. I don't much wish to marry anyone, I confess, but by no means do I want to marry him."

"Are we thinking of the same young man? He is not a repulsive creature, Jane. He's good looking, tall for his age, well spoken—in English, at least. I daresay he's fallen into bad company now and then, but that's the nature of young men his age." Harry suddenly wrenched Jane's chin up. "You have not promised yourself to someone else, have you?"

"No, Father."

"You don't fancy yourself beholden to the Earl of Hertford, do you? That would have been a fair match in its day, but that day is done. He's of no account now."

"I do not regard myself as betrothed to him."

"Then is it not right for you to accept Guildford Dudley as your husband?"

"He is commonplace."

"For God's sake, girl! You could not have spent more than an hour or two with him in your life. And he is barely older than you are. What do you expect of a lad his age?"

"I had hoped for someone different."

"Who?" Harry's voice softened. "Jane, you're not still hoping for King

Edward, are you? If so, I am sorry we ever put the idea in your head. He is destined for France. If—"

"If what?"

"If he lives long enough to go to his wedding. I'm beginning to have my doubts."

It was the first time anyone had voiced the thought that had been troubling me for some time. I interrupted the volleying between my husband and Jane. "Harry, you see him at court. Is he that ill?"

"The physicians aren't saying what ails him. Perhaps they don't know. But you can look at him and tell that something's not right. He looked a little better when he moved to Greenwich, but it didn't last long. I'm old enough to recognize the mark of death on a face. I see it on his."

"I didn't know," Jane said. She swallowed hard.

"Jane, the king himself wants this match. I don't know why. I suspect Northumberland might know, but he keeps his own counsel. All I know is that the king wants it. Unless I'm mistaken, and I hope I am, you will be thwarting the wishes of a dying boy if you do not marry Lord Guildford. Do you still refuse?"

"No, Father. I will marry him." In a small voice, Jane asked, "But must I sleep with him immediately?"

"Yes. The king wants it consummated." Harry glanced at the clock on the mantle. "Time I went to the council meeting. Your mother can answer any questions you might have."

⁓

I had barely had time to get used to Jane's upcoming marriage when Harry arranged the betrothals of my two younger daughters as well: Kate to William Herbert, the Earl of Pembroke's heir, and Mary to Arthur, the son of William Grey of Wilton. It only added to Jane's annoyance that Kate could look forward to being the Countess of Pembroke when her father-in-law died, whereas Jane had no such expectation. "If Northumberland continues in favor such as he is, who knows?" I suggested. "Perhaps Guildford might gain an earldom, too."

"In favor with whom, Mother? Father says that King Edward is worse than he was before."

"We can only hope that he will soon improve."

"And if he doesn't? The lady Mary will remember all her struggles about the Mass, and that Northumberland was the head of the council that tried to stop her from hearing it. I don't think she'll be inclined to give Guildford anything.

Or any of us." Jane glared at the blackwork smock she was embroidering for her trousseau. "What could the king be thinking?"

We were prevented from discussing the matter further by the announcement that Guildford himself had come to call.

This was the first time I had seen my daughter's fiancé since the marriage was arranged. Unlike his father and his brother Robert, who were swarthy, Guildford was fair, with hair the same nondescript shade of brown as his mother's. He had inherited his father's height, however, and he was more handsome than either of his parents. Physically, at least, I did not see where Jane had got such a bad bargain, fourth son or not.

Guildford bowed to Jane and the rest of us. "Well," he said after a few pleasantries, "it looks as if we'll be married soon."

Jane gave him a withering glance. "Yes," she said distantly.

"My father will be allowing us to stay a few days at Chelsea."

"Chelsea? That is where I spent much time when I was living in Queen Catherine's household. I had very happy memories of it."

"We'll have the place to ourselves. Well, except for our servants, of course."

"So I assumed."

Guildford turned his attention to the smock. "That's very nice looking," he ventured. He smiled. "Perhaps when we are married, you will make me shirts?"

"I am a very poor seamstress. I would not count on it."

"Oh."

"I prefer the pursuits of the mind. What pursuits do you prefer, Lord Guildford? Hunting, I suppose? Hawking?"

"I enjoy both, but only occasionally. I prefer tennis, actually. I hope to install a court when we have a permanent residence."

"Really."

"I do like music quite a bit, too, and dancing." Guildford looked at Jane hopefully. "My mother said that she recalls seeing you dance quite well."

"Yes, I do like music," Jane allowed. "And dancing at an appropriate occasion."

"Father has engaged the best musicians in London for our wedding, and two troupes of masquers, one of men and one of women. It will be quite a spectacle."

"Indeed it will be."

"I hope the king will be well enough to attend."

"Yes. It would be a pity if he were not able to witness what he has brought about."

I decided to help my future son-in-law. "Is Lady Katheryn looking forward to her marriage?"

"Oh, yes," Guildford said. "She met her husband the other day and has spoken of nothing but him since. He brought her a puppy as an early wedding present."

Jane, who was not fond of animals, looked warily around. Guildford said, "I didn't think you'd like anything like that, my lady."

"No."

"I would like another monkey," mused Kate. "I wish Lord Herbert would bring me one."

"That one creature of yours is odious enough already," Jane said. "The last thing we need is another."

"But you won't be living here. Neither will I. So it wouldn't matter." Kate smiled at Guildford. "He tore the pages of one of Jane's books once," she explained. "Jane has never forgiven him for that. Does your family have a monkey?"

"No. But Mother has a parrot. Father brought it home a couple of years ago. He's very talkative. He will perch on Mother's wrist, and Father's, too. He's not so cooperative with the rest of us."

"Oh, that sounds lovely. I would love a parrot." Kate widened her blue eyes at Guildford, who blushed.

I decided intervention was needed again before Kate captured the heart of her sister's betrothed—not that Jane seemed at all bothered by the possibility. "My younger daughter and I shall leave you for now, Lord Guildford," I said, rising and indicating that Kate should do the same. "You and Jane will have much to talk about, and no doubt will like to do it in private."

Guildford's and Jane's faces indicated the very opposite, but neither put up an objection as I hastened out the door.

To my surprise, though, Jane seemed in reasonably good spirits after Guildford had left on his barge to Sion, one of the Duke of Somerset's houses that Northumberland had recently acquired. "I think we have reached an accommodation," she announced.

"Oh?"

"Yes. I am to be allowed free time to study each afternoon. Provided I have completed my household duties," Jane added, anticipating my objection. "I shall not be expected to accompany him on the hunt, or to spend an inordinate amount of time with his friends."

"Have you appointed a particular night for sleeping with him?"

"No. Should I?"

"Goodness, no! Marriage is a sacrament, Jane, not a series of bargains. Didn't you read that in that book you translated for your father?"

"Yes. But the author of that book was not married to Guildford Dudley."

27

Jane Dudley
May 1553 to June 1553

I WILL ADMIT—THE ADMITTING OF IT CAN HARM NO ONE NOW—THAT I DID not like my daughter-in-law. It is wrong to say that, I know, for the change in my situation has not kept me from hearing news altogether, and I have heard she is spoken of in hushed, reverent tones as far away as Zurich, by men generations her senior. But I cannot help it. I found her to be self-absorbed and chilly and prideful, and yet I would have overlooked all of these things if she had shown the slightest bit of kindness to my poor Guildford. But she did not. Instead, she looked down her pert little nose at Guildford from the very day she met him. Even at the very end, she—but I grow bitter, and I promised my dear John, on the dreadful day when I took his hand for the very last time, that I would not be so.

And besides, I digress.

Guildford and Jane, Katheryn and Lord Hastings, and Kate Grey and Lord Herbert were married May 25, with almost everyone of consequence in England present, save the lady Mary, who declined the invitation, and the king, who was too ill to come. Lord Herbert himself had been ill, but he seemed happy in the company of his new bride, who fussed over his comfort and health in a touchingly matronly manner, as if they had been married for years instead of minutes. My Katheryn, who by agreement was to continue living with John and me for another year or so before going to join her husband's very large family, watched the masques that followed the wedding in a state of marital bliss, leaning on her husband's shoulder and finally dozing off. The French ambassador pronounced the wine good; the Italian ambassador, the music excellent. Only Guildford and Jane appeared unhappy.

But perhaps I was wrong about that, for the lady Frances's pretty face did not look entirely happy either, although the duchess made small talk as determinedly as I did during the feasting and entertainments that followed the ceremony. "This must be difficult for you," I ventured toward the end of the evening. "Having not one but two daughters marrying and leaving your home."

"Yes. It will be strange not to have my girls at home." Frances hesitated, then faced me straight on. "The lord Guildford. Will he be…kind tonight?"

I refrained from pointing out my true opinion, which was that the lady Jane would probably be telling Guildford what to do. Perhaps she had consulted a book. For Guildford's part, I had no idea whether he had known women before; my husband was not the sort to encourage him to visit brothels or to have his pleasure with servants, although I would not put it past his older brothers to urge him to get some experience before he faced the daunting prospect of a night with the lady Jane. "My son has never been anything but chivalrous around women," I said coolly. "I have no doubt that he will treat your daughter with respect."

"I wish the consummation could have been postponed a year. My daughter is so young in some ways."

"You and I were brides at her age, and we adjusted. She must do the same." I looked at the three couples—Kate and Lord Herbert chatting animatedly, Katheryn sound asleep on Lord Hastings's shoulder, and Guildford and Jane sitting side by side, hardly moving their mouths except to chew their food. In a kinder tone, I said, "They will learn to care for each other, as we and our husbands did. These things take time."

*

There was no grand bedding ceremony for Guildford and Jane of the sort there had been in my day; the couple simply went to Jane's chamber, Frances having given her daughter a parting kiss and my sons having given Guildford a series of sympathetic handshakes. ("Look at the lady Kate," I had heard Guildford inform Robert sadly. "Lucky Lord Herbert. Now, there's a *girl*.") John and I smiled hard, as we had been smiling all evening, aided by more wine than either of us generally consumed.

I needed John to make love to me that night, and he did, with a tenderness I hoped somehow seeped over to the newlyweds in the bridal chamber. But when it was over, I found myself sobbing uncontrollably into John's chest. "It's just the wine," I assured him when I had finally brought myself under control. "Nothing more."

*

Three days after the wedding, the Countess of Warwick sought me out—never a good sign. "I have a question I need to ask you, Your Grace."

"Yes, dear?"

"Is it true that the Duke of Northumberland intends to put me aside so that my husband can marry the lady Elizabeth?"

I stared. "Where on earth did you hear that?"

"It's all over town, I suppose, if I heard it here. They say that the king is dying and that the lady Mary will be deprived of the crown. The lady Elizabeth will be made queen, and my husband—of course, he won't be my husband then—will rule jointly with her. Or they say that the duke himself will marry the lady Elizabeth after he puts Your Grace aside."

Why did people keep saying such vile things about my John? "There is nothing to those ridiculous rumors. Hasn't my son made arrangements for you to accompany him to Warwick Castle, where you will be greeted as his countess?"

"Yes, Your Grace."

"Then that should tell you how foolish those rumors are. As for me, it would hardly serve my husband to put me aside and bastardize our children, two of whom he held weddings for just a few days ago. Don't you think?"

"Yes, Your Grace."

"Good. You are an intelligent young lady. Use that intelligence when you hear those ridiculous rumors."

"Yes, Your Grace. But—"

"Yes?"

"Is the king really dying? Is that yet another rumor?"

"He is very ill. But he may yet recover. There is always hope."

"I see, Your Grace."

I dismissed my daughter-in-law. Then I went to my chamber and wept for a solid hour.

❧

A few days later, Jane and Guildford, who had been getting to know each other at Chelsea, joined us at Sion. I looked for signs that Jane was with child, but of course it was too soon to tell, and I could not think of a tactful way to ascertain whether she and Guildford had been sleeping together regularly, though goodness knows I tried. Instead, I had to content myself with puzzling out whether there had been a thawing between the spouses. They did not chat together easily as newlyweds of a similar age and background might, but at least Guildford paid Jane the proper courtesies, and Jane accepted them politely. Perhaps another few weeks at Chelsea might do them good.

I was pondering this at supper, and determining to talk the matter over with John once the meal was over, when Guildford suddenly turned green and stumbled to his feet, then ran out of the chamber, a hand upon his mouth. Hal, sitting nearby, made it only to a corner before he retched up his meal, while poor Lord Clinton simply stuck his head under the table. His wife, who had been sharing his salad, went white and fell fainting to the floor.

Jane shrieked as I simultaneously tried to attend to the Clintons and to my sons. "Poison!"

"No," said Robert, who along with Amy had been dining with us. "A cook who has no idea what he is about with a salad." He picked up a leaf from Lord Clinton's plate and flourished it in the air. "This has no business in a salad. A proper salad requires a French chef. We in England just don't understand it."

Lady Clinton gave a little moan and sat up. "I feel ill," she announced, and promptly proved her point.

"Salad," Robert confirmed as Guildford stumbled back into the room and looked at me piteously.

"Get them all to their chambers," I ordered in relief. What ailed everyone would be unpleasant for a few days, I foresaw, but not dangerous. I turned to Jane, who still looked uneasy. It was her place more than mine to see that her husband was coddled during his illness, but a recuperating Guildford surely deserved more sympathetic company than hers. "Jane, wait a few hours to make sure you are not afflicted. If you are not, perhaps you can visit your mother for a few days while Guildford recovers."

Jane smiled, for the first time since she had entered our family, in whole-hearted approval.

∝

Guildford, Hal, and the Clintons were still recovering when John, who had been with the king at Greenwich during this gastric mayhem, summoned me to his chamber and locked the door when I arrived. "It is time to tell you," he said. "Some days ago, I called the king's physicians together and asked for their opinion of whether the king would recover."

I did not need to hear any more; the answer was in John's face and voice. "And they said he would not?"

"Yes. They said he has three months. At best."

I felt the tears come to my own eyes. King Henry might have justified his actions with other explanations, and might have even believed them, but any-one who had lived through his reign knew it was the desire for a living son that had caused him to thrust aside Catherine of Aragon so cruelly, then to send Anne Boleyn to the block. Many more had died as the result of the turmoil caused by these queens' failure to provide the king a male heir. And now this son, this much-loved and much-protected son, for whose birth so much blood had been shed, was dying, with no one but women in line for his throne. You could say one thing for the Lord: he did love his irony. "There is no hope?"

"I told the physicians not to slacken their efforts and not to cease praying for the king's life, and I have promised them a hundred crowns a month in fees. They have every incentive to hope. I have tried myself. But I do not think there is any." John's voice faltered. Then he said, in a voice so low as to be almost unintelligible, "The king wants to see us together tomorrow morning."

"Why, what could he want with me?"

"He prefers to tell you in person," John said. He rose. "The king's condition is a secret, for now, at least in theory. In practice, every ambassador in London is aware of it and is convinced I am poisoning him. In addition, of course, to scheming to marry myself and Jack to either the lady Mary or the lady Elizabeth. One thing I can't complain of is being accused of idleness."

"John—"

"I don't care, in truth. What does it matter what they say of me, with the king dying? He has become almost a son to me."

"Maybe there is hope, John. You mustn't lose faith."

John shook his head. "You won't say that when you see him."

❧

The king remained at Greenwich, which was both the healthiest place for him to be and the necessary place for him to be, as he was too ill to travel safely. Courtiers had once flirted in its halls and done more than that in some of its secluded places, but no one who stayed here now was idle or cheerful. Everyone went around his business quietly and diligently.

I was no stranger to death in all of its manifestations, having watched five of my children die young of various illnesses, but my first glimpse of the king made me gasp even as I knelt before him. Whatever sins King Henry had committed, they would have been punished tenfold had he been fated to see his son as he looked now. Edward had managed to sit up to receive guests, and the nightcap and night shirt he wore were of rich material, but they could not hide that his face was bloated and pasty or that he needed the help of two of the gentlemen of the privy chamber, Thomas Wroth and my son-in-law Henry Sidney, to stay upright. His feet, which I glimpsed as I knelt, were swollen to twice their normal size. "Rise, my lady." He glanced at me as I desperately swiped at my cheek. "Don't cry."

"I am sorry, Your Majesty. I am trying hard not to. It is just—"

"I have come to terms with my fate," the king said. With a start, I realized Edward was not using the royal "we," a clear sign of the affection he bore my husband. "We all must die, and I sooner than later. That is why I have called you here. Some time ago, I drew up a devise for the succession, excluding my sisters. It is my understanding that the Duke of Northumberland told you of it, so there is no need to explain the particulars."

"Yes, Your Majesty."

"It will not work. There is no time to wait for the lady Jane to bear a child, and even if there was, there is no certainty that she will have a boy. The lady Katherine Grey is probably too young to conceive, as is the lady Mary Grey, and the lady Margaret Clifford is not even married yet. Therefore, I have made a change."

The king nodded to John, who led me to a table and indicated a parchment lying atop it. I can still see that bit of parchment in my mind today and marvel at how insignificant the change the king had made appeared on paper: the striking out of a letter and the insertion of two words that transformed "the lady Jane's heirs male" to "the lady Jane and her heirs male." It was such an unassuming-looking change that it only slowly dawned on me what the king had done. He had made my new daughter-in-law his successor. No Englishwoman had ever ruled in her own right: the one who had tried centuries before, the Empress Matilda, had unleashed years of civil war. And Matilda had been a mature woman: the lady Jane was a girl who had just turned sixteen and who had never been bred to rule.

Openmouthed, I turned to the king. "There is no other way," he said simply. "I love my sister Mary, but she will take the nation back to the Pope. And she is of questionable legitimacy, as is my sister Elizabeth. Besides, the lady Mary and I have been in dispute about the Mass. It is my fear that if she were to come to the throne, my friends would suffer for it, most particularly the Duke of Northumberland. That I would not have for the world."

"No, Your Majesty," I mumbled.

"As your lord husband and I have been discussing, tomorrow I shall call my justices before me and order them to put this in proper form. When that is done, I shall summon Parliament to ratify what has been written. All will be in order, provided that the Lord grants me sufficient time."

Looking at the king, I could think only that this proviso was far from certain.

There were a dozen questions running through my mind, but this brief conversation had clearly exhausted Edward, and it was apparent I would soon be dismissed. John could give me the answers to most of my questions, but there was one I had to ask the king himself. "I don't understand. Why did Your Majesty call me here?"

"So that if any man dare question what I have told you today, you will know the truth. Some will say that this devise is of your husband's procuring, to put Lord Guildford on the throne through the lady Jane. It was not. The idea was mine. I will fight for it with my dying breath."

He started coughing. A foul smell began to fill the chamber. "Go, please," Edward managed.

Followed by John, I backed out of the chamber hastily.

∽

"Does the lady Jane know of this? Do her parents?"

"Not yet. Once the judges get it ready, it will be more widely known."

"And the lady Mary? The lady Elizabeth?"

"They will know in due time."

"There are no plans to—" I could not finish my sentence.

"Harm them? Confine them? No. They shall be married to men we can trust. At least, that is what we are hoping for."

"What if they do not go along? What if the emperor comes to the lady Mary's aid and decides to restore her to the succession?"

"When has the emperor ever helped Mary?"

"When she tried to flee the country."

"Yes, and what did she do? Panicked, and lost her chance. She'll be happy as long as she has her Mass. If she has a husband and a Mass, all the better." John saw the skeptical expression on my face. "Mouse," he said gently, "you worry too much. The king has time. The physicians tell him so. Parliament will meet, and the king's devise will have the force of law. The lady Mary won't resist, particularly if a sweetener is thrown in. The same with the lady Elizabeth."

I shook my head. There seemed to be far too many "ifs" in this plan, conceived by a dying lad of sixteen. Nor did the prospect of the crown passing to my slip of a daughter-in-law, who had never been brought up to such a task, fill me with confidence. "But the lady Jane can't even properly run a household," I blurted. "Just in that brief time at Chelsea, Guildford said, she drove the servants mad, telling them one thing one moment and countermanding it an hour later. She's an intelligent girl, but she hasn't an ounce of common sense."

"She will learn it, as all rulers must. She will have councilors, remember." John took my hand. "The truth is, you don't like this idea. Neither do I. It goes against King Henry's wishes—more than that, it goes against the law, until Parliament ratifies it. But if I must choose between obeying a dead king and a living king, I must choose the living one."

"Even when what the living king wants is folly?"

"Is it folly to keep the lady Mary from turning the clock back? Is it folly to prevent bastards from ascending to the throne?"

"I suppose we shall find out," I said. I stared out the window toward the direction of Suffolk Place, where our unsuspecting daughter-in-law was no doubt settling down with a passage of Greek for the evening. "In the meantime, I shall redouble my prayers for the king."

28

Frances Grey
June 1553

"Y OU SHOULD SEE THE DUCHESS OF NORTHUMBERLAND LOOK AT HER HUS-band," Jane said on the last day of her visit to us at Suffolk Place. "I call it the Lord and Master look, as if the man was Richard I and Henry V put together. She worships him. It's sickening."

I tried to recall what I had said that had set Jane upon her favorite topic as of late: the various shortcomings of the Northumberland household. It probably didn't matter, as it took little to get her started.

"They had dancing the other night, and dancing makes some old war injury of his ache, so of course she doesn't dance either," Jane continued happily. "Instead, she just stands beside him, clutching his hand as if the two were courting instead of man and wife. I even saw them kissing that evening in a corner, like a couple of peasants at the fair. You'd never guess they were a duke and duchess, but of course they were never meant to be, were they? Thank goodness you and Father don't carry on in such an undignified manner."

Jane paused for breath, but only for a moment. Had losing her virginity made her so voluble, or was it the irresistible need to complain about her new relations? "They're all like that, too—all the Dudley children and their spouses. All giving each other the same adoring looks, all stopping by every other day to sup with the duke and the duchess when they could be at their own homes. Except for the Countess of Warwick, of course. She doesn't like them, either. She and I have become good friends."

"Do you like Guildford at all?" Kate asked. Hearing that Jane had come to stay with us while Guildford recovered from eating a bad salad, she had decided to visit, too.

"He's bearable," Jane said. "At least he treats me with respect. He brought me a book before he fell ill, which was a far sight better than that talking parrot the duke gave to the duchess as a gift before I joined the family. It squawked 'Sweet Jane' the other day, and I was mortified until I realized it was referring to the duchess. It pays her little compliments all day long—a tiny green courtier with feathers. But don't get me started on that parrot; I could go on forever."

Jane sighed as Kate and I walked her to her waiting barge and waved farewell to her. Not an hour had passed when a servant arrived, wearing the royal livery. "Your Grace, the king has asked that you come to see him immediately. My lord Suffolk is with His Majesty and adds his request to the king's."

What on earth could the king want with me? I rose. "I will be ready straightaway."

❧

Not only my husband stood beside the king, but the Duke of Northumberland and his duchess. It was her presence that made me realize something truly extraordinary was going on.

I listened as the king explained with a heartbreaking calmness that he was dying, a statement corroborated by his frail appearance. I listened as he told me what everyone now knows, of his decision to disinherit his sisters. Then he told me my girl was to be the reigning queen of England.

Harry looked at me proudly as I heard the words that made my knees begin to shake under my gown. I barely knew the lady Elizabeth, many years my junior, but I had known the lady Mary almost since we were both infants. And now my daughter was to supplant her! "She cannot be queen, Your Majesty," I said. "Not a reigning queen. She knows nothing of how to rule a kingdom."

"Our grandfather Henry VII was not brought up to rule, either," Edward said. "He gained his throne only because of the cruel murder of the young Edward V by Richard III, and yet he left England healthy and prosperous. Our own father was a second son, yet he made all of England quake before him."

"But they were men."

"The king is aware of that, my dear," Harry put in.

"I beg Your Majesty's pardon," I said. "I am simply stunned by this. I have never looked to see my daughter rule."

"It does your ladyship honor that you are humble enough to question your daughter's ability to rule England," said Edward tiredly. "But she will have men to guide her, wise men like her father and the Duke of Northumberland."

I looked at the Duke and Duchess of Northumberland, who stood by the king with their heads bowed respectfully. How far had they influenced what the king was saying now?

Edward continued, "Her sex hinders her no more than would that of the lady Mary, and she is of a godly persuasion, unlike our sister Mary. It is our wish that this be carried out, and the process has started already. The justices are drawing up the necessary documents for signature."

"And my daughter knows nothing of this?"

"Not yet. It is our wish that she not be told until we are satisfied that everything is in place. We would not distress her until her smooth accession is assured."

If my daughter could rule the kingdom, could not she be taxed with the responsibility of knowing about it beforehand? But I said nothing. Instead, I knelt and kissed Edward's hand. Like the rest of his extremities, it was pale and swollen. "Your Majesty does us incomparable honor."

"Our cousin is a learned and wise young woman," Edward said sadly. "She will carry out our legacy and strengthen our religion. We know it."

I took my leave of the king soon afterward, my mind so abuzz with the news I had just been told that, at first, I did not see the crone making her way to the chamber I was leaving. She saw me, though, and kicked a quick curtsey in acknowledgment of my rank. It was then I realized what an unlikely figure she was at Greenwich Palace. She looked as if she ought to be selling charms or potions in Southwark. "Who are you?"

"Madge they call me, my lady—Your Grace," the crone corrected herself, nodding to herself in approval at guessing my rank. "I've come to dose the king."

"On whose orders?"

"On the Duke of Northumberland's orders, Your Grace. I come here every day. Reckon I've been doing it for a week or so."

"What are you giving him?"

"Healing potions, Your Grace, of my own recipe. Mind you, the physicians don't set much store by them. But the great folk, when they give up on the physicians, they call Madge, and then when my work does the trick, they praise God and slip me my fee on the sly. That's the way it's been, and that's the way it'll always be. I don't care. I'm never slack of work." The crone smiled, showing a handsome set of teeth.

"Are your potions helping him?"

"Not hurting him, at least," Madge admitted. "'Tis too soon to tell. Sometimes it's too late for even me. I won't lie to you. That's not how I work. I will tell you this—if I can't bring him through, there's no one who can."

29

Jane Dudley
June 1553 to July 9, 1553

OVER THE NEXT FEW DAYS, LIFE WENT ON AS USUAL IN MY HOUSEHOLD, AS I obeyed the king's wish and did not tell the lady Jane of the king's plans. It was not a difficult matter keeping the secret from Jane, for knowing she was to be queen would surely puff up the girl more than ever. It was Guildford I longed to tell.

It could not be kept a secret for long, I foresaw. The justices had protested when the king had ordered them to give proper legal form to his devise. So sharp had their opposition been that John, straining under the impossible role in which he had been placed, had thrown off his doublet in front of the entire council and threatened to fight in his shirt any man who dared to defy the king. Calming himself, he had instead gone and spoken to the king, who summoned the recalcitrant justices to his side the next day. Then Edward himself had demanded, in a fury that had left him prostrate afterward, that the justices and the council carry out his wishes. Nearly all of the justices and the councilors had then engaged themselves, in writing, to carry out the king's wishes.

Several days later, the justices produced the document, bearing the king's great seal, which made Lady Jane Grey the heir to the throne. A hundred and two men signed it—the Archbishop of Canterbury, the Bishop of Ely, dukes, earls, viscounts, barons, knights, lawyers, the Lord Mayor and aldermen of London.

They signed the document, and when it suited their convenience, most of the cowards forswore it.

⋄⋄⋄

The council had summoned Parliament to meet in September—the quickest this could be done, as elections would have to be held—but few believed the king would live to see it. By the latter part of June, he spent most of his time flat on his back, gasping for breath. John had even brought in a wise woman to save the king, with his permission, but she seemed only to make him worse, and was soon dismissed.

That same day, John's man came from Greenwich. "Your Grace, my lord has charged me with a message. It is time to tell the lady Jane."

I thanked him and summoned my daughter-in-law and Guildford to me. Guildford was out riding, but Jane came almost instantly—to my surprise, it being her usual policy to dawdle when I asked for her. "Your Grace, I was just going to come to you. I would like a few days to visit my mother."

"I am afraid it cannot be."

"Why on earth not? You promised that I could see her as often as I wished."

I swallowed. "You are aware that the king is very ill."

"Yes. They say he is dying. Has the lady Mary been summoned?"

"No. She has not been. She is not his heir."

"Not his heir?" Jane stared at me. "Who on earth is, then?"

"You are. He has decreed that you will rule after his death."

"He has disinherited his sisters? Both his sisters? Who told you this?"

"The king himself, and my husband."

"I don't believe you."

I was beginning to wonder whether this girl was as intelligent as she was made out to be. "Why would I lie about such a serious matter, when I could so easily be proven wrong? I heard him tell your mother the same thing. Go to her if you wish. She will confirm it for you."

"Then I will." Jane turned around with a great swishing of skirts.

"But hurry back," I called. "If—when the worst happens—you must be on hand to proceed to the Tower."

A little while later, Guildford sought me out. "Mother? Where did my bride run off to in such a hurry? Or dare I ask?"

"Guildford, I have news for you."

"She's asked for an annulment?"

"No. This is not in jest, my son. The king has made your wife his heir. She will rule England when the king departs this life, which I fear will be soon."

"You mean it is true what I have heard, that the lady Mary will not be allowed to succeed to the throne?"

"Yes. What else have you heard?"

"Not much. Some say that the lady Elizabeth will be chosen; others are saying the little Queen of Scots. Some are saying that Father will marry the lady

Elizabeth and take the throne himself. I laid out the whoreson whom I heard saying that, actually. But this is the first I've heard that my wife is to be queen." Guildford blinked. "What will that make me? *King?*"

"I believe Parliament will have to decide it. And, of course, the queen," I added dutifully.

"But you think I'd make a good king, don't you, Mother?"

"You have not been brought up to it any more than she has," I reminded my son. "We must see what happens, Guildford. There is no precedent in England for this sort of thing. It may be that you are made a duke. Or that you are known as king consort. First, you must talk to your wife."

Guildford, who apparently was already planning his coronation, scowled at the thought.

∽

Several days passed, and my daughter-in-law had not returned from Suffolk Place, even as news came from Greenwich that the poor king was much worse. I sent a messenger to Jane and received a grand reply from the Duchess of Suffolk: the lady Jane was gathering strength to assume her new duties and preferred to remain at Suffolk Place.

This would not do. Jane might be Edward's heir, but she was also a bride, with a husband she seemed to have forgotten about entirely. What sort of behavior was this for a future queen? I sent an equally grand reply back to Jane and her mother. After both of us mothers had acted up to our rank as duchesses (it was difficult to believe we'd held the titles for less than two years, I thought proudly), we at last reached a compromise: Jane, who did seem to be suffering from the strain of her impending role, would go to our house at Chelsea, where Guildford would join her.

Instead, Guildford was still with us on the morning of July 7, when Henry Sidney arrived with the dawn. He did not even stop to embrace his wife, whom he had not seen in weeks. "The king is dead."

Instinctively, I started to cross myself, but stopped just in time.

"He died between eight and nine last evening, in my presence," said Henry, wiping a tear from his eye. "Sir Thomas Wroth, his groom Christopher Salmon, and his physicians, Dr. Owen and Dr. Wendy, were there, as well. The king said a prayer of his own composition, then let me take him into my arms. He said that he was faint. Then he said only, 'Lord have mercy upon me, and take my spirit.' And the Lord did."

We stayed silent for several moments in memory of the poor king, whom I prayed was now at last in the company of his gentle mother. Perhaps, I thought optimistically, he would even find comfort in his uncles Thomas and Edward. Then Guildford broke the quiet. "Should we tell Jane—er, the queen?"

"Not yet. The duke has expressly requested that the king's death be kept a secret for a day or so, as was King Henry's death. Everyone is to stay where he or she is for now. The lord Robert has been sent to bring the lady Mary to London."

"To imprison her?"

"No. To explain to her why this must be, the duke says, and to explain the financial arrangements that have been made. She will be treated generously if she cooperates."

Almost, I thought, as if she had been one of King Henry's cast-off wives.

⁓

Over the next couple of days, we at Sion House received encouraging reports from John and the others at Greenwich. Only one unsettling piece of news arrived: Mary had abruptly left her residence at Hunsdon to head toward the coast of Norfolk, evading my son Robert. Was this journey coincidence, or had someone been giving her information? If it was the latter, was she once more planning to escape abroad? While we waited to hear more of Mary's moves, there was little for us at Sion to do but to plan Jane's coronation—and Guildford's, for it seemed eminently reasonable he be crowned as her consort (at the very least). We were in the process of listing those we thought should be appointed to Jane's household (scrupulously, we made certain all of her own relations were duly represented) when late on July 9, John ordered that Jane be brought from Chelsea to Sion.

"I'll fetch her," offered Mary. She winked at her brother. "King Guildford would probably scare her off if he went in person."

Guildford gave a regal scowl.

Presently, Mary returned, escorting Jane into the room where John conducted business, and a short time later I saw John, the Duke of Suffolk, the Marquis of Northampton, the Earl of Arundel, the Earl of Huntingdon, and the Earl of Pembroke arrive. Guildford went to meet them. My friend the Marchioness of Northampton had been deputed by the council to bring the Duchess of Suffolk to Sion, and they arrived just as John's man came to my chamber. "The men want the ladies to join them," he said succinctly.

We charged—"hastened" would give the mistaken idea we were delicate about it—into John's chamber. There Jane stood, surrounded by a group of kneeling men. "Mother!" she cried, turning so sharply poor Northampton was assailed by her skirts. "They are telling me that the king is dead! Is it true?"

"It is true," Frances said gently. "The king has gone to God."

"Well, of course it is true," I put in irritably. "Why would all these men be kneeling before you if it were not?"

Jane recovered to give me an icy stare, and I realized my place. "Your Majesty," I said, and knelt so low to the ground that every bone in my being protested.

John craved Jane's permission to allow the company to rise. She gave it in a distracted manner, and John, reading from a long sheet of parchment, outlined what all of us knew already: the king had disinherited his sisters in favor of Jane. Once again, we all knelt, the men promising to defend Jane's right to the throne with their very blood.

Jane stared down at us. Then she sank to the ground and began weeping, but only as long as was proper. After she prayed in silence, she accepted Guildford's proffered hand and rose to her feet. "I have not sought this crown, which is too great a weight for a person as insignificant as myself. But if it is rightly and lawfully mine, I beseech His Divine Majesty to grant me such grace and spirit that I may govern to his glory and service, and to the advantage of the realm."

"Long live the queen!" we shouted.

✍

After Jane accepted the crown, there was an interminable banquet that was far more memorable for its awkwardness than for the quality of the fare. The queen alternated between looking confused when the other guests did her honor and looking annoyed when they did not. No one seemed quite to know what to do with Guildford, the new royal consort, who finally ended up sitting at a table with his brothers, all of whom I suspected were drinking too much wine. John and the Duke of Suffolk sat with the rest of the royal councilors, most of whom had a dazed look on their faces. Only the Marchioness of Northampton appeared entirely happy. "Who would have thought my matchmaking would be for a queen?" she asked rhetorically.

When the banquet had at last ended, John followed me to my chamber. "Well, we've carried out the king's will. I hope we've done the right thing. I realized at the banquet tonight that I really know very little of Lady Jane—I mean, Queen Jane. Oh, she's learned, all right, but is England safe in her hands?"

"The king thought it would be."

"Yes. I hope he's right. I wish he'd been given more time, so that Parliament could have given its approval of these arrangements." Tears came to his eyes. "I still can't entirely believe he's dead. I was fond of the lad. I kept hoping for a miracle."

"I am sure it will all be well."

"I hope so. I keep picturing King Henry glowering down at us from heaven, asking what we were doing listening to a mere boy." John sighed and kissed me good night. "With that image in mind, I believe I'll keep to my own chamber tonight."

30

Frances Grey
July 10, 1553, to July 12, 1553

THE DAY AFTER ACCEPTING THE CROWN, MY DAUGHTER HELD HER FIRST council meeting, and asked me to join her. The Duchess of Northumberland was in the same room at the time, and naturally took this as an invitation to her own self, as well.

The meeting had just started when an elderly man, his quick breathing indicating he had been riding hard, entered the room. I recognized him from my visits to Mary as Thomas Hungate, one of her servants. Hungate did not kneel when he saw Jane, but handed Northumberland a letter. "From the lady Mary, who is at Kenninghall."

The council appeared to have quite forgotten about Mary. Northumberland gave Hungate a killing frown, but broke the seal. "This is the main point of it," he announced after scanning it. "'Wherefore, my lords, we require you and charge you, for that our allegiance which you owe to God and us, that, for your honor and the surety of your persons, you employ yourselves and forthwith upon receipt hereof cause our right and title to the Crown and government of this realm to be proclaimed in our City of London and such other places as to your wisdoms shall seem good and as to this case appertaineth, not failing thereof, as our very trust is in you.'"

"Good Lord," murmured the Duchess of Northumberland. "She intends to fight for the crown."

Northumberland tossed the letter aside and fixed his eyes upon Hungate. "We, as Queen Jane's loyal councilors, will compose an answer, but you will not deliver it, my lord. It was unwise for you to throw yourself away upon this embassy. For your impertinence, the council must lodge you at the Tower until your mistress is in safe custody."

"Aye, lodge me there if you will, Your Grace, but it will not stop my mistress. The crown is rightly hers as King Henry's eldest daughter, and the people know it. They will fight to defend my good and gracious lady."

Northumberland beckoned to the men standing guard by the council door. "Take him away to the Tower," he commanded.

"No matter, Your Grace. I shall see you and your fellows there soon enough when my lady is in her rightful place. Mark me well." He turned to his guards. "You have your orders. Take me to the Tower, where I shall await the lady Mary's coming in majesty."

He strode out, practically dragging the guards, who were backing out of Jane's presence as her rank demanded, in his wake. The Duchess of Northumberland stared at their departing figures and suddenly began to cry.

So did I. The man had sounded so unnervingly sure of himself...

"I think, Your Majesty, that it was a mistake to have the duchesses at the council meeting," Harry said. He rose and offered each of us a hand. "They take these idle threats too much in earnest. Come, ladies. I believe the queen will excuse you."

In the oversized chair that was serving as a makeshift throne, Jane nodded. "You are excused."

✏

Despite the disquiet occasioned by Mary's letter, servants had scurried about all morning, making the Tower ready for my daughter's arrival. At two that afternoon, the royal barge—fitted out nearly as magnificently as it had been in my uncle Henry's time—docked at the royal stairs at the Tower.

Nothing Jane owned was splendid enough for the occasion, so some of Catherine Parr's robes, long in storage, had been brought out for Jane and hastily altered to better fit her youthful figure. I bore my daughter's lengthy train as we processed toward the Lion Gate, a clutch of spectators standing by. Harry, Northumberland, and the other councilors had gone to the Tower earlier that day and awaited Jane at the gate, on their knees.

A boom, made even more startling by the silence of the spectators, caused me to almost drop the train I was carrying. "Just a salute from the guns, Mother," whispered Kate, walking close by. "Don't be frightened."

Yet I should have been; it was the last time my girl would ever walk beyond the walls of the Tower as a free woman.

✏

That afternoon, Jane, pen in hand, sat at a desk in the Tower's royal lodgings. Unused since King Edward had been crowned six years before, they had been hastily put in order but still looked slightly seedy. Beside her was a stack of letters ordering officials of each of England's counties to resist the usurper, Mary. Each letter bore the signature "Jane the Quene" in upright letters with an exuberant tail to the "Q."

As Jane added yet another letter to the pile and started on the next, the Marquis of Winchester, William Paulet, entered the room. With him was a procession of servants bearing velvet-covered caskets. "The royal jewels, Your Majesty," Winchester said to Jane. "There are more elsewhere, but these are what came immediately to hand."

Jane might be a queen, but she was girl enough to squeal at the jewels that were handed to her, one by one, for her inspection. There was a muffler of black velvet, hung with chains of gold and garnished with pearls, rubies, and diamonds. There was a clock engraved with a crowned rose and the motto *Dieu et mon droit*. There was a brooch, showing a lady coming out of a cloud. There was a gold toothpick shaped like a fish.

And there was the small crown, with ten large pearls, surrounded by pointed diamonds, set on points of gold. It was covered with rubies, diamonds, and emeralds, so many I lost count, and an enormous sapphire. "Having been a child yourself at the time, Your Majesty may not recall that three crowns were used during King Edward's coronation—the crown of Edward the Confessor, the imperial crown, and a crown made personally for the king," Winchester said. "This is the latter crown. As it was made to suit the king when he was a lad, it is more comfortable than the others. Would Your Majesty like to see if it suits you?"

Jane shrank back, no doubt thinking, like me, that the crown of a king who died at age sixteen could only be unlucky. "No. It was made for a child. We should prefer our own crown."

"So it shall be. I shall order that one be made." Jane nodded her approval, and the marquis hesitated. "Does Your Majesty wish that one should be made for Your Majesty's husband, as well?"

The Duchess of Northumberland, who had been seemingly lost in admiration of the clock, turned around sharply.

"We have not decided on this matter," Jane said.

"It is something that Your Majesty ought to decide," said the Duchess of Northumberland.

"So we shall," Jane said. "Send our husband to us."

I heard no more about the matter of Guildford's crown until the next afternoon when the Duchess of Northumberland stomped into my daughter's presence chamber, her small figure trembling with rage. Remembering just in time to kneel to my daughter, she sprang up when ordered. "What is the meaning of this, Your Majesty?"

"You must explain yourself."

"I should hardly think an explanation is warranted. My son tells me that Your Majesty and he agreed that he should be made king, provided that Parliament consented. And then, barely a half hour after he left your presence, you sent the Earls of Arundel and Pembroke to him with the message that Your Majesty would make him a duke, but never king. That is outrageous! You cannot tell my son one thing at one hour, and then another at the other."

"How dare you tell us what we can or cannot do?"

"It is Your Majesty's duty as a wife to honor and respect her husband, queen or no queen! It is but right that he be crowned, at least as Your Majesty's consort."

Guildford Dudley hastened in, followed by his brother Hal Dudley and by his feeble-minded uncle Jerome, a harmless sort who was more or less treated as the Dudleys' pet. I had heard various members of the family explain Guildford's new status to him, but none seemed to have succeeded in making him grasp it. "Mother!" Guildford protested. "You promised that you would not interfere."

"How can I stop myself from interfering when you have been treated so shabbily by this girl?"

I stepped forward. "How dare you speak of your queen so?"

"I dare because she is ungrateful and unnatural! My husband is working day and night to carry out the king's devise, and she is barely civil to him—much less my son. It is perfectly reasonable that he be king. Instead, she tries to fob him off with a mere dukedom. Duke of Clarence, indeed!"

"Drowned in a barrel of malmsey," offered Jerome, clearly proud of having acquired this piece of historical knowledge. Everyone turned to glare at him, so, thoroughly abashed, he scurried away.

"Hal, go after your uncle and tell him that no one is angry with him," the Duchess of Northumberland said tiredly.

"Your son will be lucky to get a dukedom, if you continue to speak to the queen in this insolent manner," I said.

"Indeed? Well, I tell you this, madam, my son and I are going back to Sion. If you wish to conceive an heir, *Queen* Jane, you will have to do so by immaculate conception. Until you treat him more equitably, he will not be sleeping with you. Come along, Guildford." She tugged at his arm, though Guildford was easily a foot taller than she. "Come!"

"You cannot leave our presence like this," Jane said.

"We can, and we will. Come along!"

Guildford reluctantly obeyed.

"You can't let him go to Sion, whatever that insolent little woman says," I said. "There will be scandal."

"I will send the Earls of Arundel and Pembroke after him," Jane said. "Now leave me."

"Jane——"

"Leave us, we said!"

Meekly, I backed out of the chamber.

It was not the Earls of Arundel and Pembroke who led a sheepish-looking Guildford Dudley back to Jane's chamber later that evening, but Harry. "A little row this afternoon, I hear," he commented when he came to my own chamber in the Tower later that evening.

"To put it mildly. That Dudley woman must be put in her place. And that son of hers, always harping on being made king!"

"He's not a bad sort."

I turned to stare at him. "You are standing up for him?"

"Yes. Jane can be a tall order for a boy, my dear, especially one who's not used to the ways of women, as I wager young Guildford is not. So this evening, I have played peacemaker. Someone had to, I must say."

"You have not persuaded her to make him king."

"No. I persuaded them to consummate their marriage. That's right, my dear, consummate it."

"But they have been sleeping together!"

"Yes, and that's all they've been doing—lying side by side. At least King Henry got as far as kissing Anne of Cleves; these two haven't done even that." Harry snorted. "It's our Jane who has been stalling, I fear. Guildford's been too ashamed to mention it to his own family—considering the way his mother acted today, I can see why—and he didn't want to force her. So that was step one: making Jane understand that she had to act as a proper wife to him. Step two was making Guildford understand that he has to stop nagging Jane about being king. He's not even of royal blood, and the people have to accept Jane on the throne before they accept him as king. A dukedom's a sensible start, and she's agreed to let him dine at a separate table, to assuage his pride. He's a reasonable enough lad when handled well." Harry rose. "The Duchess of Northumberland and you I shall leave to your own devices, my dear. One man can't work miracles."

I frowned as Harry suddenly grabbed his side. "Harry, you look ill."

"I do believe I am, my dear. The stone is part of it, I think. I had a fainting fit the other day, as a matter of fact. I didn't want to concern Jane with it."

"You must go to Suffolk Place and rest."

"Maybe after a day or so. First, let us get through this night. If Jane reneges on her promise to Guildford, it's going to be a long one."

∽

The next day, Guildford did appear more at ease, being served at a separate table and being addressed as "Your Grace." Jane herself seemed less skittish than she had been since her marriage, and even bestowed a royal smile upon Guildford's uncle Jerome when he timidly presented her with a red rose from the Tower garden. The Duchess of Northumberland and I managed to sit side by side without incident.

Jane and Guildford's marital relations, however, were not the chief concern at the Tower on July 12: the council was preoccupied with choosing a commander to lead the forces against Mary. They chose Harry.

"I don't like Father being chosen for this," Jane said later that afternoon when only the two of us were present, Jane having waved off her attendants. "He's been looking ill, don't you think?"

"He complained of feeling poorly only last night."

"And he has so little experience in these matters."

"That is true."

"And I would be left here with the Duke of Northumberland. I don't trust him, Mother, or his odious wife." She pointed to her hair. "Look. It's falling out in clumps."

I pulled gently on an auburn lock. Sure enough, a few strands of hair did come out in my hand.

"It's even worse when Mistress Ellen brushes it at night." Jane lowered her voice. "Nothing was wrong with my hair until I came here. I think Northumberland is trying to poison me. Or perhaps his duchess is."

There could be other reasons Jane's hair was falling out, I knew. Still, I thought of Mary telling me years before that she did not trust Northumberland. How far had King Edward been influenced by the duke in changing the succession? And what of the old woman I had seen in the dying king's chambers? Northumberland, the son of a traitor, was an ambitious man. He had successfully brought down Somerset. Might he have hastened the death of the king? Especially since the talk about Guildford becoming king had begun, it was a thought I could not repress, no matter how respectfully Northumberland treated my daughter and no matter how adoringly his duchess gazed upon him. "Now that you are queen, you should have someone taste your food for you. Everything. If Northumberland is doing you no harm, he will see no harm in it."

Jane nodded.

"But if you don't want your father to leave you—and I would feel better myself if he did not—you need to tell the council. You need not voice your suspicions about Northumberland or your worries about your father's military experience. Simply demand that he stay here with you because of his health."

"Then I will," Jane said. "Tonight." She hesitated. "Last night, I consummated my marriage. I had been putting it off."

"So I heard."

"Will I know soon whether I am with child?"

I smiled to think how little my brilliant daughter knew of such ordinary matters. Some things could not be found in books. "Probably not until you miss a monthly course, perhaps even two. Of course, you cannot pin your hopes on just one encounter. You must keep lying with him."

"Well, I know that much," Jane said huffily. "It wasn't so horrid, really. At least he didn't ask me afterward if he could be king." She hesitated again. "It's good to have you here with me, Mother. Will you stay with me at court?"

"Indeed I will, until you no longer think you need me here."

For once in her life, my daughter looked entirely humble. "I don't think that will ever happen."

31

Jane Dudley
July 12, 1553, to July 19, 1553

I PASS OVER THE DREADFUL SCENE FOLLOWING MY DAUGHTER-IN-LAW'S refusal to give Guildford the crown matrimonial. It makes so little difference now—and besides, it was not one of my finer moments.

The arrogant child who had become our queen, however, was to score another victory the following evening when she summoned the council before her and told them her own father could by no means lead the troops against Mary. He was too ill, she said, and besides, she would be lost without him. When tears welled up in her soft brown eyes, the councilors lost all will. Someone else, they agreed, would have to lead the army—and what man would be better for it than the man who had broken Kett's rebellion, my own dear husband?

As the man who had done more than anyone to fulfill King Edward's dying wish, John could hardly refuse to lead the army. "Though I would like to," he said when he brought the news. "I worry about the loyalty of some of the men here. Arundel in particular." Imprisoned when Somerset fell, he had spent a year in the Tower. Recently, he had been released and had had his fines canceled and his place on the king's council restored—generous treatment for someone who had been plotting at the very least to arrest my husband.

"Perhaps you should take him with you."

"I considered it, but there will be enough commanders going with me, and it would look as if I didn't trust him—which, of course, I don't, but it can't look as if I don't. But perhaps my suspicions are for naught. He is, after all, a close relation of the queen." John shrugged. "This shouldn't take too long, in any case. We're well prepared."

"I will be glad when you return, so we can get the queen crowned and we can leave the Tower," I confessed. "I am a little too close to the queen here for my comfort."

"Yes, I heard about that set-to the other day." I hung my head, and John grinned. "What a shrew I married. But really, you served Katherine Howard, the silliest queen in Christendom. Jane can't be much worse."

"Katherine Howard was irresponsible, but sweet natured and pleasant. And I was much more patient then, too," I admitted. "Probably because I was younger."

"Oh? I haven't noticed such a change." John drew me close to him and ran his hands along my form. "I shall miss you, my love."

A knock sounded. "Your Grace? The queen is asking for you."

"And that," I said, "is just another reason why I will be glad to leave the Tower."

The next day, July 13, John left the Tower for Durham House, where he was to muster his troops and set out the following morning. With him would be going our sons Jack, Ambrose, and Hal, as well as our daughters' husbands, Henry Sidney and Lord Hastings. Andrew, John's brother, and Francis Jobson, his half sister's husband, were also accompanying John.

John knelt before Queen Jane, sitting in her chair of state. The night before, having heard of his agreement to take her father's place at the head of her army, she had thanked him, sounding almost human in her gratitude. "We wish you Godspeed," she said now as John kissed her outstretched hand. "You will keep us apprised of the pretend queen's movements?"

"I shall, Your Majesty," said John, rising in response to Jane's gesture.

"Our trust is in you."

"And in Your Majesty's council." In a low voice, John said, "Your Majesty, do be alert for treachery. I accuse no man, but these are volatile times."

"We will be, my lord."

With a final bow, John backed out of the queen's chamber and walked through the council chamber as I and my daughters followed, wanting to be the last to see him off. The Earl of Arundel stopped his path. "I wish to say, Your Grace, that although we have had our differences in the past, I pray that God be with you," the earl said, pressing John's hand. "You may rest assured that I will spend my blood at your feet if the occasion warrants it."

"I pray it may not come to that," John said, obviously moved. "But I am grateful to hear this."

Arundel looked down paternally at John's page, Thomas Lovell, off for his first taste of battle, which I prayed would be slight. "Farewell, gentle Thomas, with all my heart," he said, and ruffled the boy's hair.

At last, I stood by the Tower landing with my daughters and my daughters-in-law as John prepared to step into the barge that would take him to Durham Place. He did not like long, undignified farewells in public, and in any case, we had given each other such a farewell in the privacy of my bedchamber the evening before, with the additional merit of it being pleasurable. So I settled for a kiss and a quick embrace, and my companions with me followed suit. "Do take care of yourself, my love," I said as we pulled apart. "The Dudley women will not rest easy until you return," I added lightly.

John smiled, then surprised me by sneaking a kiss just before he got on the barge. We stood there waving a few minutes more. Then John turned his attention to his companions, and we women filed back into the Tower. Back to the councilors waiting there, their false smiles still on their Judas faces.

❧

I need not dwell at length on those next six days in the Tower. What is to tell? The council sent out proclamations urging various men to support Jane, who nodded approvingly at the denunciation of her opponents they contained and signed them in a firm, bold hand her great-uncle King Henry might well have appreciated. The Duchess of Suffolk and I sewed shirts for the poor and kept a silent count of the occasions when either Guildford or Jane slighted or irritated the other. Bad news of various defections to Mary trickled in, but there was nothing that made me lose heart entirely. John's victory would not be as easy as we had hoped, but I had confidence there would be a victory.

Then, on July 19, Guildford came in, ashen. "The council's taken off. I wasn't asked to come along. Neither was the Duke of Suffolk."

"Where have they gone? What are they doing?"

"I don't know."

A bell started pealing insistently. Some sort of news was to be proclaimed. Had John won a victory?

Without speaking further, Guildford and I hurried through the Tower gates and to Tower Hill, where a crowd had already assembled. There, I saw with relief, was the Duke of Suffolk, mounted on a horse. We pushed closer to him but could make no progress through the mob, which had started to light bonfires in its midst. Wine, ale, and beer were being passed around freely—too freely, really. John, a temperate man, would disapprove.

Then came the cries, faint at first but growing louder as the speakers approached. "Long live Queen Mary!"

"Good Queen Mary, daughter of our King Henry!"

"Long may she reign!"

Someone shoved a bottle in my face. Unthinkingly, I took a deep draught. "Mary?" I said, passing it back to the anonymous donor.

"Aye, Mary! Take another sip, dearie, you look as if you could use it. Haven't you heard? The Earl of Arundel and the Earl of Pembroke proclaimed her queen at Cheapside just a little while ago, and they're still cheering over there, I wager. It's all up with that little slip of a girl they called Jane, poor lass. Not to mention those who put her on the throne. Whoa! Save some for the rest of us, dearie. It's going to be a long night."

A trumpet blasted. "Good people," called the Duke of Suffolk in an unexpectedly eloquent voice. "Silence!" The crowd instantly grew quiet.

"Whereas it hath pleased Almighty God to call to his mercy our late sovereign lord King Edward VI of blessed and glorious memory," the duke began, "I, Henry, Duke of Suffolk, do now hereby publish and proclaim that the high and mighty Lady Mary, daughter of King Henry VIII, is now by the death of our late sovereign of happy and glorious memory become our only lawful and rightful liege, Mary, queen by the grace of God of England, France, and Ireland. God save the queen!"

"God save the queen!"

"And the devil take the Duke of Northumberland!"

Guildford muttered a curse that fortunately went unheard by the boisterous crowd. My very ordinary face was of the type that allowed me to blend in to my surroundings, but my attire was another matter altogether. Guildford, tall, handsome, and richly dressed, was even less inconspicuous. If he was recognized as a Dudley... "We must get out of here," I hissed.

"What do you think is going to happen to Northumberland?" a man nearby asked his companion as the Duke of Suffolk tried to silence the crowd again for the singing of *Te Deum*.

"It won't be pretty, if Queen Mary's made up of the stuff of her father." The second man chuckled. "Beheading if he's lucky. Hanging, drawing, and quartering if we're lucky."

Guildford's hand went to the sword he wore at his side. I grabbed his hand. "Take me back. Now."

A head turned and stared. "Why, it's—"

I plunged into the crowd, hoping Guildford had sense enough to follow. Fortunately, he did. I felt my jeweled headdress go awry as we pushed against the movement of the crowd, then fall off my head altogether, but I could not bend to retrieve it even if I had dared. At last we were safely inside the Tower gates. Gasping, we made our way to the hall where Jane sat dining under her canopy of estate. The meal had just begun. "You are late," Jane said, frowning. "And why do you not kneel to us? What disrespect is this?" She looked more closely at our disheveled appearances. "What is this?"

I said nothing, but shook my head and sank onto the nearest bench. Guildford began, "Jane—"

The Duke of Suffolk stumbled in, head lowered and tears streaming down his face. Jane rose. Her voice climbed to a childish squeak. "Father?"

"This morning, after the council conducted its business here, most of the members left the Tower on the pretense of consulting with the French ambassador," Suffolk said slowly, as if he were reading instead of speaking. "Instead, they met at Baynard's Castle, Pembroke's home, and agreed to proclaim the lady Mary queen. They asked the Lord Mayor and the aldermen to join them, and they did. Then they all rode to the cross at Cheapside to proclaim her. I was not there, but they say the crowd went wild with joy and are still celebrating." Suffolk bowed his head even farther; I could hardly hear him speak. "The council sent a deputation to me, and I have proclaimed the lady Mary as queen just now on Tower Hill. I am sorry, my child. I could not stand against them all. I am but one man."

He reached up and began tearing down the canopy of state under which Jane was dining, sobbing as the fine cloth came tumbling to the ground. Jane watched openmouthed as the Duchess of Suffolk began to weep. "So we are—I am—no longer queen?"

"Yes, lass. It's all over." He swallowed. "The council has given orders. Your mother and I are to go to Suffolk Place and remain there until further notice—after I perform one duty. You are to stay in the Tower and await the pleasure of Queen Mary. None of us knows what that will be. The Earl of Arundel and my lord Paget are riding to Her Majesty at Framingham tonight."

"What of John?" I asked, breaking the silence that fell over the room. "What of my husband and his army? Has the council forgotten him?"

"No, they have not. As we speak, the council is preparing a letter for the Duke of Northumberland, who is said to be at Cambridge, informing him that he must disband his forces and instructing him to await the queen's orders. Signing it is the duty of which I spoke."

"We must warn John," I said, pulling myself to my feet. "Come, Guildford! We cannot just let him wait to be captured."

"My lady—"

I ignored Suffolk and ran out of the chamber, followed by Guildford. With the crowd still celebrating outside, leaving the Tower on foot or on horseback would be neither easy nor wise, but if I could go by water to one of our houses, I could take horse to Cambridge. It was a journey of over sixty miles, but I was a country girl by birth, who had learned to ride before I learned my letters, and I could cover that distance quickly if called upon. Or I could send one of our men ahead of me. Or—

"Your Grace, you cannot pass."

I blinked at the large guard who was blocking my path to the water gate. "What do you mean? Let me through!"

"I'm sorry, Your Grace. I can't. Orders of the council." Seeing my uncomprehending look, he added, "You are Queen Mary's prisoner now."

32

Frances Grey
July 19, 1553

Harry watched wearily as the Duchess of Northumberland and Guildford raced out of the hall where my daughter and I had been dining with her ladies. "She'll not get far," he said. "The guard has orders to take her into custody. Guildford, too."

"Why the Duchess of Northumberland?"

"She can be a hostage if the duke tries to flee the country or starts trouble down at Cambridge. I wouldn't give.two pence to be in his shoes at the moment. He's a dead man, if you ask me."

My food, served just moments before Harry had walked through the door, sat untouched in front of me. Now that the worst had happened, I found myself reacting with a strange numbness, almost as if I'd foreseen this happening all along. For horrid as this turn of events was, it was not entirely unexpected. The signs had been there: the coolness that had greeted Jane's proclamation, the sullen silence of the crowd who had watched Northumberland leave the city with his army. Above all, there had been two more things: the people hated Northumberland, and they had loved Mary's mother, Catherine of Aragon. No daughter of hers could ever be a bastard in their eyes.

How blind King Edward had been not to see that—but then again, he was a dying boy. Northumberland, nearly fifty, had no such excuse for not anticipating the people's reaction. It was he, I realized as my numbness began to give way to anger, who had brought this catastrophe upon England and upon our family. It was he, then, who should have to face the consequences. Not my daughter.

The door opened, and Lady Anne Throckmorton, who had been serving in Jane's stead as godmother at a christening near the Tower, started to kneel to Jane, then saw the cloth of estate lying waste on the floor. "Then it's true what I heard?"

"Yes," Jane said.

"Ah," said Lady Throckmorton, "a sudden change." She sat down and looked about. "Do you think they'll be bringing us anything more to eat?"

I pushed my plate toward her. "Here."

It soon became clear no more dinner courses were going to be brought to us that evening; the rhythms of royal life had ceased entirely. Even the musicians who normally played for us at dinner—most of them men who had served King Edward—were packing up their instruments and wandering off.

Then two men from the Tower garrison arrived and walked over to Harry. After conferring in low tones, they approached Jane. The shorter of the two cleared his throat and said, "My lady, the council has ordered that you be confined until further notice."

"Yes, that is what Father told me."

"You may take two ladies of your choosing with you, and three manservants will be appointed to wait on you." He looked around. "The other ladies are free to leave, but I would advise not doing so until the morning. The crowd is boisterous."

"I'll go with you, my lady," said Elizabeth Tilney, Jane's companion since childhood. Ursula Ellen, a widow who had served Jane for the past several years, echoed, "Please, my lady, allow me to serve you also."

"Then it is settled," Jane said. "Where do we stay?"

"The second floor of Master Partridge's house, my lady, overlooking the Green. It is comfortable and airy, and you will have ample space."

"Then let us go there now," Jane said. "I am tired."

Jane took leave of Harry, after which he disappeared from the room—going off, I suspected, to weep in private. I then took my daughter in my arms, "When I can, I will beg Queen Mary to show mercy to you," I said in a low voice. "She and I were friendly in the past, and I hope that I can appeal to that friendship. In the meantime, the best thing you can do is to write to her, explaining what has happened. Do not denigrate her religion, whatever you do. Write as her young and penitent cousin. And it would do no harm to let her know your fears about poisoning."

"But I have no proof."

"That should not stop you from telling the queen about your suspicions. Present them as such, and let her decide."

Jane nodded.

I was on the verge of breaking into tears. How could I leave my daughter a prisoner in the Tower? But I could do more for her outside the Tower than inside it, I knew. Besides, Mary would be merciful to her sixteen-year-old cousin. She knew where the blame should lie, and if perchance she did not, I would make sure she did.

33

Jane Dudley
July 19, 1553, to July 28, 1553

I AM NOT A GOOD PRISONER; I FOUND THAT OUT IN THE FEW DAYS I SPENT IN the Tower. I had been allowed to take all of the normal accoutrements of my life—my needlework, my prayer book, even a lute—with me, but all of these things sat unused in a corner, because I could not bend my mind to occupy myself with any mundane tasks. Instead, I paced up and down the room, then sat staring out of my window, and then when I tired of that, paced again.

Guildford was lodged in the Bell Tower; Jane, in the home of Nathaniel Partridge, one of the Tower jailers. I was in an almost identical house next to hers. My daughters and Jerome—all crying in terror, even Mary—had been taken to stay with Bridget, a widowed half sister of John.

My jailers had not been communicative at first, but an enameled ring had bought me the information that on July 20, John, hearing that the council had deserted Jane's cause—and him—had walked to the marketplace at Cambridge and proclaimed Mary queen, even smiling and tossing his cap in the air as the occasion required. Then the Earl of Arundel—the whoreson who had said a tearful good-bye to him a week before—had come on Queen Mary's orders to arrest him. My husband had fallen on his knees and begged Arundel to show him mercy, reminding him he had acted in everything with the consent of the council.

"My lord, you should have sought for mercy sooner," the earl had replied.

And now my husband was on his way to the Tower. He would get here before Queen Mary, I supposed; she was coming from Framingham, where she had mustered her troops. Mary was proceeding to London in majestic slowness, allowing people to flock from everywhere to join her entourage as it approached the capital. John, and the rest of us, would have to wait until she arrived to learn our fates.

There were two groups of prisoners at the Tower: the old ones and the new. Young Edward Courtenay, then only a lad of twelve, had been put here in 1538 by King Henry, who had been convinced at the time the boy's family was conspiring against him. Though no one had seen fit to let him out, his mother had been allowed to send in tutors for him, so he had grown into a well-educated young man, but one with no companions of his own age or degree. Recently he had found a new friend in Stephen Gardiner, the Bishop of Winchester, imprisoned in King Edward's time for his refusal to support the king's religious changes. With Mary's arrival impending, they were considered almost as good as free, so I often saw them walking around Tower Green, talking earnestly, their guards at a respectful distance. The Duchess of Somerset, of course, was still here, with her mother to keep her company. Her steward, Francis Newdigate, frequently stopped by, bringing her news of her children and, the guards joked, trying to fill the duke's shoes. Bringing up the quartet of important prisoners was Thomas Howard, the old Duke of Norfolk, who would have been executed had not King Henry died on the very day he was set to go to the scaffold. He was about eighty and was said to have survived this long purely out of spite. Norfolk, too, had been allowed great freedom after Mary's triumph and could often be seen sitting in the garden, smiling as if mentally counting all those he had outlived.

The rest of us—the new arrivals—had no such privileges, only our windows out of which to stare. I had not seen Guildford since he and I had been taken into custody, though I had spotted Lady Jane walking to her new lodgings under guard. Since then, I had watched as a servant of the Duchess of Suffolk bore a teetering stack of books to Partridge's lodgings. There was no doubt as to how the lady Jane was passing her time.

Around three o'clock on July 25—I had been allowed to keep the dial that hung from my girdle—I heard a rumbling sound mingled with shouts, too far away for me to understand what was being said. Then, as the sound grew louder, I made out the word "Traitor!"

I ran down the winding stairs as fast as I dared and banged on my jailor's door. He opened it with a sigh. "What is it?"

"The prisoners are coming? Is that what I hear outside?"

"Yes." The jailor sighed again. "Where they're going to put them all is anyone's guess."

"Will you let me talk to my husband? Just for a short while?"

"Your Grace—"

"For pity's sake! I do not know what will happen to either of us. It may be the last—" My voice choked. "I beg you, on your honor as a gentleman, just let me tell him that I love him. Everyone else has betrayed him."

"Very well. But don't think that means I'm going to let you out every time your heart desires."

"I won't ask again," I promised. "And I will stand right by you."

"Another thing. The crowd out there's been baying for the duke's blood. He might not be in good case when you see him."

I nodded and let him escort me outside, where the din from the crowd nearby had grown even louder. Finally, the Tower gate was flung open. Through the press of armed men remaining outside the gate rode the traitor: the Earl of Arundel, bringing in his captives.

Close behind him, mounted on his favorite horse, was John, cloakless and with his cap clutched in his hand. I clapped my hand to my mouth as I saw just how many prisoners there were and who they were—my sons Jack, Ambrose, and Hal; my brother-in-law Andrew; Kathryn's father-in-law, the Earl of Huntingdon; and her husband, Lord Hastings, to name only the ones most important to me. All were covered in filth, but none worse than John, who also bore a large, fresh bruise on his face.

While the prisoners waited silently on their horses and the cries outside grew faint and scattered, Arundel spoke at length to the constable, who gestured at various buildings. At last, John was allowed to dismount under the eye of two armed guards. He did so slowly, as if in pain. The Order of the Garter, which he had worn proudly beneath his knee for ten years, had been stripped from him.

Forgetting my promise to my jailer, I pushed my way toward John. Without a word, he took me in his arms as the guards, openmouthed, retreated. "Forgive me," he said as we huddled together. "I have cost us everything."

"There is nothing to forgive," I whispered. "Nothing."

Beside us, my youngest son, Hal, whose face was already wet with tears, began to weep afresh. "They've even got our mother," he said. "Our mother."

John stepped back. "It's true? You are a prisoner, too?"

"Yes, and Guildford and Jane."

Jack dismounted, trembling with anger. Never in my life had I seen him such. Shaking his fist, he leaned in Arundel's direction. "Why don't you go off and arrest my little sister Katheryn, you sorry turncoat, you Judas? Or are you afraid her kitten might scratch you?"

"Jack," said Ambrose, as a guard yanked Jack backward. "This isn't helping anything."

"I don't give a damn whether it helps anything or not! He gave his oath to Father, and what did he do? Ran to Mary—"

"Queen Mary," said Arundel.

"Ran to Mary and hid his head in her skirts and begged her forgiveness, then came to Cambridge—"

"Take them away," said Arundel. "The Earl of Warwick to the Beauchamp Tower, Lord Ambrose and Lord Henry to Coldharbour. The duke goes to the Garden Tower."

"You could lodge him with me," I suggested.

"No."

John squeezed my hand tenderly as the guards moved in to take him away. "For mercy's sake, my lord, can't you let my lady go free? None of this business was her idea."

"We'll see," Arundel said, looking at me but not into my eyes. He glanced at my own jailer, who had come to stand beside me. "In the meantime, my lady, I have no idea how you got here, but I will thank you to go back where you belong."

∽

Later, I heard four thousand men had been enlisted to keep order as John and the rest of the prisoners came to London, jeered at by the crowds who watched them pass and who pelted them with objects of various sorts all the way. Before entering London through Bishopsgate, Arundel, presumably not wanting the embarrassment of having his captive stoned to death, had ordered John to make himself less conspicuous by taking off his scarlet cloak, but that had not stopped the London mob from screaming vitriol at him, nor from waving the handkerchiefs stained with Somerset's blood that so many had treasured as relics.

The mob was more subdued the next day when a new group of prisoners arrived, among them my son Robert, the Marquis of Northampton, and the Bishop of London. Now all of my sons were in prison.

Their captivity meant that a couple of hours after Robert had disappeared into the Bell Tower with Guildford, a knock came on my own chamber door. "Your Grace, now that your husband and sons are safely in custody, the council has ordered that you be freed. The crown has taken possession of Sion and Durham House, but you may stay at Durham House until other arrangements have been made."

I did not much like the sound of that.

Attending me at the Tower were three ladies, a gentleman, and a groom. As the groom went to see to our horses and the others packed my belongings, I went outside and paced around, hoping to catch a glimpse of John or my sons at their windows before I left.

"It appears that your stay here has been a short one."

I turned to see the Duchess of Somerset. Now that I saw her face-to-face, I found her hair was graying in spots, and she had a line between her eyes that had not been there before, but she was otherwise dressed well, if plainly. She even carried a pair of gloves. "Yes," I said. "They are releasing me."

"Edward wanted to marry our son to that girl. It is providential for our family that he did not succeed."

"Yes."

"Being shut up for a week seems to have damaged your conversational powers. I daresay if you had been here as long as I have been, you would be completely dumb."

"I did try to influence John to release you, Anne. Your mother can attest to that."

"Yes, she has mentioned it. She was disappointed, but I was not. I expected nothing different from John Dudley after what he did to my husband."

"Anne, we have been through this! Your husband was not an innocent man."

"And yours is? Subverting King Henry's will to please the fancy of a sixteen-year-old boy is not guiltless behavior to me. But his judges will decide that. The biter may be bit."

The attendants emerged from my lodgings, my coffers of belongings in their hands. "I must leave now."

"Don't let me detain you, then." Anne Seymour turned away, then turned back to look at me. "I trust you will send my daughter back to me when I am free? With her husband in the Tower and you in reduced circumstances, it can hardly be pleasant for her."

"If she wishes, I will gladly let her go to you."

"Good," the duchess said. "It may be necessary to seek an annulment. I am sorry, as I believe your son has been good to her, but one has to be practical about these things."

"Yes," I said. "One does."

༄

At Durham Place, I found I had plenty of company: even though John had not even gone to trial yet, the Crown had already begun to seize his goods, and the house was full of royal servants, meticulously writing down anything of value John and I owned. No place—not even my own bedchamber—was exempt from their relentless inventorying: my sleeves, my cushions, even my parrot were duly counted. They conducted themselves politely enough, but the sight of them standing in John's wardrobe, patiently counting every shirt I had made for him, was hard to bear. Even harder was the knowledge that men were already inquiring about their chances of receiving John's choicest possessions, secure in the knowledge he would never be freed to reclaim them—or worse.

After two days of this, I decided I could not just wait for Queen Mary to arrive in London; I had to travel to her myself. We had never been close, but our relations had always been cordial, and she had served as godmother to a couple of my children. If I could just be admitted to her presence, I could explain to her that John had done only what her brother wished and that he would show the same sort of loyalty to her if he were allowed to serve her. As for my sons, they had only obeyed the commandment that men honor their fathers. Should they be punished for doing what the Lord himself directed?

As I mounted my horse and settled into my saddle—both carefully accounted for by the queen's men—I felt my optimism, so long in abeyance, rise. Many of the other men who had supported Lady Jane had been forgiven by the queen. The trick seemed to be seeing her face-to-face. If I could speak for John now, and at least get the queen to grant him an audience, it was entirely possible she might extend him her mercy, as well. At the very least, she might agree to free my sons.

When I set off the next day, I found that the roads toward Beaulieu, the Essex manor where Mary was staying for a few days, were lined with Queen Mary's followers. Some were soldiers, keeping an eye out for anyone who might foment trouble, for there were still pockets of England that recognized Jane as queen. Others were just admirers or hangers-on, caught up in the excitement of the queen's bloodless victory and anxious to witness her triumphant entry into the capital. I had planned to break the thirty-mile journey to Beaulieu overnight, as my horse was not accustomed to covering such distances, and my health had not been good over the past few days, but the crowds were so great, there were no reputable lodgings to be had. So I pressed on.

I was five miles outside the queen's headquarters when three armed men stopped my path. "My lady, in the queen's name, I must ask where you are bound."

"Beaulieu. I wish to see the queen."

"Your name?"

"I am the Duchess of Northumberland." If only I had lied!

The men looked at each other. Did they doubt my word? I gestured toward my groom, William Bowden, and my waiting woman, Maudlyn Flower. "They can tell you I am who I claim to be."

"I have no doubt of your identity, Your Grace, but that will do you no good. I cannot let you pass. You must turn back to London."

"On whose authority?"

"On the queen's authority, Your Grace. She has ordered that you in particular not be admitted to her presence."

"I?"

Before the men could answer, I heard horses slowing to a trot behind me, and men speaking in a foreign tongue I did not understand. I turned to see four men, richly dressed in clothing that was not in the English style, and their servants. They were accompanied by a fifth man, of an inferior rank and wearing English clothing, who said to the guards, "These are the imperial ambassadors, sir. The queen sent me to conduct them hastily to Beaulieu."

"Ah, yes. They are expected." The guards waved the ambassadors through.

"Wait, I beg of you!" I caught the queen's messenger by the arm. "Can you conduct me to the queen, also?"

The man stared at me. "And who would you be?"

"The Duchess of Northumberland. There is an absurd misunderstanding. This man says that the queen has refused to see me even before I craved permission to see her."

"There is no misunderstanding, Your Grace. I heard her give the orders myself. If you attempted to see Her Majesty, you were to be turned away and sent back to London where you belong. Now we must be off."

The ambassadorial party moved past me, looking in my direction and talking amongst themselves. I could just make out the names "Northumberland" and "Dudley" and "Suffolk."

I tried another approach. "I am not well, and there is no place to sleep around here, I am told. Please? Cannot the queen allow me the Christian duty of hospitality tonight?"

"So you can slip into her presence somehow? Your Grace, there is no point in this. We have our orders and are following them."

"But why? What harm can it do the queen to hear my plea to her, upon my knees?"

"Even on her knees, a Dudley may find a way to poison Her Majesty."

"*Poison?*"

"There are the gravest suspicions that your husband hastened the king's death. The queen is taking no chances. Now begone with you! Go to London, and do not intrude yourself upon the queen until you are asked, or you will find yourself in the Tower again."

He took my bridle and firmly guided my horse around.

There was nothing to do but obey. We rode a mile or so, tears pouring down my cheeks, and then found a place by the side of the road where we could rest our weary horses. It was well past midnight when we set out again.

As we plodded down the road, now nearly deserted of travelers, we heard the sound of approaching horses. I froze with dread. At this hour of the night, save for desperate supplicants like me, no one was out but robbers. But the face I saw in the lantern light a few minutes later was no robber. "My lady of Suffolk!"

"Yes. I am on my way to see the queen. I have been much delayed. Do you come from her?"

"No. She would not suffer me to come near her. I was turned away. She may do the same with you."

"I am willing to take my chances," Frances Grey said. "I am her cousin. That counts in my favor. I must be going."

"Wait! My lady, I am desperate. She will not see me. I have done nothing to merit such treatment. She thinks John poisoned the king! Will you tell her he is innocent of that and beg her to allow me a moment of her time when she comes to London? Just a moment? You are my last hope. Tell her that I will speak to her behind prison bars, even, if that is what it takes."

"I will mention it."

"Oh, thank you! Thank you!"

The Duchess of Suffolk nodded curtly. Then she and her companion—her master of horse Adrian Stokes, a man so handsome few husbands would have permitted him to serve in their wife's household—cantered away.

34

Frances Grey
July 28, 1553, to July 29, 1553

ON JULY 28, HARRY WAS ARRESTED. "I EXPECTED AS MUCH," HE SAID calmly as his servants hastened to pack his belongings while the men sent to Suffolk Place to seize him waited patiently. "Don't forget my books, please. I don't want to trust to the queen's taste."

Kate, who had been unceremoniously sent home by her father-in-law to await the annulment of her unconsummated marriage, and Mary, whose betrothal had been called off, were crying as Harry calmly sipped ale to fortify himself for the barge ride to the Tower. "Don't worry, chickens," he said. "The new queen's a kind lady, and I'm sure she will be merciful. Your mother is going to speak to her. Isn't she?"

I nodded affirmatively.

"They're cousins, and old friends. Something will be worked out. I'll be home in no time, and so will Jane, I'll wager. Speaking of wagering, did you pack my cards?"

༆

Queen Mary, on her slow progress to London, had reached Beaulieu, where the girls and I had visited her some years before. It was there Jane had insulted one of her ladies about the Mass, so I could only hope Mary had put that incident out of her mind or would attribute it to girlish ill manners.

"I really don't know what to say to the queen," I confessed to Adrian Stokes as we rode along the congested roads. I had followed his advice and chosen an old, plain riding habit and a nondescript horse for my journey instead of traveling in my litter, emblazoned with Harry's arms and mine. I could not remember ever traveling with so few people, and I was grateful that in addition to a lady, I had Master Stokes on horseback beside me, for not only was he athletically built and forceful looking, he was a good companion. "There is no question that I betrayed her when I allowed my daughter to be put on the throne, but what else could I do? King Edward wanted it that way. Could we have said no?"

"I do not think it would have been wise to try."

"Yet Mary herself resisted the king for many years, and her father before that for a time," I recalled. "It was foolish of us to underestimate her. I see that now."

Because our horses were good ones and any accommodation we could have managed to find would be unsuitable, we did not stop overnight to break our journey but simply rested frequently. It was well after midnight, then, when I saw a rider emerge from the mist like the ghost of our misfortunes: the Duchess of Northumberland, coming toward London. The four days her husband had been a prisoner had aged her by so many years.

"The queen would not let me see her," she said, tears running down her face. "I begged—I even humiliated myself in front of the imperial embassy. When you see her—if you see her—would you please speak to her for me?"

"I—"

"We both have children in the Tower," Jane said. "What is good for one of us is good for both of us, don't you agree? If I can only persuade her to set my husband and sons free, your Jane is bound to follow. The queen will not have a young girl in the Tower when all of the men who aided her are free. But I must see her in order to accomplish anything. Please!"

She fiddled with a ring on her finger. For a moment, I thought that she, a knight's daughter, was going to attempt to bribe me, a king's niece, with it. But she kept on absently twirling it, as she sat her horse in the chilly night and babbled about how setting her husband and sons free would solve all of our problems. I could finally take no more. "I must go. It is very late."

"Yes. I am sorry I have detained you. Please do what I begged of you."

"I will do what I can."

"Please do. The imperial embassy is there by now. God only knows what slanders have traveled with them." Her tears started afresh. "People are spreading so many lies about John to the queen. He loved the king like one of his sons. He wept for him. He would never have harmed him. He did everything to save him. He never would have harmed the queen, either. Neither he nor the king meant her or the lady Elizabeth any ill. They would have been married and given large estates, that is all. They—"

We had to finally just ride away from the Duchess of Northumberland; she would have detained us there the rest of the night, otherwise. It was not until two in the morning that we reached Beaulieu. Though the guard on the road had let me pass without incident, the lateness of the hour put me in fear I would be turned away once I arrived there. Instead, I was allowed to doze in one of the queen's outer chambers until Mary had arisen and said her morning prayers. Where I would have gone I had no idea, for so many people had gathered in the neighborhood, there was not even a barn in which to sleep for three miles round.

Having made myself seemly, I knelt before the queen, who gazed down at me mournfully. "Your Majesty, I beg you for your forgiveness," I said when invited to speak. "I have done you an incalculable wrong."

Mary shook her head. "We had thought that you were our friend."

"The king called me to him, Your Majesty, and told me that it was his decision that my daughter take the throne. It was not my decision, not Harry's, and not Jane's. It was the king's—and Northumberland's."

"I believe it was mostly Northumberland's," Mary said, momentarily slipping out of the royal plural. "I never trusted that man, and I believe that he exerted enormous power over my poor brother."

I have asked myself, many a night, if I could have done otherwise than seize upon the opportunity offered me. Perhaps a saint could have, but if I have learned anything from those dark days of July 1553, it was that I was not a saint. "There are rumors that he did worse than that. There are rumors that he hastened the king's death with poison."

"We have heard them. Do you believe them?"

I voiced the suspicions that had no place in logic, perhaps, but which were always in my heart. "I can tell Your Majesty that when I last saw the king, a woman was in his bedchamber who had no business being around the king— she spoke of mysterious potions that she was giving him, and of people visiting her in secret. Such a woman might have well been capable of poisoning His Majesty. I can also tell Your Majesty that soon after Lord Guildford and my Jane were married, Lord Guildford fell ill. Jane was not affected, but I believe it possible that the dish that was served to him was meant for her. In the Tower—when she was constantly in the presence of the Duke and Duchess of Northumberland—her hair started falling out in clumps. And, Your Majesty, my husband, too, fell ill. He is not a sickly man, and although my Jane was ill last year with the sweat, she has otherwise been a healthy young woman. I have no proof, but I cannot put aside as coincidence that Harry and Jane fell ill after they began coming in contact with the Dudley family." For good measure, I added, "There is even a rumor that after Northumberland was captured, an apothecary who had been employed by him threw himself in the Thames." I had not taken the rumor seriously when I heard it, it was true, but in my fervor to accuse, I saw no reason not to pass it along.

Mary nodded gravely.

"It is also true that the lord Guildford repeatedly expressed a desire for a crown and that his mother encouraged him openly. She was furious when my Jane—acting as a queen out of a sense of duty to the men who forced her into acting as one—refused him the crown matrimonial. If my Jane had been got rid of, I believe Guildford would have claimed the right to rule England. Your Majesty's right to rule England."

"Northumberland will die," said Mary.

I looked up at her.

"He may die in the true faith or as a heretic, as he chooses, but he will die. Whether or not he actually poisoned the king, we could not keep such a man alive, for he deliberately subverted the law of succession set down by our most noble father. Such treason cannot go unpunished except by death. His wife has attempted to come to us, we hear. The imperial ambassadors met her upon the road. She is not a bad woman, but it is common knowledge that she is deeply in love with the duke"—a shadow of sadness passed over the queen's face—"and that she would likely do anything for him. We will not risk our person in her presence."

I shut out the Duchess of Northumberland's tear-stained face, begging for me to intercede with Queen Mary. "Jane?" I ventured. "She never asked for the crown. It was Northumberland's manipulations that put it on her head. And Harry—he loves Jane dearly, Your Majesty, more than me or my other daughters. She is the pride of his life. He could no more resist the chance to put a crown upon her head than a child can resist a sweet, but he truly meant no harm to Your Majesty. He proclaimed Your Majesty upon Tower Hill and tore down Jane's canopy himself, although it broke his heart to do so."

"Rise, Cousin." I obeyed, and the queen embraced me. "We will grant your petition as to your husband. We do not forget that your mother was a friend to our mother when others had gone to that great whore, Anne Boleyn. Nor have we forgotten your silence when we confided to you our foolish plan to flee from England."

"Oh, thank you, Your Majesty."

"Our pardon is not without conditions. Until we can trust your husband, he must stay away from court—and we will not tolerate any insolence from him against our religion. Let that be known to him."

"I will, Your Majesty. I thank you. But Jane—"

Mary shook her head. "We cannot let your daughter leave the Tower at this time. Not until the kingdom is stable under our rule and before those who were most culpable have paid the price. Even if she was manipulated by Northumberland, your daughter acted as a queen, and she was old enough to be held responsible for her actions. We cannot free her at this time. It would be a sign of weakness."

I could realistically not ask otherwise, I knew. "But will Your Majesty spare her life?"

"Yes," Mary said without hesitation. "The girl shall not suffer for the mistakes of her elders." She smiled. "You must be very weary and famished after your journey. Stay and rest the night before you set off back to London."

⁓

I rode back to London the next day, well rested and well fed, bearing the news to my daughters that Harry would be released and that Jane, though she would have to remain a prisoner for now, was safe from death. I had barely settled in when the Duchess of Northumberland arrived at Suffolk Place. "Did the queen see you?"

"Yes. She agreed to free Harry."

"Did you ask her if she would consider seeing me?"

I could not quite bring myself to lie. "I am sorry, my lady. There was no opportune time."

The Duchess of Northumberland stared at me. For a moment, I thought she was going to scream or strike me. Then, worse, I thought she would begin to cry. Instead, she said, "I will trouble you no more with my pleas, your lady. I wish you and your family well."

As she turned, leaning on a servant, and slowly walked to her barge, I wished she had struck me.

35

Jane Dudley
August 3, 1553, to August 21, 1553

I DID NOT ENTIRELY GIVE UP HOPE OF SEEING THE QUEEN AFTER THE DUCHESS of Suffolk refused to assist me. I could not give up. When there is no hope, the soul dies. Once the queen was in London, I told myself, she might be more amenable to my petition. To this end, I had decided to be among those greeting her. I would have to stand in the crowd, of course, but I took care to dress every inch the duchess, and to have my much-reduced household standing with me. If I could just catch her eye...

At seven in the evening of August 3, Mary at last arrived, preceded by hundreds of men in velvet cloaks and heralded by triumphant blasts from the Tower guns that made the ground shake beneath my feet. Overnight, the workaday streets of London had blossomed with rich cloths of arras and silk, and fresh, clean gravel crunched beneath the hooves of the horses. There were stages set up for musicians to play and sing—vying to be heard over the guns. The members of every city guild appeared in their best livery, but they were nothing compared to the hundred poor children, dressed in blue and wearing red caps, who greeted the queen at Aldgate. It was nothing like the chilly reception that had greeted Jane's progress to the Tower, and I could not help but think it was rather unkind of the Lord to keep reminding me of this.

The traitor Arundel had so far redeemed himself that he carried the sword of state before Mary. I hoped he would fall and impale himself upon it, but he did not oblige. Riding next to Mary were the lady Elizabeth, the Duchess of Norfolk, and the Marchioness of Exeter. The lady Elizabeth had prudently said nothing in favor of either Jane or Mary until the victory had gone to Mary. I hoped she spared some thought for her old friend Robert, my imprisoned son. The Marchioness of Exeter was the mother of the long-imprisoned Edward Courtenay; if all went as predicted, her son would soon go free. The Duchess of Norfolk's husband would also go free today, but the duchess did not wear the same look of anticipation the marchioness did: the Norfolks' marriage had been legendary for its acrimony long before the duke entered his cell.

As for Mary, I had seen her many times since she was a young girl; it is safe to say that I had never seen her happier. She was clad in a French gown of purple velvet, with matching sleeves, and her kirtle of purple satin was covered with goldsmith's work and pearls. And her train! It was so long that Sir Anthony Browne, leaning over her horse, had to drape it over his shoulder. Her horse was enveloped in cloth of gold that extended all of the way to its hooves.

But I was not here to gawk at the queen. Waiting for a break in the gunfire, I raised my hand and cheered, so hard my throat ached for two days afterward, "The Lord Jesus save Her Grace! Long live the Queen Mary!"

Too late, I remembered Mary was badly shortsighted. She turned to Sir Anthony, who whispered a reply, and I saw Mary's joyous face suddenly turn cold. Then she turned her head and waved at the people lining the other side of the street until she was safely past me.

There would be no audience for me, I finally realized.

✍

By mid-August, the council had ordered me to vacate Durham Place. My new home, at least until someone decided I could not live there any longer, was Chelsea, where Guildford and Jane had spent part of their married life together. It was from there I traveled on August 18 to Westminster Hall, where John and Jack, along with the Marquis of Northampton, were being tried for high treason.

"Forty-three years and a day before this, Dudley's father perished on the scaffold," a man behind me whispered happily. "Like father, like son, eh?"

Having been released from the Tower, the Duke of Norfolk had been put to work immediately; he was presiding as High Steward over John's trial. On his right sat the Lord High Treasurer, the Marquis of Winchester, who had brought the crown jewels to Jane, and the Earl of Arundel, who had sworn to spend his own blood at John's feet. On his left were John Russell, Earl of Bedford, George Talbot, Earl of Shrewsbury, and Richard Rich, all of whom had signed King Edward's devise for the succession.

John, dressed in a black satin gown and preceded by a man carrying an axe, walked into the court under guard. Having touched his knee three times to the ground before arriving at his place before his judges, he stood impassively while his confession was read out, and then knelt again. Invited to speak, he asked, "I have confessed to the charges against me, and nothing I say is meant in defense of myself. I wish to understand the opinion of the court upon two points."

Norfolk, who had been glaring at John throughout these proceedings, grunted. "Speak."

"May a man doing an act by the authority of a prince's council, and by a warrant of the great seal of England, and doing nothing without the same, be charged with treason?"

The Duke of Norfolk said coldly, "The great seal you speak of was not the seal of the lawful queen of the realm, but the seal of a usurper. It therefore can be of no warrant to you."

I clenched my fists. John, I knew, had been speaking of King Edward's great seal, placed on the devise for the succession. Norfolk had deliberately misunderstood him.

John, however, must have expected such an answer. His voice calm, he asked, "May such persons who were equally culpable in my crimes, and by whose letters and commandments I was directed in all of my doings, be my judges, or try me as my peers?"

Arundel had the decency to avert his eyes from John. Norfolk responded in the same voice as before, "If any are as culpable as you, it remains a fact that no attainder is of record against them. Therefore, they are able at law to pass upon any trial, and are not to be challenged except at the queen's pleasure."

"Very well," John said. "I thank the court for its opinions on these matters."

"As you have confessed, I now pass sentence upon you," Norfolk said. He cleared his throat. "You are to be drawn to the place of execution, hanged, your heart and entrails cut from your body while you are still alive, and quartered."

I had known this sentence would be given; I also knew it would most likely be commuted to beheading. Nonetheless, it was all I could do to keep my sickness inside me.

John asked again to speak. Given permission, he said calmly, "I beseech you, my lords, to be humble suitors to the queen's majesty, to grant me four requests, which are these: first, that I might have the death which noblemen have had in the past, and not the other; second, that Her Majesty will be gracious to my children, who may hereafter do Her Grace good service, considering that they went by my commandment as their father, and not of their own free wills; third, that I might have appointed to me some learned man for the instruction and quieting of my conscience; and fourth, that she will send two members of the council to me, to whom I will declare such matters as shall be expedient for her and the commonwealth. And I beseech you all to pray for me."

Norfolk nodded curtly and asked that the next defendant, Northampton, be brought to the bar. His defense, that he could not have defied Jane's orders without committing treason, met with a chilly response, and he was likewise condemned to die. Jack, the last of the three, simply confessed his guilt and begged that the queen pay his debts out of his confiscated property, so the innocent should not suffer from his treason. My son was sentenced to the same horrid death as his father had been.

Norfolk, to give the customary signal that he had completed his task, reached for his white staff of office. He cracked it in two pieces, the snap of it like a human heart breaking.

✍

John was condemned on a Friday. A few hours after I returned home from his trial, I heard his execution was set for Monday.

In three days, the man who had been my companion since I was three years of age would no longer walk the earth. I wanted to hang my head and weep. Instead, I said, "Have pen and paper brought to me immediately."

In my own uncertain hand, shaking from anxiety, I wrote to Lady Anne Paget. Lord William Paget and John had quarreled after the Duke of Somerset's fall, and he had been one of the first to desert John after he left London, but Lord Paget had taken it upon himself to assist me in recovering some of my goods from Durham Place and Sion, and his wife and I had been friendly. She had even contacted Susan Clarencius, Mary's most trusted lady, in hopes of getting me an audience with the queen. Lady Paget was my last chance to save John.

Now, good madam, for the love you bear to God forget me not, and make my lady Marquis of Exeter my good lady, and remember me to Mistress Clarencius to continue as she has begun doing for me. And, good madam, desire your lord as he may do in speaking for my husband's life. In way of charity, I crave him to do it.

Madam, I have held up my head, for all of my great heaviness of heart that all the world knows cannot be light, so that now I begin to grow weak, and also have such a rising in the night from my stomach upward that in my judgment my breath is like clean to go away, as my women well can say. They know it to be true by the pains they take with me.

Good madam, of your goodness remember me, and so God keep your ladyship with long life with your lord and yours.

Your ladyship's poorest friend, Jane Northumberland as long as it please the queen.

The tears beginning to blind me, I wrote a postscript:

And good madam, desire my lord to be a good lord unto my poor five sons; nature cannot do otherwise but sue for them, although I do not so much care for them as for their father, who was to me and to my mind the most best gentleman that ever living woman was matched with all, as neither those about him nor about me can say the contrary and say truly. How good he was to me that our lord and the queen's majesty show their mercy to them.

That last sentence did not make much sense, even to me, but I had no time to make it better. I summoned a servant and watched as he sped away.

Two days later, a response came in the person of Lord and Lady Paget themselves, standing in my chamber at Chelsea. "We are very sorry, Your Grace," Lady Paget said quietly, touching my hand. "We have done our best. The queen is adamant. The execution will go on as planned."

So on Monday, August 21, all was ready on Tower Hill: the scaffold, the executioner, the sand to soak up my John's blood, the coffin in which to lay his broken corpse, the crowd of ten thousand to cheer and gloat. I was ready, too, standing in the throng to see my husband give up his life while those who had betrayed him and his king lived on. But as I stood there, my face veiled closely, an armed man mounted the scaffold and cried, "There will be no execution today! Go back to your homes."

The queen has agreed to pardon John after all, I thought wildly. A surge of hope knocked me to the ground in a faint. When I came to myself, my man John Rogers was bending over me. "Is it true? John will not die today?"

"Not today. The duke has declared his faith in the Catholic Church."

"Then he is saved?" I sat up slowly. Though I had followed the new religion for years, I cared not a jot for that now; if a Mass would save John, I would hear four a day. Six! We would be better Papists than the Pope himself, which given what I had heard about the present Pope wouldn't be all that hard.

"I can't say, Your Grace. It may be that it is only postponed. Please don't hope for too much."

"Queen Mary would surely not bring my husband into her church only to destroy him," I said stubbornly. "If nothing else, it would be a waste."

⨌

In front of a crowd of clergy, royal and city officials, courtiers, and prisoners, John had renounced the Protestant faith and heard the Mass. It was an enormous triumph for the queen: her brother's chief minister admitting King Edward had been wrong about the religion he held so dear. But John Rogers had been right to caution me. Whether John was Protestant or Catholic, it mattered not in the end, for late that afternoon, as I knelt praying that my husband might be spared, a message came from Lord Paget that John's execution had been rescheduled for the next morning.

I was sitting in my chamber, weeping next to the clock that had once been John's, when Maudlyn Flower came. "Please dry your eyes, Your Grace, and hurry. The queen has allowed you and your daughters to see the duke. Her men are waiting for you."

⨌

As my daughters and I entered the Tower late on Monday evening, the place where my husband awaited death was bustling with life. Royal servants were scurrying about, trying to finish the day's business before night fell. How could the world be going on so normally, when the man I loved best was to die?

Beside me, Katheryn faltered as we came closer to the Garden Tower. "Will he be in chains? Will they have"—she swallowed—"tortured him?"

I cursed myself for not having realized the mental torment my daughter must have been suffering all of these days; I had hardly seen the poor child, leaving her to the care of her attendant, Mistress Blount. "The queen does not do that to people, Katheryn. He will look just as he always looks, and he will be very glad to see you."

As soon as we entered, Katheryn ran forward and flung herself, sobbing, at John. He backed onto a window seat and took her into his lap, where she wept against his chest while Mary and I struggled to keep our composure. "Child, you must try to be brave for your mother," John said at last, his own voice shaking. "She will need you to be so in the days to come."

"I hate the queen! Mama has been begging to see her—has been begging everyone to urge her to spare you. The queen will not listen. I hate her! I hope she dies!"

"Katheryn!" Mary wrung her hands.

"Katheryn, you must not say that." John managed a stern look. "I have wronged her. I made a great mistake, and she is within her rights to punish me. She has been more merciful than many would have been under the circumstances. Don't grow bitter and angry over this. It helps nothing and could only make things worse. You will promise me never to say something foolish like that again?"

"Yes, Father," Katheryn mumbled. "But I still don't like her."

"Well, that is understandable, I suppose, under the circumstances." He brushed my daughter's cheek with the back of his hand and settled her more comfortably against him. "When I was younger than you are, my father was executed, too, you know. I thought I would never be happy again, but I was. I went to live with your mother, for one thing. So you see? There will be hard days for you, but they will not last forever." He turned to Mary and with his free hand drew her closer to him. "I was angry when you ran off with young Sidney, you know."

"Oh, Father, I meant no disrespect."

"I know. And you chose well—better than I might have chosen for you. He is a good man. I am glad to know you will be in his care." John smiled at my daughters. "I have had six sons grow to manhood, but only two daughters grow to womanhood," he said. "That has always made the two of you doubly precious to me."

I walked to the other side of John's chamber as John and the girls talked quietly. After a little while, John called the guards. "Take them to the chamber upstairs for a short while, please. I just want a few moments alone with their mother."

As soon as the door shut behind my daughters, John and I came into each other's arms and remained there, the room silent except for the beating of our hearts against each other. Finally, I drew back. "Is there any chance that the queen might pardon you?"

"You never give up, do you? No. There's none at all. Read this. It's a draft of a letter I wrote to both Arundel and Gardiner."

Honorable lord, and in this my distress my especial refuge; most woeful was the news I received this evening by Mr. Lieutenant, that I must prepare myself against tomorrow to receive my deadly stroke. Alas my good lord, is my crime so heinous as no redemption but my blood can wash away the spots thereof? An old proverb there is and that most true that a living dog is better than a dead lion. O that it would please her good grace to give me life, yea, the life of a dog, that I might live and kiss her feet, and spend both life and all I have in her honorable service, as I have the best part already under her worthy brother and her most glorious father. O that her mercy were such as she would consider how little profit my dead and dismembered body can bring her, but how great and glorious an honor it will be in all posterity when the report shall be that so gracious and mighty a queen had granted life to so miserable and penitent an object. Your honorable usage and promises to me since these my troubles have made me bold to challenge this kindness at your hands. Pardon me if I have done amiss therein and spare not I pray your bended knee for me in this distress, ye God of heaven it may be will requite it one day on you and yours. And if my life be lengthened by your mediation and my good Lord Chancellor's (to whom I have also sent my blurred letters) I will vow it to be spent at your honorable feet. O my good lord remember how sweet life is, and how bitter ye contrary. Spare not your speech and pains for God I hope hath not shut out all hope of comfort from me in that gracious, princely and womanlike heart; but that as the doleful news of death hath wounded to death both my soul and body, so that comfortable news of life shall be as a new resurrection to my woeful heart. But if no remedy can be found, either by imprisonment or confiscation, banishment and the like, I can say no more but God give me patience to endure and a heart to forgive the whole world.

Once your fellow and loving companion, but now worthy of no name but wretchedness and misery.

JD

John watched my face as I read, knowing what it had cost my husband to beg in that manner. "I know it doesn't show me at my most dignified, but I didn't want to die. I couldn't help but make one last plea. It was hopeless, though; I received my answer a few hours ago. The queen had made up her mind, and I had no right to expect mercy. But she offered me something else."

"What?"

"You. The chance to say good-bye."

I laid my head on his shoulder and wept as John patted my back. Then he said, "I knew on the first day I saw you that I would marry you. Someone told me that guardians often did that with their wards, marry them to their daughters. I wasn't pleased about it at the time."

"Oh?" I said dully.

"Later I changed my mind."

"When?"

"When the old Duke of Suffolk knighted me. Your father was there. My friend—my friend Edward Seymour was there, the people who'd never had much to do with me because of my father were there, but you weren't there.

I missed your presence. I wanted you there to kiss me and tell me you were proud of me. That's when I realized that I did want to marry you."

I twined my fingers into John's. His grasp was as strong as ever. "I can't even think of when I decided I wanted to be your wife. It seems that I always did. I don't know how I will bear this."

"You will. You are strong. Were you there today?"

"Yes."

"Promise me you won't come tomorrow. Someone from here will come to tell you once it's finished. I don't want you to see me behe—like that."

"I promise I will not come." But what did one do while one's husband was being executed? Read? Sew? Practice the virginals? Perhaps I could consult the Duchess of Somerset. I pushed back the nervous laughter that was beginning to overtake me; if I started laughing in such an insane manner, I might never stop.

"Sit in your garden where it's pretty, you and my girls, when the time comes near. It is the picture I will hold in my mind. It will be a comfort to me."

"Very well. I will sit there." To calm myself, I looked around the chamber. Hanging on a clothes rack next to the bed were a light gray gown and a matching doublet—the clothes John would wear tomorrow.

Like a good husband, John asked, "Do they meet with your approval?"

"Yes."

"Good." John was silent for a while, stroking my hair. Finally he said, "I requested that the Duke of Somerset's sons come here today, to see me take the Mass. I asked them for their forgiveness for executing their father."

"But he plotted against you."

"I know. But his death has gnawed at my conscience nonetheless. It eased it a little, speaking to them. Of course, they probably won't forgive me, any more than Katheryn will forgive Queen Mary. But at least I tried."

"And you have really embraced the old religion?"

"Yes. It wasn't that way at first. I renounced my Protestant faith in the hopes of saving our sons. And it has, at least one of them. Jack won't die with me tomorrow as I had feared. But it has brought me comfort since then. After all, so much has gone ill with England under the new." He touched my cheek. "I don't expect you to embrace the old religion straightaway. These things take time. But I hope someday you will."

I was silent. New religion, old religion were the same to me now; they shared the same cruel God, who was taking away from me the man I loved better than anything else on earth. Or maybe there was no cruel God. The wicked thought that there might be none at all was one I was trying very hard not to let push its way into my mind. But I would not distress my husband in his last hours of his life with my newfound doubts. "I will try."

"That is all I can ask." He reached into a drawer and pulled out an inexpensive rosary. "Everything I have here will go to the Crown, but the queen won't mind if I give you this."

I wound it around my wrist before John locked me into another embrace. We stood there for a while, whispering loving words to each other through our tears. Then John said, "The girls will be getting weary up there, and the guards might think we've gotten up to something. We'd best call them back."

"Yes." But I did not move until John gently disengaged me and knocked at the chamber door as a signal to his guards.

The girls silently came in, and John kissed and embraced each of them in turn. Then he turned, for the last time, to me.

"Good-bye, Mouse," he said and kissed my lips. "God keep you."

The guards pressed around us and hurried us downstairs to our waiting boat. It was a mercy, I suppose, that they did not allow me to turn and look backward, for the last sight I had of my John was his smiling face as he bid me farewell.

36

Frances Grey
August 22, 1553

WHEN THE DAY APPOINTED FOR THE DUKE OF NORTHUMBERLAND'S EXE-
cution came round, Harry insisted we should be there. It was necessary, he said, to show our loyalty to the queen so she would prove more
sympathetic toward our imprisoned daughter. "And to us, as well, my dear!
We are not exactly basking in royal favor at the moment." So on August 22,
we rode to Tower Hill, leaving kindhearted Kate and squeamish Mary at our
house at Sheen, a former priory. I wished I could have found an excuse to stay
there with them.

Over days of interrogation, Northumberland had denied poisoning the king.
There was nothing, he had said repeatedly, he had wanted more than to see the
king live to an old age. The old woman had been a desperate measure to cure
the king, who had consented to her ministrations when all else failed. Asked
whether he had poisoned Harry, he had snorted with laughter; asked whether
his wife had poisoned Jane, he had lost his temper for the first time since his
arrest and had demanded to know the name of the whoreson who had made
such an allegation. Reluctantly, the queen and her council had decided there
was no ground for charging him with the king's demise. In any case, there
was no need; there were plenty of other grounds on which to sentence him
to death.

There were at least ten thousand people at Tower Hill, I guessed, but Harry
and I stood well away from the common people, who were busy jostling for
a better view and taking bets over how many strokes it would take to sever
Northumberland's head. We were in a little stand by the scaffold that had been
set up for the nobility, for many others besides Harry and me had decided this
would be an apt occasion to demonstrate their loyalty

Beside me stood the Earl of Hertford and his younger brother. Somerset's death, like everything else that had gone wrong in England since the death of King Henry, was now being blamed entirely on Northumberland's ambition and greed, and it had been deemed fitting that the former Protector's sons attend the beheading. People kept coming up to the boys to grasp their hands and congratulate them, as if the duke's downfall and execution had been arranged especially for their gratification, and I had seen that they looked more uncomfortable than triumphant. I smiled at Hertford, who looked resigned to yet another congratulation upon the duke's imminent demise. "Your mother must have been thankful beyond words to see you again."

Hertford looked startled, then smiled—the first genuine smile I'd seen from him that morning. "Yes. And I was glad to see her, too." He paused. "Is Lady Katherine here?"

"No. She stayed home. She is very softhearted. She cannot stand to see people suffer, even traitors."

"I like a soft heart in a woman."

I resolved to invite the young earl to supper one day.

A beating of drums sounded, and we all turned to see the Duke of Northumberland, wearing a gown of pale gray damask and surrounded by armed men, as he slowly made his way up Tower Hill. Beside him, chanting in Latin—to the puzzlement of the crowd, which had grown used to English—were Nicholas Heath, the Bishop of Worcester, and several other priests.

Northumberland climbed the scaffold where the executioner, wearing a white apron, limped as he stepped aside to make way for the duke and his party. The duke quickly removed his gown, revealing a black jerkin and gray doublet, and handed it to an attendant. The crowd grew still and silent as he walked to the east rail of the scaffold. "Sirs and friends," he said, "I have come to die as you see, having been condemned by the law, and I declare and confess that I have grievously offended God, and I beseech you earnestly that you would implore God for my soul, and if there be any here or absent whom I have offended, I crave their forgiveness."

"God forgive you," the people chorused dutifully.

Beside me, the Earl of Hertford stared at the ground. I patted him on the shoulder.

Northumberland went on, "I beg you to accept humbly the work of God, because He does all for the best, and as for me, I am a miserable sinner and have deserved to die, and I am rightfully condemned by the laws. But although it is true that I was chief in bringing those things to pass for which I have been condemned, it is also true that I did it by the instigation of others." He paused, and I felt everyone on the platform with me tense. "But I will not name them, for I will hurt now no man. I forgive them as I myself desire the forgiveness of God. And I beg you all to bear witness that I am taking leave in perfect love and goodwill with everybody, and to aid me with your prayers in the hour of death."

The duke paused and stared out over Tower Hill before he continued, "Brethren, you are not ignorant in what troubles this realm has been and now continues, as well as in part of the reign of King Henry, as from then until this day, all of which are notorious. I know well that there is no one of you but knows what has befallen us for having departed from the true Catholic church, and believed false prophets and preachers, who have persuaded us of their false doctrines, and have brought me as the chief offender in this and other things to the extremity which you behold, as they have done to many others, as you know. For which I ask God's pardon, and declare to you that I die a true Catholic Christian, and confess and believe all that the Catholic Church believes."

Harry started to snort, and then recalled himself.

"And I warn you, friends and brothers, that none should believe that this great novelty and new conscience arises from being urged upon me by any or that any have persuaded me in this, but I tell you what I feel at the bottom of my heart, and as you see I am in no case to say aught but truth. And thus I charge and enjoin you straightly that you give no credit to the preachers of such false doctrine. And consider, brethren, what I say, and do not forget that I charge you to have no let or shame in returning to God, as you see that I have not, and to consider what is written in the Apostles' Creed, 'I believe in the Holy Ghost, the Holy Catholic Church, the Communion of Saints.' And I, though ignorant, could say more upon this, but you may reflect and consider it with an impartial mind. And if this does not satisfy you, think upon the miseries in which so great a multitude has lived and died in Germany, one against another, and that they have been trampled down for having forsaken the Catholic faith, wherefore God has forgotten them as he has forgotten us. And if this does not move you to feel as I have declared to you, let each one make his private reckoning and consider how it has fared with him in his own condition. And if he is not utterly blind, I am sure that he will come into this my true knowledge. And therefore I again charge you to embrace what the Catholic Church believes, which is what the Holy Spirit has revealed from generation to generation from the time of the apostles until our days, and will continue until the end. And live peaceably, and be obedient to the Queen's majesty and her laws, and do that which I have not done.

"I could go on with this talk, my dear people, as I have a thorough experience of the evil which has befallen this kingdom, but you know that I have something else to do, to which I must prepare as time is running short. And now I ask the queen's majesty to forgive the offenses committed against her. And I have a firm hope of obtaining it, as she has already extended her mercy and clemency towards me so far that whereas she could have made me die, without any judicial proceeding or examination, in the most infamous and cruel way by dragging, hanging, and quartering, as I have been up in arms against Her Majesty, nevertheless by her mercy and goodness she has been contented to have me brought to my judgment and to have my case settled according to the law, by which I am rightfully and fairly sentenced. Her Majesty has also extended her clemency and mercy towards me in the way of my death. Therefore I hope that by her graciousness and bounty she will remit her anger and indignation against me, for which I heartily ask you all heartily to pray our Lord to preserve the life of our majesty so that she may reign on you for many years to come, in honor and happiness."

Northumberland moved away from the rail and knelt in the fresh straw in the middle of the scaffold. Flawlessly, as if he had been practicing in his cell, he recited a series of psalms and prayers in Latin. Then, having stripped to his shirt and tied the blindfold the lame executioner handed him, he crossed himself and lay down on the beam, then abruptly rose up. The crowd gasped. Was he going to declare all he had just said and done to be a sham?

The duke's blindfold had slipped down over one eye. Without pausing to take a last look at the summer sun beginning to break through the morning clouds, Northumberland adjusted it, lay down quickly, and struck his hands together. As I cringed against Harry, the executioner—stronger of arm than of leg—swung his axe, dispatching the duke with one stroke as the crowd roared its approval.

Harry winced as the executioner raised Northumberland's head. "I hope he wasn't looking to get himself a last-minute pardon with all that Catholic twaddle," he whispered to me.

"Harry—"

"Oh, I know, my dear. There but for the grace of God—and the queen—go I. But there's no need to keep reminding me of it."

In a very short time, John Gates and Thomas Palmer, two underlings of the duke, followed him to the grave. As the crowd slowly dispersed, I watched as the executioner tossed Northumberland's rich clothing over his arm and as the three bodies were laid inside a cart. The most guilty had paid for their sins— and, I could not help but think, for ours, as well. Now, I prayed silently as the mingled blood of the three traitors ran down the scaffold and the death cart rattled toward the Tower, England would be at peace. We could begin afresh, and my girl would soon be free.

37

Jane Dudley
August 22, 1553

I DID NOT SLEEP THAT NIGHT AFTER LEAVING JOHN AT THE TOWER. I STAYED in my chamber, praying and weeping. When dawn came, I dried my eyes and dressed, using more care than I had as of late. Then, followed by Henry Sidney, my daughter Mary, and my ladies, I took Katheryn's hand and walked out to the garden, where we sat watching as the sun broke over the Thames.

The church bells tolled seven, and John's half sisters joined the vigil. Eight, and a couple of my cousins came to sit with us. Nine—the hour John was to proceed to the scaffold.

I fingered my rosary. It was a string of beads to me, nothing more, but it was a string of beads my John had held, at least. Unbidden, the Latin prayers I had said as a much-younger woman came back to me, and I began to repeat them in a whisper. Perhaps John, dying his Catholic death, was saying them, too.

The sun was high in the sky when John's servant from the Tower arrived by skiff at Chelsea's landing. As I went to meet him, he took off his cap and held it to his heart. "It is done, Your Grace. I am most heartily sorry."

I realized then that the entire household had come out to the garden, the same garden where Catherine Parr and Thomas Seymour had courted and giggled in what seemed now to be a more innocent time. Everybody stood silent, their heads capless and bowed. Some were weeping. I managed to command my voice. "Please take the rest of the day to mourn my husband," I said, blinking back tears. "He was a good and fair master."

"Aye, he was," my servants muttered.

Henry Sidney took Mary into his arms, while Mistress Blount offered similar comfort to Katheryn. Maudlyn Flower took my arm. "Please go in and lie down, Your Grace. I will give you something to make you sleep."

I shook my head. "I would like to walk for a while. By myself."

"My lady…"

"I need to be alone."

I turned away and set off walking aimlessly down the bank of the river. Someone from my household was protectively dogging my footsteps, I soon realized, but he stayed at a respectful distance, so I did not care. Most of the time, I was crying. At last, I grew so tired I could walk no longer, so I sat on the riverbank, where I childishly hugged my knees and watched the water-craft go by. *Most people in London travel by water*, John's seven-year-old voice informed me.

How cruel my father had been, to marry me to someone I would come to love so dearly.

Grief, I found, would not keep me awake. Too exhausted from my sleepless night and from weeping and walking to hold my eyes open for long, I drifted off. For a few happy hours I was transported to my childhood in Halden with John until a touch awoke me. "My lady? It's getting ready to rain. Please let me take you home."

I looked up to see one of my servants, leading my horse. I nodded and let him help me to my feet and into the saddle. Then, as the rain began to fall, I rode back to a home to which my John would never return.

38

Frances Grey
October 1553

O N OCTOBER 1, 1553, THE CROWN KING EDWARD AND THE DUKE OF Northumberland had wanted to go on my own daughter's head was put on that of Queen Mary. With Jane in the Tower, Harry and I took no part in the coronation; doing so would have been too awkward for words. Yet a couple of weeks later, Harry was allowed to take his seat in Parliament—albeit belatedly—and I was summoned to Mary's presence.

My cousin smiled at me and quickly ordered me to rise. "Your daughter has written us a letter," she said, handing it to me.

I read the long letter slowly, tracing the perfectly formed letters with a finger and imagining the voice of the daughter I had not seen since July.

> *Although my fault be such that, but for the goodness and clemency of the queen, I can have no hope of finding pardon, nor in craving forgiveness, having given ear to those who at that time appeared, not only to myself, but also to a great part of this realm, to be wise, and now have manifested themselves the contrary…Although my fault may be great, and I confess it to be so, nevertheless I am charged and esteemed guilty more than I have deserved. For whereas I might take upon me that of which I was not worthy, yet no one can ever say either that I sought it as my own, or that I was pleased with it or ever accepted it…*

As I had urged her to do when we had parted, Jane had offered a full explanation of the events that had put her on the throne, without once speaking disrespectfully of the queen's religion. I sighed with relief as I read on, then winced when I reached these words, written perhaps at my own advice:

I know for certain that, twice during this time, poison was given to me, first in the house of the Duchess of Northumberland, and afterwards here in the Tower, as I have the best and most certain testimony, besides that since that time all my hair has fallen off.

I at last handed the letter back to Queen Mary. "I hope, Your Majesty, that this letter shows you that my daughter was innocent of any ambition to wear the crown."

"It shows us that the plan was concocted by others, which we already knew. That your daughter was entirely unhappy about being queen is something of which we are not completely convinced." Mary folded the letter. "And those who have seen her at the Tower report that she has an abundant head of hair."

I blushed. "My daughter has been known to exaggerate on occasion, but I do believe, Your Majesty, she genuinely believed that malicious forces were working against her. She was greatly agitated and unsure of what was going to happen next. I myself believed in the possibility of poison at the time, as I told Your Majesty at Beaulieu."

"And there is nothing about you or your husband in this letter! To believe your daughter, neither your husband nor you played any role in this business. Why, you yourself have admitted the contrary." Mary stopped me before I could speak. "It is of no matter. We merely say these things to inform you that although we are inclined to mercy, given your daughter's youth and relative blamelessness, we are not a fool."

I hung my head. "Your Majesty, might you be willing to set my daughter free, or at least allow her to come to live with us under our supervision? I promise Your Majesty she will be a loyal subject to you if given a chance."

"That we must wonder at, given her heretical views. It was the talk of the Tower, what she had to say of Northumberland's conversion."

I sighed. Though neither Harry nor I had been allowed to see Jane since her imprisonment, we did have friends who were in a position to let us know of her daily doings. Having been dining with her jailer, Master Partridge, and his friend Rowland Lea the week after Northumberland's execution, Jane had heard with irritation that the Mass was again being heard in London. Then she had turned to the subject of Northumberland, whom she had called the most odious of all men, and had pronounced with relish, "As his life was wicked and full of dissimulation, so was his end thereafter."

"Northumberland's good end was the one redeeming aspect of his life,"

Mary said firmly. "It has brought many Londoners back to the true faith. If your daughter believes his death was a wicked one, what hope is there for her? We do not like to refuse you, Frances, as you are our cousin, but for now, your daughter must remain where she is. We promised you her life, and we intend to keep that promise, though there are several on the council who would have her dead."

I shuddered.

"So be content with that for now," Mary advised. "We called you here to let you see your daughter's letter, and we also called you here for another reason. The Duke of Suffolk is being very difficult on the matter of religion. You must know we wish to put the state of religion back to where it was at the time of our father, King Henry, and to repeal the statutes that were enacted under our misguided young brother. Your husband is opposing these measures, and quite vocally. If you have any influence over him, we wish you would use it, for he is irritating us. He should remember that he has a daughter in the Tower."

"I will try, Your Majesty." I hesitated. "Your Majesty, may I ask what is to become of the lord Guildford and his brothers?"

"The Duchess of Northumberland has been wearing poor Susan Clarencius to rags, asking her to intervene with us on their behalf," said Mary. "She is a devoted mother, and we must sympathize with her, but we are not ready to decide these matters. She must be patient." Mary smiled. "As you must be yourself."

That afternoon at our house at Sheen, I caught my husband when he returned from Parliament. "Harry, I have spoken with the queen today. She is still disposed toward clemency for Jane, but she must remain in the Tower for now."

"What, does the queen think our Jane is going to don armor and challenge her? Jane of Arc?"

"She is mainly concerned about Jane's views on religion, and your own, as well, Harry. She says you are speaking against her in Parliament."

Harry shrugged. "Someone has to."

"Why does it have to be you? Harry, you could have died on the scaffold with Northumberland! Can't you give way on this? She wishes only to turn back religion to the way it was in King Henry's time, and she herself proclaimed that she would not compel her subjects to follow her religion."

"For now. Do you think that's going to continue indefinitely? This Parliament will only be the nose under the camel's tent, I'll wager, if she's encouraged in her changes. And she's already complaining that the lady Elizabeth does not have the proper motive for attending Mass. The poor lady can't win. If she doesn't go to the Mass, Queen Mary squawks at her, and if she does go, she gets squawked at for not being sincere in her devotion. No, my dear, I'm afraid that if we do nothing, it's only a matter of time before the queen brings England back under Papal control."

"But you are angering her, Harry. She told me so. You are putting our daughter at risk."

"Our Jane wouldn't want me to keep silent. You might say I'm doing this for her."

I shook my head. "That may be so, but her approval shouldn't force you into imprudence."

"The truth is, my dear, you have no strong feelings about these things, and you can't understand those of us who do."

"Perhaps I can't. But I can understand that you are alienating the queen at a time when we should be treading carefully."

Harry snorted. "Treading carefully? If the queen goes through with the marriage to Philip of Spain, as it is rumored that she will, it will be she who has to tread carefully. Mark my words, the English people won't stand for it."

39

Jane Dudley
November 1553

IT IS SHAMEFUL TO ADMIT, BUT MY SONS' IMPRISONMENT WAS PROBABLY THE only thing that saved me from following John to the grave. Working to free them gave me a purpose to get out of bed in the morning. Without that cause to occupy me, I might well have just lay there each morning, listening to John's clock tick beside me and dreaming of an impossible revenge against those who had made him their scapegoat. I might—there were days I contemplated it— have even died at my own hand. Only the knowledge that this would make my poor daughters the children of a traitor *and* of a suicide stopped me, I think.

As it was, my thoughts were loathsome, especially toward the one male Dudley who was not locked up or dead: Jerome. On the surface, I was as kind to Jerome as ever—mending his shirts, making certain he was taken for the rides he loved, letting him win large sums (in his eyes) from me in the very simple card games he could play—but each time I looked at him, with his face that would have been so much like John's if it had had a glimmer of intelligence in it, I wondered why God had been so unfair as to take John while leaving Jerome. Useless Jerome, who had never had a woman's love, who would never father children. Why, if the Lord had to take a Dudley brother, could he not have taken Jerome? That I hated myself for thinking such things did not prevent me at all from thinking them, especially since at least once a week, I had to retell Jerome the pretty little fiction I had invented for him about John's death and Andrew's and my sons' imprisonment: John had fallen ill while traveling and had had to be buried abroad, but he had died peacefully and happily and would be waiting for us all in heaven. Andrew and the boys, as Jerome still thought of my five sons, were traveling on very important business for the queen. No, I did not know when they would be coming back: the business was that important.

Jerome would nod solemnly and return to his cards. But I had underestimated even his capacity for observation, for one day he asked, "Jane, why do you cry so much lately?"

Caught off guard, I could say only, "I miss John very much."

Jerome looked at me reproachfully. "I miss him, too," he said sternly. "But he is happier where he is now. You told me that yourself, so you should not cry."

"I will remember that," I promised. "And I will try my best not to."

The other story I had woven for Jerome's benefit was that I regularly went to court to visit the queen—which was half-true, at least, for on the days Mary received petitions, I went to court and stood in the most outer of the queen's outer chambers, alongside all of the other motley supplicants begging for a crust of royal favor. The kinder of the guards, recalling that I was a duchess in name, at least, and seeing that I was no longer young, would pull me a stool, but that was the only concession I received. Each afternoon, after several hours of waiting, I would be told the same thing. "The queen is not seeing anyone else today. You must go home."

I did not confine my begging to the queen herself, though. There were those who knew the queen who could put in a word for me at the opportune time, and I pursued them shamelessly. Poor Susan Clarencius! In those days, when no one wanted to be associated with anyone connected with John, she was the only person in the queen's circle of women who showed me any favor, and as a result, I bombarded her with petitions—and gifts. If she used half of the sleeves I worked for her in the evenings, when I sat in my chamber at Chelsea with none but my ladies and John's clock for company, she must have never needed another pair in her lifetime, and if there was a bad smell anywhere around her, it was certainly not my fault, for I made her sweet bags for every corner of her wardrobe. Yet as kind as Susan Clarencius was to me, even she could bring me no more satisfactory answer than: "She is inclined to show your sons and Sir Andrew mercy, but she will not make any decisions just now. You must be patient." Then it turned to: "She is disposed to show them mercy, but this must wait until after her marriage."

The queen's marriage had been the leading topic in London that autumn, pushing aside even the fraught topic of religion. There had been two leading candidates, one an Englishman and one a foreigner, both of them about a decade younger than the queen: twenty-seven-year-old Edward Courtenay, now restored to his family earldom of Devon, and twenty-six-year-old Philip of Spain, the heir of the emperor Charles.

The most enthusiastic promoter of the match with Courtenay was Stephen Gardiner, the Bishop of Winchester, who had spent time in prison with him. Since their release upon Mary's arrival in London, the bishop had assumed a positively paternal attitude toward the fatherless Courtenay and lost no opportunity to praise him to Mary. He had a hard task ahead of him, for Courtenay, shut up for all of his youth in the Tower, was completely without judgment. Told what to do by others for all of his formative years, he had no difficulty in following the commands of the tricksters, whores, and flatterers who collected around him once he was free and at last had money to spend. Yet he was an Englishman and a great-grandson of Edward IV, which for many was enough to make him an ideal husband for the queen. For my part, I suspected Courtenay would be a disaster for Mary: a Katherine Howard in breeches.

Philip of Spain was a different proposition. Already a widower with a young son, he had been helping to govern his father's vast domains for several years. Simon Renard, the imperial ambassador, had been pressing him upon Mary as a husband since the very day the ambassador had arrived to Beaulieu to meet with her. By mid-November, I and the rest of the people learned what had already been known to those at court: Mary had decided to marry Philip.

My, what a furor that caused! The Londoners' imaginations ran wild with tales of Philip emptying the treasury and sending its contents to Spain, of Mary herself being dragged screaming from Westminster and hauled (sometimes in a sack) to be imprisoned abroad as Philip put the crown on his own head, of Philip's son by his first wife being made the Prince of Wales, of Englishmen being thrown out of their houses in the dead of the night to make way for the hordes of Spaniards who would be coming over with the king. And this was all before the details of the marriage treaty had even been negotiated.

I was one of the few people I knew who did not regard the Spanish marriage with dread. By all accounts, Mary had had no desire to marry one of her subjects, even if a mature man of the suitable rank could have been found. Philip was the son of the man to whom Mary had been betrothed as a young child and to whom she had never ceased to regard with warm feelings. A happy marriage for the queen could only bode well for my sons, for surely then she would be more kindly disposed toward me, who had been so happy in my own marriage. And if Philip could get Mary with child despite her relatively advanced age, then that augured even better for the future, for I would be able to appeal to the queen's maternal instincts.

So I continued to haunt the court and to shower Susan Clarencius with gifts, and to pray each day that the marriage the queen desired so much would soon come about. In the meantime, on November 13, three of my sons and the lady Jane went to trial at London's Guildhall. Jack already had a judgment of death upon him, and Robert's trial had not yet taken place.

With Ambrose's and Hal's wives, I sat on a bench that gloomy November morning, waiting for the prisoners to be brought from the Tower. In addition to Jane and my sons, there would be a fifth defendant: Thomas Cranmer, the Archbishop of Canterbury. He had quarreled with John over a revision to the canon law and had been but a reluctant supporter of Jane, so it was generally believed the queen was finally exacting revenge for Cranmer's long-ago support for the marriage of King Henry to Anne Boleyn. The archbishop had not helped matters, however, by circulating a letter denunciating the Mass.

As we waited, I saw Frances, Duchess of Suffolk, making her way to our bench. Apparently the Duke of Suffolk had been unable to come, or perhaps had not trusted himself to keep his temper at his daughter's trial. Frances had two escorts: the ubiquitous Adrian Stokes, and Jane's former Italian tutor, Michelangelo Florio. How many good-looking men did the woman need around her? Reluctantly, I moved down to allow her and her swains to sit, and the duchess gave me a tremulous smile of acknowledgment, which I failed to return.

Never could I forgive the woman for not saying anything to Mary in favor of John, futile as I knew it would have been.

With the Duchess of Suffolk settled into place at last, it was time for the prisoners, who had been led on foot from the Tower through the streets of London, to make their entrance, preceded by a man bearing an axe. At the forefront of the dismal procession was the Archbishop of Canterbury, followed by Guildford, then by Jane and her two ladies, and then by Ambrose and Hal.

Jane, wearing a black velvet gown and a black French hood, with a black velvet prayer book hanging at her belt and yet another black book in her hands, looked more an archbishop than the archbishop himself, save for her disadvantage of gender. She nodded at Frances, who dabbed at her eyes with a handkerchief Stokes passed to her while Florio heaved a Florentine sigh.

I drank in the sight of my three sons, whom I had not seen since July, although their wives had been given permission to visit them. Their imprisonment was not harsh, and they all looked well-tended, though the exercise they were allowed—walking on the Tower leads—was far less than the sort of vigorous activity to which they had been accustomed. My sons each had a taste for fine clothing, and since the days of their young manhood, they had never gone to an event together without consulting with each other about what to wear. This trial was no exception. All wore short gowns over black embroidered doublets. The three of them sought me out with their eyes as they entered the room, and smiled.

I smiled broadly in return.

Sitting in judgment of the prisoners were the Duke of Norfolk, who had sentenced John to die, and fifteen others. One by one, the accused were brought to the bar. None had lawyers to assist them; it was not the way of a treason trial.

The archbishop pleaded not guilty. Then came Guildford's turn. "Raise your hand."

Guildford obeyed.

"Thou, Guildford Dudley who stands there are accused of taking possession of the Tower and of proclaiming Lady Jane Grey, daughter of the Duke of Suffolk, as queen. How do you plead? Guilty or not guilty?"

My son did not hesitate. "Guilty."

Jane was next. Accused of taking possession of the Tower and proclaiming herself queen, with the additional charge of signing writings as the queen, she asked, "My lords, if I plead guilty, may I speak afterward?"

"You may."

"I plead guilty," Jane said, as easily as if she appeared in court every day of her life. "Yet I would like to add that although I accepted the crown, I never sought it, and that some of those before whom I stand sought to place it on my head."

Norfolk, who could congratulate himself on having had the foresight to be a prisoner in the Tower during the events in question, nodded curtly. "You are finished?"

"Yes, my lord."

"Stand down."

Jane obeyed. Her reproof to the judges had been no more successful than John's, but I could not begrudge her a speck of admiration for having made it.

Ambrose and Hal, each charged with taking the field against Queen Mary and proclaiming Jane as queen, also pleaded guilty.

Because the archbishop had pleaded not guilty, the other prisoners had to wait until his trial was finished before their sentences were pronounced. At last—Cranmer having changed his plea after the Crown presented its evidence—each of the prisoners was called to hear his or her sentence. "Guildford Dudley, as you have pleaded guilty to high treason, I hereby sentence you to death by drawing, hanging, and quartering."

Hal's wife, sitting next to me, clutched my hand. I fought back nausea.

"Jane Dudley, approach the bench!"

The only sound in the Guildhall was Jane's skirts swishing against the floor. "Jane Dudley, as you have pleaded guilty to high treason, I hereby sentence you to be burned alive on Tower Hill or beheaded as the queen should please."

Frances Grey slumped over in a faint on Adrian Stokes's shoulder. Jane's face had not even changed.

My two other sons were sentenced to die the same grim death as Guildford. Then the prisoners once again formed a neat line and exited the Guildhall, this time with the axe facing them as a signal to the crowd that they had been sentenced to death.

Under the devoted ministrations of Master Stokes, who had all but knocked the curious out of the way so that his lady could come to herself in peace, Frances was reviving as I began to make my way out of the Guildhall. She looked up at me as I passed. "The queen promised me she would spare my daughter. Do you think her majesty will do so now that my child and your sons are under this dreadful sentence?"

"You know her better than I do, my lady. Unlike you, I have not been allowed into her presence."

I had struck home. Frances blushed. Then she said, "I will beg for all of their lives if I see the queen again. In the meantime, I can at least pray that she spares my daughter's life, and your sons', as well. Will you do the same?"

"I shall pray for all of them." Then I added, "But it is the queen we must convince. God may be an easier matter."

40

Frances Grey
November 1553 to January 1554

JANE'S CONDEMNATION AT THE GUILDHALL MOVED HARRY TO DO WHAT none of my own pleadings could accomplish: make his peace with the queen on the matter of religion. While he did not go so far as to consent to begin hearing the Mass, he did agree not to interfere with the legislation that was making its way through Parliament. Just as important to the queen, he promised not to oppose her marriage to Philip of Spain. In return, he received a public assurance of the queen's goodwill and a private assurance that Jane would be safe. The dreadful sentence that had made me faint at the Guildhall was merely a formality. In time, Jane would go free. The queen was less certain about Guildford and the rest of the Dudleys—this time I had kept my promise to the Duchess of Northumberland and asked that she show them mercy—but no moves were made to carry out the sentences against them.

I had no reason to doubt any of this. Indeed, when I came to court in late November, I found, to my immense embarrassment, that Queen Mary gave precedence to me and my cousin Margaret, Countess of Lennox, over the lady Elizabeth, who glared at us as she took her seat at a lower table.

"It's been like that ever since I came," Margaret informed me as we relaxed in her chamber at Westminster later that evening. The queen was feeling poorly and had retired early. Margaret fingered the material of her rich gown, a gift from Mary, guiltily. "She has pampered me shamelessly since I have come to court. I can't say I find it disagreeable, but she snubs the lady Elizabeth at the same time. It is awkward, to say the least. I pity the lady Elizabeth, but it is hardly my fault that the queen sees Anne Boleyn in her face whenever she looks at her." Margaret lowered her voice. "The queen has even said that if she dies without issue, I will be the heir to the throne."

"Better you be anything else, Margaret! Trust me, you would be better off going back to Yorkshire and staying there for the rest of your life."

"I had forgotten how much you have suffered for your royal blood," admitted Margaret. "But the queen always speaks highly of you, and she speaks very indulgently of the lady Jane. Surely she will free her soon."

"I hope so. Christmas will be dismal without her."

"Wait until the queen marries," Margaret said confidently. "She will be in a humor to grant anything, maybe even get the lady Jane's marriage to that Dudley boy annulled and let her marry someone whose family isn't knee-deep in treason."

"Is she that pleased about the Spanish match?"

"Pleased? She talks of nothing else among her women these days but Prince Philip. And I can't blame her. His portrait arrived a few days ago, and I don't know whether the credit is due more to Titian or to Prince Philip himself, but it certainly is a feast for the eyes. Mind you, no one else, other than Simon Renard, is happy with it. The marriage, I mean, not the portrait."

"So I have heard from Harry."

"Oh, my dear! Courtenay alternates between sulking and pursuing the lady Elizabeth, who can't abide him. The French ambassador's nose is out of joint. Gardiner is unhappy because the queen refused Courtenay, and the queen is unhappy because the Commons have been badgering her not to make the marriage. And, of course, the Commons are unhappy because the queen refuses to give up the idea of this marriage."

"Do you think she will be prevailed upon to change her mind?"

"Not a chance," Margaret said. "The more people cry out against her marriage, the more she digs in. The queen is as mulish as her father ever was, and King Edward, too, from what I hear." She laughed. "Not that I lack a stubborn streak myself. In fact, I believe you are the only one of us cousins who escaped it."

♥

After Parliament recessed, we stayed at Sheen instead of going to Bradgate, as Harry's health had been suffering lately. Besides, with a daughter languishing in the Tower—though Jane was well fed and well supplied with comfortable furnishings and her beloved books and paper—neither of us had the heart to go to Leicestershire as if nothing were amiss.

As Christmas drew near, Harry's brothers paid us their accustomed visits, along with several men who had not visited us much before: Sir Peter

Carew, Sir James Croft, and Sir Thomas Wyatt. They were more soldiers than scholars, not Harry's usual choice of companion, I thought. But as they were congenial and well bred, and their presence was a distraction, I welcomed them to Sheen.

As we played cards a few days before the anniversary of our Lord's birth and the men enjoyed the wide varieties of wine we had on hand, the subject, despite my best efforts to the contrary, soon turned to the queen's marriage. "Any news of the Spanish invasion?" asked Thomas Grey, Harry's younger brother.

"Nothing you haven't heard," said Harry. "Probably the Spaniards are arguing over who's going to get which part of England once Philip coaxes the queen into handing it over."

"Oh, Harry," I said. "Really."

"My wife lives in a state of happy illusion," Harry said, picking up a card. His voice was slurred. "She believes that the queen is going to keep Philip in his place, and that England won't be handed over to the Pope."

"I believe the queen will exercise common sense and not alienate the people."

Thomas Wyatt smiled at me. He was a handsome man in his early thirties, the son of the poet who had narrowly escaped being accused of adultery with Anne Boleyn. "We can hope."

"I think we should give her a chance to do what is right for England," I said. Perhaps I had had a cup of wine too much myself, for I added, "After all, Harry has pledged to support her marriage."

Thomas Grey turned to his brother. "Is that true, Harry? I wouldn't have thought it of you."

Harry shrugged. "It could be worse. The queen's husband could be one of the savages the Spaniards bring over from Africa."

"No," said Thomas. "It would be better. She could teach him how to worship that bread of hers, and dress him up and put a crown on his head, and then she could leave the governing of England to Englishmen, while the savage begets a child upon her—or tries. That might be a bit much, even for a savage."

"This is abominable," I said, pronouncing the word too carefully. I rose. "How can you speak of the queen so? She has been merciful to our daughter. We owe her gratitude, not vile jokes like these."

"Now, Fan, let us have our fun," said Harry as I turned to stare. To call me "Fan" in front of men I hardly knew, he had to be well and truly drunk. "God knows we won't be having it for long, once the queen takes all that's ours back and gives it to the monasteries. Not once she milks us to pay for Spain's wars and puts us at war with the French. Not once she sacrifices England so that she can find a little pleasure between her leg—"

As regally as I could with my head beginning to ache, I swept from the room.

∽

Late the next afternoon, Harry, looking so hung over I might have felt sorry for him were he not my husband, appeared in my chamber. "Have you got anything else vile to say?" I asked.

"Yes. I mean, no. I mean—oh, I don't know what to say. Just read this letter. I received it yesterday before my brothers and the rest came."

I stared at the familiar handwriting, confident and upright as ever despite the fact that the author was imprisoned in the Tower. "Jane wrote this?"

"Yes. It's a fair copy of a letter she sent to Harding when she heard of his apostasy."

Thomas Harding was one of our former chaplains. Like a number of other clergy, he had abandoned his Protestant faith when Mary came to the throne. "How did she hear of that?" Though we wrote to our daughter from time to time, we—or at least I—carefully avoided any topics that might offend the queen. I thus spent a great deal of time writing about the weather, my plans for my garden, and Kate's pets, all subjects I knew thoroughly bored Jane but at least would not send her to the scaffold.

Harry shrugged. "We have friends in the Tower guard. But read the letter."

So oft as I call to mind (dear friend and chosen brother) the dreadful and fearful sayings of God, that he which layeth hold upon the plough and looketh back again, is not meet for the kingdom of heaven; and on the other side to remember the comfortable words of our Savior Christ, to all those that forsaking themselves do follow him, I cannot but marvel at thee and lament thy case; that thou, which sometimes wert the lively member of Christ, but now the deformed imp of the devil; sometimes the beautiful temple of God, but now the stinking and filthy kennel of Satan; sometimes the unspotted spouse of thy Savior, but now the unshamefast paramour of Antichrist; sometimes my faithful brother, but now a stranger and apostate; yea sometimes my stout Christian soldier, but now a cowardly runaway. So oft as I consider the threatenings and promises of the Divine Justice to all those which faithfully love him, I cannot but speak to thee, yea, rather cry out and exclaim against thee, thou seed of Satan, and not of Juda,

whom the devil hath deceived, the world hath beguiled, and desire of life hath
subverted, and made of a Christian an infidel.

For pages Jane went on like this; the letter never seemed to end. Finally, I folded the epistle in half. I wanted to tear it in two.

"Well?" Harry said. "Our girl minces no words, you'll have to admit. A pity women can't take the pulpit; she would be a natural for it."

"Harry, this is insane! How can she write foolish tirades such as this, when she is living under a sentence of death?"

"But your precious queen is merciful, isn't she?"

"She is merciful, but she can be pushed too far, and Jane is trying her forbearance to the utmost. How could you encourage her to write this?"

"I didn't, as a matter of fact. She took it upon herself. But don't you see? She may be writing to Harding, but it's me she is thinking of, as well. I and all of the others who have sold our souls to Queen Mary."

"Harry, she means no such thing! You have not renounced your faith."

"Not yet."

"You have only agreed not to oppose the queen's legislation and to support her marriage."

"Doesn't that amount to the same thing, my dear?"

"It does not."

Harry shook his head. "In our Jane's eyes, it does."

"Harry, it does not! Jane is an intelligent young woman. She surely realizes that you are acting for her own good. If she doesn't, whoever is smuggling those letters out for her should be told that. What is wrong with you? I can guess. You've been ill lately and had too much wine the night before on top of it all. You need to rest."

My husband ran a weary hand over his beard. For the first time, I noticed it was beginning to develop flecks of gray. In a few weeks, he would be seven and thirty. "Perhaps you're right."

"I know I'm right. Please go to your chamber and lie down." I indicated Jane's letter, which I still held in my hand. "This is seditious, Harry. Please, let us burn it, and hope that the original goes no farther than Harding."

Harry took it from me swiftly as I moved to the fire. "No. I want to keep it."

꩜

Over Christmas, Harry and I went several times to Richmond, where the queen was holding court. It was just a short distance from our house at Sheen. The lady Elizabeth had chosen to spend Christmas at Ashridge in Hertfordshire, so I was not put in the uncomfortable position of having to take precedence over her. Harry made no awkward comments about religion or the queen's marriage, and our visits went smoothly.

Then, around the third week of January, Adrian Stokes came to my chamber, his face grim. "Your Grace, I do not know how to tell you this."

"My daughter? She is ill?"

"No. Your Grace, I have never known a kinder master than the Duke of Suffolk. No one who knows him can truly say otherwise."

"I don't understand."

"No. How could you? I have not told anyone besides Your Grace what I have learned. It pains me to say it. I have struggled for the last day or so about whether I should even say it, but Your Grace has been as kind to me as the duke has. It is something you should know."

I looked at Master Stokes a little impatiently as he stumbled on. "Those men who were here before Christmas. Sir Thomas Wyatt and the rest."

"Yes?"

"They have induced the duke to turn traitor to the Crown."

I sank down into a chair, with Master Stokes's assistance. "In what way?" I managed.

"These are men who are bitterly opposed to Queen Mary's Spanish marriage. I'm not entirely sure exactly what their objective is. To be honest, I'm not sure they are, either. Some want to force the queen to listen to her people and to break off her marriage plans to Prince Philip. Others want to force the queen to abdicate and put the lady Elizabeth on the throne. Still others want to marry the lady Elizabeth to the Earl of Devon and have them rule together."

"Oh, for mercy's sake, tell me that they don't want to put Jane on the throne again!"

"No. At least none are saying so if they do. She's too closely associated with Northumberland and his schemes, I think, for anyone to dare to propose that. The lady Elizabeth is a different matter. The people like her, even the ones who hated her mother, and because she wasn't involved in any of last summer's business, there are many who would gladly see her on the throne."

"Is she involved in this?"

"Not that I can tell. Wyatt approached her, but she never replied."

"And how are they to accomplish this?"

"Wyatt is to lead a rising in Kent, Carew in the southwest, and Croft in the

Welsh marches. The duke will be leading one in the midlands. Then they are going to converge upon London. The French are said to be involved, too. The risings are to take place on Palm Sunday."

"You are sure of this?"

"Yes, Your Grace," Master Stokes said, reverting to formality. "You may ask me what business I had hearing of this in the first place. I will tell you honestly—none. I accidentally heard scraps of things which made me suspicious, and I remained alert for more, because I knew Your Grace would be concerned—and because I thought you should know."

"He has told me nothing. Nothing! I believed he would be faithful to the queen."

"I know. But, Your Grace, that is not the worst of it. It was not hard for me, a mere servant, to learn of this. I believe others may have learned of it, too, and at the highest levels. There are rumors that men are being arrested already. My lord Thomas Grey was here just now. He did not stay to dine with the duke, as he usually does. I believe he brought a warning."

"I must speak to Harry," I said, rising. But when had Harry ever listened to me? I turned to Master Stokes. "Please come with me," I begged.

Harry had been ill with the stone, and I expected to find him in his bed when I was admitted to his chamber. Instead, I found him dressing and in conversation with his secretary, John Bowyer. "Harry. I must speak to you."

Harry nodded, and Bowyer hurried away. "Very well, my dear, but there's little time to chat. I must go to Bradgate."

"Bradgate? Without me?"

"I am afraid, my dear, some business has come up. It shall be accomplished quickly—"

"There is no business," I said, gathering courage from Master Stokes standing beside me. "I know what your intentions are, Harry."

"Intentions?"

"For mercy's sake, Harry, do not play these games with me! You have joined a conspiracy."

"Who told you of this?"

"I did, Your Grace," said Master Stokes.

Harry glared at Master Stokes. "Sometimes, sir, I have thought that you get above your place with my wife. This is one of those times. I hope that is the worst you get up to with her."

Master Stokes spoke before I could. "Why are you going to Bradgate?"

"And now my wife's master of horse examines me! You should have gone into the law, Master Stokes. But as you seem to have learned so much, I'll tell you. Our plan is going off prematurely. Help me dress, will you? There you go, pretend I'm a horse. Carew took panic when he was summoned before the council, and headed down to the West Country and started to agitate against the queen. Renard's been snooping about, too, and he told the queen what he knew. And that idiot Courtenay told Gardiner what he knew. Why we approached him— Anyway, it's now or never. Wyatt and Sir William Pickering have already left for Kent. I must do my part now."

"Harry, this is insanity! The queen has been warned. She raised men against our daughter's cause in days. Don't you think she will be able to do the same now?"

"That was before this Spanish marriage. I can't linger to discuss this, my dear. Thomas tells me that Sir Edward Warner has already been arrested."

Someone knocked hesitantly at the door. "Good God, what now?" snapped Harry.

A messenger entered, wearing the queen's livery. "Your Grace, I come bearing the queen's desire that you attend her at court. The matter is urgent."

"You can see that I was just on my way to court," Harry said. "Just let me break my fast, and I will go." He nodded to the servant who had accompanied the messenger. "Give him some money and refreshment, and I will join him shortly."

"So you are going to court?" I asked when they were gone.

"Certainly not. Don't you know a trap when you see one, my dear? I'm for Bradgate."

"Harry, no! Go to the queen. Tell her you repent of your foolishness."

"Is it foolishness to stop England from becoming a principality of Spain? Is it foolishness to want my girl freed from the Tower?"

"This won't help her!"

"Nor will it hurt her. She knows nothing of this. But I'll be damned if I'll keep playing the good Catholic while she rots there as a hostage for my good behavior."

"You can serve Jane best by being loyal to the queen! You must have patience, Harry! The queen will free her, if only you give her time. Please."

I dropped to my knees in supplication. Harry just shook his head and smiled. He bent to brush his lips against the top of my head.

"Get off the floor, Frances," he said, not unkindly. "My mind is made up. It's been made up since I got that letter to Harding."

He turned toward the door. "I may be sending for some plate to sell," he called over his shoulder. "I'm probably going to need it."

⋙

The next morning, a group of armed men came from the queen. "Your Grace, your husband has been proclaimed a traitor to the Crown. We've been sent here to look around."

I nodded.

The queen's men went from room to room, searching everything in which anything incriminating could be concealed. I watched as every coffer at Sheen was ransacked and its contents thrown onto the floor. The men did not even spare the chambers of Kate and Mary, who watched, terrified, as the searchers rooted through their belongings.

Numbly, I wandered into the library. There, men were lifting Harry's books and shaking them, alert for any incriminating piece of paper that might fall onto the floor. "If you see something that looks heretical, throw it into this pile," said the man who was in charge of the others.

"That's just about everything," grumbled another man. "Wait, what about this?"

"Don't bother with it."

I watched as the men tossed to the floor a beautiful illuminated volume of *The Canterbury Tales* that had belonged to Edward IV's queen, who was my great-grandmother as well as Harry's. It was followed by a Latin grammar Jane had used when she was very young. Finally, I got the courage to ask, "Have you heard what is to happen to me and my girls?"

"You're to stay here until the duke is captured. As he will be, the fool. No books about military strategy here, you'll notice."

"And Jane?"

"No idea." With a final shake, the man tossed the last of the books to the floor. "We'll be back for the heretical ones later," he said over his shoulder as he left. "Don't you be trying to hide them while we're gone."

I nodded. Then I sank to my knees among Harry's savaged books and cried.

41

Jane Dudley
January 1554 to February 12, 1554

I WAS AT WHITEHALL, MAKING MY USUAL FUTILE EFFORT TO SEE THE QUEEN, when someone hurried in and whispered something to the guard. "You'll have to go home," the guard said then, addressing all of us petitioners. "The queen can't see you today."

By this time, I had become friendly with most of the palace guards. "What is going on?" I asked when the other supplicants had stomped or shuffled away, depending upon their humor.

"Treason, my lady. On the part of Sir Thomas Wyatt. Don't know exactly who else is involved, but they say the Duke of Suffolk is up to his knees in it."

"Suffolk? Surely to God he is not trying to put his daughter on the throne again?"

"No, my lady. This is to stop the Spanish match, I hear. But you'd best get home. Wyatt's approaching London, they say. This could turn nasty."

I thanked him and hurried toward the landing. I no longer had my own barge, but my months of going back and forth to court had won me the acquaintance of many of the men who carried passengers on the Thames. One of those boatmen, seeing me, put in where I stood waiting. "Yes, Your Grace, there's trouble about," he said cheerfully as my page helped me into the boat and Maudlyn Flower helped to arrange my voluminous skirts in the little skiff. "This man called Wyatt raised a force in Kent, and the old Duke of Norfolk was sent out to stop him."

"Norfolk? But he's at least eighty!"

"Yes, and he fought as if he was ninety. Well, you can't blame the man, I guess, shut up in the Tower as long as he had been. But it wasn't his finest moment, that's for certain. Got to Rochester with five hundred Londoners in white coats, and what do you think happened?"

"I can't imagine."

"Deserted, most of them! Their own captain stood up and made a grand speech about how the Spanish would ravish their wives and deflower their daughters if the queen was allowed to marry Prince Philip. Sent the white coats right over to Wyatt, and sent the duke back to London with his tail tied in a knot. So now it looks like Wyatt will be paying a visit to London. There's trouble elsewhere, I hear, but I can't tell you much about it, Your Grace."

"And the Duke of Suffolk is involved?"

"So they say. He's clean left his place at Sheen. Something's up, I reckon."

"I thank the Lord my sons are shut up out of harm's way," I said grimly. "Or else suspicion could fall on them. Do these people really believe the Spaniards are going to snatch their daughters from their beds if the queen marries abroad?"

"This is what you get when a woman rules," said the boatman philosophically. "Trouble." He grinned as I glared at him. "No offense meant, Your Grace."

"Mind your boat," I snapped.

❧

Back at Chelsea, I stocked up with supplies and ordered the gates shut—not that my house was fortified by any means. The news we got over the next few days was wildly contradictory. One hour, Wyatt and his men were vanquished in the field; the next, the country had plunged into civil war, like that between the houses of Lancaster and York of the previous century. Mary had been taken to the Tower; then the lady Elizabeth had been taken to the Tower. Someone even claimed Edward VI was being held there, and by the time the story came down the river to Chelsea, an octogenarian Edward V had been spotted in the Tower, as well, having been patiently waiting all of these years for an opportune time to reclaim the throne for the white rose of York.

Some truth, however, did leak through, and it was certain that on February 3, Wyatt's men arrived in Southwark, where they found London's great bridge tightly secured against them. For three days, Wyatt's troops remained in Southwark, enjoying the hospitality of the residents there and behaving as decorously as a convent of elderly nuns on pilgrimage. Meanwhile, inside the walls of London, life went on in an eerily normal manner; the lawyers were even arguing in the courts at Westminster, albeit with armor under their robes.

At last, Wyatt, growing tired of this inaction, abandoned his post. He took his men to Kingston, where they managed to cross the river. By dawn on February 7, they were at Knightsbridge, not far from my house at Chelsea. I stood on the walk on one of my house's turrets and watched them marching toward the city. Would this be the end of Mary's reign?

For those inside the city, it must have seemed for a while as if it was. As Wyatt's troops, exhausted from their all-night march and hungry, passed down Fleet Street, citizens in full harness stood immobile by their doors, letting them pass. At Charing Cross, Sir John Gage's forces, a thousand strong, panicked when Wyatt's men shot at them. Inside Whitehall, Mary's ladies screamed and wailed, while Mary herself calmly prayed. Only Lord Clinton, John's old friend, distinguished himself by making a cavalry attack on Wyatt's main forces.

At Ludgate, Wyatt and his depleted army found the gates shut against them and retreated to Temple Bar. There, the queen's forces at last brought him to surrender.

Suffolk, meanwhile, had been captured without ever being brought to battle. The other leaders were in captivity or had fled abroad. Mary was safe on her throne.

❧

Even from a distance at Chelsea, I had anxiously kept up with the events in London, so after a few nights of barely closing my eyes, I slept later than usual on Thursday, February 8. I was breaking my fast, somewhat sleepily, when Lord Paget was announced. I rose as he entered, his dark eyes looking more like those of a sad dog than ever. "My lord?"

"My lady, I wish with all my heart I did not have to tell you this. You will recall that Lord Guildford lies under sentence of death."

I felt myself begin to shake. "I recall," I managed.

"Because of this rebellion, the queen has determined to carry out the sentences against him and the lady Jane. She has commuted their sentences to beheading."

I opened my mouth. No words came out.

Lord Paget went on quietly, "I have asked the queen to spare them, as all know that they had nothing to do with the rebellion, and indeed had nothing to gain from it. But more powerful voices have prevailed."

"But why? Surely she understands that they are innocent!"

"She does. I have told her this, and so have others. But there is the fear that others may rise in their names."

"They are innocent." These seemed to be the only words I could manage.

"I will ask her again to spare them, but I am in a minority. There have always been many on the council who believed that their lives should have been taken at the same time the Duke of Northumberland's was, and this has given them a justification they lacked before. I can plead with the queen for mercy, but I can offer you no hope."

"No. There is no hope whatsoever in this world." I fingered my wedding ring. "My other sons? Does the queen feel the need to exterminate them, also?"

"No, my lady."

Not yet. I managed to say, "Thank you, my lord, for telling me about this. I hope you did not put yourself at risk by doing so."

"No. If there is anything I can do for you, please let me know. I shall pray for you."

"You can if you wish. But I truly think that God has deserted me, so I will not ask you to waste your time."

Paget put his hand on my shoulder as I stared stonily ahead. "I will anyway," he said quietly.

∽

The executions had been scheduled for the next day, February 9, but they were postponed three days while the queen tried to get the lady Jane to convert to Catholicism. It was just like the girl, I thought sourly, to prolong everyone else's agony.

While the queen was working on Jane's soul, I occupied myself as best I could. I still had Guildford's belongings, save for those possessions that had been sent to the Tower for him. No one had deemed them incriminating enough, or valuable enough, to take away. Over the next several days, I sorted through them again and again, as if they would somehow furnish a clue as to why a young man with no claim to the throne had to die for someone else's conspiracy.

I managed to go through the motions of life. I even composed a letter to the queen, begging for my son's life. Unlike the letter I'd written begging for John's, it was calm and coherent; I was vaguely proud of my effort when I looked at it afterward. But it produced no effect whatsoever. On February 12, as scheduled, my son, just a couple of weeks short of his seventeenth birthday, went to the block. I had not been allowed to visit him in the Tower. If I wanted to see him again in this life, I would have to go to Tower Hill to see him die, and so I did.

My ladies and servants begged me not to attend the execution, but I proved as stubborn as Jane had been on the question of religion. So on a freezing morning, I came early to Tower Hill so I could be as close to my son as possible. Jane was to be executed in the privacy of Tower Green as an acknowledgment of her royal blood and, I thought, as a precaution against the possibility of a volatile crowd taking exception to the death of a woman barely past girlhood.

"It's still not too late," Maudlyn Flower urged as the beat of drums shortly before ten in the morning signaled that Guildford was on his way. "Please, Your Grace, let us go home. Your health has been poor lately," she added as a gust of wind made me shiver.

"No." And then I saw my boy, being led to the scaffold by Thomas Offley, the sheriff of London. Some men, angry at the queen's decision to execute him and anxious to show him sympathy, had been waiting to greet him as he was led out of the Beauchamp Tower, and they still trailed behind him, though he was surrounded by guards. He had no priest with him, and I felt a pang of satisfaction that he had denied the queen this concession. His expression was somber but not fearful, and he had his chin slightly up. *Like a Dudley*, I thought.

Guildford was dressed well, as I'd expected, in black velvet. Probably he had discussed what to wear with his brothers, who had all been moved to the Beauchamp Tower to accommodate the press of prisoners from Wyatt's rebellion. I pictured them in their crowded prison quarters, laying out one gown, then another, my Robert snorting, "I wouldn't be seen dead in that! Pick another."

Taking leave of his well-wishers, Guildford mounted the scaffold steps quickly and nimbly, like the young man he was, leaving his guards behind. I caught myself wondering how Jane would mount her own scaffold. Would she shake out her skirts in the fastidious little manner of hers that had so annoyed me?

But it was not the time for thinking unkind thoughts.

"Why, he's little more than a lad," said a woman standing near me to her companion. A few minutes before, she had been happily munching on a hazelnut. She lowered her voice. "They'll be executing babies next, for God's sake."

"He's a young 'un, all right. His poor mother will be heartbroken."

He is, and she will be, I thought. But I kept staring at the scaffold.

Guildford walked to the rail of the scaffold, just as his father and Somerset and countless others had done before him. He cleared his throat once, then twice; he had never liked it when his tutors forced him to make speeches. I found myself nodding at him encouragingly, willing the words to come out of his mouth as if he were in his chamber with his tutor instead of standing atop Tower Hill.

"Good Christian people, I am come hither to die, according to law," he finally said, and I hoped he had not decided to appropriate Anne Boleyn's execution speech for himself. But he continued in a voice that was louder and clearer than it had been at the outset. "I took no part in this recent unrest, but I am guilty of wishing to wear the crown matrimonial on my head, and for that arrogance and presumption I deserve to die. I thank the queen, who is good and gracious, for allowing me a nobleman's death, instead of the traitor's death to which I was sentenced. Oh, and I should say I was justly condemned by the law, and I bear malice to no one, and if I have offended anyone, I hope he will forgive me." Guildford paused and stared at the crowd, plainly considering what to speak of next. "I guess that's all I have to say," he said after a moment and knelt quickly to say his prayers. They took considerably longer than his speech. Guildford prayed so earnestly and with so little self-consciousness, holding his eyes and hands up to his Maker again and again, I felt my own faith returning, if just barely.

My son rose, took off his gown and doublet, and neatly turned down his shirt collar. The black embroidery on it was my own handiwork. Then Guildford forgave his kneeling executioner—the lame one who had beheaded John—and considered the blindfold that was offered to him. He shook his head, refusing it, and laid himself on the block. The executioner slowly raised his axe.

"Spare him!" I pushed forward. A man was blocking my path to the scaffold, and I began to beat on his back. "For pity's sake, don't take my boy! He is innocent. He has done noth—"

The axe fell, and I crumpled to the ground.

42

Frances Grey
February 8, 1554, to February 23, 1554

I DID NOT SEE MY GIRL DIE AT TOWER GREEN, AND FOR THAT I WILL NEVER forgive myself. I should have had the courage she did.

Harry's part in what became known as Wyatt's rebellion had been short and disastrous. Ill prepared for the sudden change of plans, short of money and men, and suffering from poor health, my husband had tried his best. With the help of his brothers, he had issued proclamations against the danger of the queen's Spanish marriage and managed to get Leicester to shut its gates against the queen's supporters. But the queen in her letters to the counties claimed he was trying to put Jane back on the throne, which was only too easy to believe. The Earl of Huntingdon, whom Harry had hoped would support his cause, arrived instead in pursuit of him. With the walls of Coventry closed against him, Harry had divided his money with his fifty followers and had determined to flee abroad. Aided by a servant, who brought him food, he had hidden in the hollow of a tree on our property at Astley until he could leave without being detected. But Huntingdon's dogs had sniffed him out, as they also did his brother John, who was found hiding under a stack of hay. On February 2, Harry was Huntingdon's prisoner; on February 10, he was back in the Tower, where he heard the news I had learned two days before: our daughter was to be executed.

I begged to see the queen. But this time her door, and her heart, were shut as firmly against me as they had been against the Duchess of Northumberland the summer before. My daughter would be given the chance to meet with the queen's chaplain, John Feckenham, who would attempt to save her soul. That was all.

There was nothing stopping me from seeing my daughter die. Oh, I would have had to get permission to get into Tower Green, but surely a mother would have been allowed that privilege. But I did not dare. Perhaps I feared I could not stay sane after seeing such a sight; perhaps I feared something more mundane, that I might collapse and embarrass my daughter in her last moments. Instead, I spent the night, and much of the morning, in prayer, though I knew Jane hardly needed my intervention with the Lord. It was Adrian Stokes who went to the Tower that Monday, February 12, first to see Guildford Dudley die on Tower Hill and then to see Jane die on Tower Green.

It was past noon when Master Stokes arrived at Sheen, where Kate and Mary sat with me in my chamber. With him were my daughter's waiting women, Ursula Ellen and Elizabeth Tilney, both of their faces creased with tears. We women came together in a wordless embrace as Master Stokes slipped from the room.

Later that day, when prayer had made me strong enough to hear about my daughter's last hours, Jane's women and Master Stokes told me of them. For three days, Feckenham, a kindly man, had disputed theology with Jane and found her intransigent. But approaching death had softened Jane, and when Feckenham, unable to convert Jane and unable to persuade Mary to pardon her, had begged to do her the last service of accompanying her to the scaffold, she had agreed. Wearing the same black dress she had worn to her trial, Jane had walked to her place of execution calmly, reading from the book of Esther as her ladies trailed sobbing behind her. Only the sight she had seen a little while before, that of her husband's headless body being carted back from Tower Hill, had discomfited her, and that only for a short time.

On the scaffold, my daughter had given a speech, which Master Stokes had scribbled down himself for me. In my chamber, I listened as he delivered it in his Leicestershire accent:

Good people, I am come hither to die, and by a law I am condemned to the same. The fact, indeed, against the queen's highness was unlawful, and the consenting thereunto by me: but touching the procurement and desire thereof by me or on my behalf, I do wash my hands thereof in innocence, before God, and the face of you, good Christian people, this day. And therewith I pray you all, good Christian people, to bear me witness that I die a true Christian woman, and that I look to be saved by none other means, but only by the mercy of God in the merits of the blood of his only son, Jesus Christ: and I confess, when I did know the word of God I neglected the same, loved myself and the world, and therefore this plague or punishment is happily and worthily happened unto me

for my sins; and yet I thank God of his goodness that he hath thus given me a
time and respite to repent. And now, good people, while I am alive, I pray you
to assist me with your prayers.

"She knelt and said the fifty-first Psalm, with Feckenham helping," said
Elizabeth Tilney. "Then she rose and thanked him for keeping her company.
She said that during the last three days she had been more bored by him than
frightened by the shadow of death. Then she said that she hoped God would
reward him for his efforts."

I blinked. My daughter had made a joke on the scaffold?

"She gave Thomas Bridges her prayer book, then handed me her gloves
and handkerchief," Elizabeth continued. She still clutched the gloves. Mistress
Ellen was stroking the snow-white handkerchief, embroidered crookedly *JG*.
"The executioner offered to help her untie her gown, but she gave him a look
and had us ladies do it. Then she forgave her executioner and—and begged
him to be quick. He promised her that he would, and he also promised her
when she asked that he would not take her head before she lay down.

"The only time she lost her composure was when she put on the blindfold
and couldn't see where to put her head. She fumbled around the block. None
of us thought to help her—it was as if we would be sending her to her death.
So someone finally stepped forward, and she tossed her beautiful hair in front
of her, to bare her neck, and said, 'Lord, into my hands I commend my spirit.'
And the headsman was quick."

"Everyone on Tower Green was weeping," Master Stokes said. "There were
no cheers." He paused to give me time to weep, but I reached a point beyond
tears. "The lieutenant gave me some things," he continued. "Another handkerchief of your sister's for you, Lady Mary, and this for you, Lady Katherine."

Mary sniffled into the handkerchief while Kate stared gloomily at the New
Testament in Greek Master Stokes handed her.

"There is a letter written in it to you, Lady Katherine," Adrian said. He
handed another little book to me. "And there is one written inside here for
you, Your Grace."

Late that night, I read my letter. Jane's letter to Kate has since been published. It was an exhortation to the godly life, kindly meant but perhaps misad-
dressed to a pretty young woman who wanted only to marry a kind young man
and have his children. Mine never has been published and never will be, for it
was of little interest to the greater world, only of immeasurable consolation to

me. It told me my daughter loved me and she would pray for me in the next world to have the courage to face the trials to come. On that bleak February night, this was what I needed to hear. I wear that book on my girdle today, and when I need heart, I only have to open the book and hold it before my eyes. It will be placed in my hands when I am laid in my grave.

∽

On the same day Jane died, gallows rose ominously everywhere around London. Even they would not hold all of the men who would die for their part in Wyatt's rebellion; some would be hanged in their own doorways.

Harry's trial came five days later. I did not go; my heart was too bitter against him. It was not only that I held him responsible for Jane's death, by far the worst of his sins: he had wreaked other destruction, as well. With his treason, all the worse after he had been forgiven for his role in the events of last summer, he had blighted my other daughters' futures. What men of substance would want to marry them now?

And he had blighted my life, too. Bradgate, where my baby son and daughter lay at rest, was forfeit to the Crown: never would I be able to visit their graves. So were the rest of Harry's lands. For the time being, I had a home at Sheen, but that was bound to be taken from me any day. I would soon be like the Duchess of Northumberland, who I had heard was living on the queen's sufferance at Chelsea and selling her plate to keep her increasingly small household fed.

All this, when I had pleaded on my knees for Harry to abandon Wyatt's cause and make his peace with the queen. Why, for once in his life, couldn't he have listened to me?

The verdict came as no surprise: Harry was found guilty, after he argued that preserving the realm from strangers was not treason. The Earl of Arundel, who had arrested Northumberland, sentenced Harry to death. He was to die on February 23.

I pleaded for Harry's life, but more, I am ashamed to admit, for form's sake than out of affection; in my grief and anger, I truly did not care much whether my husband died. Yet a more impassioned plea would probably have not met with any better result. I heard nothing from the queen until the morning of February 22, when she sent word that if I wished to see Harry before his death, I could.

"Should I go?" I asked Adrian Stokes, who sat preparing a list of horses and stable goods I hoped to keep for myself and my daughters.

"You are thinking of not going, Your Grace? It may have been his last request."

I winced at the reproach in his voice. "I cannot forget that it is his folly that brought us to this. If only he had listened to me."

"He is the father of your children. The lady Jane loved him dearly."

"She was the only person who meant anything to him, I think sometimes. And his stupidity killed her."

"Your Grace, if you do not go and wish him well, you may forever regret not having made your peace with him in this life." I shook my head, and Master Stokes continued. "You know that is true, or you would not be asking me for my opinion. Go, my lady. He and you will both be better for it."

I sighed. "Will you go with me? I do not think I can face the Tower by myself."

"I was going to offer to accompany you, Your Grace."

Harry sat at a table, reading, when I was shown into his cell. Before his rebellion, he had been tending toward stoutness; now, he looked thinner and coughed when he spoke. His doublet was torn and dirty. It must have been what he was wearing when he was caught hiding in a tree. "Is that all you have to wear?" I said as he rose.

"I'm saving my best for tomorrow. It's not much better, but it's clean."

"I will have some things sent over for you this afternoon."

"Thank you."

I looked around the chamber. Save for a few books—some, I supposed, sent from Jane's rooms after her death—it was comfortless. I could have at least thought to inquire about my husband's material needs after he was taken prisoner. "I would have sent some of your things here to you earlier, if you'd asked for them."

"I didn't want to trouble you." Harry looked at the ground. "Truth is, I wasn't sure you'd come here today."

"I wasn't sure, either."

"I know you must hate me for what I did. Trust me, I hate myself for it. It never occurred to me that Jane would be in danger."

"It should have."

"Yes." Tears were running down Harry's face. "I saw her die, saw her pay the price for my folly."

"You watched?"

"From beginning to end." He indicated the window seat behind him. "I could see everything from there."

For the first time, I realized Harry's chamber looked directly onto Tower Green. I glimpsed Jane's scaffold, still standing, before I quickly turned my head. "The guards made you watch?"

"No. I made myself watch. It was the worst punishment I could think of, other than having to swing the axe myself." Harry wiped his hand against his eye—he had no handkerchief—and continued, "I saw Guildford walk to the scaffold, too. They were both so calm, Frances. They'd looked more uneasy the day of their wedding." He reached for a small prayer book that was lying on the table. "This is what Jane brought to the scaffold. I can't give it to you. Jane inscribed it to the lieutenant, as he had become fond of her, and he will be keeping it for himself. But there are two messages there for me, one from Guildford and one from Jane. I keep reading them. They have brought me indescribable comfort."

Harry turned to first one page of the book, then to the other.

> *Your loving and obedient son wishes unto Your Grace long life in this world, with as much joy and comfort as ever I wished to myself, and in the world to come joy everlasting. Your most humble son till his death.*
>
> *G. Dudley*

> *The Lord comfort Your Grace, and that in his word, wherein all creatures only are to be comforted. And though it hath pleased God to take away two of your children, yet think not, I most humbly beseech Your Grace, that you have lost them, but trust that we, by leaving this mortal life, have won an immortal life. And I for my part, as I have honored Your Grace in this life, will pray for you in another life. Your Grace's humble daughter,*
>
> *Jane Dudley*

My husband carefully folded the little book and smiled. "Writing those messages was the only thing I think the two of them ever cooperated in together. Poor Guildford. Jane wouldn't even see him before their executions. The lieutenant told me she preferred to focus on spiritual matters, but it would have been kind for her to say good-bye to the lad. I would have liked having him as a son-in-law. I got on rather well with him. I always thought our Jane was rather unfair to him. The worst you could say of him was that he wanted to be king, and I daresay he'd have done a better job of it than that turncoat Courtenay would have."

"I wonder how their marriage would have turned out."

"Probably better than ours, I fear. I haven't been the best husband in the world."

"You weren't that bad," I protested.

"No, I didn't beat you, I didn't shout at you, and I was never unfaithful to you, but I sometimes think I could have been more to you." Harry sat on the window seat and drew me to sit beside him, our backs to the scaffold. "I was remembering our wedding night. I took you with all of the finesse of a Southwark tomcat. You cried for hours."

"I was afraid that it would always be that way, that's all. But it did get better."

"Well, I'm glad to hear that much. I wanted you, you know. That's why I broke off my betrothal with Arundel's sister to marry you."

I turned to him, shocked. "I was always told that was your mother's doing."

"No, it was mine. I insisted upon it, and my mother had no choice but to agree. You were the king's niece, of course, and I liked that, but I also liked you more than I did Arundel's sister. You had the better nature, poor girl." Harry turned aside and coughed.

"You're ill."

"A bit. I should have asked you to bring along that potion of yours. It always put me right. Did I ever tell you that?"

"Yes," I lied. I touched his forehead. "You're feverish, too."

"I'll feel better this time tomorrow." Harry sighed. "My brothers are here, too, you know. I'm glad my mother isn't alive to see this. She never did approve of much I did to begin with, and now she would be furious with me."

"Has the queen tried to get you to convert?" I said, hoping to divert my husband to a less gloomy subject.

Harry managed a smile. "Oh, yes. As a matter of fact, I'll be visited by a priest later today, I hear. I'll be damned if I will join the Papists. At least I can do that much right by our girl." He squeezed my hand and rose. "I am glad you came, but I think I should be alone now, so that I can prepare myself to make a good end. Who accompanied you here?"

"Master Stokes."

"I thought so."

I bristled. "Harry, you were unjust to him—and to me—the other day. I have never been anything but a faithful wife to you. He has never spoken or acted with anything but the greatest respect for you."

"Yes. It was wrong of me, I suppose. But there are times I've wondered, especially since I've been here, whether he might fancy you in his bed."

"It is all in your imagination."

"Maybe," said Harry. "But it would be pleasant to have been right about something for once in my life." He drew me to my feet and placed a hand on each of my shoulders. "Thank you for coming, Frances. Pray for me, my dear. I shall need it."

"I shall."

"But not after I am dead. Superstition."

"I won't," I promised.

"I'd prefer you not to come tomorrow, in case you were planning on it. I'd rather you remember me as I was in less awkward circumstances."

"All right, Harry."

Harry swallowed. "And will you be so kind as to forgive me for the wrongs I've done to you and the girls? It's a kindness I know I don't deserve, but it would make these last hours better for me."

I thought of Harry watching as our daughter died. He was right: there had been no greater punishment he could have undergone than that. "I will, Harry."

"Thank you." Harry smiled at me. In his relief at being forgiven, he looked almost boyish again.

Master Stokes had also been right; it would have haunted me forever if I had not bothered to come to say good-bye. "I'm glad I came here."

"So am I." Harry kissed me, more gently than passionately, and then led me to the door, where Master Stokes stood outside, talking with the guards. "Take care of her, Stokes."

"I will, Your Grace."

Harry gave me a knowing, almost mischievous look, and raised his hand in farewell.

❧

"The duke bore his execution bravely," Master Stokes reported to me the next day. "He was steadfast in his Protestant faith to the end, even though the queen sent a priest to accompany him. He made a short speech, very dignified." An odd look came across his face.

"What is it? You are not hiding something?"

"No. Well, there was a moment just before he climbed the scaffold, he tried to keep the priest from following him. They got into a shoving match."

Yes, that was my Harry.

"And at the end, just before the duke took off his gown and doublet, a man popped up on the scaffold and asked, 'My lord, how should I get the money that you owe me?' How he managed to get up there, I have no idea. The duke didn't lose his temper. He just said, 'Good fellow, trouble me not now, but go to my officers.' He was a good man, Your Grace, and deserved a happier fate. I shall miss him."

So, I realized when I prepared to climb into my empty bed that evening, would I. Instead of settling into bed, I dropped to my knees and, breaking my promise to Harry, prayed for his soul.

It couldn't hurt. And if he was already in heaven and didn't need my prayers, he surely wouldn't hold a grudge against me for offering them anyway.

43

Jane Dudley
February 1554 to June 1554

FOR A DAY AFTER GUILDFORD'S DEATH, I LAY IN MY BED, UTTERLY UNDONE by the cruelty of this world. What was the point of going on? But after a day of weeping, I knew this self-pity could avail me nothing. I had four sons left on Earth. It was up to me to get them set free.

And so, a few days after Guildford's remains were buried in an unmarked grave at the Chapel of St. Peter ad Vincula, I was back haunting the court.

It was hardly a promising place to be. In London, one could not turn a corner without running into a hanging corpse; the air was so rank with the smell of rotting traitors, no one went out without a pomander clutched to his or her nose. The lady Elizabeth, pale and ill, had been forcibly brought to Whitehall. Suspected of complicity in the Wyatt rebellion, she remained shut off from her sister. Rumors flew that she would soon follow Lady Jane to Tower Green, where the scaffold remained. Wyatt, in captivity, was being questioned daily, but so far had refused to implicate the lady Elizabeth, even, it was said, under torture.

In the midst of all that uncertainty, my daughter Mary and her husband, Henry Sidney, came from Penshurst. With them was Katheryn, who had been staying with Mary since John's death. I had hoped that the change of scene might do her good. "Is Guildford really dead?" she asked as soon as she dismounted from her horse and embraced me.

"Yes, my child. He is with your father now. We will meet them both again, never fear."

"That is what Lord Hastings said." Katheryn sniffled.

"Lord Hastings wrote to you?"

"Yes, Mama, the most beautiful letter. It was very kind, and he sent me a pair of sweet gloves, too." Katheryn extended her hands proudly.

"They're lovely," I said, sniffing the fine perfume emanating from the gloves. I, too, had had a letter, this one from Lord Hastings's father, the Earl of Huntingdon. Although he had not broken off the betrothal, it was plain he held no great enthusiasm for it. He would leave the matter, he wrote me coolly, for his son to decide when he was a little older. Or, I had surmised, until a better prospect came along, which it was bound to do if the earl continued to rise in Mary's favor. And if Reginald Pole, the cardinal who was Lord Hastings's long-exiled uncle, returned to England, as expected, he would likely take an interest in the marital prospects of his nephew.

But I would not let these thoughts intrude upon the hopes of Katheryn, especially when she was still mourning her father and now Guildford. "So I understand you have business for the queen?" I asked Henry after we had spoken quietly of my dead son for some time.

"Yes. I am among those appointed to escort Prince Philip from Spain to England. I owe my appointment mainly to my ability to speak good French and Italian."

I smiled. "There is no need to be modest in our company. I know you had served King Edward on embassies and had won praise."

"Well, yes." My son-in-law flushed, and Mary beamed at him. He leaned forward. "I do have hopes of turning this assignment to the good of our family. The prince will want English allies when he comes here, and I will do my best to impress upon him the advantage of allowing my brothers to go free and to serve him."

My eyes filled with tears as Henry referred to my sons as his brothers. It was a precious thing these days, when so many others had distanced themselves from our family. Save for John's half sisters and a few old friends, hardly anyone visited me except for a handful of paupers at mealtimes, which was just as well, because I barely had enough to feed the few guests I did receive. "If you can manage that, you will have my undying gratitude. For I am certainly making no headway," I admitted. Time, it was said, could wear down a stone, but Queen Mary remained as obdurate as ever. It was me, I sometimes thought, who was being worn away. Riding for more than short distances tired me, and there were days when I had pains in my chest that would not cease. These were matters I preferred to keep to myself for now, however. There was no need to add my own secret fears to my family's misery. I smiled at my son-in-law. "Running off with you was one of the best decisions my daughter ever made."

❧

Just a few days after Henry Sidney and the rest of the English embassy left for Spain, the lady Elizabeth came to the Tower, not as Mary's guest but as her prisoner. I wondered whether she and her old friend, my son Robert, ever glimpsed each other there. Even after Wyatt went to the scaffold the next month, using his dying speech to exonerate both the lady Elizabeth and Courtenay from guilt, the queen's sister remained a captive.

In mid-April, a few days after Wyatt's death, I went to join the crowd of the queen's petitioners and was placed on my usual stool. I was sewing a shirt for Hal (his wife sewed them, too, but not as well as I could) when the guard approached me. "Her Majesty will see you, Your Grace."

I blinked. "Me?"

"Yes."

After all of the months of waiting, I now had but moments to compose myself. I patted down my clothes, hoping I looked seemly. Quickly, I checked to see if the rosary I always carried to court was prominently attached to my girdle. Perhaps this was what John had had in mind in the first place when he gave it to me.

I sank to the ground in obeisance before the queen, fighting back the dizziness that had begun recently to overtake me when I changed position. "Rise, my lady." I complied, swaying slightly as I did. The queen looked at me closely. "You are not ill, my lady?"

"I have attacks of giddiness at times, Your Majesty. They pass quickly."

Mary quickly turned her attention to my waist. "We see you have embraced the true faith, my lady." Her voice hardened. "Are you sincere in doing so?"

"It is not the religion I have practiced over the last several years, as Your Majesty knows, but I am reacquainting myself with its majesty and beauty. And I promised my husband I would follow his wishes and adhere to the Catholic faith."

"Do you hear the Mass in your household?"

"I keep no priest in my household; I cannot afford to do so. But we go to our parish church faithfully."

"You wished to put a petition to us."

"Yes, Your Majesty." I hesitated, wondering whether I was about to ask too much at a time. But who knew when if ever I might get to meet the queen again? Not even the lady Elizabeth had been allowed this privilege since arriving at the Tower. "I would like to ask that my sons, my husband's brother Sir Andrew, and I myself be pardoned, and be allowed to show how loyally we can serve Your Majesty."

"We will consider a pardon for you, as you were but an obedient wife. Your sons and Sir Andrew must wait our further consideration and consultation with our council."

"I thank you, Your Majesty. While my sons continue in confinement"—*prison*, I decided swiftly, would sound too harsh in the queen's ears—"may I request that they be allowed to hear the Mass?"

"The guards at the Tower do not report that they have shown any signs of embracing the true faith. Why, your son Guildford refused a priest."

He was sixteen, dying for a conspiracy he knew nothing of. Would you deprive the boy of that one last satisfying act of defiance? "He was young and foolish about such things. My older three sons have greater understanding of these matters, being, well, older, and my youngest son will likely follow their example."

"So you believe they will hear Mass if permitted to?"

They will if they have the sense God gave a sheep, I thought. "I should like to have them given the opportunity, Your Majesty."

"We shall consider it."

"Thank you, Your Majesty. There is one more matter—my livelihood. I have the support of my daughter Katheryn and of my late husband's youngest brother, Jerome, who is a natural. There is a household dependent upon me, as well. All have suffered for my husband's treason." *John, forgive me.* "Your Majesty has generously allowed me the use of Chelsea, but we are in straitened circumstances. I would ask that you allow me to enjoy some of the lands that formed my jointure."

"Bring a petition in the Court of the Exchequer, and it will be attended to."

"Thank you, Your Majesty."

I started to drop to my knees, but the queen forestalled me. "You need not trouble yourself," she said in a voice that held more warmth than it had before.

I thanked her again. Impulsively, I added, "I am very happy Your Majesty's marriage is coming to fruition. There is no greater happiness than the married state."

"We shall soon find out," Mary said dryly. "God be with you, my lady."

"Your Majesty? I do have one last request."

"Yes?" Mary's voice was sharp again.

"I would like to visit my husband and my son in their resting place."

❧

I said my prayers over the body of Guildford, who lay a distance from the high altar at the Chapel of St. Peter ad Vincula, and dutifully added a prayer for his wife, as well, although she probably would not have approved. Then I walked a few feet forward, where, in graves marked only by four small crosses, lay two dukes between two queens: Anne Boleyn, the Duke of Somerset, John, and Katherine Howard. *The silliest queen in Christendom*, I heard John say. Perhaps lying next to her for all eternity, instead of me, might appeal to his sense of humor. I hoped so.

"I miss you so much, my love," I whispered. "I try to put a brave face on things, but it is very hard. But I am making progress with the queen, you will be glad to hear. I have finally been allowed to see her, and she didn't outright refuse to free our sons. That is something, at least—"

I heard a rustle behind me. Standing at a respectful distance, clad in black, was the Duchess of Somerset. "I am sorry to have disturbed you," she said. "I usually come here at this time. I will leave you in private, if you wish."

"There is no need. I was just leaving. The Countess of Warwick is well, I hope?"

"Yes. She visited the Earl of Warwick not long ago. She said he was in good spirits, all things considered."

"I am glad to hear that." I started to move away.

The Duchess of Somerset stopped me. "I am glad to have found you here. Do you remember me cursing your husband?"

"How could I possibly forget? And you got your wish."

"I saw how foolish a wish that was when I came to visit my husband and saw your own husband's newly made grave beside his. His death did nothing to fill the void in my heart, and your grief made mine none the lesser." Anne reached out her hand to me. "I wish you the best. I hope with all my heart that your sons are soon free. They are fine young men."

"Thank you," I said, not trusting myself to say more without giving way to emotion. I once again turned to leave, but the duchess again stopped me.

"I quite often talk to my Edward here, too," she said softly. "It does me more good than anything. Stay here until you have told your husband all you wish to tell him. I will leave you alone to do so."

☙

In May, I received my pardon, and in June, I was allowed some of my jointure lands and the manor of Hales Owen. Now I could live more comfortably and, better yet, have something to pass down to my children. My sons were also allowed to hear Mass, though how enthusiastically they responded I did not know. At least it gave them another opportunity to pass out of the Beauchamp

Tower, and if they heard Mass in the right spirit, it might please the queen to pardon them.

I had another source of interest that June: my daughter Mary, who had remained with me at Chelsea while Henry was abroad, appeared increasingly indisposed, in the best of ways. I watched with satisfaction as she waved away her food and dozed over her embroidery, as she wrinkled her nose at every strong smell. Finally, I could bear it no more. I pulled her aside one morning and asked, "Have you had a monthly course lately?"

"No. Do you think—"

I poked my daughter's bosom, which was noticeably fuller. She winced, and I nodded with satisfaction. "Having borne thirteen children, I can think of no other possibility."

Mary came into my arms and began crying. (*Moodiness*, I thought approvingly.) "Child, what is wrong?" I said.

"Everything has gone so badly for our family lately. What if my baby dies? What if I die?"

I was silent. Five of my own offspring had died as children, some as mere infants. Two of King Henry's queens, Jane Seymour and Catherine Parr, had been claimed by childbed fever. There were many more examples I could bring to mind, though I did not care to. "I can only tell you that you must hope for the best, and not give in to despair," I said finally. "I thought it would claim me when your father died, and then again when your brother died, but something brought me through. I can only assume that it is the Lord who did that, and that he also had a reason for taking away those I loved so much. What it is, I could not possibly guess. It would be kind of him to tell us occasionally, but perhaps we would not want to know the answer." I patted Mary's cheek. "You are healthy and young, but not too young, and those are two things in your favor. I, for one, intend to rejoice in this coming birth."

Mary smiled faintly. "I do, too." She paused. "But would it be too much to ask that there be no cheese allowed in the house until my child is born?"

44

Frances Grey
March 1554 to September 1554

IN EARLY MARCH, MY STEPMOTHER, KATHERINE, CAME TO STAY A LITTLE while at her manor at Kew. While there, she came to visit me. After she had spent some time condoling me upon the loss of my daughter and my husband, and I had spent some time asking her about the baby, Susan, she had borne Master Bertie in January, Katherine cleared her throat. "Have you thought about your future?"

"Future?" I asked blankly.

"Don't you realize how vulnerable you are? You're as close to the crown as you ever were—closer, with King Edward gone and the lady Elizabeth suspected of plotting with Wyatt. I don't think the queen would put you in the Tower to keep herself safe, as she's had plenty of opportunity to do so, but I do think that she will put you in bed with a Papist. Personally, I'd as soon be in the Tower, but that's just my own taste."

"She would never force me to marry."

"How can you be sure? Didn't she as good as promise you that Jane's life would be safe?"

"Yes. But that was before Harry committed treason." I dabbed at my eyes with a handkerchief.

"Well, has she ever promised you that she wouldn't have you remarry?"

"I've not seen her since Jane's and Harry's deaths. But I can't believe—"

"Frances, think! The queen's no fool. Northumberland found that out the sharp way. Unless she has a child, which is about as likely as my little dog giving birth to a litter of kittens, your royal blood is going to be a threat to her—unless she can marry you to someone she trusts. Or to someone she wants to keep sweet. Why, I wouldn't be surprised if she didn't have the Earl of Devon in mind for you."

"He's a prisoner."

"Prisoners can be set free. And you don't need me to tell you how he acted after getting set free last time. Do you want his whores lounging in your great hall, taking up the guest chambers? Do you want him putting his prick inside you after it's been God knows where?"

I shuddered. I was beginning to realize that in some ways, I had led a very sheltered life in my marriage. Faults he might have had, but Harry had never subjected me to such indignities. "But this is sheer speculation."

"True, but I wouldn't take the risk. Why not be certain? Do as I advise you now. Marry a man of your own choosing."

"Marry? But poor Harry is barely cold!"

"You can wait on consummating the marriage. It's best if you wait, anyway. If you got with child, it might be considered Harry's." Katherine looked at me sharply. "You are not with child, are you?"

"No. We had not had relations in a while. Harry had the stone, and with Jane in the Tower..." I sighed, then lifted my head. "What is all of this about my conceiving a child, when I haven't even remarried? And you say, remarry, as if it were as easy as getting a new gown!"

"For you, it could be," Katherine said. "There's a man in your household who would marry you in a trice if you asked. Master Stokes."

I blinked. "Harry said almost the same thing. But that's nonsense."

"Why?"

"He is not of my station—"

"Oh, pshaw on that! Look at my marriage to Master Bertie; I couldn't be happier. Mind you, I was fond of your father. But there were all the other entanglements that went with being married to the king's close friend. I had enemies among people whom I wouldn't know if I met them in the courtyard of St. Paul's, just by dint of my marriage. And—well, may I speak freely?"

"When have you ever done otherwise?"

"Your father wasn't chaste at the best of times, as you know, and having a young wife didn't change his stripes in that respect. There is none of that with Master Bertie. He sleeps in one of two beds, mine or his, and attends to two spheres of business, mine and his, and that suits me fine. Master Stokes, I daresay, would treat you just as well as my Master Bertie does me."

"But what makes you think Master Stokes would agree?"

Katherine snorted. "Considering that you're of royal blood and haven't lost your looks, I can't think of any reason why he would refuse. Besides that, he's fond of you; all anyone has to do is look at your horses to see that. I'd wager the stable boys live in terror of anything being the slightest bit amiss."

"That Master Stokes is very competent at his position hardly means that he is sighing with love for me."

"He accompanied you to your daughter's trial. He attended her execution. He was the one who warned you of your husband's rebellion. What more proof do you need of the man's devotion? He will do anything you ask—and you're not asking him to do anything disagreeable, after all."

"I can't decide this now. I must think about it—and pray about it."

"Of course you must," Katherine said. "I will leave you to your thoughts, then."

⁂

I did pray and think about my decision, all through that night. I had been a widow for only three weeks. If I remarried, I would be rushing to the altar more quickly than my own parents, who had been considered too precipitate by many. Yet my stepmother had a point: the longer I remained unmarried, the more I risked having a marriage arranged for me by the queen. I knew she would not wed me to a brute, but she might well marry me to one of the men who had betrayed my daughter, or one of the men who had watched scornfully as Harry walked to the scaffold. The idea of giving my body to such a man repelled me. With Adrian Stokes, I knew I would be getting a husband who had always been loyal to me and who was kind, as well.

And I would be getting a man whom I liked—nay, a man whom I had even imagined in my bed. Even as I flushed at the memory, I realized a woman could do far, far worse than to share her life with such a man.

I knelt and prayed once more. This time when I arose off my knees, I felt I had received a heavenly answer at last. Or at least, I hoped it was a heavenly one, and not my own desire speaking.

⁂

Master Stokes stood before me in the chamber where I conducted my business. Beside me, silent for once, stood my stepmother. I had asked her to be with me lest I lose my nerve. Besides, if Master Stokes refused, at least he would not have the ill manners to laugh in front of a third person.

"I have called you here to ask you to do me a great favor, Master Stokes," I faltered.

"Ask it, Frances," Katherine hissed.

"I want you to marry me," I blurted.

"Your Grace?"

"That's what she's asking," Katherine said. "She—"

"I can speak for myself," I said. I looked pleadingly up into Master Stokes's fine blue eyes and saw astonishment, but not unfriendliness, in them. "I fear that the queen will force me to remarry someone I do not care for, even someone who might use Harry's treason as an excuse to treat me unkindly. I would much rather be married to someone I trust and respect and like, and that person is you."

"Your Grace, you must know you could do much better. I am merely a gentleman's son."

"I know I could be truly miserable. And there is another reason I want to marry you. No one will ever try to put Mistress Stokes, or her children, upon the throne. I want no part of any more such schemes. Please, Master Stokes. You will be doing me the greatest of kindnesses."

"In that case, I will be pleased to marry you, Your Grace."

"Frances."

"Frances," Adrian agreed. He stepped closer to me.

I drew back. "But there is something else. Two things. I would like to delay consummating the marriage. I am still mourning my husband."

"And if she quickened with child so soon," Katherine put in, "the babe might be thought to be the duke's."

"Yes, that's reasonable. The other thing?" Adrian asked quietly.

"Some will say that I married for lust, or to spite Harry's memory. I do not want to hear such unkind comments. For that reason, I would like to keep our marriage secret for now. Will you agree?"

"Yes." He hesitated. "Let me speak to you alone for a moment, Your—Frances."

Katherine obediently exited the room.

Adrian looked at me, his blue eyes grave. "Are you sure about this, Frances? I have little love for Queen Mary, but I do not honestly believe she would force you into a marriage with someone you disliked. Nor do I believe that after this latest rebellion that anyone would attempt to seize the throne through you. I am honored to be your choice, but there may be no need to take such a drastic step as you are thinking of taking."

"I would prefer not to risk it. Besides, there is another reason, which I could not admit to in front of Katherine." I swallowed. "She did very well on her own after my father's death. I am not like her. The thought of managing in this world all alone terrifies me. I know that makes me a foolish creature, but that is what I am."

"I do not think you do yourself justice. But do you believe you would be happier if you were married?"

"Yes," I admitted.

"Then may I kiss my future bride?"

I nodded. Gently, Adrian put his lips to mine. "I'll take good care of you, Frances," he said, patting my cheek. "Just as I promised your husband."

ℭℴ

Two days later, on March 9, Katherine and my two most trusted ladies rode to Katherine's house at Kew, accompanied by Adrian in his usual position as my master of horse. No one could have guessed that we were a wedding party.

Katherine had a priest—one who would soon be going into exile abroad—waiting for us. As Katherine, Master Bertie, my ladies, and Adrian's younger brother William looked on as witnesses, we said our vows, Adrian in a firm voice, mine slightly shaking.

Afterward, we had a small celebration—very small, lest those in Katherine's household not in the secret suspect something odd. Then we rode back to Sheen as if this had been nothing more than a social visit to my stepmother. Adrian looked at me a little wistfully as our odd wedding party began to break up, but asked in his usual manner as a groom led my horse away, "Will your grace wish to ride tomorrow?"

"Yes, I believe so."

At the ceremony, Adrian had slipped a lovely gold ring—one upon which he must have spent a considerable part of his earnings—onto my finger. I had concealed it under my glove when I returned to Sheen. Alone in my chamber, I sat twisting the band, wondering what on earth I had gotten myself into. Then I slipped my wedding ring from my finger and placed it in a little coffer.

ℭℴ

Though Harry's brother Thomas was executed in April for his part in the rebellion, my own position remained little changed. Bradgate was forfeit to the Crown, but I was given nearby Beaumanor and other lands, and I was allowed to remain at Sheen. I even had three girls in my care again: Harry's niece Margaret Willoughby had joined my household.

In early June, soon after Margaret arrived, my stepmother again visited, having been doing business in London. It was important business, I soon learned: Richard Bertie had left England. "And I am going to join him as soon as I can wrap up my affairs here," said Katherine. "Bishop Gardiner called Master Bertie to him and made it very clear that if we did not conform to Papist teachings, England would be a very unpleasant place for us. He even dragged out the old story that I dressed up my dog in priestly robes and named him 'Gardiner' and taught him to beg." Katherine sighed. "Master Bertie denied it, which was quite honest on his part. That was a prank of my eldest son, the clever boy, not one of my doing."

"You would leave your country? Your little daughter?"

"Not my little Susan, certainly. She will go with us. My country—well, with Prince Philip coming, it may not look like my country anymore. I know, I know!" I had raised my hand. "You don't want anything said against him here after what happened to your husband and to Lady Jane, and I don't blame you. But I do wish you would consider taking your girls—oh, and Master Stokes, too, of course—and leaving. You would be most welcome abroad, as Lady Jane's mother. Do you know that your daughter's letters are being printed, here and abroad?"

"I am well aware of that." I had my own printed copy of the letter to Harding, hidden well away in some old account books. "I allowed them to be placed into the printer's hands. It was what my daughter—and Harry—would have wanted. But they would not want me abroad. Harry once told me that I had no strong feelings about religion and could not understand those who do. He was at least half-right. I have gone without Mass, and I have gone with Mass, and I feel exactly the same way about our Savior with either one. Why would I leave my country and wander abroad merely to avoid hearing a Mass?"

Katherine shook her head.

"Besides, I have already let you talk me into one great change."

"Ah, yes. How do you and Master Stokes get on?"

"Very well," I said. In fact, except that he no longer addressed me in private as "Your Grace," and that we made the major decisions about the running of my estates together, our relationship had scarcely changed since we married.

"Do you share a bed with him yet?"

"No."

"Don't make the poor man wait forever," Katherine advised. She sniffed. "He's a good man, Frances, but he's not *that* good."

"I'm not ready yet," I said firmly. "It is far too early."

⁂

In July, Mary finally married Prince Philip at Winchester Cathedral. The girls and I were not invited—that would have been unthinkable, as this was a marriage my husband had died trying to prevent—but after the queen and king, as Philip would be known, arrived at Richmond in August, I was commanded to see the queen.

I had never seen Mary looking better in her life, or dressed more colorfully. She was festooned from head to toe in scarlet, relieved by lace and gold trim. "We regret having to execute sentence upon your daughter and your husband, my lady," she said. "It was a necessity. We cannot encourage future rebellions by appearing weak."

There was nothing I could say to this except for, "Yes, Your Majesty."

"But now we wish to put the past behind us," the queen continued, and I realized this was the last I would ever hear of Jane and Harry from her lips. "How old is the lady Katherine?"

"She is almost fourteen, Your Majesty."

"She is an attractive girl, as I recall?"

"Very much so, Your Majesty."

"She plays and dances well?"

"My daughter dances better than she plays, but no one has ever found fault with either, Your Majesty."

"She is biddable?"

This was not my Kate's strong point. "She is willful, Your Majesty, but her nature is good."

The queen considered. "We should like to have her serve as one of our maids," she said finally. "We will soon be making our entry into London with the king, and from thence we will go to Hampton Court. Can you have her ready by September? Our mother of the maids will inform you what is necessary in the way of clothing."

"Yes, Your Majesty."

"You and your younger daughter, of course, are welcome at our court any time you wish to come."

Dismissed by the queen, I made the short trip to my house at Sheen, lost in thought. For Jane's sake, and Harry's, should I have refused the queen's invitation to Kate? Even if I had dared to decline—and Mary had given me no chance to do so—I could not justify such an action. Kate and Jane had never been close, and I knew Kate's mourning for her sister had been more dutiful than deep. As for Harry, he had been a kind father to all three of our girls, but his deepest attachment had always been to Jane. Kate's main grief, it had to be admitted, had been for the death of her own prospects. Now she would be at court, with young men and their matchmaking parents to remark upon her beauty and to watch her dance and play...

So at the beginning of September, I watched my second daughter get on a barge—sent for her by the queen—bound for Hampton Court. Even her monkey was making the journey. Queen Mary had given the royal permission for it to accompany Kate to court. She had made it a jaunty red cap and matching doublet especially for the occasion. "Don't let that creature pester the bargemen," I called in farewell as it showed great interest in an oar.

Kate, who normally took great offense at the term "that creature," simply laughed. Her coffers had been packed for days.

Beside me, my youngest daughter pouted as the barge began to pull away. "Kate won't be able to see me wave good-bye!" she complained. Her lip began to wobble. "Father would have put me on his shoulders."

"May I, Your Grace?"

I nodded, and Adrian, who had been standing with the rest of the household to see Kate off, lifted petite Mary high into the air. She waved happily until Kate's barge pulled out of sight. Then Adrian carefully set my daughter back on her feet.

"Thank you," I said. "That was so kind."

Adrian shrugged. "Kind? After all, I am Lady Mary's stepfather," he said into my ear.

45

Jane Dudley
October 1554 to December 1554

Since the Spanish entourage had arrived in England ("an invasion," the malcontents liked to call it), I had acquired a new friend at court: María Enríquez de Toledo y Guzmán, Duchess of Alba. Fortunately, I was allowed to call her Maria.

I had sought out the duchess for purely selfish reasons, as yet another contact to be cultivated to free my sons. I was granted an audience so quickly, I felt almost ashamed as we each settled on a stool.

"There are few of us Spanish ladies here," the duchess informed me after we had discussed King Arthur's Round Table, which the Spanish had enjoyed seeing at Winchester, for a while. (You must not think this conversation went so smoothly as I report it. I was speaking my barely adequate French, the duchess was speaking Spanish, and a member of her household, who knew both languages and a little English, was gamely interpreting for us.) "The English ladies do not like us. They avoid us. We get homesick here."

"We English can be unkind to foreigners," I admitted. "But we are all not like that."

"No, I see you are not. But you must pardon me. I did not understand who your husband is, my lady."

Even in English, much less fractured French, I was at a loss to explain. Everyone in England knew perfectly well who John was, or who they thought he was: a traitor who had manipulated the poor little king into changing his will and paid the price. The interpreter came to my rescue. He bent and whispered something in the duchess's ear, finishing off with a cutting motion of his own neck that he was probably not aware of making.

I sat there miserably, waiting to be turned out of the house, for the Spanish had enough enemies without receiving the wife of an attainted traitor, as well.

Then the duchess at last spoke. "You must grieve his loss greatly, my lady. I can tell from your eyes, even though I do not understand a word that comes out of your mouth."

"Indeed I do." Something in her own eyes made me add, "Each day when I wake I have hope, just in those first few moments before I am fully conscious, that it is all a bad dream, and that he is just away in his own chamber."

I expected the interpreter to smirk, but he nodded gravely and rendered my words into Spanish. Then the duchess dabbed at her eyes. "I love my husband," she said. I could make out the words even before they were translated. "We ladies were not supposed to be on this expedition. We were told that it would anger the English to come with too large an entourage. But I insisted on following my husband. Everywhere he goes, I go, if it is humanly possible." When I had been made to understand this, the duchess spoke again. "Some people dislike my husband, the duke, too. He is a soldier, not a courtier. He has a foul temper sometimes, but never with me. He is the kindest of husbands. Did your husband leave children?"

"Two daughters and four sons, now. All of my boys are in prison."

"In prison? For what?"

"For obeying the Lord's command that we shall honor thy father."

"The poor lads!" The duchess shook her head angrily. "They should not suffer for that. I have seen the queen but seldom, but my husband is King Philip's chief advisor, and I will ask him to say a word on their behalf. My own sons are dear to me—but not, I confess, as dear to me as my husband."

In that moment, I knew I had made a friend for life.

⁂

I would have been delighted to have Maria visit me at Chelsea, but the Spanish in London did not like to venture far from their lodgings in the city's guildhalls except in large numbers. Though there was little actual violence, save for the occasional scuffle, between the Spanish and the English, there was a great deal of hooting and mockery, especially by the city's boys, who had the miraculous ability to melt into nowhere when someone arrived to keep the peace. The London cutpurses had also discovered there was something in the make of Spanish purses that was peculiarly advantageous to their trade. So in the middle of October, I was rowed to the stairs near Maria's house by one of my regular boatmen. "There's some news, Your Grace," he said. "Don't know if it's true, mind you. I guess you don't want to hear it, though."

"William, don't torture me like this! Of course I want to hear it."

"They say the queen's expecting."

Expecting what? I almost asked. Then I realized what he meant. "You mean she is with child?"

"So they say. No disrespect, but she looks a little old to breed to me. Roger over there thinks so, too." He nodded at one of his compatriots a ways off.

I could not help but share the boatmen's expert opinion. "Nonetheless, I hope it is true, and I will pray that she bears a healthy babe," I said. "My own daughter will soon be having a child," I added proudly.

"Aye, that's good, Your Grace." He handed me out of the boat with a flourish. "Don't let me hear that you let that George take you home as you did last week. Young fool almost overturned you, didn't he?"

"It was pouring," I said apologetically. "I should have waited for you to come along, though."

The Duchess of Alba greeted me in a torrent of Spanish before anyone could come to assist us. By now, I could pick out a phrase here or there, and I distinctly heard the name "Penshurst," or Maria's version of it. "Penshurst? That is where my daughter lives." I stared at the approaching interpreter. "Is there something wrong with my daughter that you have heard?"

"No, no! The queen has agreed to set free three of your sons. The Earl of Warwick, Lord Robert, and Lord Henry. They are to go to Penshurst, pending further orders."

"God be thanked," I whispered.

The duchess took me into her arms.

"But there is one thing you need to know," she said softly, her tone echoed by the interpreter. "The Earl of Warwick is very ill."

⌘

By the time I arrived home, a royal messenger had come to confirm the news of my sons' release. I would have taken horse and ridden for Penshurst as quickly as I could, but my servants flatly ignored my orders and got my litter and mules ready for me instead. They had been coddling me lately, and fussed each time I went to the court or to the Duchess of Alba's, but they could hardly complain about this journey.

Even in the mule cart we made good time, though—better, I heard the driver say to my groom, than we would have made if I had slid off my horse in a faint—and we arrived at Penshurst before my sons were expected to arrive.

Mary took my arm when I got out of the cart. "You're the one who needs an arm," I protested. "You're huge."

"I feel fine, Mother. Why don't you lie down until Henry gets here with the boys?"

"No. I want to be here when they come through the gate. Not sound asleep."

Mary gave Katheryn, who had come with me, a look.

At a little past three, I heard the sounds of approaching horses. Before I could disentangle myself from the baby clothes I was stitching, Robert and Hal stood before me.

I have no words to describe how it was seeing my sons for the first time in months with no guards beside them. We clung to each other and wept for what seemed to be hours. Finally, I managed, "Jack?"

"They're bringing him upstairs, Mother," Mary said. She had been talking in a low tone with her husband. "Let him get settled first. Then you can see him."

"No! If he is ill, I need to nurse him."

"Mother—"

Henry moved closer to Mary. "Let her, Moll," he said softly. "It can't make her any worse."

∞

Jack was not merely ill; he was dying. I knew that as soon as I stepped through the door. He had the same wasted look King Edward had worn in his last days, except the desperate remedies tried on the king had not been tried on him, so he would be dying in peace, at least.

"I didn't get to finish my carving," he said as we all sat in his chamber.

"Carving?"

"Jack carved our bear and ragged staff into the wall of the Beauchamp Tower," Robert said, patting his brother's shoulder. "It's beautifully done. Not that I ever want to go back and see it again."

"And a border with roses for Ambrose, gillyflowers for Guildford, oak leaves for Robert, and honeysuckle for Hal," said Jack. "There's a verse, too."

"'You that these beasts do well behold and see / may deem with ease wherefore here made they be,'" recited Hal. "'With borders eke wherein are to be found / four brothers' names who list to search the ground.'"

"And poor Guildford carved 'Jane' into one wall," said Robert. He glared at the wall of the chamber. "And then the little wench wouldn't even see him."

"She said it would have caused too much grief for them both," Hal said.

"Still, she could have at least waved to him from the window."

"Boys!" I said.

"It's all right, Mother," Jack said. "They've been arguing about this since

Guildford died. I like hearing them." He closed his eyes, then opened them. "Anne...my wife. Is she coming?"

"We sent for her," I said. All of my sons' wives were here now, or on the way.

"Good."

I walked out of the chamber with Henry and my younger sons as Jack dozed. "I have not had a chance to thank you, Henry, for helping to get my sons released. You and the Duchess of Alba have done so much."

"I believe your petitions did as much as the rest of us combined. The queen respects tenacity."

I turned to Robert and Hal. "How long has Jack been ill?"

"Not that long, or even the queen would have probably released him earlier than this. He'd been looking peaked for a while, now that I think of it, but the way you see him now, it came upon him quickly," said Robert.

"And Ambrose?"

"He's being kept in the Tower as sort of a hostage for the good behavior of the rest of us," Hal said. "There's been no talk of releasing Uncle Andrew."

"Then we must keep trying."

Robert cleared his throat. "You're not looking well, Mother," he said bluntly.

"Naturally, your father's and Guildford's deaths have aged me."

"Katheryn said that you fainted a few days ago. Fell off your chair while you were sewing."

"The room was too warm. I told her that at the time."

"Henry and Mary would like their physician to see you. So would the rest of us."

"So I can get poked and prodded and dosed? I believe that physicians only make one sicker. You know that." I met Robert's eyes defiantly. "When Ambrose is free and when my grandchild is born, I will let a physician see me. I promise, if it will make you and the rest happy."

"It will."

"Then that is settled. Now, tell me. Did you see your father before he died?"

"No," Hal said. "He sent us a letter begging us to forgive him for bringing us to this. He converted for our sake, you know. Jack, at least, would have been executed with him otherwise."

"I know."

"He was gone by the time we got the letter. We couldn't reply. But we were allowed to pay our respects at his grave before we left the Tower. We spent a long time there. What did we have to forgive him for, anyway? Being loyal to the king?"

I wiped my eyes with my handkerchief, one of my husband's. "Now tell me about Guildford."

Robert said, "He wouldn't say a thing against Father when the lieutenant told him that his sentence was being carried out. Nothing against the fool Duke of Suffolk, either, who deserved it. He even insisted on sending him a farewell message. He said that Suffolk was about the only person in the Grey family who didn't treat him like something the cat spat out." My son snorted. "I think he was half in love with Jane by the time he died, judging by that carving of his, but of course he didn't actually have to spend any time with her. That helped, in my opinion. As I said back there, he begged to meet her one last time, but she decided it would be a distraction." Robert rolled his eyes. "Poor Guildford. It wouldn't have been easy, married to a Protestant saint. Anyway, he sent his love to you, of course—I should have said that from the start—and made us promise that we remaining brothers would always be loyal to one another, that we would always speak of Father kindly, and that we would take care of you." Robert patted my hand as I at last began to give way to my emotions. "He didn't need to make us promise those things, Mother. We would have done them anyway."

⁂

Aged seven and twenty, Jack died in my arms on October 21, 1554. His wife had come just in time to spend a few minutes with him alone. What the two of them said I never asked, but Jack seemed at peace as he said his dying prayers, surrounded by his wife and family.

We buried him at Penshurst—Warwick Castle, where we might have otherwise taken his body, was forfeit to the Crown. I was not present at the funeral, for his death did send me to my bed, from which I found myself too weak to arise for nearly a month. By the end of November, however, I was able to be present while my daughter Mary labored to bring her first child into the world.

It was a long labor, but my daughter remained strong through it all. On November 30, she brought forth my grandson.

King Philip agreed to be one of his godfathers; the Duke of Bedford, who had led the embassy to Spain a few months ago, the other. They served by proxy. I, the godmother, was there in person as we gathered in the chapel of Penshurst in December to christen him.

I bore my grandson to the altar and carefully placed him in the arms of Philip's proxy—my son Robert. "What name do you give this child?" the priest asked.

"Philip," Robert said, staring proudly down at his baby nephew. "Philip Sidney."

46

Frances Grey
October 1554

WITH KATE SETTLED AMONG THE MAIDS AT COURT AND THRIVING, ADRIAN and I traveled to Beaumanor in Leicestershire. Although it had belonged to Harry and me, we had seldom stayed here, and I was pleased to find the house more attractive than I remembered. It did not have Bradgate's mellow beauty, but it was a place where I could be at peace. "It does need some repairs, though," I told Adrian that afternoon. "And it could be made more comfortable, also. It is rather old-fashioned. I think we can afford some work to it, don't you?"

"I suppose."

"If you think we cannot afford it, tell me so."

"If you think we can, we can. You're careful with money."

I smiled modestly, for I always had been meticulous with our household accounts. "Harry once said that I took after my grandfather," I said, referring to the seventh King Henry. "Mind you, I don't think he meant it as a compliment."

Adrian did not smile. "I was joking," I said lightly.

"Yes, I know. There is something else we need to talk about."

"Adrian?"

"I am considering leaving England, just as so many have."

"Leaving? With me?" Adrian shook his head no. "But we are married!"

"Are we?"

"You know we are! We had a priest, we exchanged our vows, and you gave me a wedding ring."

"Which is nowhere on your hand."

"Of course not. We agreed to keep our marriage a secret." I looked up at Adrian, puzzled. "Didn't we?"

"Yes, of course we did."

"Then why are you speaking of leaving? Why are you acting so peculiar?"

"Why do you think I married you?"

"Why, because I begged you to."

"No. Because I've wanted you in my bed since I first laid eyes upon you."

I drew back, shocked.

"When you and your stepmother made that very businesslike proposal to me, I did want to oblige you. Who could resist two duchesses? But I never would have agreed if I thought that I would never get to take you to bed at some point. Why, our marriage could easily be held invalid, being that we've never consummated it. Has that ever occurred to you?"

"Yes," I admitted. "But —"

"I didn't expect you to lie with me when we first married, not so soon after your husband's and your daughter's deaths. I've been patient, knowing that you needed time to grieve. But as each day goes by and we're as businesslike as we've ever been, I've been asking myself, is this really worth it, this being not quite a servant and not quite a husband? Is it ever going to change? Would I be better off just going abroad and forgetting we ever exchanged vows?"

"Harry... Jane..."

"The Duke of Suffolk himself urged me to take care of you; you heard him. The lady Jane? She's happy in paradise. Why would she begrudge you a little happiness on earth?"

"But—"

"Our marriage was your idea. Or was it? Was your stepmother merely putting words in your mouth?"

"She did give me the idea. But I wanted to marry you. I thought it was a good idea. I do want to be your wife—a true wife. I just—" I gestured hopelessly, feeling tears come to my eyes. "Perhaps this was a mistake, marrying you so hastily. I have only caused you pain, and I never meant to. I—I like you. Better than any man I've ever known."

Adrian's voice softened. "Did you bring your wedding ring here?" When I nodded, he asked, "Can you find it?"

I went to my chamber and retrieved the coffer where I kept my ring, wrapped inside a handkerchief. It had sat there undisturbed since our wedding day. When I returned, I held it out to Adrian.

"Did you ever look inside it?"

"No. It never occurred to me to look."

"Well, look now."

I obeyed. Inside the wedding band, engraved in a fine italic, were the words "A to F: *Amor Vincit Omnia*."

"'Love conquers—'"

"I know what it means. I always did like Chaucer's Prioress." I looked up from the engraving at which I'd been gazing. "Are you saying—?"

"I love you, Frances. I've loved you for a very long time. I can remember the very day I fell in love with you, as a matter of fact. It wasn't long after I came to your household. I'd been looking for horses for your new litter, and I found two fine ones. Matched greys, I told you, and you said, 'How appropriate.' When I chuckled, you gave me the sweetest smile, as if you were so pleased, and so surprised, to have someone laugh at your joke. From then on, all I wanted was to have you smile like that at me again." He shook his head. "I never even dreamed of the possibility of you marrying me. All I could ever hope for was that I'd always be able to serve you faithfully, as the lady of my heart. Then out of nowhere you asked me to be your husband, and that's when you gave me that sweet little smile of yours again, when I accepted."

My eyes were filling with tears again, but they were not tears of sadness. I stepped forward and raised my lips to Adrian's. He accepted my invitation, and we kissed. It was not like our previous polite efforts. This time, we kissed as passionately as though our lips had been made for no one else's. "Adrian?" I said when we pulled back at last.

"Yes?"

"Will you take me to bed with you?"

My husband took my hand. "I thought you'd never ask."

⁂

"Tomorrow we shall start living as man and wife," I told Adrian much later. For hours after consummating our marriage, we had lay entwined, talking not of business but of ourselves, of those we had lost and what we had gained in each other. "I am sorry I have waited this long. Will you forgive me?"

"Only if you will forgive me."

"For what?"

"I hadn't the slightest intention of leaving you, Frances. I could never do that. It was a lie I told you back there."

"I am very glad you told it." I snuggled closer to Adrian. "The whole household shall know me as your wife when I rise from this bed. But I am so comfortable, I don't want to rise."

"Will you tell the queen of our marriage?"

I hesitated. Even with Adrian's arms around me, the prospect of facing my cousin was a daunting one. "I should like to wait a little longer, to find a good time."

"Very well." Adrian held me closer. "As long as you are truly mine now, the queen can wait."

I leaned over Adrian and shook my hair over my shoulders and breasts so it tickled his belly. Earlier in the evening, when we had first disrobed, he had stared at my hair in awe as I let it fall to my waist, and for the first time in my life, I had felt beautiful. "What if I asked you to make love to me again tonight?"

Adrian smiled up at me and tapped my nose. "I'm not one and twenty any longer, sweetheart, but I think I can manage that."

47

Jane Dudley
December 1554 to January 22, 1555

IN DECEMBER, MY ONE SON REMAINING IMPRISONED, AMBROSE, IS FREED FROM the Tower. It is then, and only then, I keep my promise to Robert and let a physician examine me once the Christmas and New Year's festivities have passed. What he tells me, I have figured out for myself long ago, without having to pay a fee.

When he leaves, I go to my desk and begin writing my will.

⁂

It is not hard to write my will once I get into the flow of it. Money to the poor, money to the prisoners in London's various jails. Gowns to my dear John's sisters, to my daughters, and to my daughters-in-law—all but Jack's widow, who has proven only too eager to cut the last tie between my family and hers, except for the title of "countess" and her jointure lands. Those things will probably make her happier than anything I could give her, I tell myself, and write on.

John's clock, ticking peacefully as I write this, will go to our daughter Mary. A tawny velvet jewel coffer to Susan Clarencius, a gown to Lady Paget, and a black enameled ring to Lord Paget: all were kind to me and helped me intercede for my boys, though none could save my John. I leave my lands to my children but remember, just in time, that all are under attainder and cannot inherit: I must leave my lands to my executors.

My green parrot, looking at me with interest as I write, I leave to the Duchess of Alba. She is a wealthy woman and will have no need for more fine gowns or beds. I have nothing else worthy of her.

I am not quite sure it belongs here, but I beg my executors to give my thanks to those men of the privy chamber who helped my sons, and to ask that they continue to do so. God, I know, will requite them for it.

It occurs to me that someone, after I am dead, may decide to open me up for embalming. That will not do. Although circumstances have forced me to assert myself when needed, I have not liked to be bold even before women, nor do I want any man's hands upon me when I am dead. All I want is to be wound up in a sheet and put in a wooden coffin, then given such a funeral as my executors see fit, seeing that none of my children will inherit John's forfeited title.

I would rather that my debts be paid, and the poor given their due, than that any pomp be showered upon my wretched carcass, that has at times been too much in this world full of vanities, deceit, and guile. For whoever trusts to this transitory world as I did, may happen to have an overthrow as I did. Yet I am smiling as I write these words, for each one of them brings me closer to my John.

⁐

My will is witnessed and safely in the hands of Henry Sidney, one of the executors. This feat accomplished, I am dozing when someone glides into my chamber. I open an eye. "Andrew!"

"Yes, it is I."

"You are free?"

"Yes."

This is indeed my brother-in-law Andrew, a man of few words. Imprisonment turns some men voluble after they are freed, but not this one. I push myself farther upright. "You have been pardoned?"

"No. I'm still in that no-man's-land between prison and freedom. I'm on a bond for good behavior, and I daresay I needn't behave very badly to find myself back in the Tower."

"Jerome will be so glad to see you. Even with my sons back, he has still missed you. I have been afraid that he will pine away."

"I'll take good care of him."

"I am sorry about the Clifford girl," I say gently. Her engagement to Andrew was broken off after his arrest and trial; evidently God did not intend her as a Dudley bride. Perhaps it is just as well. She stands after the surviving Grey sisters in line for the crown.

Andrew shrugs. "Probably she would have talked too much anyway."

My sons and Jerome soon follow my brother-in-law into the room. For a while, they sit around my bed, talking of a tournament Robert and Ambrose were in recently—thanks to the king, who had invited them personally to take part. Then they all drift away except for Robert. "I wanted you to know that I heard from the lady Elizabeth the other day."

"I thought she was still under house arrest."

"She is, but she has her sympathizers."

"Robert, you are still under attainder. Not to mention a married man."

"The lady Elizabeth and I are old friends, Amy knows that. And it's not treason to send my good wishes to the queen's sister, surely?"

"If you put it like that, no, but do be careful."

"I will. I can't help but think, though, that someday my friend Elizabeth will be queen. No, we haven't spoken of it!" he says, forestalling my protest. "Not to each other or to anyone else. I'll do nothing to shorten Queen Mary's reign. But I think God means Elizabeth to rule, and years ago, she promised me that if she did, I would be one of the first she calls to her side." He smiles at me as fatigue begins to make me sink back into my pillows. "It will be a golden age, Mother."

⁂

Over the next few days, letters come while I slumber. Many of them are from people who have studiously avoided contact with me since John was arrested and who deem it safe to renew our acquaintance now that I am so soon to pass out of this world. *Vanity, deceit, and guile*, I think to myself and order Katheryn to toss them—the letters, that is—into the fire.

But there are other letters. My daughter Mary writes to inform me that while she was holding little Philip in the nursery and reading—it strikes me as entirely natural that my daughter should be doing these two things at once—the child grabbed the edge of her book and held it fast. *He displays a most encouraging interest in the written word*, Mary writes smugly.

Another letter, however, makes Katheryn, who is reading it to me, break out crying. Good Lord, I think, has the Earl of Huntingdon chosen this time to dissolve our daughter's marriage to his son? "Tell me what it says."

"It is from the Countess of Huntingdon. She writes that she is very sorry to hear of your illness, and that when you can no longer take care of me, she will welcome me to Ashby-de-la-Zouche as her very own daughter. She has set aside a pretty chamber for me there, which I may furnish just as I like. And there is a postscript by Lord Hastings, telling me he will come to take me there himself whenever I please. He calls me his very own sweetheart and his darling wife."

I join my daughter in her tears, thinking that sometimes, the goodness of human beings can make one weep harder than their follies.

⁂

It is the twenty-second day of January, a miserable day outside. Even behind my bed curtains, I can hear the sleet coming down and the wind beating against my windows. Faintly, I feel sorry for anyone who is abroad on this bleak day, but I myself am quite content, for John's clock ticks steadily and John himself is holding me tight in the bed we shared for so many years, keeping me safe from all that is without. *Patience*, his voice tells me. *Soon*.

All it took to bring him back to me was to do *this*, just as Anne Boleyn taught me so long ago. Why did I not try it sooner?

There are footsteps and a jumble of voices. "Has she been like this long?"

"Most of the day, my lords. I don't believe she can last for much longer." Nurse Stacy, my laundress who also attends me in my illness, adds uncertainly, "She received the last rites, my lords, when she could still respond to them. The Catholic rites, of course."

Someone grumbles about this, but not too strenuously.

"Can she hear us?"

"You can try, my lords."

Someone bends over me. He is speaking too loudly, really, for my hearing is perfect, but under the circumstances, I can be forgiving. "We have received our pardons from the queen, Mother."

Pardons. I have done all I can do on earth for my sons; there is no need for me to linger here any longer. I start to smile, and just as my mouth crinkles upward, my John bears me away.

48

Frances Grey
January 1555 to April 1555

T HE DUCHESS OF NORTHUMBERLAND HAS DIED," ADRIAN INFORMED ME ONE morning in January as we sat breaking our fast in my chamber at Sheen. "A heart malady, it is thought."

I stared at my lap. We had not liked each other or the other's children, but for a few short months, we had been bound together by the will of one young king, and now that Jane Dudley was gone, I felt peculiarly bereft.

"She died in comfort. Her children were with her, all of them, and the queen pardoned the sons the day the duchess died. She did so out of compassion for their mother."

"We should have parted in this life as friends. After all, we each lost a husband and a child to the headsman."

"Will you go to the funeral?"

"No. It might grieve her children to see me there. I will send someone from our household to pay our respects." I sighed and pushed my untouched plate away.

"Are you ill? This is the second day in a row that you have not eaten."

"No. I am not ill." I touched my belly. "I have suspected for several weeks that I have been blessed far more than I deserve, but now I am quite certain. I am carrying our child."

Adrian abandoned his own breakfast and wrapped me in his arms. "God be thanked," he whispered.

⁓

There was a funeral for the Duchess of Northumberland on the first day of February, with two heralds and many mourners, but it was not what was spoken of that month. Three days after the duchess was laid in her grave at Chelsea's church, the burnings started.

They began with John Rogers, a canon of St. Paul's, at Smithfield on February 4. It was a matter no one at court was supposed to speak of, but one everyone was speaking of three days later when the court gathered for a grand wedding: that of my niece Margaret Clifford to Henry Stanley, Lord Strange. People watched the jousts and the Spanish cane-play put on for the occasion, but their minds were plainly not on the grand spectacle before them.

"His wife and eleven children were standing along the route, watching him go to the stake," I heard Jane Seymour, the Duchess of Somerset's daughter, whisper to my Kate.

"He bathed his hands in the flames, as if they were cold water," Lord Paget murmured to his companion.

"People collected his ashes as mementoes. Just as they collected the Duke of Somerset's blood," Lord Hastings told one of his sisters.

I went home to Sheen that night fancying the smell of Rogers's burning flesh lingered in London's air.

Perhaps, I prayed, his death was an aberration. Instead, on February 8, the day after the wedding, Laurence Saunders, the rector of All Hallows in Coventry, was burned. He was followed the next day by Dr. Rowland Taylor, the rector of Hadleigh in Suffolk, who had supported my daughter's accession to the throne, and by John Hooper, the Bishop of Gloucester and Worcester, who had given the Duchess of Somerset spiritual comfort while she was in the Tower. It had taken the bishop, crying out for more wood because that which he was provided had failed to ignite properly, forty-five minutes to die.

Yet even as the burnings continued, Mary sat serene and happy, her hands folded over her belly—for the queen was now expecting a child, a state of affairs many regarded as miraculous, as the queen was well in middle age. Each time I came to court before my own condition began to show itself, I saw the Mary I had always liked, the Mary who lost graciously at cards, the Mary whose women were comfortably housed and never overtasked, the Mary who visited the poor in disguise and never failed to make certain something arrived after she had left—a sum of money, a draught of medicine for an ailing child, some warm blankets. My daughter Kate, who like my Jane was strong in her likes and dislikes, never spoke of Queen Mary with anything other than warmth. How to reconcile this Mary with the one who roasted human beings to death?

"It's not that hard to do," said Adrian. "The government gives them the chance to recant. I doubt that the queen gets any pleasure from these burnings." He shook his head. "But the fact remains, she goes on with them."

And indeed she did. At the end of March, Robert Ferrar, the Bishop of St. David's, was burned in Wales.

Two bishops in two months, I thought. And God only knew when it would all end.

 ⌒

In April, Kate, along with her new friend Jane Seymour, came to visit me at Sheen. "We thought we had better come while we had the chance," Kate explained. "The queen's going to go into confinement soon, and then we'll be boxed up for weeks."

"She is doing well?"

Kate frowned. "She's not showing much more than she did a couple of months ago. You're showing more than she is, in fact. I heard…"

"Well?"

Kate lowered her voice. "I heard one of her ladies, Mistress Strelly, asking her if she might not be with child at all. The queen was furious. She boxed Mistress Strelly's ears. She hardly ever acts like that. But how could she be mistaken, Mother? She does have a great belly. Have you ever heard of such a thing?"

"Of a woman growing a great belly, yet not bearing a child? Yes, I have. It happened years ago to our kinsman Arthur Plantagenet's wife." I was silent, not wanting to think of this possibility as it concerned Queen Mary—or me, for that matter. "But this is different. The queen has had the best physicians in England examine her."

"True," said Kate. She giggled. "Anyway, I have another piece of gossip, and it is about you, Mother! They say there are plans afoot to marry you to the Earl of Devon."

The Earl of Devon was Edward Courtenay, the foolish young man who had been released from the Tower when Mary came to the throne. Although he had revealed to the queen what he knew about the Wyatt rebellion, or at least some of what he knew, he had later been imprisoned. A week or so ago, he had been released in the hope he had learned his lesson.

Kate continued, "Devon said he would rather leave the country than be married to a woman ten years his senior whose husband and eldest daughter had been executed as traitors."

I snorted. The earl appeared to have forgotten that his own father had been executed as a traitor. "And who proposed this?"

"Some of the queen's council, but others were against it. They said that if, God forbid, the queen should die in childbirth, along with the child, there

would be a contest for the crown between the lady Elizabeth, the Countess of
Lennox, the young Queen of Scots, and you. If Devon was married to you,
they said, he might try to seize the crown in your name."

"There will be no contest for the crown on my part," I said. "It belongs to
the lady Elizabeth."

"It will be quite the joke when everyone finds out that you're married
already," Kate said. During her last visit, I had told her of my marriage and of
my coming child. To my relief, she had reacted with no more than an indulgent smile at the folly of her elders. She glanced at my belly. "Are you going
to tell the queen about Master Stokes soon?"

I had been stalling, half hoping that the news of our marriage, known to our
small circle of close friends and relations, would reach the queen on its own. It
might well have, had not the burnings and the queen's pregnancy preoccupied
the court. But the time for stalling was past. "Tomorrow," I said. "It is time
the queen knew the truth."

⁓

The next morning, Adrian and I went to Hampton Court. It was the last time
the queen would be seen in public before she withdrew to her private apartments, accompanied only by her female attendants. Her chamber was crowded
with courtiers attending to last-minute business. No matter: a large audience
suited my purpose.

Mary had a great belly, but not of a size commensurate with the May date
that had been predicted for the birth. I had the sickening conviction Mistress
Strelly was correct: there was no child on the way. Poor Mary, there would be
sorrow ahead for her, I feared.

Unconscious of the burst of pity I felt, Mary smilingly bade us to rise. "I
believe we have seen this gentleman before. He accompanied you to Beaulieu?"

"Yes, Your Majesty. He is Adrian Stokes, my former master of horse. He is
now my husband." I pushed back my cloak, revealing the distinct bulge under
my gown. "As Your Majesty can see, we have been married some time."

A silence settled over the court. "You did not ask permission of us for
your marriage."

"No, Your Majesty, I did not, but I believed it would be agreeable to you.
I am asking now for your blessing upon it."

"You must surely know that your marriage is a matter of great concern to
us, as you are so close to the throne."

"It is because I am so close to the throne that I married a good, honest man who will put me far away from it." I took Adrian's hand and placed my other hand against the child who grew within me. "I want nothing of crowns, Your Majesty. Not for me, not for those I love. They cost too much."

Mary placed her hand on her own belly and nodded.

"You and your horse master have our blessing, Cousin Frances," she said. "Go in peace."

And so we did.

Author's Note

FRANCES GAVE BIRTH TO A DAUGHTER, ELIZABETH STOKES, ON JULY 16, 1555—the anniversary of Frances's own birth. Sadly, the child died on February 7, 1556, and Frances and Adrian seem to have lost other children in infancy, as well. Frances herself died in November 1559 and was buried in St. Edmund's Chapel at Westminster Abbey, where the fine tomb erected by Adrian in her memory can still be seen today. In her will, she made Adrian her sole executor.

In 1572, Adrian Stokes married Anne Carew, the widow of Sir Nicholas Throckmorton. (She makes a very brief appearance in this novel as Jane's proxy at a christening.) Adrian's stepdaughter, Elizabeth Throckmorton, married Sir Walter Ralegh (or Raleigh). Adrian served in Parliament and on local commissions before his death in 1585. He was buried at Beaumanor.

Two different death dates are recorded for Jane Dudley: January 15, 1555, in a postmortem inquisition, and January 22, 1555, on her memorial inscription at Chelsea's Old Church. I chose the latter date, which allowed her to hear the news her sons had been pardoned. The January 22 date also seemed more compatible with the date of her funeral, which took place on February 1. A resilient woman, Jane Dudley would be pleased to know her tomb survived a Nazi bombardment of the church in 1941.

Andrew Dudley died in November 1559, having spent his last years at his house in Tothill Street in Westminster. His disabled brother, Jerome, was still alive in 1556, when Andrew left him a bequest in the will he wrote that year.

Katherine Brandon, Duchess of Suffolk, returned to England with her husband, Richard Bertie, and their two children, Susan and Peregrine, after Queen Mary's death. She died in 1580, having remained an outspoken Protestant.

Anne Seymour, Duchess of Somerset, followed the examples of the two

Duchesses of Suffolk and married her husband's steward, Francis Newdigate, late in 1558. Having outlived her second husband, she died in 1587, leaving behind masses of magnificent jewels. Her daughter Anne, Countess of Warwick, widowed when Jack Dudley died at Penshurst, remarried in 1555 and had seven children by her second husband, Sir Edward Unton. The countess suffered from bouts of mental illness in her later years.

In 1557, the surviving Dudley sons, Ambrose, Robert, and Henry, fought for King Philip at St. Quentin, where Henry was killed. Following this, the Crown reversed the attainders of Ambrose, Robert, and their sisters.

The Dudley children and the Grey children fared very differently in Elizabeth's reign. Robert Dudley became the Earl of Leicester. His volatile but enduring relationship with the queen, which ended only with his death in 1588, has fascinated readers for centuries. Elizabeth marked the final letter he sent to her before his death as "His Last Letter" and kept it for the rest of her life. Ambrose Dudley became the Earl of Warwick. He survived his younger brother Robert, to whom he was devoted, by two years, dying in 1590. Ambrose had no children.

Mary Sidney and her sister Katherine Hastings (which I spelled "Katheryn" in my novel to distinguish her from the many other Katherines of her day) each attended Queen Elizabeth. Mary lived until 1586. Her firstborn son, Philip Sidney, gained fame as a poet and critic and as an embodiment of the chivalric ideal. His literary works are still studied today. Her daughter Mary, who eventually married Henry Herbert, the Earl of Pembroke, was both a poet and a literary patron. Katherine Hastings's long marriage to Henry Hastings, who inherited his father's earldom, was happy but childless. As Countess of Huntingdon, Katherine took many well-born young girls into her household and prided herself on her ability to "breed and govern young gentlewomen." Widowed in 1595, she outlived her husband by a quarter of a century and was buried in 1620 at Chelsea's Old Church alongside her mother.

For Katherine and Mary Grey, Elizabeth's reign was disastrous. Katherine Grey fell in love with Somerset's son, the Earl of Hertford. Frances, approving of the match but recognizing the need to gain royal approval, drafted a letter to Elizabeth seeking permission for the couple to marry. Before she could send the letter, she died. Instead of seeking another means of gaining the queen's approval, the couple secretly married in 1560 with the assistance of Hertford's sister Jane. When their marriage came to light, both spouses were imprisoned in the Tower, where the pregnant Katherine gave birth to a son. Katherine spent the rest of her life in custody, first at the Tower and later in various private homes, though a sympathetic Tower guard had allowed the couple to meet, resulting in a second son. Katherine died in 1568, at about age twenty-eight. Hertford eventually was freed and was allowed custody of his two sons by Katherine. Having remarried, he died an octogenarian in 1621. Hertford and Katherine Grey were finally reunited that same year when their grandson, the new earl, moved Katherine's body to Hertford's tomb at Salisbury Cathedral.

In 1565, Mary Grey likewise made a secret marriage, hers to Thomas Keyes, a widower who was a sergeant porter at court. The match also resulted in the couple's imprisonment. Although the spouses were eventually freed, they were never allowed to resume living together as a married couple. Keyes died in 1571. Mary, who had set up her own household at Aldersgate, died in 1578. She was buried at Westminster Abbey in her mother's tomb.

Except for Mary Sidney's letter to her mother and the letters mentioned by Katherine Hastings, all of the letters and other writings quoted in this novel are genuine, although I have modernized spelling and punctuation in some cases. Likewise, all of the execution speeches are taken from contemporary accounts, except for Guildford Dudley's speech, the substance of which was not recorded.

My depiction of the Lord of Misrule's antics is based upon contemporary accounts of the festivities. The December 1551 celebration featured "an infamous tabernacle, a representation of the holy sacrament in its monstrance, which [was] wetted and perfumed in most strange fashion, with great ridicule of the ecclesiastical estate." This is as good a place as any to make clear (if anyone is in doubt) that the religious bigotry expressed by various characters echoes their own beliefs, not mine.

There is no evidence that Jane and Frances attended the trials or the executions I have depicted them as attending, but there is nothing putting them elsewhere at the time. Likewise, the execution-eve visits each woman makes to her husband are products of my imagination, but it is possible such visits were allowed. Mary's refusal to give an audience to Jane Dudley in July 1553, and Frances's arrival at Beaulieu at two in the morning to see Mary, are both recorded by contemporary sources.

Mary did indeed make plans to escape from England in 1550, but her confiding her intentions to Frances is purely my invention.

Jane Grey's exact birth date is unknown, but Eric Ives convincingly places it in the spring of 1537 rather than the October date of tradition. The birthdates of the children of John and Jane Dudley are also unrecorded. An unnamed

Dudley son was christened in March 1537, and Diego Hurtado de Mendoza, who was Guildford's godfather, was in England from May 1537 to September 1538; I think it possible then that Guildford was the Dudley son born in March 1537 and that Diego served as his godfather, not at his christening, but at his confirmation on a later date. With the other Dudley children, I have followed the estimates of their ages given by Simon Adams, a specialist on Robert Dudley, or, failing that, those given in the *Oxford Dictionary of National Biography*.

Anne Seymour, born in 1538, was only twelve when she married Jack Dudley. I therefore think it likely her marriage had yet to be consummated when her husband was imprisoned in 1553.

Robert Dudley's marriage to Amy Robsart was later characterized by William Cecil as a "carnal" marriage, a love match, and that it was not a particularly illustrious match for an earl's son is further evidence the couple married for love. That Mary Dudley's marriage to Henry Sidney might have also been a love match is suggested by the fact that she had two wedding ceremonies: one at Esher, the other at Ely Place. It may be that the first was secret, the second public. Her marriage was certainly less distinguished than that of her younger sister, Katherine Dudley, who married the heir to an earldom.

A supposedly contemporary description of Jane Grey's physical appearance states she was thin and very small, with reddish-brown eyes and nearly red hair. As Leanda de Lisle has observed, however, this description may have been the invention of Richard Davey, a modern biographer of Jane, so I have not relied upon it. No portrait has been definitively identified as being an authentic one of Jane, but John Stephan Edwards makes a good case for a portrait at Syon House as being a true one of Jane. I have therefore followed that portrait, which shows an auburn-haired young woman with brown eyes, in my own novel.

There is no historical evidence that Adrian Stokes suffered the loss of a fiancée. That is my invention.

A "Mistress Ellen," who is otherwise unidentified, accompanied Jane Grey to the scaffold. As Leanda de Lisle points out, the story about her being Jane's nurse is a modern invention, possibly inspired by Juliet's nurse. I supplied her with the first name of "Ursula."

Recently, several historians, including Eric Ives and Leanda de Lisle, have questioned the story that Frances married Adrian Stokes on March 9, 1554, just weeks after her daughter's and husband's deaths. It has been suggested the wedding actually took place in 1555 and there was confusion caused by the official practice of dating the New Year from March 25. In researching this book, however, I found in the United Kingdom's National Archives a 1560 inquisition post mortem for Frances. To my dismay, it gave the March 9, 1554, wedding date as well as precise birth and death dates of Elizabeth Stokes, her place of birth and death, and the ages of Katherine and Mary Grey—and because it used regnal years, not calendar years, it was unlikely there was confusion over new style/old style dates. While it is possible this information is incorrect, as it sometimes is in inquisitions post mortem, it also seemed likely the dates could have come from Adrian Stokes himself, who would have known this information better than anyone else.

There is, however, evidence that contradicts the March 1554 marriage date. A land grant to Frances dated April 10, 1554, makes no mention of Stokes. As late as April 21, 1555, Frances was still thought to be free to remarry: Simon Renard, the imperial ambassador, passed along the news that the Earl of Devon had been proposed as a husband for her. As Judith Field, a commenter on my blog, pointed out, however, these discrepancies could be readily explained if Frances kept her marriage secret for a time. After wrestling with the matter, I finally chose to use the March 1554 date as the historically more likely one, along with the scenario of a secret marriage.

∽

Several of the characters who have appeared in this novel have traditionally been treated harshly in historical fiction, as well as in history. The reader may wonder why I have chosen to treat them differently.

For centuries, John Dudley, Duke of Northumberland, was viewed as one of history's villains, whose insatiable ambition led him to destroy the innocent Somerset and to manipulate the hapless Edward VI. In the past few decades, however, historians have taken a much more balanced view of this man. As Susan Brigden and other historians have pointed out, there is evidence that Somerset was involved in some sort of plot against Northumberland in 1551, even if its actual details were exaggerated by the government. Far from ruthlessly engineering the downfall of Somerset, Northumberland arranged for the marriage of their children and restored the duke to his position on the council, although his attempt at reconciliation failed.

It continues to be debated whether the plan to alter the succession originated with Edward VI himself or with Northumberland, but it is beyond question the young king held rigidly Protestant views and made it clear to Mary he disapproved of her Catholic practices, berating her in person on occasion.

Certainly once his "devise" was revealed, Edward VI himself demanded his councilors put it into effect. Thomas Cranmer would later tell Mary it was not Northumberland, but other members of the council and Edward, who pressured him into supporting Jane as queen. He wrote that the king himself required him to sign the document supporting the king's will. Furthermore, while the devise certainly benefited the Dudley family, it should be noted that Northumberland's first choice of a bride for Guildford Dudley had not been Jane Grey, but Margaret Clifford, who was much further from the throne than her cousin Jane. William Cecil indicated that the idea of a match between Guildford and Jane originated with the Marchioness of Northampton.

As Edward VI sickened, rumors swirled that Northumberland, hated by many because of his role in executing the popular Somerset and because of his suppression of Kett's rebellion, was poisoning him. (Even Frances alleged that Northumberland had poisoned her husband, and Jane claimed to have been "envenomed" in the Duchess of Northumberland's house.) The charges against Northumberland at his trial did not include regicide, and modern historians give the rumors of poison little credence, although it may be that a wise woman was called upon when conventional physicians failed to cure the king. An associated story, which still is repeated today, even had it that the duke switched Edward VI's body with that of a youth murdered for that purpose. This story is most improbable. The merchant John Burcher, the only contemporary source to record this particular rumor, was residing in Strasburgh at the time and did not name his informant. Edward VI was buried on August 8, long after Northumberland had been imprisoned in the Tower. Had there been doubts the body was the king's, it would have been simple for Mary's government to ascertain the truth.

Northumberland's private life does not support the notion of him as a scheming, coldhearted man. Jane, his wife, loved him deeply, as her letter to Lady Paget pleading for his life, and her will, make heartbreakingly apparent. In a revealing letter, the duke, ailing and depressed, wrote, "Surely, but for a few children, which God has sent me, which also helps to pluck me on my knees, I have no great cause to desire to tarry much longer here." He was indulgent to his son John when he ran into debt, telling him to inform him of his bills so they could be paid. Facing execution, he begged for the lives of his children, and though his motives for his last-minute conversion to Catholicism will likely never be known, it has been speculated that he did so in hopes of saving his sons from his fate.

As for the Dudley son most affected by the king's devise, little is known about Guildford Dudley's personality. Jane Grey's letter to Mary suggests he might have been a bit of a mother's boy, but her account is hardly impartial and was written at a time when Jane had no reason to think kindly of her husband or his family. There is certainly no historical basis for depicting Guildford as dissolute, cruel, or cowardly, as he is characterized by many novelists. The gracious note he wrote to Jane's father after Henry Grey's ill-judged participation in Wyatt's rebellion surely says something about Guildford's character, as does the quiet dignity with which he went to the scaffold, according to an anonymous chronicler who was probably employed at the Tower. The chronicler Grafton, who may have known Guildford, wrote, "that comely, vertuous, and goodly gentleman the lorde Gylford Duddeley most innocently was executed, whom God had endowed with suche vertues, that even those that never before the tyme of his execution saw hym, dyd with lamentable teares bewayle his death."

Finally, we come to Jane Grey and her family, a subject about which fiction has come to overlay fact so heavily that distinguishing between the two has become difficult if not impossible. In my own attempt to do so, I have been heavily influenced by the research of Leanda de Lisle and Eric Ives, who have done much to clear away the myths that permeate most modern works about Jane and those who brought her to the throne. I am indebted to their research for much of what I say below, though any errors I may have fallen into are of course my own.

There is a widespread notion, stated as a matter of fact in most modern accounts of Lady Jane, that Adrian Stokes was a pretty boy half Frances's age. A friend of Adrian's recorded his birth to the hour in a horoscope: Adrian was born on March 4, 1519, making him less than two years younger than Frances, born on July 16, 1517. A portrait of a stout, middle-aged lady and a much younger man, for centuries described as one of Frances and Adrian Stokes, was identified recently as a portrait of Mary, Lady Dacre, and her son, Gregory Fiennes.

Adrian Stokes is named variously as Frances's steward and as her master of horse, but in either case, such a position in a noble household was a responsible one requiring a man of ability, not a sinecure for the decorative and vacuous. Indeed, privy council records show that in the 1540s, Adrian Stokes served in France as marshal of the garrison of Newhaven (now Ambleteuse), where he had command of ten men.

There is no evidence Frances's match with Adrian offended Queen Mary or caused Frances's daughters to be taken from her care, as is claimed by some authors. It seems to have been understood as a means for Frances to distance herself from the royal succession. Queen Elizabeth's early biographer, William Camden, wrote that Frances's marriage was "to her dishonor, but yet for her security."

The most enshrined legend about Frances and, to a much lesser extent, her husband Henry Grey is that they were brutal parents who made young Jane Grey's life a miserable one. This belief is based chiefly on Roger Ascham's book *The Schoolmaster*, written long after the deaths of Jane and her parents, in which Ascham recalled Jane complaining about the "pinches, nips, and bobs" she received from her parents, in contrast to the lessons she received from her kindly tutor, John Aylmer. Yet in a letter to John Sturm written a few months after the visit, Ascham commented only on his admiration for Jane's command of Greek: "I was immediately admitted into her chamber, and found the noble damsel—Oh, ye gods!—reading Plato's *Phaedro* in Greek, and so thoroughly understanding it that she caused me the greatest astonishment." If anything disturbed Ascham about his recent encounter with Jane, he did not see fit to mention it to Sturm at the time.

Contemporary correspondence by those who knew Jane shows a father who took pride in his daughter's intellectual accomplishments and who shared her religious views. In July 1551, Jane wrote to thank the reformer Heinrich Bullinger in Zurich for "that little volume of pure and unsophisticated religion" which he had sent to her and her father; both were reading it, she added. Earlier, in May 1551, while Jane's father was in Scotland, John ab Ulmis wrote to Bullinger that he had been visiting Jane and her mother at Bradgate, where he had been "passing these two days very agreeably with Jane, my lord's daughter, and those excellent and holy persons Aylmer and Haddon [Jane's tutor and the family chaplain]." Ulmis went on to gush, "For my own part, I do not think there ever lived any one more deserving of respect than this young lady, if you regard her family; more learned, if you consider her age; or more happy, if you consider both." The previous year, in December 1550, Ulmis noted Jane was translating a treatise "On marriage" from the Latin to the Greek as a New Year's gift for her father, whom Holinshed described as "somewhat learned himself, and a great favorer of those that were learned." Henry Grey himself wrote of Jane in December 1551 to Bullinger, "I acknowledge yourself also to be much indebted to you on my daughter's account, for having always exhorted her in your godly letters to a true faith in Christ, the study of the scriptures, purity of manners, and innocence of life."

Robert Wingfield, in a contemporary account of Mary's victory that is hostile to Henry Grey, described Jane as the duke's "favourite daughter."

It needs to be remembered that Tudor standards of child-rearing were very different from our own: the smart-mouthed children lording it over their hapless parents who are staples of modern television and film would have been regarded with horror by Jane's contemporaries. The humanist Juan Luis Vives, who had been asked by no less a personage than Catherine of Aragon to advise her on her daughter Mary's education, wrote, "Never have the rod off a boy's back; specially the daughter should be handled without any cherishing. For cherishing marreth sons, but it utterly destroyeth daughters." Even John Aylmer, the tutor whom Ascham recalled Jane speaking of so fondly, wrote letters indicating his belief that the adolescent Jane needed a firm hand.

Frances Grey is a much more shadowy figure than her husband and Jane, but contemporary sources do not support her portrayal as a vicious and rabidly ambitious woman who terrorized her hapless daughter. Though she is often depicted as a dominant figure in making her daughter queen, at least one source, the Marian sympathizer Robert Wingfield, wrote that she was "vigorously opposed" to the match of Jane and Guildford Dudley. Significantly, she never spent any time in prison for her role in the succession crisis of 1553, an indication, perhaps, that she was believed by Mary's government to have been a reluctant participant. There is no evidence she shared her daughter's or her husband's intellectual interests, but there is equally no evidence she discouraged her daughter's intellectual development or that she resented her because she was not a boy, although she certainly must have grieved for the loss of her infant son. (For that matter, despite the prevailing notion that Frances spent most of her time slaying sad-eyed does when not beating her daughter, there's no evidence she particularly enjoyed hunting, other than her one recorded absence on a hunting excursion on the day Ascham showed up at Bradgate.) Unlike Anne Seymour, Duchess of Somerset, whose difficult personality elicited negative comments from everyone from Catherine Parr on down, none of Frances's contemporaries are on record as disliking her. When Sir Richard Morison groused about "Lady Suffolk's heats" in May 1551, he was referring to the sharp-tongued and quick-tempered Katherine Brandon, not to Frances, who did not bear the Suffolk title at that time.

It is often stated that Frances's callousness toward her daughter is shown by her failure to plead with Mary for her release and by her remarriage just weeks after the death of Jane and Henry Grey. As we have seen, however, a near-contemporary believed Frances married for her own security. As for the former charge, it is recorded that Frances successfully pleaded with Mary to free her husband in 1553, but it does not necessarily follow that Frances did not plead for her daughter on that occasion or she did not plead for Jane's life in 1554. There is no evidence Frances visited her daughter in the Tower, but there is likewise no evidence the Duchess of Northumberland, whose desperate attempts to save her husband and her sons are well documented, visited her imprisoned children, either. It may simply be that permission for such visits was denied.

Before her death, Jane wrote a message to her father in her prayer book (Eric Ives has suggested that a purported second letter to Henry Grey, stylistically different from the one in the prayer book, may not be genuine) and another one to her sister Katherine. No letter to Frances survives, but Michelangelo Florio, Jane's erstwhile tutor in Italian, stated that Jane wrote to her mother. It is quite possible the letter has been lost or Frances destroyed it, perhaps because it was purely of personal, not of religious, value. The absence of a surviving letter, then, does not indicate that Jane and her mother were estranged at the time of Jane's death.

What of the story that Jane refused to marry Guildford until being beaten into submission by her parents? As Dr. John Stephan Edwards has written in his dissertation, no contemporary English source records Jane's reaction to her marriage. Giovanni Commendone, a papal nuncio from Italy who arrived in England in August 1553, wrote that Jane was "compelled to submit [to the Dudley marriage] by the insistence of her Mother and the threats of her Father." As Ives notes, the story of an actual beating appears only five years later, in a pirated account by Raviglio Rosso, another Italian, and the official 1560 text by the same writer mentions no beating. Notably, Jane, in her letter to Mary, made no claim that she was compelled to marry Guildford Dudley by physical force, although it would have been to her advantage to emphasize that she was a reluctant bride. While Jane may not have been happy about her marriage, there is little reason to suppose she was treated differently from other noble girls, who were expected to marry in accordance with their parents' wishes. Frances herself made her arranged marriage before she was sixteen.

It may well be, of course, that Jane's parents were strict disciplinarians—as indeed, Tudor parents were expected to be. It may be that they were perfectionists. It may also be that Jane, as an unusually intelligent girl, resented being treated as an ordinary daughter from whom misbehavior or slacking off would not be tolerated. But to damn Jane's parents as cruel and unloving based on a single outburst by a teenage girl, recalled by a listener years after the fact and after an aura of martyrdom had already settled around Jane, is hardly fair to them—or, for that matter, to Jane, who in later life might have regretted her youthful comments had she been spared her tragic death on the scaffold.

For more about the historical figures in this novel, please see my website, www.susanhigginbotham.com, and my blog, History Refreshed, at www.susanhigginbotham.com/blog.

Further Reading

Adams, Simon. *Leicester and the Court: Essays on Elizabethan Politics*. Manchester and New York: Manchester University Press, 2002.

Beer, Barrett. *Northumberland: The Political Career of John Dudley, Earl of Warwick and Duke of Northumberland*. Kent, Ohio: Kent State University Press, 1973.

Berkhout, Carl T. "Adrian Stokes." Notes and Queries, March 2000.

Bridgen, Susan. *London and the Reformation*. Oxford: Clarendon Press, 1989.

Edwards, John. *Mary I: England's Catholic Queen*. New Haven and London: Yale University Press, 2011.

Gunn, S. J. "A Letter of Jane, Duchess of Northumberland, in 1553." *English Historical Review*, November 1999.

Ives, Eric. *Lady Jane Grey: A Tudor Mystery*. West Sussex: Wiley-Blackwell, 2009.

James, Susan E. *Kateryn Parr: The Making of a Queen*. Aldershot and Brookfield: Ashgate, 1999.

de Lisle, Leanda. *The Sisters Who Would Be Queen: Mary, Katherine, and Lady Jane Grey*. New York: Ballantine Books, 2008.

Loach, Jennifer. *Edward VI*. New Haven and London: Yale University Press, 1999.

Loades, D. M. *Two Tudor Conspiracies*. Cambridge: Cambridge University Press, 1965.

Loades, David. *John Dudley, Duke of Northumberland, 1504–1553*. Oxford: Clarendon Press, 1996.

———. *Mary Tudor: A Life*. Cambridge, Mass., and Oxford: Blackwell, 1989.

Porter, Linda. *The First Queen of England: The Myth of "Bloody Mary."* New York: St. Martin's Press, 2007.

Skidmore, Chris. *Edward VI: The Lost King of England*. New York: St. Martin's Press, 2007.

Whitelock, Anna. *Mary Tudor: Princes, Bastard, Queen*. New York: Random House, 2009.

Websites of Interest

The Lady Jane Grey Internet Museum

www.bitterwisdom.com/ladyjanegrey/

   This site, by Sonja Marie, has an extensive gallery showing how Jane has been depicted by artists throughout the centuries. It is also an invaluable resource for finding books about Jane and the rest of the Tudors.

Some Grey Matter by John Stephan Edwards

www.somegreymatter.com/

   Maintained by a historian who did his doctoral dissertation on Lady Jane, this site offers a rich array of materials about Jane, including a listing of primary and secondary sources, a transcription of Jane's prayer book, and a discussion of the various contemporary portraits alleged to be of Jane.

Reading Group Guide

1. Frances overhears Jane's famous "nips and bobs" speech to Roger Ascham but decides not to confront her daughter. Would you have done so?

2. In begging Lady Paget to intercede for her in saving her husband's life, Jane Dudley frankly admits that her husband is more dear to her than are her sons. Did her admission make you think less of her?

3. Frances tries to reconcile the kind and charitable Mary she knows with the queen's burning of heretics. Nearly three hundred people would be burned to death on Mary's orders before her reign ended. Do you believe Mary was psychologically damaged, or was she merely acting in accordance with the values of her time, which did not look favorably on religious tolerance?

4. Desperate to save her family, Frances tells Mary what she knows are dubious stories about Edward VI being poisoned and encourages Jane Grey to do the same. Did this make her a less sympathetic character to you?

5. Prisoners facing execution in Tudor England were expected to express their penitence on the scaffold and to profess their loyalty to the monarch, even if the prisoner believed his sentence was unjust. Most of the people executed in this novel dutifully follow this convention. Could you have done this?

6. Despite his misgivings, John Dudley carries out the dying Edward VI's wishes and puts Jane Grey on the throne. Setting aside for the moment the hindsight that informs us of the disastrous consequences of his decision, do

you believe he was right to do so? Or should he have honored the provisions of the dead Henry VIII's will?

7. Though Henry VIII is dead when *Her Highness, the Traitor* opens, he casts a shadow over the novel. In what ways does the king continue to influence events?

8. Frances tells her stepmother that her relationship with the Lord is no different no matter whether she goes to mass, and Jane Dudley readily changes her religion in hopes of seeing her sons freed. Others choose to die for their religious beliefs. Are there principles, religious or otherwise, that you would never compromise?

9. Certain characters in this novel, especially Frances Grey and John Dudley, have traditionally been depicted hostilely by novelists and by popular historians. Were you surprised to see them treated differently here? What about the depiction of Jane Grey, who has often been depicted as meek and helpless?

10. What sort of ruler do you think Jane Grey would have been if Mary had not claimed the throne?

11. Mary promises to spare Jane's life but executes her after Henry Grey participates in Wyatt's rebellion. Was her action necessary to prevent future rebellions, as she tells Frances? As a ruler, would you have spared Jane's and Guildford's lives?

12. At the end of her life, Jane Dudley writes, "For whoever trusts to this transitory world as I did, may happen to have an overthrow as I did." How, if at all, does Jane's reversal of fortune change her? What about Frances's reversal of fortune?

13. Which heroine did you prefer, Frances Grey or Jane Dudley? Did your feelings about them change as the novel progressed?

14. Most of the writings in this novel, such as Jane Grey's letters, Northumberland's last letter, Somerset's prayer composed on the eve of his execution, and Jane

Dudley's letter to Lady Paget and her will reflect the actual words of the historical figures involved. Likewise, Somerset's, Northumberland's, and Jane Grey's execution speeches are drawn from contemporary reports. Did you find that this brought you closer to the characters?

15. Henry Grey loves his daughter Jane dearly but puts her life—and his own—at risk by joining Wyatt's rebellion. Do you believe that he willfully blinded himself to the consequences of his actions, that he underestimated Mary's strength of will, or that he was simply naïve?

16. Frances Grey has often been criticized for her hasty marriage to Adrian Stokes. Did you find the motives given here to be convincing? Do you think she found happiness in her second marriage?

Acknowledgments

When I left behind medieval England (for the time being) to write about the Tudors, I worried that those I had enjoyed discussing history with online might fall silent. Happily, I found that I was wrong: the conversations only grew livelier. I would like to thank those with whom I have discussed the Greys and the Dudleys in the course of writing this novel. A special thanks must go to Judith Field, a commenter on my blog who pointed out that the discrepancies involving the date of Frances's marriage to Adrian Stokes could be accounted for if the marriage were a secret one.

I would also like to thank Simon Neal, who has done a number of transcriptions of contemporary documents for me, thereby saving both my eyesight and my sanity, and Dr. John Stephan Edwards, who kindly answered some questions I had about Jane Grey. Several of my Facebook friends in a long-buried thread provided translations of a short Italian passage; I am grateful for their assistance.

As ever, my deepest thanks go to my family, particularly to my mother, Barbara Higginbotham, who did not live to see this novel in print. Although my mother would have much preferred me to write about Regency England and to leave all my characters with their heads intact, she gamely read each of my novels upon publication. I inherited my love of books from her and would probably not be writing this today had it not been for her influence. If I ever write that novel set in Regency England, it'll be for you, Mother—but I can't make any promises about the heads.

About the Author

Photo by Tim Broyer

Susan Higginbotham lives with her family in North Carolina and has worked as an attorney and an editor. She has written two historical novels set in fourteenth-century England, *The Traitor's Wife* and *Hugh and Bess*, and two set during the Wars of the Roses, *The Stolen Crown* and *The Queen of Last Hopes*. Her first novel, *The Traitor's Wife*, won the gold medal for historical/military fiction in the 2008 Independent Publisher Book Awards. Susan maintains a popular bulletin board, Historical Fiction Online, and writes regularly about medieval and Tudor England on her blog, History Refreshed.

The Traitor's Wife

by Susan Higginbotham

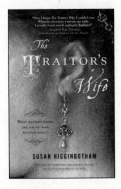

From the bedchamber to the battlefield, through treachery and fidelity, one woman is imprisoned by the secrets of the crown.

It is an age where passion reigns and treachery runs as thick as blood. Young Eleanor has two men in her life: her uncle King Edward II, and her husband Hugh le Despenser, a mere knight but the newfound favorite of the king. She has no desire to meddle in royal affairs—she wishes for a serene, simple life with her family. But as political unrest sweeps the land, Eleanor, sharply intelligent yet blindly naïve, becomes the only woman each man can trust.

Fiercely devoted to both her husband and her king, Eleanor holds the secret that could destroy all of England—and discovers the choices no woman should have to make.

Praise for **The Traitor's Wife:**

"Conveys emotions and relationships quite poignantly... entertaining historical fiction." —*Kirkus Discoveries*

For more Susan Higginbotham, visit:

www.sourcebooks.com

Hugh and Bess

by Susan Higginbotham

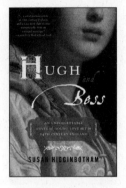

An unforgettable novel of young love set in 14th-century England.

When forced to marry Hugh le Despenser, the son and grandson of disgraced traitors, Bess de Montacute, just thirteen years old, is appalled at his less-than-desirable past. Meanwhile, Hugh must give up the woman he loves in order to marry the reluctant Bess. Far apart in age and haunted by the past, can Hugh and Bess somehow make their marriage work?

Just as walls break down and love begins to grow, the merciless plague endangers all whom the couple holds dear, threatening the life and love they have built.

Award-winning author Susan Higginbotham's impeccable research will delight avid historical fiction readers, while her enchanting characters brought to life will be sure to capture every reader's heart.

Praise for **Hugh and Bess**:

"Following in the footsteps of Jean Plaidy and Norah Lofts…filled with a gentle, dry, very subtle sense of humor." —*Dear Author*

For more Susan Higginbotham, visit:

www.sourcebooks.com

The Stolen Crown

by Susan Higginbotham

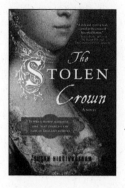

It was a secret marriage...one that changed the fate of England forever.

On May Day, 1464, six-year-old Katherine Woodville, daughter of a duchess who has married a knight of modest means, awakes to find her gorgeous older sister, Elizabeth, in the midst of a secret marriage to King Edward IV. It changes everything—for Kate and for England.

Then King Edward dies unexpectedly. Richard III, Duke of Gloucester, is named protector of Edward and Elizabeth's two young princes, but Richard's own ambitions for the crown interfere with his duties...

Lancastrians against Yorkists: greed, power, murder, and war. As the story unfolds through the unique perspective of Kate Woodville, it soon becomes apparent that not everyone is wholly evil—or wholly good.

Praise for Susan Higginbotham:

"Beautifully researched and incredibly captivating, *The Traitor's Wife* is a book you won't want to put down. Susan Higginbotham's vivid portrayal of life during Edward II's tumultuous reign makes for fascinating reading. Highly recommended!"
—Michelle Moran, bestselling author of *The Heretic Queen*

For more Susan Higginbotham, visit:

www.sourcebooks.com

The Queen of Last Hopes

by **Susan Higginbotham**

History would call them the Wars of the Roses. But the story began with one woman's fury...

Margaret of Anjoy, Queen of England, does not want immortality. She does not need glory. All she desires is what rightfully belongs to her family—and that is the throne of England. Her husband the king cannot rule, but the enemies who doubt her will and dispute her valor underestimate the force of a mother's love. Her son is the House of Lancaster's heir and last hope, and her fight for him will shake the crown forever.

Award-winning author Susan Higginbotham will once again ask readers to question everything they know about right and wrong, compassion and hope, duty to one's country and the desire of one's own heart.

Praise for Susan Higginbotham:

"A beautiful blending of turbulent history and deeply felt fiction, Susan Higginbotham's *The Queen of Last Hopes* brings alive an amazing woman often overlooked or slandered by historians. Higginbotham has given readers of historical fiction a gift to treasure." —Karen Harper, *New York Times* bestselling author of *The Irish Princess*

"A compelling, fast-paced, and well-written saga that is destined to both entertain and educate anyone interested in the spirited and fascinating Margaret of Anjou for generations to come!" —D. L. Bogdan, author of *Secrets of the Tudor Crown*

For more Susan Higginbotham, visit:

www.sourcebooks.com